BONKPOCALYPSE
A Red Darkling Jam

L. A. Guettler

ISBN-13: 9798815904484

Cover design by: Jason Kemp
Printed in the United States of America

DEDICATION

To everyone, everywhere: Have faith. Trust Fardus.

Chapter 1
The Best Improv Mechanic in Six Systems

A bone-shuddering impact slammed through the *Wart*. A dozen alerts popped up on the vidscreen and an alarm shrieked to life. Red Darkling glanced at them and let loose a string of profanities rarely heard outside a Fardic monastery on St. Cripps Eve. She blew a strand of hair out of her eyes and flipped some switches. A few more alerts appeared, but the alarm stopped.

"You know, you don't get any bonus points for hitting every asteroid."

Red glared at the scruffy man lounging in the copilot's chair. "Maybe if you'd quit jerking off and lock down that plasma damper, I could focus more on flying."

"Nag, nag, nag." Mark Woodman stretched and pretended to yawn, but at least he pulled the cover off the tech panel and started poking around inside. For the fifty-seventh time, Red regretted asking him to help out with this job.

She turned her attention back to the field of icy asteroids that filled the viewport. She yanked the control stick hard left to avoid a particularly gnarly one, then hauled the stick straight back and shot over another, even more gnarly than the first.

"What's the status on our forward shields?" Red asked, not taking her eyes off the viewport.

"Kinda busy with the plasma damper right now," Woodman muttered.

"I need to know—" She pulled right on the stick. "—the shield status—" Left, then a quick right. "—so I can tell—" Up and left. "—how many of these little guys I can hit—" Down. "—without killing us both."

"Don't hit any of them and we'll be fine." Woodman yanked a snarl of wires out of the tech panel. "Aha! I think I found the problem. I just have to bypass—"

"Shut up and do it already." Red risked a peek at the shield status: thirty-five percent. Not too bad, but a solid hit from one of the big ones would wipe them out completely. She looked back at the viewport just in time to see a grum-sized asteroid bounce off seemingly inches from her nose. She didn't dare look back at the shield status, but she knew it had to have dropped another six or seven percent.

"Woodman, I need that plasma damper locked down yesterday!" she shouted over some new buzzing alarm. "If the engines overheat, these asteroids will have a cookout on our burning corpses."

Suddenly, he pumped a fist and let out a whoop. "Who's the best improv mechanic in six systems? Me, that's who!"

"What do you mean, improv?"

Woodman sat back in his chair and put his hands behind his head. "The damper is fried, babe. Lucky for you, I worked around it."

Red caught the reflection of his disgustingly smug grin in the vidscreen. "What did you *do*, Woodman?"

"Get this: the plasma damper keeps the engines cool, right? And it's cold in space, right? So I overrode the automatic lock on the engine room's exterior hatch and presto! Instantly cooled engines. We'll just have to pick up a new damper before we—"

"You grumstained idiot!" Red stomped on his foot with one heavy black boot and swung the ship around a cloud of tiny asteroid particles. "Are you saying the back of the ship is *open*?"

"Gee, don't thank me or anything," he grumbled.

Red ground her teeth. "You realize these are icy asteroids, yeah?"

"So?"

"So, what happens if the ice gets into the—"

She was cut off by a loud chunking sound from the back of the ship. She felt her ass lift off the captain's chair and grabbed the edge of the control panel with her non-steering hand to keep from heading straight to the ceiling. Beside her, Woodman clutched the arms of his own chair. Empty beer cans, FlinkBar wrappers, and cigar butts drifted around the cockpit.

"Grav plate. Ice in the grav plate, Woodman."

"Oh. Right." He grinned sheepishly. "Sorry."

Note to self: pick up a new copilot at the next sewage dump. "Can you see the edge of the asteroid field yet?"

Woodman glanced at the scopes. "Looks like another few clicks and we're home free."

"What about our friends back there?"

He switched to rear scopes and squinted. "Hard to tell. Asteroids, you know."

"Yeah, I'm familiar with the concept." Red jigged the ship around a cluster of debris. "Let's hope they either gave up or had worse shields than we do."

"What did you do to piss them off, anyway?"

She cleared her throat. "Ah, well, I may have sort of, accidentally, kind of insulted their royal family."

"*What!?*"

"It was a compliment, really, if you think about it." Red swung the control stick hard left. "I mean, technically, the prince wouldn't screw his mother if she wasn't at least a little hot, right?"

"Oh, lord . . ."

"And lots of people enjoy that particular technique for— finally!" The asteroids outside the viewport had thinned to a few small fragments. "So, anyone make it through besides us?"

Woodman shook his head. "Nope, looks like we're clear." He punched a button. "Okay, engine room's sealed up again. How's the shields?"

"Don't ask." Red slipped past one final asteroid crumb and popped on the autopilot. She shook out her stiff fingers, letting herself drift out of the seat. "Let's go see if we can de-ice the grav plate. Floating makes me want to throw up." She pulled herself through the doorway out of the cockpit.

"Don't throw up until we get gravity back," Woodman warned, following. "In fact, don't throw up at all. You get all ugly when you throw up."

Red punched his arm, spinning them both in opposite directions and making her stomach twist up unpleasantly. She bumped into the wall, steadied herself, and pushed toward the rear of the ship.

Woodman joined her at the engine room door, and they both peered through the round window.

"The room's pressurizing now," Red said. "Should be back up to normal range in a minute. Temperature will take longer."

He shifted his grip on the door frame. "I really am sorry about the grav plate," he mumbled.

Red rolled her eyes. "It's okay," she sighed. "You can make it up to me by buying a replacement plasma damper, Mr. Improv Mechanic."

"Deal." He paused. "That was some epic flying."

"Thanks."

"How many did you hit? I lost count around fifteen."

Red chuckled. "You suck at math."

"That's hardly my fault," he protested. "You never let me look at your answers at school. I had to cheat off Buck."

A green light blinked on in the engine room. Red pressed the hatch release and the door slid open with a soft hiss. The icy air raised goosebumps on her arms and made her shiver, but it was breathable.

"Let's get this done," she said, cracking her knuckles.

Over the next few hours, the temperature in the engine room rose enough to melt the ice. Red and Woodman disassembled the grav plate, dried off the components with the least grungy towels they could find, and pieced it back together. When it kicked on again, the gritty asteroid water floating around the room fell to the floor like the galaxy's most localized cloudburst. Red and Woodman fell with it, though with significantly less poetic grace.

"Remind me to get some carpet in here," Red groaned, sitting up and rubbing the back of her head. She'd be lucky not to get a lump.

"Better yet," Woodman said, cradling an elbow, "a mattress." He stared at Red. "Uh, I don't know how to tell you this, darlin, but your shirt is wet."

She glanced down. Her favorite t-shirt—the vintage Poly Torrents one from their first tour—was soaked with grey water.

"Dammit," she spat. "Does asteroid juice stain?"

Woodman rolled on his side and ran a hand up her leg. "Let's find out. First, you'll need to take it off."

Red scowled, but she didn't pull away when he squeezed her thigh. "We really should clean up this mess before we do anything else."

"Why, *Mild*red Darkling," he purred. "Cleaning? That doesn't sound like you at all." He squeezed a little higher, a little tighter.

Nnnngh. "But I might have a concussion."

He unzipped his pants. "How many am I holding up?"

Red's mouth twitched up at the corner. "One."

"See? Dr. Woodman's diagnosis is that you're perfectly healthy."

"Oh, you're a doctor now? What happened to improv mechanic?"

"Look, are you gonna jump my bones here, or are you just gonna talk all day?"

She looked around the engine room at the grey puddles, then pushed Woodman down and straddled him. "Just a quick one."

"Darlin, I can't make any promises."

Chapter 2
You'll Get Fazzer Piss and Like It

They did clean the engine room eventually.

Red tossed her filthy Poly Torrents shirt on the pile of even filthier towels. Time to swing by Granny's again. Red's ship, the *Wart*, didn't have its own laundry. Those kinds of accessories were generally included on big family ships, like an Air Skimmer. The *Wart* was a lot of things, but a family ship it was not. It was more of a garbage disposal with a sublight drive and currently busted plasma damper.

She headed to the shower, but Woodman had beaten her there. She poked her head through the curtain. "Don't use up all the hot water, asshole."

"If you're worried, you could join me." He winked, scrubbing an armpit.

Red stifled a groan. "Whatever. Just hurry up, I think that asteroid juice is giving me a rash."

"You sure it's the asteroid juice?"

"Shut up. I'm gonna make coffee, you want some?"

Splashing. "You mean that fazzer piss you *call* coffee? No thanks. I'll take a beer instead."

"It's nine in the morning!"

"So?"

"You'll get fazzer piss and like it."

She swiped the fresh shirt Woodman had tossed on the back of the toilet and pulled it on as she walked toward the kitchen. She was struggling to find the head hole when something hard and metal dodged between her legs. She flailed around desperately trying to keep her balance, but gravity asserted itself yet again and she hit the floor.

"Dammit, Bonk!" She finally got the shirt on properly and saw her cat standing a few feet away, tail swinging lazily from side to side. It blinked its mismatched eyes and made a mechanical gargling sound.

"Don't talk back to me, buster," she scolded. "That's the second time I've landed on my ass today."

Bonk turned and walked directly into the wall. Again. And again. And again.

Red pushed it with her foot so it could get through the kitchen doorway, grimacing at a sharp twinge in her ankle. Great, add *that* to the list. She stood, gingerly, testing her weight on the ankle. Not broken, but definitely screwed up. She limped into the kitchen and punched the coffee button on the beverage dispenser. A weak trickle of liquid dribbled into a crusty mug.

Bonk wiggled its rear end and jumped to the top of the fridge. Well, tried to, anyway. Its trigonometric servos failed to calculate the correct trajectory, launching the cat instead into the side about halfway up. It left a dent and probably would have ruined the finish, too, if there had been any finish left to ruin.

"Holy grumshit, Bonk!" Red cried. "Are you okay?" She crouched down to check it for new damage. She hadn't had the cat very long, really, only a year or so. It was a total pain in the ass, tearing up mattresses to get at vermin and driving her crazy with its incessant bonking. A normal person would have junked it ages ago.

Still, Red liked having someone to talk to when Woodman wasn't around. And of course there was the time the cat had saved her life. She touched the scar that ran along her jawline, a souvenir of the encounter that started with picking up a hitchhiker for some quick cash and ended with Bonk violently disassembling the murderous insect into his component parts.

Bonking aside, Bonk was a good cat, and deserved better than a face full of fridge.

Luckily, the cat seemed completely unconcerned by its epic, circuit-quaking failure. It settled on its haunches on the grimy kitchen tile, lifted a leg casually into the air, and began its standard exhaust port maintenance routine.

"Guess that's a yes." Red grabbed the freshly filled mug of coffee and took a sip. Yurk. She forced it down, suppressed her gag reflex, then shrugged and drained the rest of it.

"Bonk," she said as she refilled the cup for Woodman, "we need a pitstop. Like, big time. You need anything?"

The cat scoured its exhaust port with renewed enthusiasm.

"All right then." Red pointed to a pile of dishes in the sink. "There's a nest of dugger mites in there you might want to take a look at. You know, when you have the time. No rush."

Bonk ignored her completely. She flipped it off and wandered back to the bathroom, where Woodman was toweling off. She thrust the mug of coffee at him and tried not to look at his abs.

"Thanks, babe. I think."

She grunted and got in the shower. She took off Woodman's shirt and tossed it over the curtain. Please, let there be some hot water left.

There wasn't.

After a two-minute rinse that left her teeth chattering and her lips blue, Red bundled up in a shiqwool blanket and shivered to the cockpit. Woodman was in the copilot's chair, feet up on the control panel, watching *Port Desire* on the vidscreen.

Red sank into the captain's chair. "I'm worried about Bonk. It's getting worse. I want to—"

"Shh, they're just about to reveal who's the father of Goldova's baby."

On the screen, a half dozen men in bad suits stood around an elaborately coifed woman in a hospital bed. She clutched an infant to her chest and shot dark looks at the men from under her double layer of false eyelashes.

"It's obviously the Glorreen guy's baby. Look at the green skin."

"Can't be Thad's. That clomis attack on Rutfala 13 put him in a coma so he wasn't at the contessa's funeral where the baby was conceived."

"How can you watch this junk?"

"SHH."

A doctor entered the room holding a clipboard, and the organ music swelled dramatically. "Ms. Gregory," he said, "The test results are back. Your baby —"

Red clicked off the vidscreen and smirked at Woodman's strangled howl of objection.

"Oh, stop it. I've got something better for us to do anyway."

"I'm not seventeen anymore, you know. I need time to recover."

Red ignored this. "We're on our last case of beer, and we're out of real coffee, FlinkBars, and a few other necessities, like a plasma damper."

"Market day?" Woodman raised an eyebrow.

"Market day. And I want to find someone to fix the cat. It just dented the freaking fridge."

"Where d'you want to go?"

She shrugged. "What's close?"

Woodman flipped on the navbox and scrolled through the neighboring systems. "G'qshu? There's a good junkyard there."

"Nah, too small. I'm thinking Andar."

"We'd never make it all the way to Andar," he pointed out. "We're stuck on impulse power until we get a working damper. Unless you want to get a nice crispy plasma tan?"

"I guess not. Lut?"

"Uh." He coughed. "Not Lut. Anywhere but Lut. Unless you think the warrant has expired."

"Good point." She thought a minute. "There's really nothing else around here except . . ."

Woodman groaned. "Ugh, Magross."

"It won't be that bad," Red said, tapping some coordinates into the nav. "I bet Granny will make us dinner. And you can see your parents."

"Gee, can't wait." The nav beeped, and he squinted at the travel time it spat back. "Three hours. Well, at least I'll have time to squeeze in a few more episodes of *Port Desire*."

Red snorted and stood up, stretching. "You do that. If you need me, I'll be in the storage compartment setting my eyeballs on fire."

The soap was already back on the vidscreen. "Sounds good," Woodman said vaguely, chewing a fingernail. "Have fun."

Port Desire. Ha! Who watches that crap? What a loser.

Chapter 3
Interestinger and Interestinger

"I still can't believe the baby's father was the C'longi drug lord." Red eyeballed her bottle of Hamstel Lite in the dull brown light that managed to penetrate the filthy windows of the bar.

"Right? I don't think it's physically possible," said Woodman, gesturing wildly and slopping beer down his shirt. "Do their parts even line up? Where do the tentacles go?"

"It's a terrible show," Red muttered, shaking her head. "Totally unrealistic."

"I know. Ain't it great?"

Red drained her beer. "How're we doing on our shopping list?"

"Not bad." He pulled a limp paper from his pocket and unfolded it. "We got the grocery stuff done, but there's still the plasma damper." He wiggled his beer. "We should probably pick that up before we drink away all the credits."

"Pfft," Red sputtered, spraying beer-scented spittle. "Chuck'll run us a tab. Right, Chuck?"

Chuck looked up from organizing the liquor bottles behind the bar. This didn't look promising. "You still owe me fifty credits from the last time you swung through this system."

"Do not."

"Do too."

"Well, what about him?" She jerked a thumb in Woodman's direction.

Chuck flickered and faded a bit, the way all cross-dimensional beings did when they were checking in with their other selves. At least Red assumed they all did. Chuck was the only one she'd met, at least as far as she knew. Maybe it was a glitch unique to Chuck, like a disease. Or maybe it was because he stretched himself so thin, tending bar at dozens of establishments of varying degrees of repute across multiple systems. Or maybe Red was always just a little drunk when she saw him.

Chuck snapped back into focus. "Nope, he owes me twenty-five from the ShiqShack."

Red's eyebrow shot up. She turned to Woodman, who was intently examining the label on his beer. "The ShiqShack?" she asked, trying like hell not to laugh. "What were you doing at the ShiqShack?"

"I'll leave you two to talk."

"Aw c'mon, Chuck—"

A voice interrupted her. "Their next round is on me. And I'll have another icewine."

Red spun on her stool. A woman she didn't recognize handed Chuck a few credits. He nodded, popped the tops off two fresh beers, poured a glass of wine, and turned back to sorting his bottles.

"Uh. Thanks, I guess." Red tipped her beer at the woman. "Cheers."

"You can pay me back with a few minutes of conversation," the woman said, taking a sip of her drink.

"Do we know you?" Red looked at Woodman, who shrugged and shook his head.

"No, but we have someone in common."

Red squinted at her. She was about Red's own age, maybe a few years older. Her hair was blue—not the deep royal blue of an Orgullan, but pale. She wore a crisp suit that didn't quite hide the bulge of a blaster holster under the jacket. Red hadn't seen her before, but there was something vaguely familiar about her anyway.

"Come on. Just a few minutes. Bring your beer." She glanced at Woodman. The corner of her mouth twitched. "Leave your boyfriend." She walked to a table by the window and sat down.

"He's not my boyfriend," Red muttered.

"Now hold on a minute," Woodman protested. "I'm not?"

Red blinked. "You are?"

His forehead wrinkled in confusion, then he shook his head. "Never mind. What does she have to say that I can't hear?" He started to stand up, but Red put a hand on his arm. She'd seen that twitch before. Somewhere.

"Dude, it's okay," Red said. "I'll be right over there. Five minutes."

"But—"

"I can take care of myself."

"I know, but—" Woodman scowled and picked up his beer, avoiding Red's eyes. "It's just . . . I'll be here if you need me."

"Drink up." Red winked. "I want to hear all about the ShiqShack when I get back." She grabbed her beer and left him sputtering.

The woman smiled as Red kicked out a chair and plopped down at the table. "Is he going to be okay?"

"Who, Woodman? He's fine." She swallowed a mouthful of beer. "So, not to be rude, but who are you, and what do you want?"

"I wanted to ask you about your relationship with the man who goes by the name John Smith."

Shit. "John who?"

The woman's smile widened. "I think you know, Ms. Darkling. Or may I call you Red?"

"You can call me anything you want," Red said with a burp.

"Fine. There's no need to worry, Red. I'm not after you. I just want to clear up a few things about the events of last November."

"I'm out of here."

"Wait, no. Please." The woman's voice cracked slightly. Beneath that crisp suit and icewine-sipping demeanor, she was desperate.

Interestinger and interestinger.

Red leaned back in her chair and crossed her booted feet on the table. "Why don't you start by telling me who you are."

"I thought I had."

"Nope."

The woman extended a neatly manicured hand. "I'm Samanthya. You can call me Sam. Most people do."

Red said nothing. Sam lowered her unshaken hand and continued. "My interest in John Smith is strictly professional."

"Is that so."

"Yes," she said, flashing a badge. "I've been looking into John Smith's activities for several years now, without much luck." She sighed, tucking the badge back in her pocket. "Every lead I dig up either goes missing or turns up dead."

"That would be a problem."

"Every lead except you."

Red shifted in her chair. "I have no idea what you're talking about."

"Yes, you do."

Red lifted her eyes to meet the woman's level gaze, scenes from the year before flashing in her mind: Smith carving a grum loin with a flashing blade, Smith walking atop the clouds of Crysallia, Smith cursing her among the moldering ruins of her childhood home, Smith, Smith, always Smith . . .

She gulped some beer to cover her emotion. "Maybe. Maybe not."

"You and Smith were seen together at a coffee shop called Scarpio's." She slapped a photograph across the table.

"Holy crap," Red spat. "Was everyone following me?"

"That's you, correct?" the woman pressed.

Red picked up the photo. It was fuzzy, obviously shot from a distance and through at least one window. Still, Red couldn't forget that corner booth, the smell of Smith's coffee, and the offer he'd made.

Red pushed the photo back. "Yeah, that's me. So?"

Two more photographs appeared on the table. "These were taken two days later at your parents' house in Magross." She pointed at the figure in the first picture. "That's you again, correct?"

Red shrugged.

"You had just exited the building. And this," Sam said, pointing at the second photo, "this is John Smith, exiting the same building a few minutes after you." She tapped the time stamp. "What did you talk about at these two meetings?"

Red considered a moment. "He wanted me to work for him," she finally said. "With him, actually."

"I see."

"I said no."

"I know."

Red threw up her hands, nearly knocking over her beer. "If you already know everything, why are you here?"

Sam leaned forward, both elbows on the sticky table. Her suit would need a good dry-cleaning after this. "You said no . . . and lived."

"So what?"

"No one tells Smith no and lives."

"I'm lucky, I guess."

"Hmm." The woman gathered up the photos and tucked them back in her pocket. "Why did you tell him no? He'd have made you rich. Powerful. You wouldn't have to argue with bartenders over the cost of a beer. You could take care of your grandmother for a change, instead of the other way around."

Red's face flushed with anger and, if she was being honest, not a small bit of shame. "Who the hell are you?" she demanded.

"If you decide you want to talk, let me know." She slid a business card across the table and stood up. She hesitated a second, then left the bar.

Red took a slow pull off her beer. "Yeah, I'll be in touch real soon, Sam . . ." She glanced at the card. "Anyanama." She tucked it into her bra and headed back to the bar. She tried to focus on how hard she wanted to ride Woodman about the ShiqShack.

Chapter 4
Time for Some Diplomacy

"So that's it?" Woodman asked, shoulder-deep in a crate of used ship components. "That's all she said?"

"Yep." Red shrugged. She turned to the Fylaran merchant sitting in a dark corner of the booth. "This all you've got for a StarMaster Blip series light utility vessel?"

The veiled figure spread his thin hands.

"Any plasma dampers at all?"

The merchant remained silent and still.

"Let's go." Red grabbed Woodman by the arm.

"Wait," Woodman protested as she dragged him away from the crate. "There was an old PV-394 navcomp processor in there. You know how hard those are to find? It's practically an antique!"

"Plasma dampers," Red said, picking her way through the crowded market. "We're looking for plasma dampers. Remember, Mr. Improv?"

"Yeah, yeah." He shot a final longing look over his shoulder, then turned his attention to a mountainous display of bakery they passed. "You want a quusberry tart? My treat."

"The only treat you can give me is a new plasma damper."

"Your loss." He bought a tart and crammed it into his mouth whole. "Whough ee anna oog esh?" he said, crumbs spilling down his chin and getting caught in his stubble.

Red wrinkled her nose. "You're disgusting."

"Hnh." Woodman swallowed and licked sticky quusberry juice off his fingers. "Where you wanna look next?"

She glanced around. The Magross marketplace was Red's childhood hunting ground. She, Woodman, and the rest of the guys had spent entire days lifting wallets from shoppers, sneaking food from vendors, smoking stolen cigarettes, and generally having a great time. The market itself centered on an airy pedestrian square and snaked outwards through the surrounding streets. Red recognized many of the booths that had been setting up in Magross for decades, but there were always new merchants with new pitches for new products. The market was always the same, and always different—like an old, comfortable t-shirt with a few new stains.

"Let's head toward Scrappers Row," she decided. "There's a couple guys over there I usually have luck with. If not, we can zip over to Septimal City and check out their market."

Woodman groaned theatrically. "I'm not dragging my ass over to Septimal City today. If we can't find a plasma damper here, I'm planting myself on my parents' couch with the biggest, greasiest pizza I can find, and I'm not leaving until I'm caught up on *Port Desire*."

"Live the dream, man." Red started walking toward the row of scrappers' tents squatting along the eastern edge of the square.

Pickings were slim. Apparently the *Wart* was the least popular model of the least popular ship ever produced by the least popular manufacturer in this quadrant, because no one had parts for it. Red found a Twist series plasma damper she might be able to rig up to fit, and a plasma inducer that could be flipped to a damper by slapping a couple A-130 screwbolts to the powerboard and covering the gaps with electroputty. Eh, too much work, and she didn't think she had any A-130 screwbolts left. She picked up the Twist damper and waved it at Woodman. "You think we could patch this in?"

Woodman looked up from the array of assorted hatch relays scattered on the next table. "Are you kidding? Give me half an hour and a sonic wrench and I'll have that puppy damping more plasma than a quashtoad on steroids."

"You need to work on your metaphors." Red turned to the vendor, who was reading a newspaper. "Hey," she said, waving the damper. "I'll give you sixty credits for this."

The newspaper dropped, and so did Red's jaw. "Holy shit, I know you!"

The C'longi blinked his single bloodshot eye. "Hnh. Many know me. I work many market."

"What do you mean, you know him?" Woodman raised an eyebrow.

"His name's Tom," Red explained. "At least that's what he says it is." Her eyes narrowed. "He's the one who sold me Bonk."

"I not know dis Bonk."

"A glitchy cat."

The eye widened, then glanced away. "My tings always good. If cat glitchy, is user problem."

"User problem? It walks into walls!"

Tom chuckled, causing the tassels on his floral headscarf to dance merrily.

"I don't think it's very funny." Red crossed her arms. "I paid eighty credits for it."

"Is good price."

"It was a total rip-off. But you can make it up to me by fixing it."

Tom ran a tentacle over his slug face, rearranging the pungent slime into a new and interesting pattern. "I no can fix. Fix is not my job. My cousin, mebbe, he fix. Good price."

Red shook her head. "Oh no, you don't. I'm not getting sucked into some C'longi family gangbang. I've been screwed before, but never by so much ugly at once."

Tom rose up off his stool. "What you say bout family?" His tentacles waved menacingly at Red from across the merchandise table.

Woodman touched her arm. "Hey, babe, why don't we just buy the damper and go?"

Red shook him off. "No way. He owes me." She jabbed a finger into Tom's spongy chest and immediately regretted it. "I paid for a cat, and instead I got a metal box of claws that can't find its way through a door."

"I tell you, my tings always good." He sank back onto the stool. "You have problem? Go to manufacturer. Mebbe recall. Mebbe patch to fix." He shrugged.

"Okay. Fine. Who's the manufacturer?"

More tassel-swinging laughter.

"Look," Red said, gritting her teeth. "I just want to fix my cat."

Tom stroked his multi-layered chin with the tip of his least-crusty tentacle. "I have idea. Mebbe I know where is previous owner, if you have fifty credits."

"Fifty!? Red, come over here for a minute." Woodman dragged her across the street by the jacket sleeve and spun her around. "Don't you dare give this guy fifty credits," he whispered fiercely. "He's a scrapper. He's not going to remember where that stupid cat came from."

"Shut up," Red hissed. "I know what I'm doing."

"Do you? It's just a cat. Who cares if it's glitchy?"

Yeah, it's just a cat. A machine designed for one thing: pest control, which it mostly managed to do even with the glitches. Anyway, it's not like Bonk's a person or something, with feelings. She could scrap it and get a new one for less than she'd probably end up spending to fix it.

Then Red's brain played a little vid of Bonk crashing into the fridge. "I care," she said. "It's my cat. It's Bonk."

Woodman threw up his hands.

"Is okay," Tom said loudly. He was sweeping his merchandise into crates. "I mebbe not remember anyway. You want buy plasma damper or no?" He pointed at the device still clutched, forgotten, in Red's hand.

"Tell you what," Red said, returning to the table. "I'll give you seventy credits—"

"RED!"

"—Seventy credits for the damper *and* the info."

Tom paused and adjusted his headscarf. "Hundred."

"No way. Seventy or I walk. Without the damper." She tossed it casually from hand to hand.

"My girlfriend kill me, I get so little."

Woodman snorted. "You've got a girlfriend?"

"Look, Tom, no one else is begging to buy your crap today anyway." Red gestured at the emptying streets around them. "What do you say, buddy?"

The C'longi let out a juicy noise that must have been a sigh. "Show me credits."

Red elbowed Woodman, who dug a stack from his pocket and slapped it on the table. As Tom scooped up the bills, Woodman grumbled something about zuranfruit-for-brains and heading back to the ship before stomping away.

Tom smoothed out the crumpled bills and counted them under his breath. He nodded, sending ripples down his gelatinous body. "Take damper. Is yours." He tucked the credits into a beaded purse at what Red assumed was his waist.

Red slipped the device into her leather bag. "And the cat? Where is the previous owner?"

"Don't know. Cat, ah, showed up at booth one day. I put in cage and sell to you."

Damn the Fourteen gods of Penthus. "You lying sack of grumshit. You told me you knew where the previous owner is."

"I said *mebbe* I know. But no. Am sorry, girl, but booth closed now." Tom snapped the lid on the last crate. "Enjoy damper. Mebbe it work better than cat."

Red's hand itched to grab her blaster and make a lot of very small holes in the C'longi's sluggy face. But that would bring the cops, and the cops might remember those outstanding warrants, and then things would get really messy. Besides, she didn't really savor the idea of finding out what Tom's insides looked like. It couldn't be any better than the outside, and was probably a lot worse. Woodman once told her that C'longi had grey blood the consistency of clotted pus. She shuddered at the thought.

But he couldn't get away with this, either. He had to know something.

Time for some diplomacy.

Red's hand grabbed her blaster and made a lot of very small holes in the C'longi's merchandise table, then leveled the barrel at Tom's eye. Vendors at the surrounding booths suddenly remembered they'd promised to pick up dinner on their way home, and decided they'd better leave now if they wanted to beat the rush.

Red adjusted her aim and smiled. "Now," she said, "let's try this again."

Tom licked sweat from his upper lip with a forked tongue. "I tell you. I take cat from market."

"Which market?"

"Gambora."

"You sure about that?" Red asked. "You don't want to make a mistake, Tom."

"Yes, Gambora. I always sell at Gambora market, every week. Rich people, government people, good quality scrap to pick."

"Okay, Gambora. Anything else?"

The C'longi played with his tassels nervously. "There was—"

"Yes? There was what, Tom? You can do it."

"Anodder piece. Piece mebbe you need for cat to work right." He gestured vaguely at would have been a throat on any species with a body shape less potato-y.

"What kind of piece? What did it do?"

Tom shrugged. "Don't know."

Red's shoulder ached from holding up the blaster. This was the stupidest conversation she'd had in years, including her one-sided arguments with Granny's washing machine when it refused to dispense the soap. "You took a piece of the cat out before selling it? Why?"

"To sell. Eighty credits for cat, mebbe twenty for piece." He shrugged. "Is how Tom makes living."

"And did you? Sell it, I mean?"

"No. No one want. I have with other merchandise, mebbe?" His goopy eye narrowed. "I can find, for price."

Her jaw twitched. Typical. Why did she never end up haggling with Fardic monks who'd just taken a vow of poverty and selflessness? It was always some C'longi sleazebag or Andarian prince with sky-high gambling debts. At this rate, she'd go broke. Well, broke-*r*. She almost regretted spending so much on FlinkBars.

FlinkBars. Her stomach growled. Time to wrap up and get back to the ship so she could get to Granny's in time for dinner. She could almost smell the roast darna, garlicky and swimming in gravy. Or was that the yozzie stand down the block?

"Better be more than 'mebbe.' Find it and we'll talk price." She slipped the blaster back in its holster. "How long do you need?"

Tom sank back on his stool and pulled a stained handkerchief from the sleeve of his muumuu. "One week. Will be at Gambora market then. You want missing piece, I see you there." He mopped the goop from his eye, inspected the handkerchief, and licked the contents.

Red swallowed a bit of vomit before nodding in agreement. "I'll see you then."

Chapter 5
Feline Malware Virus?

Back on the *Wart*, Red found Woodman with Bonk between his legs. The cat was on its back, stomach panel open, electronic guts spilling across the floor.

"What the hell are you doing?" Red demanded, throwing her bag on the couch and squatting next to him.

"Well," Woodman said, loosening a screw. "I thought, you're so worried about Bonk, maybe I could take a look."

A twinge shot through Red's rumbling stomach. Woodman may be a sex-crazed asshole, but he was a thoughtful sex-crazed asshole.

"Tom said it's missing a piece," she said. "But he's got it. I'm supposed to meet him at the Gambora market next week to negotiate a price."

Woodman paused, a particularly crusty circuit board in his hand. "Oh, yeah?"

"Yeah. Problem?"

"No." He blew some grit off the board and clicked it back into place. Then he turned to Red. "I'm really trying, you know. To be less . . . helpful."

Red punched him in the arm, but lightly. "It's okay. What d'ya say we go to Granny's? I'm so hungry I could eat a raw fazzer."

"Another time," Woodman said. "I promised my mom I'd have dinner there tonight. Dad's home, and she's on this togetherness kick because   . . . anyway, I'm afraid I'm in for an intense night of jester's scrap and hot cocoa."

"Sounds fun," Red snorted. "I'll probably stick around Granny's, get the plasma damper in, before I head out to Gambora for that piece. You coming with me?"

"Aw, babe, you know how much I love to watch you throw perfectly good beer money away on busted-up junk, but I've got a job lined up for next week." He smirked. "Someone's gotta keep fuel in the tank."

Red's eyes rolled hard enough to see her own eyebrows. "You mean, contribute to expenses? Why start now?"

"I bought that plasma damper, didn't I?"

"Well, if you hadn't sucked ice all over the last one . . ."

"Details, details." Woodman tossed his sonic wrench down on the floor with a clank. "I give up, babe. I don't know anything about cats. You need to talk to a vet tech. I hear Dr. Mn is good. He's over on Jiljala Street. I bet you can get over there before they close."

Red peered into the cat's gaping stomach cavity. "Put it back together, then."

"If I can."

"Improvise."

~ ~ ~

The door to Dr. Mn's Vet Clinic and Oil Change Emporium swooshed open, blasting Red with a wall of cold air. She shivered despite the sweat dripping down her back. She hauled an inert Bonk across the packed lobby and dropped it on the desk with a crash. Her arm muscles quivered in relief. Mental note: start exercising more. Especially weights. Her lift max was pathetic.

The Ulatan receptionist jumped at the noise. "Are you here for an oil change?" they asked, readjusting the glasses on their left head. Their name tags read 'Ya3t' and 'Yo1nck.'

"Not today." Red wiped her forehead with her sleeve. "I'd like to see Dr. Mn about my cat here."

"Dr. Mn isn't in today," Yo1nck said. They had to shout to be heard over the shrieks of a purple-breasted tagram that appeared to have broken its auxiliary neck. "I'll see if I can get you in with one of our other techs." Ya3t turned to tap frantically on a massive triple-decker keyboard. The complex alphabet used by most people on Ulatu used almost two hundred unique symbols that could be combined across three dimensions, which made translation into most galactic languages impossible at best—a major reason Red avoided doing business with Ulatans who—unlike Ya3t and Yo1nck—couldn't be bothered to learn basic GalactiStani.

"Oooookay," Ya3t said. "Dr. Oe is currently molting, but if you're not allergic to dander, he can see you now. Otherwise you'll have to come back tomorrow."

Red's stomach growled. That FlinkBar she'd horked down on the way over hadn't been enough. "Dr. Oe is fine."

"Excellent!" Yo1nck said. "Fill this out while I get a room ready for you."

Red filled out the form: her name, Bonk's name, its serial number (no idea—she left this blank), date of manufacture (also left blank), date of last oil change (she made this up).

The receptionist returned and reviewed the form. "Exam room two," they said, gesturing toward an open door. It was flanked by two chairs, one occupied by a woman with a nervous Non-Newtonian poodle oozing around her ankles, the other by a boy cradling an alarmingly buzzing cardboard box.

Red sighed, shook out her arms, and picked Bonk back up with a grunt. The poodle tried to slime up her ankles as she walked by. "Shoo," she said. She kicked at it and stubbed her toe—hard. She cursed under her breath.

"Shh, it's okay, Pookie-ookums," the owner crooned, scooping the dog into her lap. "Did that mean lady hurt you?"

"Keep your dog in a pail, like a responsible pet owner," Red muttered as she elbowed the door shut behind her. She laid Bonk on the exam table and glanced around at the dials, wires, tubes, syringes, soldering irons, rubber hoses, and other equipment. She wondered if all those shiny buttons did anything cool.

Before she could find out, the second door opened and the vet tech flew in, a clipboard held tight in his beak. "Good morning!" he chirped, settling on a perch across the table and setting the clipboard down next to the cat. "Are you Red Darkling? I'm Dr. Oe." He extended a scaly foot for her to shake. "And this must be . . ." He checked the clipboard. "Bonk, is it?"

Red nodded.

"Nice to meet you both." He fluffed his feathers, sending a few scraggly ones to the floor. "I apologize for the mess. Molting never seems to come at a convenient time. Of course, there is no convenient time." He warbled at his joke. "So, what seems to be the problem today? Feline malware virus? There's a lot of FMV going around the last few months."

"I'm not sure," Red said. "I got Bonk second-hand about a year ago, and it's always been glitchy. But lately it seems to be getting worse. I guess I just want to know if there's anything you can do to, I dunno, fix it."

"All right, let's take a look." Dr. Oe opened the stomach panel with one talon and tilted his head to peer inside with a beady black eye. "Did you have it serviced recently?"

Red rubbed her neck. "Uh, no, not exactly. My—a friend opened it up to see if he could find the problem. Oh!" She dug a small bag out of her pocket and placed it on the table. "He said he couldn't remember where these went back in." She grinned sheepishly. "Sorry."

Dr. Oe clicked his beak. "I strongly recommend that all cat owners trust the service of their animals to professionals." He opened the bag and dumped out a few gears and bolts. He pushed them around a bit on the table with one claw. "None of these look like they belong in a cat in the first place. Are you sure these came out of Bonk?"

"No, I suppose not," Red replied as the tech poked around in Bonk's innards. "Woodman was working on the floor of my ship, so I guess it's possible he picked these up by mistake."

Another beak click. "Hm," he said thoughtfully. "That's odd."

"What?" Red leaned over to see what the tech was looking at.

"It's . . . hold on." Dr. Oe pulled a corded tool from a drawer and touched it to something inside Bonk. He checked one of the dials, then moved the tool to touch something else. "Okay, that doesn't make sense," he said, scratching his head with a claw. "This voltometer must be defective. I've got another one here, let's see if that does the trick."

He repeated the process with another tool—touch, check, touch again. This time his crest flared out and he tossed the tool on the table. "I don't know how to tell you this, Ms. Darkling, so I'll just say it," he said briskly. "Bonk isn't a cat."

Chapter 6
SECS Would Just Have to Wait

"What the hell do you mean, Bonk isn't a cat?" Red demanded. "What is it?"

"That I cannot say." Dr. Oe shook his head. "A cat has a combined electrical frequency signature between 52.9 and 63.2 hertz. It won't function outside those parameters." He tapped the dial with a claw. "This machine has a combined frequency of just 43.5 hertz."

"What does that mean? It's obviously a cat. Look at it!"

"I'm not finished, Ms. Darkling." The tech pointed at something in Bonk's cavity. "See these wires? They don't connect to anything but themselves. No cat has this. No cat has a panel like this, either. Can you see it?"

Red looked where Dr. Oe pointed. Sure enough, there was a slightly raised piece of metal attached to the inside of the hull. "What is it?"

"No idea. All I know is, in my fifty years in this business, I've never seen a cat with one of those."

"That looks like an empty port on the side, there. Like for a data chip," she said, nose inches from the chassis. "And is it just me, or is there something written on the side?"

Dr. Oe tilted his head again, then pulled a magnifying scope from a hook on the wall. He angled it over the mysterious panel and switched it on. A hologram appeared, showing an enlarged view of the panel and four letters etched into the metal.

"SECS . . ." Dr. Oe mumbled to himself. He ground his beak in thought.

"I didn't think Bonk could do that."

Dr. Oe warbled. "S.E.C.S. It's probably an abbreviation or acronym."

"The name of the manufacturer?" Red asked.

"Probably not. I'm familiar with most cat building companies, even the ones that work in rare models. None use this name."

"It does sound vaguely familiar, though." Red touched the hologrammatic letters with a finger. "And you're absolutely sure Bonk isn't a cat?"

"At best, it is something carefully designed to look like a cat, but it is no cat." He waved one wing. "You're welcome to consult other vet techs, of course, but that is my professional opinion." Dr. Oe closed the stomach panel with a click that resonated with finality. "I'm sorry I can't help you, Ms. Darkling."

"Hey, no, that's okay," Red stammered, her brain busy trying to figure out what SECS stood for. Special Equipment for Cat Stuff? Secret Entry for Component Service? Secondary Employment Compensation System? She'd seen it somewhere before, but she couldn't drag it from her memory. She'd have to search the database back on the *Wart*.

"Thanks anyway, Dr. Oe." She gathered the random hardware bits back into the bag and stuffed it in her pocket. "What do I owe you?"

"Not a thing," he said. "No actual cat, no actual exam." He extended his foot again and Red shook it. "I hope you figure out Bonk's secret." And he left the exam room in a small cloud of dander.

Her stomach rumbled angrily. Start eating cookies soon? SECS would have to wait. Red needed to get to Granny's before she put the leftovers away in the fridge.

~ ~ ~

Red left the clinic and headed across town to Granny's humble but comfortable home. She parked the *Wart* in front of the house and sat a moment, taking in the faded paint and shaggy lawn. She'd have to take care of the mowing while she was here, or maybe ask Buck to do it, if he was still around. Granny enjoyed good health, considering her age, but there were limits on what she could do herself. Mostly she kept busy with knitting, cooking, and playing bingo down at the senior center.

And, apparently, tending her roses. Red walked up the sidewalk lined with huge yellow blooms. The rich scent brought her back to the childhood she'd spent here with Granny. One time, she'd found a can of spray paint and turned every rose black. She winced at the memory. That was years ago. Granny'd probably forgotten it by now, right? She knocked on the door.

"Why, Mildred!" Granny cried, patting her hair. "What a nice surprise!"

"Hi, Granny." Red hugged her gently. "Your roses are gorgeous this year."

The old woman smiled and waved her hand. "Oh, they're all right, I suppose. This year I tried putting coffee grounds in the soil. Marge Blattz told me about it. At first I thought she was pulling my leg. She's always been jealous of my roses, you know. Remember that time you painted them all black? Marge won the Garden Club contest that year. You should have seen her face. Oh!" She patted Red's arm. "Listen to me, rattling on. Come in, come in!"

The smell of food hit Red like a wall as she stepped through the door.

"Are you hungry?" Granny asked, walking into the kitchen. "I've just finished, but there's plenty of leftovers."

"Oh, is it dinner time?" Red said. "I hadn't noticed."

Granny laughed. "Dear Mildred, I could hear your stomach talking to me from two systems away. Now, sit down and relax while I make you up a plate. It's only a casserole, I hope that's okay."

"It's perfect." Red sank into her usual place at the table.

Granny slid her hands into the pink-and-white checked oven mitts Red had given her for Christmas ages ago. "Why don't you get some new mitts, Granny? Those've got to be . . ." She squinted as she did the quick mental math. ". . . eighteen years old?"

"They may be old, but they still work fine," Granny said, removing the lid from a chipped dish. "Besides, they remind me of you."

Red shifted in her chair. The mitts had been, er, liberated from a warehouse near the docks on a dare from Woodman one boring Saturday night when she was ten. Granny found them under a pile of laundry in Red's closet, forcing Red to improvise a story about doing chores for her friends' parents to earn money for them. She wasn't surprised that Granny still pretended to believe that after all these years.

Granny slid a spoon through the golden topping of the casserole with a small crunch. It was still warm enough to release a wisp of fragrant steam.

"Tell me, what have you been up to lately?" she asked, placing an overflowing plate of creamy darna and noodles in front of Red.

Red shoveled in a bite. "Not much, really."

"You'll burn your tongue, eating that fast." Granny put a glass of milk on the table.

Red swallowed hard and grabbed the milk. "Too late."

Granny tutted and shook her head, then sat down to fold a stack of dishtowels. "How's Mark?"

"Mmph," Red mumbled, her mouth full. "He's fine. Visiting his parents right now."

"That's nice. Have you heard from . . . anyone else?"

Red burped. "Like who?"

"Oh, I don't know." Granny fiddled with the edge of a towel. "Anyone."

"Look," Red said, "if you're talking about Smith, I already told you, I took care of that."

Granny's brow wrinkled even more than it normally was. "I know, dear. It's just that I know how Johnny is."

"Everything's fine." Red chewed a moment. "Funny you mention it, though. Someone was asking about him earlier today."

"Oh?" Concern filled Granny's voice.

"Yeah, Woodman and I were at Chuck's and someone named Sam Anyanama buys me a drink. She's probably galactic police." Red paused. "She wants to know what happened with Smith. Why he's been leaving me alone."

"How does she know about that?"

Red stabbed a chunk of darna. "Apparently she's been following me. I'm starting to wonder if I've got a fan club or something. Stalkers of Red Darkling, Local 256."

Granny shook her head. "What did you tell her?"

"Nothing," Red shrugged. "Same as everyone else."

"I wish I knew what you'd done, dear." She sighed. "But I suppose you have your reasons to keep it all a secret."

Red avoided Granny's searching eyes and scraped the last bits of casserole onto her fork. She thought about the massive bluff she'd pulled out of her ass to make Smith back off. It was probably the stupidest thing she'd ever done, trusting his own fear and pride to keep him in check. But she'd played it well, and it worked. So far. But she couldn't risk telling anyone the details, not even Granny. One little slip and they would all be dead.

"Yeah," she said finally. "I do."

Granny pushed aside the stack of folded towels. "Well, then. Would you like more casserole? Or are you saving room for butterscotch cake?"

Red groaned and clutched her stomach. "Why didn't you tell me there was butterscotch cake! I'm already stuffed. Maybe later?"

"Later? Are you planning to stay?" Granny asked, picking up the empty dishes and putting them in the sink.

"Yeah, I mean, just a few days. If that's okay with you."

"Of course! I'll go put fresh sheets on your bed."

"You don't have to do that."

Granny waved a hand. "Oh, it needs to be done anyway."

Red rolled her eyes but said nothing. She knew from years of experience that there was no stopping Granny from changing sheets once she decided they needed changing.

Chapter 7
Empty Cigarette Lighters and Other Childhood Detritus

Red woke up the next morning to discover it was already afternoon. The summer sun splashed across the tattered band posters, 'hopper magazines, empty cigarette lighters, and other childhood detritus. She stretched. Her back let out a series of satisfying pops—proof that she'd slept harder than a hibernating gazellope.

Her body ached for coffee and a smoke, but she was too comfortable to get up yet. She made a mental list of what she wanted to get done today: install the plasma damper, get Buck to come mow the lawn, shower, look for SECS.

Too much. Coffee first.

She stumbled downstairs in her bare feet, face splitting in a massive yawn. A note from Granny stuck to the refrigerator with a "Bingo Queen" magnet explained that she'd gone to the senior center for a presentation on traditional Lufarian knitting patterns. A pot of coffee simmered on the stove. Red poured herself a giant mug and inhaled the steam. The slightly sludgy consistency and nosehair-curling smell made Red suspicious that the coffee had been keeping warm since Granny made it at whatever godforsaken time she usually woke up. One sip proved her right—it was strong, dark, and bitter. In other words, perfect. Well, almost. A splash of whiskey wouldn't hurt. Granny only kept cooking sherry around the house—which had been an acceptable alternative to real booze during many a youthful adventure, but Adult Red had standards. Low ones, sure, but not cooking-sherry-in-the-coffee low.

Especially when she had a perfectly good bottle of Finebock on the ship.

Red slipped a slice of butterscotch cake onto a plate, grabbed the mug of coffee, and headed out to the *Wart*. She activated the hatch with her elbow and somehow managed to climb into the ship without spilling anything. She was congratulating herself on not wasting any of the precious coffee when her little toe discovered the ammo box under a haphazard slew of skin mags and catalogs. Hot liquid splashed over her front, adding another layer of stain to her shirt. She flinched at the heat, causing the cake to fly from the plate in a gentle arc. Without thinking, Red dropped the empty plate and threw out her hand to catch the gooey cake before it hit the floor.

Red caught her breath and looked around. She was wet, had possibly scalded her tits, and her little toe throbbed dully. Granny's plate had shattered, its hundred tiny pieces scattered among the rest of the coffee-sprinkled garbage. But it could be worse: her mug was still more full than not, and the cake, while no longer strictly recognizable as cake, was certainly still edible.

She shrugged, took a bite, and limped into the cockpit. She sank into the captain's chair and balanced the mug carefully on the control panel. Taking another bite of cake, she groped under the chair with her free hand for the bottle of whiskey she kept there for emergencies. She used her teeth to unscrew the cap, then topped off her coffee with a hearty shot. Okay, probably closer to two shots. She deserved it, especially since she'd only been awake for half an hour and had already hurt herself and made a mess. A bigger mess. Whatever.

Plus she had to ping Buck. She groaned. Buck was a cool guy and all, but damn, he hadn't changed at all since they were twelve and he thought no one else had either. Maybe she'd just send him a message. Avoid that whole 'hey, you wanna get together with the old gang and hang out like old times' crap. That never went well.

Yeah. She'd send a message.

Red crammed the rest of the cake into her mouth and washed it down with the heavily spiked coffee. She pulled up Buck's number on the vidscreen, licked most of the frosting from her fingers, wiped the rest on her shirt (it was already beyond hope), and tapped out a quick message:

```
HEY,  BUCK,  HOW'S  IT  GOING?  SAME  OLD
STUFF  WITH  ME.  CAN  YOU  SWING  BY  GRANNY'S
AND  MOW  THE  LAWN?  I'D  DO  IT  MYSELF  BUT
I'M  ONLY  IN  MAGROSS  FOR  A  DAY  OR  TWO  AND
I'M  SUPER  BUSY.  I  KNOW,  I'M  GRUMSHIT.
I'LL  BUY  YOU  A  PIZZA  NEXT  TIME  I'M  IN
TOWN.    ANYPLACE    BUT    SHELLCHUCKERS.
THANKS,  MAN,  YOU'RE  THE  BEST.
```

She sent the message and sat back, lighting a thin, black Crolinian cigar. Smoke twisted toward the ceiling in lazy curls. Assy task number one: done. Next up: plasma damper. She really wanted to chill out with Granny for a few days, but without the plasma damper she'd have to leave last Tuesday to make it to Gambora in time to meet Tom.

"Sorry, Granny," she said, blowing a smoke ring at the screen. "Your turn to wait."

~ ~ ~

Three hours, two more pieces of butterscotch cake, and several bruised knuckles later, Red had the plasma damper installed. Well, installed was maybe too formal a term. 'Beaten into submission' was better. Or 'held together with a quart of electroputty and the confidence of Vladmir V after a few shots of blood rum.' Not her prettiest work—the casing stuck out of the engine block at a weird angle and was held up by some old, mismatched tools pressed into service as legs. But hey, it was done, and it worked.

She flexed her sore hands. While she'd been fighting the damper into place, her mind kept returning to SECS. She'd seen it somewhere, and recently. If she could just remember . . .

Screw it, that's what databases were for.

Grabbing the half-empty Finebock bottle, she slumped into the captain's chair. She opened the research portal and activated the voice controls. "Search SECS," she said, taking a sip.

Results immediately flooded the vidscreen. Red sprayed whiskey all over the control panel. "No!" she cried, wiping her chin with her hand. "Not SECS, S.E.C.S.! Ess ee cee ess!"

An icon spun while the database searched. After a few seconds, a message blinked on. OVER 9 MILLION RESULTS— CONTINUE?

Figures. "Add search string 'cat.'" Another few seconds, then OVER 500,000 RESULTS—CONTINUE?

Red groaned. This was going to take forever. "Prioritize location 'Slovar.' Display." The Slovar market was where she'd picked up Bonk in the first place. It wasn't likely the cat originated there, but she had to start looking somewhere.

The list popped up on the screen. Red took a slug of whiskey and scanned the results. Nothing looked promising. Half of them didn't even seem to have anything to do with cats at all. Sanitation Engineers of Central Slovar? No. Stange Enterprises: Cat Socks? Maybe. Red tagged it, just in case. Stereo Experiences in Culinary Science? Probably not. Supersonic Endoplasmic Cathode Sequentializing—what the hell did that even mean?

One hour, 2,156 listings, and only three tagged possibilities later, she threw a cigar butt across the room in frustration. It was hopeless. Whatever SECS was, she wouldn't get it this way. If only she could remember where she'd seen it before . . .

Hungry for real food to ease the post-whiskey buzz headache, Red closed the database portal and stretched. Her nose wrinkled at the smell of stale coffee, butterscotch, and B.O. that wafted from her body. She checked the time: just enough to take a quick shower before seeing what Granny had planned for dinner.

She went into the house and stuck her head in the kitchen. She found Granny humming to herself and stirring something on the stove.

"Oh! Mildred! There you are," she said. "Thought I'd try a new recipe tonight. Spoo aloo? The girls at bingo all rave about it. I can't tolerate the spice myself, of course, so you'll have to put in your own peppers."

Red peeked into the pot at the stew, brimming with unrecognizable chunks. "I don't think I've ever had Podnarian food before," she said. "Give me ten minutes. I need a shower. I stink like a quashtoad."

Granny sniffed. "Is that butterscotch cake on your sleeve?"

"Fifteen minutes, tops." Red raced up to the bathroom, shedding her socks and jacket along the way. She cranked the water up to scalding and peeled off the rest of her clothes, tossing them like a jatball into the corner. Something small and white fell out onto the tile floor. Red picked it up. It was the business card from the woman at the bar, Sam something. It was stained with coffee and sweat, but still legible. Red squinted at the small type through the steam pouring from the shower and gasped. It said:

```
Sam Anyanama
S.E.C.S.
GAM-8-182-28183-9-A12
ext 706
```

Chapter 8
Reverend Skulkington

"Mildred!" Granny scolded, recognizing Red's stained clothes and unique aroma. "I thought you were taking a shower before dinner."

"I can't stay to eat," Red said. "Something's come up. I've got to see Woodman."

"But—"

"Save some spoo aloo for me?" She shrugged into her jacket.

"But—"

She kissed her grandmother's cheek. "Sorry."

"Well, at least take something with you."

Red grabbed a zuranfruit from the bowl on the kitchen table and waggled it at Granny. "I gotta go. Love you!"

"I love you—" The door slammed. "—too." Granny looked at the bowl of spoo aloo in her hands and sighed.

~ ~ ~

The *Wart* made record time to the Woodmans' place, thanks to the lack of traffic cops in central Magross. Red dropped the ship onto the private landing pad in the yard, near the professionally manicured aggrippinia trees. She knocked on the back door. A few seconds later, she knocked again, harder. She stretched out her hand to try the knob herself when the door swung open.

"Red? What are you doing here?" Woodman frowned. "Babe, you stink."

"Yeah, cool," she said distractedly, pushing past him into the hallway. "We need to talk about SECS."

"Hey!" He threw a hand over Red's mouth. "My parents are right in the other room!"

Red slapped his hand away. "No, you grumbrained idiot. It's letters, etched into this weird panel in Bonk's stomach cavity."

"Oh, this is about the cat?" Woodman glanced over his shoulder. "Look, it's not a good time, babe."

"Pfft. Jester's scrap with mom and dad can wait. This is important! I looked it up in all the databases, right? A billion results." Woodman raised a skeptical eyebrow. "Maybe not that many, but too many for me to slog through one at a time."

"Okay, so?" He shook his head and rubbed his stubbled chin.

"So I gave up, yeah?" Red paced the floor, waving her hands. "But I knew I'd seen that somewhere before. I just had to remember where. Then I was getting ready for a shower and that business card fell out of my bra. The one from the chick at the bar. The card, not the bra. Anyway, I'm sitting there, naked on the toilet—"

"Shut *up*, Red!"

"Mark?" A voice called from another part of the house. "Is everything all right?"

"Yeah, mom, it's just . . . it's . . . a bear."

"A bear!?"

"I mean, I'll be right there."

Red choked back a laugh. "A bear?"

He shot Red a dark look. "I told you, it's not a good time. Can't this wait until tomorrow?"

"Why, what're you guys doing?" She leaned around Woodman's body, trying to see past him. "This isn't about jester's scrap, is it?"

"Look, just tell me what you need to tell me."

"Fine, fine. So like I said, not a single hit on the databases, but on that card it says—you'll never believe this—Sam Anyanama, SECS."

He blinked. "Okay, what does it mean?"

"I don't know. But she does."

"Who?"

"Sam Anyanama!" She snapped her fingers in front of his nose. "Are you even paying attention?"

"Yeah, sorry, I'm a little—"

"There you are, Mark," said his mother, walking into the room. "You're missing everything."

"Hi, Mrs. Woodman," Red said, trying not to stare at the sequined eye patch she wore, and failing miserably.

"Oh, hello Red. I didn't know you were here." Mrs. Woodman's eyes widened slightly at the state of her shirt, and her nose wrinkled. But she must have decided it wasn't that far out of Red's ordinary appearance because she regained her composure almost immediately. "It's Joe's birthday next week, but since he'll be, ah, out of town, we're celebrating early. Just a couple of friends from the club. We're playing one of those old-fashioned murder mystery role-playing games. I'm the Duchess of Merivale." She touched the eye patch. "I was partially blinded by a rapier during the Duke's duel with Admiral Bartlett over my hand in marriage. Caused quite a bit of tension at court, as you can imagine."

Red nodded, biting her lip hard and struggling not to meet Woodman's eye.

"If you'll excuse us, please, Red. Mark—I mean, Reverend Skulkington—was about to reveal the owner of the dagger he found behind the credenza in the maid's quarters." Mrs. Woodman took her son's arm and put an elaborately beribboned Blixic Fundamentalist liturgical hat on his head. The red cord at the brim matched his furious blush.

"No problem. Sorry I busted into your party. Tell Mr. Woodman I said happy birthday." She glanced at Woodman and couldn't tell if he was about to laugh his guts out or melt into a puddle of shame on the carpet. Probably both. "I'll ping you tomorrow, Reverend. Maybe we can grab some drinks. I'll buy if you wear the hat."

She managed to wait until she was safely back on the *Wart* before laughing so hard her stomach muscles ached and she got the hiccups.

Chapter 9
Chip Lipley Is On the Scene

The next day, Red met Woodman at Chuck's Tap again.

"No hat?"

"Ha ha," he said, settling into a chair across from her.

"Maybe you can swipe it. I've always wanted to fool around with a Blixic priest."

Woodman said nothing. Just stared at his empty hands.

Red eyed him suspiciously. "Don't you want a beer or something?"

"Nah." He picked at a coaster advertising the Purple Radish Microbrewery in Septimal City.

"Oooookay." Red took a swig from her own sweating bottle. She watched the jatball game showing on the grimy vidscreen behind the bar. A bunch of guys running around in shorts, how exciting. "So," she said, trying to fill space. "Who died?"

Woodman looked up from shredding his coaster. "What? Why would you ask that?"

She leaned back in her chair and threw up her hands. "Dude, weren't you playing some murder mystery game?"

"Oh. That."

"Woodman, what the hell is wrong with you?"

His face seemed to collapse, and he sighed. "It's my dad. He's, well, they think he's got the rikk."

Holy shit. "How the hell did he get the rikk?"

Woodman shrugged, poking the shreds into little piles. "Picked it up somewhere, I guess. You know how he's always traveling for work."

"I had no idea he was sick."

"I wanted to tell you sooner, but . . . We don't even really know if that's what's going on," he said, starting on a new coaster. "He's got the classic symptoms. You know, swollen toes, nausea, can't stand bright lights. But the doctors need to get in there and see his spleen to be sure one way or the other."

"When will they know?"

"He goes in for surgery next week." He paused. "I'm sorry, Red, but I gotta stick around here for a while. Mom's really having a hard time. And if he does have the rikk—"

"Dude." Red took his hand across the table. "You do what you gotta do."

"Yeah." He sniffed.

"Do you want me to stay?"

A hint of a grin twitched Woodman's lips. "Nah, it'll just be a bunch of us moping around in a hospital room. Totally boring, you'd hate it."

"But—"

"And you're not exactly good at handling that kind of thing. You know how you get around doctors. Remember when we were kids, and Schnozz fell off his roof and broke his arm?" Red nodded. "You kept insisting that he was fine, tried to keep the MediTeks from taking him to the hospital? You gave that guy a bloody nose!"

"Wait, but that—"

"They had to sedate you!"

"Okay, yeah, you've got a point."

He squeezed her hand. "Babe, I know you want to help, but go do your shit on Gambora. I'll be fine."

"You sure?"

"Absolutely."

Guilty relief washed over her. She really did want to help. She'd known his parents since she was a kid. She and Woodman had spent hours shaving obscenities into their cats and switching labels on their canned goods. And they never seemed to mind—much, anyway. Red teased Woodman all the time about being a mama's boy, but they really were a close family. This had to be eating him alive.

Still, Woodman was right about her being weird in hospitals. Something about the overly bright lighting, and the crappy art in the lobby, and the nurses in their scrubs with the cartoon characters, like they were doing everything they could to pretend that no one was hurting or dying behind all those closed doors. It made her want to punch stuff. Her hands clenched up just thinking about it.

The last thing the Woodmans needed right now was a bunch of angry doctors with bloody faces.

"All right. But you ping me if you need anything, deal?"

"Deal. Want to tell me more about SECS?"

Red squelched yet another dirty joke. It didn't seem the time. "Not much to tell, really. It's on that Sam's business card. She said she works for . . . she didn't actually say. She gave off heavy government vibes, though. And she had a badge."

"What kind of badge?"

"I dunno, it was shiny. I only saw it for a second."

Woodman smiled a little. "Must be a rare one, if you didn't recognize it."

"Hey!" But it was good to see him joking again. Almost like things were normal. "There's a number on it too. I'm gonna ping her as soon as I figure out what to say. I thought 'Hey, d'you know my cat?' might make me look a little crazy."

"No crazier than half the stuff you say." He glanced at his watch. "Hey, babe, I gotta go," he said, standing up. "Mom dragged out all the old home movies. She's extra excited to see our trip to Crysallia when I was two."

"Can't honestly say I'm too upset to be missing out on that." Red stood too. Before she could decide what was appropriate to say or do when your best (only) friend and sort-of-maybe-boyfriend had just shared potentially devastating news about his parents, Woodman threw his arms around her and buried his face in her hair. She hugged him back, trying not to notice the raggedness of his breathing. And when he finally broke away and walked out of the bar, she pretended his eyes were always that wet.

She sat back down, drained her beer, and waved at Chuck for another. While she waited, her thoughts dragged her back to when her own parents died, when she was twelve. Died? Ha. Murdered, more like. Right in front of her. No chance to say goodbye. Was that better or worse than a slow, painful death from the rikk? At least she'd had Granny to help her pick up the pieces.

Chuck derailed her train of thought by dropping a bottle on the table with a clank. "D'you see me wearing a name tag and a twitchy little skirt?"

Red glanced at his greasy pants. "No, but I think you could pull it off. You got the legs for it."

"I'm not your damn waitress." He pointed a filthy finger in her face. "Get your ass up to the bar for your drinks like everyone else." He stalked away, muttering.

"Aw, c'mon, Chuck!" she called after him. "I'm getting hot over here just thinking about your quivering thighs!" A couple shady guys in tattered coveralls turned toward her with thinly veiled interest, but she flipped them off. The jatball game had ended and the broadcast switched to the day's headlines. Red watched mindlessly as the teased-blonde anchor with too many teeth told the greater Magross area about a string of shipjackings, flooding along the Corgan River, Ephrasia Pfeff's most recent divorce, a deadly gas leak at a vet tech's office—

"Holy shit." Red scrambled over to the bar. "Chuck, turn it up." She waved a frantic hand at the vidscreen. "Turn it UP, dammit!"

The bartender pointedly refused to look in her direction, but did nudge the volume up a few decibels.

"—baffled by the incident, which claimed the lives of at least five people and hospitalized a dozen more." The anchor was using her serious face for this story. "KMAG ActionMagross reporter Chip Lipley is on the scene. Chip, I understand you're speaking with a survivor of the leak."

The vid cut to a scene outside the vet tech's office—at least, Red assumed it was the office underneath the giant tarp with hazmat signs all over it. Lights from the emergency response ships hovering overhead cycled through red, blue, white, and back again. The reporter, wearing a pristine hard hat with the price tag still on it, pressed a hand to his ear.

"Yes, I'm here outside Dr. Mn's Vet Tech Clinic and Oil Change Emporium," he shouted into his microphone to be heard over the sirens. "As you can see behind me, this long-time cornerstone of the Magross business community and frequent winner of the Mayor's Choice Award has been shut down following an unexpected and deadly gas leak."

The camera pulled back to reveal someone sitting on the bumper of an ambulance, breathing through a respirator. Red recognized them despite the masks covering their faces. "I'm here with Ya3t and Yo1nck," the reporter continued, "the Ulatan native who worked as a receptionist at the doomed establishment." He turned to them with a frown of sympathy. "Tell me, what happened?"

"It was awful," Yo1nck said, pulling the mask away from their face. "I'd just stepped outside for a coffee break. When I came back in, everyone was on the ground, gasping for breath. The air smelled funny, sort of sour, so I ran back out." They paused to take a few breaths through the respirator. "I wasn't supposed to go on break until two, but Dr. Hp said I could go early. If she hadn't . . ." The seemingly unharmed Non-Newtonian poodle ran through the shot, yipping and dragging its leash.

Ya3t removed their mask and sniffed. "Now they're all dead," they said. "Dr. Hp, Dr. Oe, Sarah—" Their voice broke and they turned away, waving off the camera.

Chip was unfazed. "Sources within the emergency rescue team have suggested this was not an accident. Can you think of anyone who might have done this?" the reporter asked, pushing the microphone closer. "A disgruntled employee? A bereaved client? The Vandrosian mafia?"

Ya3t dabbed their eyes with a tissue. "We're vet techs. We did oil changes. We helped people and their pets. We're good people. Who'd want to kill us?"

"Who, indeed?" He turned to Yo1nck. "This must be difficult for you," he said, tutting in sympathy. "How does it feel to lose so many of your coworkers—people you've worked with for years, friends even—in such a sudden and likely excruciatingly painful way?"

"How do you think I feel?" Yo1nck snapped. "Get that microphone out of my face."

The reporter turned to the camera. "As you can see, emotions are high, and a lot of questions remain unanswered. Chip Lipley, reporting for KMAG ActionMagross. Back to you, Haelae."

The anchor reappeared. "Thank you, Chip. We'll be sure to keep an eye on this developing story." Her somber expression shifted to a brilliant smile. "Speaking of pets, today marks the fiftieth anniversary of Lardie the Gnar's major motion picture debut. We'll be talking to his handler's grandson, Hank Farkle, after a brief word from our sponsor."

The screen filled with disturbingly happy children skipping around maniacally while singing a jaunty jingle. "Before you head off into space, stuff a FlinkBar in your face—"

Red hissed in disgust. "You can turn that trash off now, Chuck," she said, "and gimme another beer. Better make it two."

She had a lot of drinking to do.

Chapter 10
Talked to Death

Drunk-dialing a possible government agent who works with the cops isn't recommended for anyone, let alone a lifelong delinquent and career criminal like Red Darkling.

That doesn't mean she didn't do it, though.

Back at the *Wart*, Red fished the business card out of her pocket and immediately dropped it. She fumbled through the damp drifts of trash on the floor, finally finding the card stuck to the not-quite-empty whiskey bottle. Red eyed the bottle suspiciously, sniffed it, and took a sip. She shuddered and spit out a soggy cigar butt.

Still, better than Granny's cooking sherry.

It took several tries to get the number right. The first one turned out to be a grum rancher in the middle of castrating his yearlings. The second went to the inbox of aging actress and hotel spokesperson Ephrasia Pfeff. Red left a rambling video message describing her idea for a *Port Desire* storyline where Pfeff would play an aging actress and hotel spokesperson who ends up as a cheerleader for the Crolinian Psycats when the evil twin she didn't know she had steals her identity, her husband, and her favorite shoes.

After she hung up, Red spent a few frantic minutes trying to remember who she was supposed to be calling and why. Luckily, the business card was still legible, despite being soaked in various layers of coffee, boob sweat, and whiskey. Red squinted at it, reading each letter and number out loud as she tapped them in.

"Anyanama." The woman didn't look up as she answered the ping. She sat behind a desk covered in neatly stacked piles of papers. A galactic flag stood in the corner behind her. Even in Red's current state of substance-inspired confusion, she could tell she was at work.

"Hey!" Red hiccupped. "Anana—Amaya—how do you say that name again?"

"Red?" Sam looked up at the vidscreen, frowned, and put down her pen. "Just call me Sam."

"Okay, Sam. Do you know my cat?"

She let out an exasperated sigh. "Red, are you drunk?"

Red hid the now-empty Finebock bottle behind her back. "Pfft, nah. Okay, maybe a little. But not, like, *drunk* drunk. I'm not even horny."

The woman took off her glasses and folded her hands on the desk. Red suddenly felt like she was ten years old again, about to be grounded for some stupid prank. "Red, I'm glad you pinged me, I really am. Are you ready to talk about John Smith?"

"No, dammit, just listen. This is important." Red squinted, concentrating hard against the spinning in her head. "Tell me about SECS."

"I'm not sure I'm the right person—"

"Gah, not sex! What's with everyone?" Red rolled her eyes. "S.E.C.S.! It's on your card?"

"Right." Sam unfolded her hands and glanced toward the vidscreen controls. "We usually just spell it out."

"So anyway," Red said. "My cat's name's Bonk. Got it used from a C'longi named Tom. Pretty sure that's not his real name. Tom, not Bonk. Anyway, Bonk's kind of glitchy? Not a big deal really, just annoying, but it's getting worse. So I take it to a tet vech, I mean vet tech, yeah? And he finds this weird panel in its stomach that says SECS."

"Your *cat*?" Sam's hand froze over the disconnect button. Her face hardened and she stared at Red through the vidscreen. "You're saying your cat has S.E.C.S. parts."

Red clapped her hands. "Yes! Exactly! Well, not exactly." She frowned. "It's not a cat."

Sam closed her eyes and seemed to take several deep breaths. "It is a cat, or it's not a cat?"

"Yes! No! I don't know, it's hard to think when you're spinning around like that." Red shook her head. "So what does it mean? Is Bonk's SECS the same as your SECS?"

"Maybe." The woman's eyes narrowed. "I'd have to see the . . . Bonk." She tapped her pen on the desktop, started to say something, then fell silent again. After a minute she gave a little nod. "Can I meet you somewhere?"

Ugh, just what Red needed—wasting fuel cruising across the galaxy to yet another meetup and getting talked to death in a rambling conversation that went nowhere. "Tell you what. I'll be at the Gambora market on Tuesday."

Sam nodded. "I can do that. Where? What time?"

"I dunno. How about the Royal ErotiStar Theater? It's at the corner of Eighth and Rabaalast."

The woman's mouth did that same familiar twitch again. Where had she seen it before? "I'll see you there at ten o'clock local time. Hopefully we'll beat the lunchtime crowd. Oh, and Red?" She slid her glasses back on and brushed back her fringe of blue hair. "Try to be sober this time. Just for something different."

The vidscreen went dark as she hung up.

"I'm sober plenty of times," Red grumbled, sitting back in the captain's chair. She grunted and pulled the bottle out from behind her. Tossing it on the floor, she picked a cigar from her boot. It wasn't until she had a lungful of smoke pumping nicotine into her blood that she realized Sam never said what SECS stood for.

Maybe she had a point about the drinking. Dammit.

Red stuffed that thought away in the same mental place she put all her guilt and shame. No time for that shit now. She had to get her ass to Gambora on Tuesday. First, though, she had to raid Granny's fridge to stock up for the trip. She stood up and stretched. She yawned hard enough to pop her jaw. Maybe a nap, too. And a shower. Definitely a shower.

Chapter 11
Hence the Blaster

Red blew a strand of sweaty, electroputty-crusted hair out of her eyes. She'd been working for hours, and all because she couldn't resist taking another look at that panel. Stupid. Just one more wire to reconnect and Bonk would be ready to power up. Who knew cats were so complicated? And how many screwbolts did one cat need, anyway? Red swore next time Woodman decided to pull apart an elaborate electro-mechanical device, she'd be sure to watch him do it.

She poked her tongue out the corner of her mouth and cycled up the cold fusion torch. Sparks flew. One threatened to ignite the large yozzie-grease stain on her pants, but she brushed it away impatiently before it could add to the intricate pattern of holes. When the smoke cleared, she checked her work. Yep, the yellow autosensor wire now attached to the eye servos. About damn time.

As Red waited for the weld to set, she took a swig of boozeless coffee. Her eyes were drawn yet again to the SECS panel, now almost completely reburied in rusty components. She'd seen plenty of scrap in her day, but nothing quite like this.

She checked her weld—it was good, of course. Seventeen years patching up one crapbucket ship after another with whatever parts she could scrounge will do that to a girl. She picked up the stomach panel, wiped it off on her shirt, and snapped it back into place. Then she hauled Bonk back on its feet and pressed the power button at the base of its tail. After a few seconds, a whirring sound came from the cat, and its mismatched eyes glowed to life.

Red cocked her head to one side, waiting for something to go wrong. But no smoke poured from its ears, and the rear exhaust port didn't emit a foul odor. It seemed okay.

"Bonk? You good?" she asked, running a hand down its back. Not overheating—another good sign.

The cat blinked at her and began to make the horrible gargling noise that passed for its purr. It walked straight into Red's chest, head-first, nearly knocking her backward. She rubbed her ribs and groaned. Another bruise for the collection.

From the cockpit, the nav beeped. "Just in time," she said, staggering to her feet.

Gambulon 2 loomed outside the viewport. Most of the galactic government's highest officials lived here, and it showed. The planet oozed money and power like a blister oozed pus. Vast cities sprawled across the surface, each one glittering in the twin suns. The populace long ago outsourced all its ugly to nearby moons. They relied on millions of freighters and other service vehicles to connect the planet to its heavy industry, manufacturing, and sanitation services. But even these had to be fancied up—who wants to see regular cargo ships flying by as you're sipping aggrippinia tea on your penthouse veranda with the undersecretary of the Interplanetary Relations Department's subcommittee on trade deficits? Not Gambulonians. Some people from less wealthy systems (which was all of them) paid cold hard cash to book a vacation on a Gambulonian freighter. Even sewage tankers had waiting lists several years long.

Red plopped into the captain's chair and ground her teeth. She hated Gambulon 2—the whole nebula, really. Bunch of grumstains, most of them far too willing to call the cops on a simple trader just trying to make a living. You'd think they'd be glad to have some of their clutter taken off their hands, but no. Plus dodging the freighters was a major pain in the ass. Worse than an asteroid field, and that's on a slow day.

She switched off the automatic pilot and took manual control of the *Wart*. Immediately a construction freighter cut her off, causing her to veer left to avoid being plastered on its polished hull. Her cursing was cut short by another freighter squeezing into her designated lane. Red punched the boosters to zoom past it, limits be damned. Wouldn't be her first, last, or worst speeding ticket.

Luckily, the nav had delivered her right above Gambora so she didn't have far to go. Red dropped into the approach pattern and circled the city center. She passed the Modern Mandrake Hotel and wondered if her good friend Spencer was working the front desk today. Maybe she'd drop in later to say hello. Then she remembered being tossed out on her ass by a couple of musclebound thugs the last time she'd been there. So yeah, maybe she'd skip drinks with Spencer.

Red found a parking space behind an office complex, close to both the theater where she was meeting Sam and the market where she was meeting Tom. The smug sense of victory at finding the perfect spot evaporated when she saw the price.

"Fifty freaking credits," she grumbled, watching her account balance drop on the vidscreen. She'd have to pull another job soon if she felt like eating something other than Granny's leftover casseroles at any point in the near future. She'd have to keep an eye open for an opportunity at the market. You never know when a nice piece of jewelry or some bootleg Indar Skjov movies might find their way into her pockets.

Speaking of pockets, time to gear up. Red went back to her tiny bedroom and changed into her favorite pants: the ones with the built-in blaster holster and reinforced linings that deflected holo-based weapons and made her butt look good. After a minute's thought, she pulled on a jacket too. A little warm for a Gambulonian summer, and it smelled like a sick shiq had taken a dump on the sleeve, but she might need the extra pocket space for, well, whatever she might find.

After tugging on her boots, she pulled her ammo box from under the bed. She'd take the blaster, obviously. And the holoknife—that always got a good reaction. She debated about the mini faze cannon, then decided against it. Too much risk of collateral damage, and it wasn't like she was joining Zaldroni'i separatists on a raid or anything. It should be a simple chat with Sam Anyawhatever, then a quick negotiation with Tom, then back to the *Wart* to give Gambora a front-row view of the backside of her ship.

Never mind that what *should* happen rarely *did* happen. Hence the blaster.

Red shut the ammo box, then quickly reopened it to grab the size D4 screwdriver. She slid it down into her boot. Not sure why, exactly. Its odd size made it almost useless as a tool, it wasn't sharp or heavy, and it didn't even look intimidating. Pull that out in a fight, and the other guy might die just from laughing. Still, she couldn't deny a certain silly sentimental feeling for the stupid thing, sort of like what she felt about Bonk and all its glitches. Weird, but there it is. Besides, no one would expect a screwdriver in her boot. Surprise had its charms.

The last thing she had to take wouldn't fit in any pocket: Bonk itself. Red had given this some thought on the trip. The cat could be carried—she'd done that before—but hauling its metal bulk through crowded city markets wasn't exactly how Red enjoyed spending her time. And you never knew when it would sense some gnars and go into Psycho Kill Mode. So, she'd rigged up a carrier from a battered but relatively sturdy Hamstel Lite crate, a spare semi-grav servo she had laying around, and a couple of batteries borrowed from the vidscreen's remote. Red had done something similar for the fourth-grade science project she threw together an hour before the deadline. She'd gotten a D because the teacher was a fazzer-loving grumstain who wouldn't stop bitching about making an effort, taking pride in your work, yadda yadda. But it worked, even if it wasn't pretty enough for Mrs. Margill's lofty standards.

She found the cat curled up in the copilot's chair. It had engaged its recharge cycle and did *not* want to be interrupted. "Let go!" Red said, struggling to unhook its claws from the fake grumskin upholstery. Ten minutes, six scratches of varied severity, and one near-escape later, Red slammed the lid of the crate on a seriously pissed-off Bonk.

"And stay there." Red latched the lid and flipped on the semi-grav. It rose a few inches from the floor and hovered there. Red pushed it easily out the hatch of the ship and into the streets of Gambora.

Chapter 12
That Certainly Is Convenient

The walk to the theater was short, but Red was forcibly reminded why she avoided Gambora whenever possible. People stared at her crusty hair and aromatic jacket with barely concealed horror. Bonk's crate, now steadily emitting a low, gurgling growl, shed moldy splinters all over the sidewalk. One woman clutched her bag to her chest and crossed the street when she saw Red coming. Red smiled, waved, and suggested something else she could clutch instead. She gestured helpfully, just to make sure the woman understood. Her response made it clear that Red would never be invited to the Gambora Ladies Society's annual luncheon and charity auction. Damn, that's a shame, but totally worth it.

Unlike Red, the Royal ErotiStar Theater offered nothing offensive to the Gambulonian eye. Your average Gambulonian enjoyed porn as much as the next person, maybe even more—they were government employees, after all. But like everything else on the planet, they preferred to disguise it in pretty wrappings. Elaborately carved columns of fashionably pink marble flanked the filigree doors. A large stained-glass window depicted several tastefully naked people engaged in stylized acts of sexual experimentation usually found in unpasteurized form on the outer channels of the low-res band.

Sam had been wrong about missing the crowd. The sidewalk was bustling with people ducking in and out of the theater, not to mention the regular shoppers going about their business. Red finally found Sam perched on a bench near a decorative fountain. When she saw Red, she stood up quickly. "Thank you for coming," she said, putting out her hand.

Red shook it and nodded at the fountain. "I heard it was modeled after Indar Skjov, but I think it looks more like Sancho della Coque. Especially from this angle. Don't you think?"

Sam glanced back at it. "It's very evocative." She cleared her throat and gestured at the growling crate. "Is this . . .?"

Red smirked and kicked it lightly. "That's Bonk." The noise intensified. "It's not too happy about all this crate stuff."

"I can see that." Sam looked around the crowded street. "Is there somewhere we can open this without putting anyone at risk?"

"We could go inside," Red shrugged. "The weirder kinks are generally pretty empty unless the senate's in special session. I think today they're showing a modern interpretation of ancient C'longi mating rituals. That could work."

"Uh. That's certainly a possibility, but—"

"Or I could just switch it off and you can look at it here."

"Let's do that."

Red pushed the crate over to the bench and sat down. Bonk fell suspiciously quiet. She unlatched the lid and peeked inside. The cat's green and gold eyes glittered in the semidarkness. "It's okay, Bonk," Red said, poking her hand tentatively into the crate. "It's okay—ouch!—just going to deactivate you for a few minutes, dammit, hold still . . ."

"Is it always this aggressive?" Sam asked, peering into the crate.

Red sucked on a bleeding scratch. "Only when it sees some vermin." She glanced at Sam. "You should be fine."

Sam smiled faintly. She lifted the cat out of the crate and set it next to her on the bench. Red couldn't help but notice she didn't have any problem with the weight. She probably worked out, the bastard. "You said there's a panel?"

"Yeah." Red flipped Bonk over on its back and popped open the stomach. She pointed at the panel through the general corrosion. "The letters are pretty small, but you can see if you get close. There's a slot in the side, too, about this big." Red held up her fingers about an inch apart. "Looks like it could take a data chip."

The woman bent her head closer to the cat. Her pale blue hair swung down, nearly brushing the rusty circuits. "Have you noticed any unusual behavior?"

"You mean besides the bonking? Not really," Red said. "I mean, I've never owned a cat before, but it seems to do normal cat stuff. Y'know, takes out gnars, dugger mites, that kind of thing. Saved my ass from this giant bug once."

Sam looked up sharply. "What kind of giant bug?"

"I didn't ask," Red shrugged. "It was a hitchhiker. Picked it up to earn a few credits. It claimed to be stranded, but once it was on my ship it tried to eat my face." She tilted her head to show Sam the scar along her jawline. "Bonk took care of it before I could ask about its pedigree."

The woman chewed on her lip. "And how big would you say this bug was? Two feet? Three?"

"Taller than me. Six feet, maybe?"

"Human size? You're absolutely sure about that?"

Like Red could somehow forget the details of being attacked by a nightmare with too many legs and not nearly enough squishy parts. "I couldn't find my tape measure so I might be off a few inches. Why?"

Sam poked thoughtfully at the cat's innards. A man approached, waving some flyers for the theater under their noses. Red fingered her blaster and he backed away, muttering something about just trying to do his job.

Eventually Red got tired of waiting. "So? Does this have anything to do with your organization? And what exactly is your organization, anyway?"

Sam blinked, as if she'd forgotten where she was. "I'm a special agent for Strategic Elimination Command Services. Technically we're an independent extra-governmental task force, but my boss reports to the Galactic Council of Generals."

Red's eyebrow shot up. She'd guessed some government drone, not the military. "What do you do over there?"

Sam lowered her voice. "We deal in the neutralization of hostile forces to maintain peace and stability throughout the galaxy."

Aha. "You kill people who make trouble."

Her face got hard. "No, we neutralize—"

"No no, I got you." Red shifted on the bench. "So what's the deal with Bonk? Is it yours?"

Sam shook her head. "I can't say I've ever encountered cats in my line of work."

"Bonk's not really a cat, though," Red said. "The vet tech told me it's got the wrong frequency or something, I don't remember exactly. And I can't ask him because—"

"Let me guess," Sam said. "Because he's dead."

It was Red's turn to narrow her eyes. "You know something."

"Let me put it this way," Sam said. "It's possible I might suspect there's something to know, but I can't confirm that right now."

Red laughed. "Do they teach you to talk like that in assassin school?"

"Lower your voice!" Sam hissed, eyes darting around the oblivious crowd.

"Sorry, it's just—" Red clutched her stomach, still laughing. "You sound like a mob informant on *Port Desire*."

"I'm trusting you with some serious shit here, Red." She jabbed a finger at Bonk. "If this is what I may or may not think it could be—stop laughing!—then you're in serious danger. You and anyone who knows this cat—this device—could disappear in a heartbeat. I've seen it happen." She glanced around again. "I've *made* it happen," she whispered.

Red wiped her eyes on her jacket sleeve. "Sam, I survived John Smith. I can survive you and your SECS squad."

"About that." Sam tucked her hair behind her ear and shifted back to Business Mode. "Have you reconsidered cooperating with my investigation?"

Oh, right. Red had forgotten about that whole thing. "How do I know you're not working for Smith? Trying to finish the job he couldn't?"

Sam's mouth twitched. "Red, if I wanted you dead, you'd already be dead."

"Why does everyone always tell me that?"

"Look," Sam said, leaning toward Red over Bonk's open stomach cavity. "I understand how hard it can be to trust people."

Red snorted. "No, it's true," she continued. "I'm a lot like you, Red, whether you believe it or not. There are reasons you can trust me. But this isn't the place to go into that."

"That certainly is convenient."

Sam sighed. "Tell you what. I'll do some digging into this cat business. Call in a few favors if I have to. In return, you tell me what's going on with Smith. Sound like a deal you can make?"

This wasn't a decision Red could make on a bench outside the Royal ErotiStar Theater with her cat's guts open and the parking meter ticking away. She might not even need Sam's help, if the piece from Tom—

Shit.

"What time is it?" she asked Sam, scrambling to get Bonk's stomach panel back into place.

Sam checked her watch. "A little after eleven. Why?"

"The C'longi who sold me this thing said it's missing a piece," Red explained. She dumped Bonk into the crate and let the lid drop closed. A whirring noise rose and fell, replaced by another gargling growl. Dammit, she must've hit the power button by mistake when she tossed it in there. She debated turning it off again, if only to get rid of that annoying growl, but decided she'd lost enough blood for one day. Let it growl.

"Anyway," she continued. "I'm supposed to meet him at the market today but it closes at noon. I'll miss him if I don't get my ass over there now."

Sam stood up and smoothed her suit. "Care for some company?"

"Sure," Red said. "But keep your mouth shut and let me work. I've dealt with this guy before, and hundreds of others just like him."

Sam nodded. "I can do that."

"Then let's go."

Chapter 13
I'll Stick with ARSE

Unlike most markets, which spread into side streets and alleys like a creeping fungus with an intergalactic visa and a trust fund, the Gambora market was confined to a single large plaza. The crowds of shoppers were already thinning out when Red and Sam arrived with Bonk's crate.

"Hang on a sec," Red said, stopping next to a table stacked high with shining zuranfruit. She did a quick pocket inventory of her gear. Everything still in place. She drew her blaster and checked the charge.

Sam watched her curiously. "Expecting trouble?"

Red shrugged. "Not really, but you never know, you know?"

"Absolutely." Sam reached under her suit jacket and pulled out a strange device, vaguely blaster-shaped but with interesting little wiggly things at the business end.

Red's mouth dropped open. She knew weapons tech. She'd fiddled around with traditional ballistic, sonic, holo, and faze weaponry since before she could fly a ship. Her personal collection represented all the major classes across scores of systems. But this wiggly-ass blastery thing was unlike anything she'd seen. Maybe if she played it cool . . .

"So," she said casually, trying not to stare too hard. "Whatcha got there?"

"It's Automatic Restraint and Suppression Equipment." Sam twisted a knob on the thing's handle. "Officially speaking, it doesn't exist. At least not yet. I'm field testing it for R&D. One of those favors I'm going to call in." She slid it back into her jacket.

Red's fingers itched. "What does it do?"

"In theory, it immobilizes the subject with a focused biometric pulse. Knocks them out, like a blow to the head, only more sophisticated."

"Can I hold it?"

"No."

"Aw, come on. Just for a minute?"

"No!"

"Fine," Red said. "Keep your piece of ARSE."

"It's an Automatic—"

Red waved her hand. "I can't remember all that. I'll stick with ARSE."

Sam rolled her eyes. "Where's this guy we're supposed to meet?"

"You'll know him when you see him. Trust me."

It didn't take very long to locate the tentacled guy with a single giant eye, less goopy and bloodshot than usual. He wore an Orgullan-blue plaid kimono and flowered sunhat, and his hygiene seemed under control. He must've cleaned up a bit for the upscale Gamboran shoppers. They weren't big on slime. Or turquoise muumuus, for that matter.

"Hey, Tom. Remember me this time?" Red parked Bonk's crate next to his booth.

"Ah. Is you." His eye shifted in Sam's direction. "Who dis?"

"No one you need to know about." Red leaned over the table "You got the piece?"

"Mebbe. You got credits?"

"Maybe. Let's see the piece."

"Let's see credits."

"Not until I see the piece."

Tom leaned back in his chair. "I tink you not trust Tom."

Understatement of the freaking century. Red crossed her arms and waited.

"Is okay," Tom said, waving a tentacle expansively. "Am man of business. I show piece. Then talk price." He reached a tentacle into his kimono.

Red dropped a hand casually toward her blaster. She glanced at Sam, who was browsing Tom's sales display. She picked up a navbox labeled CHEAP. Sam turned it over in her hands, but Red noticed her eyes never left Tom.

After a few seconds of rummaging in the kimono, Tom pulled out a small paper sack. Red relaxed; so did Sam. "See? Is piece." He opened the bag and held it out.

Red peered in the bag. Aha, it *was* a data chip! Just like millions of others, only most didn't have a hole punched through one end with a frayed string tied to it.

"That could be anything. How do we know this is the piece we need for the cat?" Red demanded.

"You don't," Tom said.

"No shit, Exaius."

Tom rubbed a tentacle over his face. "You buy or no? Mebbe Tom have other customer who buy chip."

Red snatched the bag and dangled the chip by the string in front of Sam. "What d'you think?"

"I think that's definitely a data chip."

Professional detectives, these two. A regular Dalton and Crummly. Inside the crate, Bonk started thumping around. "Not now," Red spat. She rubbed her eyes. "If you're scamming me, Tom, so help me—"

"No!" He heaved himself up and paced the booth, squelching. "Is piece that come with cat. Tom no deal with chips in business. I sell to you cheap." A canny look crossed his face. "Only fifty credits."

"Fifty!? That's ridiculous." Red threw the chip back in the bag and looked at Sam, still holding the CHEAP navbox. The agent shrugged. "I'll give you twenty. Did—cut it *out*, Bonk!"

Tom glanced at the thumping crate. "Why cat do that? Never do to Tom."

"It gets angry when people try to scam me." Red kicked the crate, unleashing a new level of screeching fury from its occupant. Beads of slime broke out on the C'longi's face like sweat.

"Um, Red?" Sam suddenly dropped the navbox on the table. "Something's not right here."

"You're damn right," Red snapped. "He's trying to get fifty credits for some skeevy data chip with a hole in it that might not even be the piece we need."

"No," Sam insisted, grabbing Red's arm. "We've got to get out of here. Now."

Red pushed her away. "I'm not going anywhere until this asshole comes down in price."

"You don't understand. The navbox. It's—"

Things happened fast. The lid of the crate shattered, showering splinters all over the booth. Bonk leapt onto the table. Tom's merchandise flew everywhere. The navbox hit him square in the chest with a sickening plop.

"Bonk, what the hell—" Red just had time to notice a yellow light flashing on the bottom of the navbox before Sam shoved her, hard. Red stumbled a few steps away from the booth, tripped on the remains of Bonk's crate, and fell. She caught herself with her arm. A sharp pain shot up her shoulder, but she barely noticed because the booth behind her exploded in a burst of green flame. Something person-shaped hit the pavement next to her. A different something, small but heavy, landed on her stomach, knocking the wind out of her.

Woodman was right, she thought on her way out of consciousness. C'longi blood looks just like grey clotted pus.

Chapter 14
Freaking Cats

When Red came to, thick smoke still filled the air. It smelled like burning grease. She figured she hadn't been out long. She coughed and took stock of herself. Her ears rang, but experience with explosions (now that's a strange thought) taught her that would go away in a few minutes. Her arm hurt, too. She flexed it, wincing, and decided it probably wasn't broken or dislocated.

Red's main concern was the crushing weight on her stomach. Between her watering eyes and the fact that there was at least two of everything, it took a minute of blinking to see what was holding her down. Two mismatched eyes blinked back at her.

Bonk.

The tips of the cat's facial sensor filaments looked charred, but otherwise it seemed undamaged. Well, no more damaged than usual, anyway. Red groaned and pushed the cat away so she could sit up. She patted out a small fire on her bootlaces, then turned her attention to the scene around her.

Smoke billowed from what was left of the booth. People ran screaming among the debris. Bonk's broken crate, no longer hovering, burned merrily. A siren wailed in the distance. Or maybe it was close; hard to tell with your ears concussed.

Something moved nearby, catching Red's attention. It was Sam. Red crawled over to her. Blood oozed from a gash under Sam's eye. Her hair and clothes smoldered, and her shoes were missing. Red reached to check her pulse and realized she still had the data chip bag clenched in her hand. She stuffed it down her pants and felt Sam's wrist. Her pulse was strong.

"Sam?" Red croaked.

Sam's head flopped to one side. Her eyes cracked open. "Red," she rasped, then fell to coughing.

"Hey, are you all right?"

"I think so," she said. One hand fluttered to her face and came back bloody. She managed a small chuckle that turned into another coughing fit. "There goes my modeling career."

The siren was definitely louder now, and joined by a couple of friends. "I hate to be the asshole," Red said, "but we gotta go. I'm not real keen on explaining all this to the cops. Where's your ship?"

Sam rolled over and struggled to her knees. "No ships . . . not safe." She coughed again. "They'll be watching the launches from this area. They've probably already . . . shut down traffic."

"We need somewhere to lay low until this grumshit circus dies down." Red tested her shaky legs. Her brain fought to think. Where could they hide for a few hours? It's Gambora. This wasn't turf she spent a lot of time in. Too many authorities with access to criminal records and mug shots. "You got any ideas?"

"Yeah. I know a place." Sam got to her feet, leaning heavily on Red until she got her balance. "It's not far. I can make it. You?"

Red nodded. She'd crawl across broken glass to get away from the burning market. Which wasn't entirely outside the realm of possibility, given the mess.

Sam waved a hand at Bonk. "What do we do about the cat?"

Oops. Good question. For the moment, Bonk was curled up on the shrapnel-strewn cobbles, tail flicking idly, as if it were relaxing in the bathroom sink in the *Wart* instead of at the epicenter of a public bombing surrounded by wailing sirens and falling ash. Freaking cats. The antigrav crate was in no condition to transport anything this side of a bockluan salamander, and she could barely haul Bonk around herself when her limbs cooperated. And it's not like she could trust it to follow them on its own.

Wait. Or could she?

Red grabbed the tattered hem of Sam's jacket and tore a strip free. "Hey!" Sam objected.

"Gimme a break. It's ruined already, and I need it for the Senso-Trak." Red approached the cat. "C'mere, Bonk, I gotta rub this on your nose—" But the cat switched into Ass-Hauling Mode and took off across the plaza, knocking Red over on her own ass in the process. In seconds, it disappeared into the Gamboran streets.

"Shit," Red spat, picking herself up with a groan. She started staggering after the cat, but Sam grabbed her arm.

"We'll find it later," she said. "We've got to get the hell out of here *now*."

"We can get the hell out of here that way." Red pointed after Bonk. "That's *my cat*."

"I promise we'll find Bonk," Sam said, shifting her weight and wincing. "But we're injured. We need to find out how badly. I have a safehouse nearby. We can regroup there." She paused. "Red, you're *bleeding*."

As if to make the point, something dark and sticky ran into her eyes. Red wiped it away and winced at the bolt of pain in her forehead.

"Heh. We're twins," she said. She allowed Sam to lead her away from the destruction and death in the marketplace, and didn't notice the odd look on her face.

~ ~ ~

The safehouse wasn't as close as Sam made it sound, but eventually she turned up a nondescript walkway to the nondescript door of a nondescript building on a nondescript street in a nondescript neighborhood. Red didn't think she could find it again if you gave her a map and told her Indar Skjov was waiting there for her, naked and sweaty.

Bonk sat on the doorstep. What the hell. "How—never mind. Don't do that again," Red scolded, swaying slightly on her feet. The cat just blinked.

Sam tapped the door in a complicated rhythm involving the knuckles, palms, and fingertips of both hands. After a moment, a similar series of taps answered back from the other side of the door. Sam waited a beat, then responded with a second flurry of tapping.

Red felt the urge to check the watch she didn't have. She needed a drink. And a smoke. And a shower. A run through a medscan might be nice, too. The bleeding seemed to have stopped but her arm ached like hell. But first she needed to get through this damn door.

The code-tapping finally wrapped up, apparently, because the door cracked open. An Andarian woman peered out at them. She was short, even for one of her species; the top of her head barely reached Red's waist, though her wildly curly red hair piled several inches higher. But Red didn't spend much time looking at her hair because she was distracted by the acres of iridescent scaly flesh bursting out of her vee-neck blouse. Red made an effort not to stare and failed spectacularly.

"Fritzi, thank the Fourteen," Sam sighed with obvious relief.

"Sam! What—" The Andarian noticed Red and her gills flared in surprise. She gave her a long up-and-down look, studied Bonk a moment, then hissed, "Get inside."

Sam limped past her. Bonk followed, managing to get through the door on the first try. Despite this minor miracle, Red hesitated, clutching the doorframe to stay upright. Walking into any unknown building was enough to set her teeth on edge, and this was the secret hideout of a professional assassin. She peered over Fritzi's head into a nondescript hallway. Seriously, who were these people? Had they ever heard of a painting or a houseplant? Sam and Bonk disappeared around a corner and Red was left alone with the redhead.

"You can trust her," Fritzi said, startling Red out of her mental interior designs.

"What?"

The Andarian didn't answer, but gestured for Red to enter.

She did. What choice did she have?

Chapter 15
What the Hell is a Plestene Bogmeadow

Red followed Fritzi through a maze of doorways, hallways, staircases, and rooms. At one point she swore they went into one closet and came out another. Her head was clearer now, but she was still too tired and sore to do more than continue her observations of the décor. A few times, something in the corner of her eye caught her attention, but when she turned to look, there was nothing there. Nothing stuck in her head. Details slipped in and out like eels, too slippery to grasp and hold. Red wondered if the head wound was worse than she'd thought.

One final door swung wide to reveal a sumptuously furnished room. After the unbroken blandness of the rest of the building, the rich colors and sparkling lights assaulted her eyes. The best part of the room was a pair of matching couches, the kind that invited a person to sit and maybe take a nap for a while, you've earned it, and here, use a pillow, that's what they're for. Bonk, already taking advantage of the upholstery's offer, curled into a rusty metal doughnut on one cushion.

In one corner, Sam stood at a small but well-stocked bar. Forget the couches—this was the best part of the room. Sam handed Red a glass of amber liquid.

"To survival," she said, raising her own glass.

Red eyed the drink. "What is it?"

"Don't tell me you're turning down a free drink."

Fair point. Red threw back the entire glass in one gulp. Almost immediately, her knees forgot how to work. Fritzi took the glass before she dropped it and led her gently to the couch.

Sam chuckled and sat down across from her. "Zuran cider. Sneaky, isn't it?"

"Ugh, it's like something Granny would have with her bingo friends. Fruity and nasty." Red sank back into the cushions and squinted at Sam. "Is it really that strong, or am I just concussed?"

Fritzi scowled at her wife. "She's injured. Alcohol is the last thing she needs." She settled next to Sam, then reached up to brush a strand of blue hair back from her face. Concern rippled through her gills when she saw the blood-encrusted wound. Sam flinched at her touch. "It's fine. I'm fine."

Fritzi looked skeptical, but let it go. "I believe introductions are in order," she said to Sam.

"Of course." Sam waved her glass at Red. "Fritzi, this is Red Darkling. Red, this is my wife, Fritzi Giggler."

"Your wife?" Red quirked an eyebrow.

"Red Darkling?" Fritzi's gills flared again, but she recovered quickly. "It's wonderful to meet you, Red. I've heard so much about you from Sam."

"I bet you have." Red said. Gotta love when you're the topic of conversation between a government-sanctioned hitman and her porn-star-looking wife. "Are you a SECS agent too?"

"Oh, no no," Fritzi chuckled, smoothing her skirt over her knees. "I'm a psychologist. I do mostly pro bono work these days, with people who are victimized by their sociopolitical systems. You know, Zaldroni'i activists living in refugee camps, Fardic monks who are the victim of workplace discrimination, that sort of thing."

"And you're . . . okay with what Sam does for a living?"

"You'd be surprised how often our professional interests overlap," Fritzi answered.

Well, that would make for some interesting dinnertime conversation, at least.

Sam swirled her cider around the glass. "If everything follows standard protocols, we've got at least a few hours before local law enforcement loosens its watch on the area," she said. "For now, we're stuck here. Let's all get some rest. We'll talk later to figure out our next move."

"Unfortunately, we don't have a guest room to offer you," Fritzi said, shaking her head slightly. "These sofas are very comfortable, though." She rose and crossed the room to a discreet door. "I'm sure you'll want to freshen up a bit," she added. "There's a bathroom through here. It should have anything you might need."

Even through her possibly concussed and definitely buzzed mental haze, Red was impressed at the tactful way Fritzi asked her to please stop leaving dirt, blood, and clots of C'longi guts all over the upholstery. Fair enough. "Thanks, yeah, I'll wash up and crash on the couch."

Fritzi smiled, and she and Sam left Red and Bonk to themselves.

Red headed for the bathroom, where she found a positively immense shower and an assortment of soaps, lotions, and towels. A fluffy white robe hung on a hook by the sink. Red stripped down, cranked the water up to scalding, and started scrubbing the grime from her skin.

Her thoughts wandered over the day, picking idly at threads left unresolved. Who planted the bomb? Was it meant for her? Sam? Tom? Did it have anything to do with the data chip? What did Sam the SECS agent really want from her? Why did Bonk go crazy and bust out of its crate? If it's not a cat, then what exactly is it? Why does Sam seem to know? Why won't she tell Red anything about it? And what the hell is a Plestene bogmeadow and why did anyone think that making a soap that smelled like one was a good idea? She wondered what Woodman would say about all this.

Woodman. On top of everything else, she worried about the doofus. She wondered if his dad had the spleen surgery yet. The rikk wasn't something doctors tossed around lightly—if it was a possibility, it meant trouble.

It wasn't just worry, though. There was something else, too, like a hole in her middle, one she knew from experience wouldn't be filled by all the zuran cider in the galaxy. She missed him. Hard.

What a ridiculous thing. She liked being alone; thrived on it, really. Woodman drove her crazy with his dirty mind and cocky attitude. The sex was good, but not that good. Heh. No, it was pretty damn great, actually, thank you very much. But that wasn't it. She could find great sex in a hundred bars on a dozen systems. What made Woodman special was he understood her. Always had, since they were kids. When she was with him, she could relax. She had nothing to prove to him. He knew she was a super badass and a horrible slob and an emotional disaster, and he didn't care. If she (gods forbid) needed help, he's the one she wanted at her back with a fully-charged blaster, or simply to bounce ideas off of over a beer at Chuck's.

By the time she tied the robe into a sloppy knot around her waist, the swirling questions had distilled down into Sam's single phrase: *our* next move. She still wasn't sure if she wanted her next move to involve Sam, but at this point it didn't seem like she had much choice. She was Red's only possible lead on Bonk now that what was left of poor Tom was probably being scooped into buckets by the Gambulon Sanitary Authority. Besides, Sam's interest in her connection to Smith made warning bells go off in Red's head. Best to keep a close eye on that.

She wasn't sure what kind of next move Sam had in mind, but by the Fourteen gods of Penthos and St. Cripps herself, she'd find out about it smelling like a Plestene bogmeadow.

Chapter 16
The Fourth Potential Target

The market burned. Red turned a navbox over and over in her hands. Something was missing. "This is incomplete," she shouted. "I need the other piece."

Frustrated, she thrust the device across the table at the vendor, who had a C'longi body and Woodman's face. "Sorry, babe," he said. "We need to figure out our next step." He pulled an ARSE from a paper bag and pointed it at her. She tried to duck but the weapon discharged, sending out a blue plaid kimono that wrapped itself around her body so tightly she couldn't move.

She looked around frantically for Bonk. Where was it? It would know what to do. But she was alone in a vast blank room. "Bonk!" she cried, but her voice was muffled. Someone said her name, but she kept screaming. "Bonk! Bonk!"

"Red, it's okay. Wake up."

Her eyes flew open to see Sam leaning over her. Slowly she remembered where she was: on the couch in Sam's hideout.

"Nrgh," Red groaned. She used her knuckles to scrub the dream out of her eyes, along with a substantial collection of grit. "Nightmare. Bad one."

"I could tell," Sam said, nodding. "You were shouting for your cat."

It's not a cat, Red thought, but kept that to herself. "Where is it?"

Sam nodded at the back of the couch. Red glanced up and saw the familiar green and gold eyes blinking down at her. Not creepy at all, perched like a vulture, inches from her head, watching her sleep.

"Jeez, Bonk, get a life already." Red rolled to a sitting position and cracked her neck. She noticed she was still wearing the robe. Panicked, she patted herself for any sign of her blaster, holoknife, or even the D4 screwdriver. Hell, even the data chip was gone.

"Oh, don't worry about your gear," Sam said. "We took the liberty of washing your clothes while you were out, and made sure to empty the pockets." She pointed to a small canvas sack on the floor. "It's all there, including the data chip and the screwdriver we found in your boot. I'm not going to ask why you had a screwdriver in your boot."

Red let out a shaky breath. "Thanks. Not sure I could tell you anyway."

"How do you feel?" Sam asked.

Red did a quick bodily inventory. Her injured arm seemed okay, if a bit stiff. A few bruises bloomed here and there, probably from stuff thrown by the explosion. She touched her forehead and winced. At least it wasn't bleeding on the couch. "A little sore. You?"

"Fritzi cleaned up my cheek," she said, pulling back her hair to show Red a fresh bandage. "And I twisted my knee when I fell. I'll limp for a few days, but it's nothing permanent. I've had worse flipping the mattress." She shrugged. "Are you up for a debriefing?"

"I guess so," Red said, but her stomach complained. "You got anything to eat around here? I like something salty and crunchy when I'm debriefing."

"Fritzi's been bugging me about what to feed you." Sam stood. "I'll go grab her."

Red glanced down at the robe. "Um."

"Your clothes aren't done yet. You really want to wait? I thought you were hungry."

"Hey, no wool off my shiq," Red said, tightening the robe's belt. "You're the one with a wife who's going to see all this hotness."

Sam laughed. "Somehow, I think she'll manage to restrain herself." She crossed to the door and stuck her head out into the hallway. Red caught a glimpse of startlingly red hair against utterly forgettable walls.

"How come this place is so plain?" Red asked as they both entered the room. "Everything looks the same. There's no color or decoration or anything, except here." She waved a hand around the room. "I can't even remember what the outside looks like, and I'm pretty sure it's not because I had a head injury."

Sam's eyebrows shot up. "Most people don't notice the C.L.I.T.," she said, settling on the couch across from Red, Fritzi at her side.

"You're bringing the wrong people home, then."

Once, years ago, Red slipped up and swore around Granny. The look she'd gotten then matched the one Sam gave her now. "It stands for Covert Light-Interruption Tower," she explained. "It intercepts the visible light spectrum before it hits your eye and diverts any wavelengths that fall within pre-determined parameters. Basically, it makes objects in its broadcast range slip right past your optic nerve's attention, so to speak, so it doesn't have a chance to register in your brain. You see it, but you don't really *see* it. A perfect way to camouflage a safehouse, don't you think?"

"What about this room? And why can I still see you as, well, you?"

"All our living spaces are shielded against the C.L.I.T., and it doesn't affect living tissues for some reason." Sam paused. "I admit I don't understand all the science behind it. My own fault; the R&D guys gave me a book on it once, but I misplaced it before I could read it."

"If I ever meet your R&D guys, I'm buying them a round of drinks."

"I suspect you'd get along well."

Fritzi smiled warmly at Red. "Please accept our apologies about the delay in returning your clothes," she said, nodding at Red's robe.

"No big deal." Red stretched and cracked her neck. "Did someone say something about food?"

"Of course," Fritzi replied. "Under normal circumstances, we'd have something already prepared. But in the chaos earlier, I neglected to ask you about any special dietary needs or preferences you might have. And Sam was no help whatsoever in that regard." She shook a scolding finger at her wife, lips curled in a smirk.

Sam rolled her eyes and eased back into the cushions. "You're right. Should I have asked Red to design a detailed menu with color-coding and explanatory footnotes *before* the bomb detonated, or after?"

"I'm not picky," Red said, her stomach yet again announcing its demands. "I'm so hungry I could eat my own tits, with or without slak sauce, so whatever you've got'll be fine, thanks."

"Your flexibility is much appreciated," Fritzi said dryly. She got up and pressed a button on a control panel near the door. Almost immediately a uniformed man entered. "Imon," she said. "Please bring an assortment of finger foods, nothing heavy." She turned to Red. "Do you drink coffee?"

The man's eyes widened a bit, as if he hadn't noticed Red until that moment. Guests were probably pretty rare at Sam and Fritzi's secret SECS lair. Or maybe it was the robe, which had slipped open a bit wider than reasonably appropriate for a light supper in a CLIT-free room.

"Only when there's no whiskey," she said, pulling the robe closed a bit. "Wait, is there any whiskey?"

Fritzi turned back to Imon. "Coffee will do. Thank you." He nodded and disappeared again. Fritzi returned to the couch, crossing her legs delicately.

"Let's get down to business." Sam said. "What happened with John Smith?"

Not this again. "That's what you want to talk about? Really? Because I can think of about a dozen—"

"Perhaps," Fritzi interrupted, placing a hand on Sam's arm, "the most pressing item of business right now is the explosion." She turned to Red and shook her head. "Sam shared with me what happened at the market. Who do you think could be behind the attack?"

Thank the Fourteen for Fritzi. "That depends on who you think the target was," Red said. "The way I see it, there's three possibilities: Sam, me, or Tom the C'longi." She held up three fingers. "I've had plenty of people try to kill me, but no one currently on my scopes." She put her ring finger down. "And I can't imagine anyone wanting to kill Tom. He was a cheap, shady bastard, but the markets are full of guys like that, and they hardly ever end up as burning jelly." She put her index finger down. "That leaves Sam the government assassin, who needs a shielded hole to hide in." Red wiggled the remaining finger slightly.

"Cute," Sam said flatly. "But you're forgetting the fourth potential target."

"Who?" Red followed Sam's gaze to Bonk, who disengaged its chassis-locking mechanisms and extended its body panels beyond their normal range for a moment, jaws wide enough to display each razor-sharp blade. The cat then retracted back to standard dimensions and began cleaning its exhaust port. "Oh, you've got to be kidding me."

"Not at all. What do we know about Bonk?" Sam asked, rubbing the back of her neck. "It looks like a cat and acts like a cat, but isn't a cat. The vet tech who noticed the anomaly is dead. How did they die, by the way?"

"Gas leak. It was on the news."

Sam nodded, as if this made perfect sense. Hell, maybe it did, if you were in that line of work yourself. "The cat's got at least one part marked with the S.E.C.S. insignia. And there's a data port with a matching chip."

"We don't know if that's even the chip that goes with the cat," Red pointed out. "Or what's on it."

"True," Sam conceded. "But if Bonk is S.E.C.S. tech, it's likely that it has sensitive material, almost certainly highly classified. Something people kill over every day, either to destroy it or protect it from discovery."

Red flashed back to being twelve years old, hiding in the basement of her parents' house, watching the life fade from her mother's eyes. Yeah, people got killed every day over data chips. She swallowed to bury the memory.

"Okay," she said, "But why would a cat need a data chip?"

"You said yourself it's not actually a cat," Sam said. "And from what you've told me, it's committed acts of violence far beyond the capabilities of any normal cat. A six-foot insect? That's no dugger mite or weevil. That's serious tactical elimination-level power."

Chapter 17

One Rule You Never, Ever Break

"Wait, you think Bonk's something your guys cooked up? One of your acronyms?" Red laughed so hard she nearly fell off the couch. "You think it's an *assassin bot*?"

Sam frowned. "It *is* stamped with the S.E.C.S. insignia."

"That doesn't make sense. It can barely—I mean, just look at it!" Red waved a hand at Bonk, currently trying to walk into a wall. "If that's SECS tech, I wouldn't trust that ARSE if I were you."

Sam looked offended. "Our R&D guys have an excellent track record."

"Everyone screws up sometimes."

Fritzi cleared her throat. "Let's work the problem. Could the chip contain coding necessary for accurate navigation?"

"I don't know enough about robotics to know if you can decouple guidance from propulsion," Sam said.

"Um," Red raised her hand and wiggled her fingers. "I don't know robotics either, but a gnar chewed up the guts of my ship's navcomp once. I had to fly blind, no idea where I was or where I was going." She shrugged. "So, it's possible for something to be going but not under control."

"But then the question is why you'd put code essential to proper function on a chip that can be removed so easily," Sam said.

"Even if the navigation code is on the chip," Fritzi added, "no one would kill over that. There must be something else on that chip."

"One way to find out," Red said, brushing off her hands on her robe. "Let's plug that thing in and see what happens."

Sam laughed. "Great idea," she said when she caught her breath. "We have no idea what might be on that chip, but sure, let's plug it into a known killer and potential assassin bot. What could possibly go wrong?"

"Got any other ideas?" Red got up and paced the room. "We don't even know for sure that Bonk's SECS tech. I mean, sure, it's got that panel, but the whole cat is nothing but a bunch of mismatched scrap. It could be some backyard mechanic's weekend project, slapped together with salvaged parts and electroputty. Hell, it's probably nothing more than a fancy radio and the chip is someone's slow jams playlist."

"Oh, right," Sam sneered. "That's totally plausible. And here I was thinking the chip is someone's porn collection and Bonk shows the vids out of a projector in its ass."

"I wasn't serious, dipshit. It was just an example."

"Who are you calling a dipshit, asshole?"

"Stop it," Fritzi snapped. "You two are behaving like children."

Red flushed and sank back onto the couch. She and Sam exchanged a guilty look.

The Andarian folded her hands in her lap. "If I might," she said, "I'd like to make a professional observation before this debriefing goes any further. At first, I thought the underlying issue between you was one of mistrust. But now I'm not so sure." She paused a beat, then continued. "You do trust each other, but you don't realize it. Red, you've trusted Sam with your very life by accepting our hospitality here. And you," she said, turning to Sam. "You have trusted Red with not only details about your job, but also the location of your safehouse and identity of those closest to you.

"The real problem is pride," she continued. "You are both overly concerned with posturing. You want to be the smartest, the strongest, the toughest in the room. You see vulnerability as weakness and imperfection as failure, not to be tolerated. But vulnerability is not a weakness, and imperfection is inescapable. What is the purpose of trust? To allow vulnerability in an environment of mutual support that minimizes risk of harm, both physical and emotional. You must learn to trust the trust, so to speak. Otherwise, the trust is for naught."

It was true, but Red didn't like it. Freaking shrinks. There was a good reason she'd never gone to therapy, despite a freighterful of emotional baggage to justify it. Having her brain dissected wasn't her idea of a good time. It made her feel like Granny's Sunday afternoon roast darna: cut open, devoured, and likely picked over again later that night. Nope, far better to head to Chuck's and bury it all under a mountain of booze, tobacco, and sex. It worked for her so far. Sort of. Red almost felt sorry for Sam, being married to a psychologist. She wondered how often she'd been analyzed like this before.

Anyway, maybe Fritzi had a point about the whole trust thing. She'd been sound asleep on their couch not an hour earlier. She could've woken up dead. They even let her keep her weapons. Still, the situation with Smith hinged on no one—not Woodman, not even Granny—ever finding out she'd bluffed him. They'd be in as much danger as Red herself if things went sideways.

The awkward silence was thankfully broken by the servant returning with a cart piled with platters of food, dishes, and a giant carafe that smelled of strong, bitter coffee. Red waited in impatient silence as he arranged everything on the low table between them, trying to ignore the empty ache shooting through her belly.

"Thank you, Imon, this is lovely," Fritzi said. "You may go. I'll summon you if we need anything else."

He nodded slightly and turned to leave. Red caught his eye, just for a split second, but she thought she saw something odd in his face, a tightness around his mouth. "Yeah, thanks, man," she said, trying to catch his attention. But he was already gone, without acknowledging her. Something stinks. Or he's just a jerk.

She didn't have time to figure it out, because Bonk jumped up onto the food-laden table. The dishes rattled and the carafe tipped alarmingly, but nothing spilled or broke. "Bonk, what the hell?

Get down from there!" Red shouted, flapping her arms at the unconcerned cat. She barely noticed the robe fall open again.

Fritzi placed a hand on Red's shoulder. "It's fine," she said. "No harm done." She stroked Bonk between its ears, causing it to emit the ragged mechanical gargling that served as its purr.

Red hitched up the robe and glared at Bonk, who sat calmly among the finger foods like it owned the place. Red flashed it a rude gesture and suggested it may want to perform certain activities typically available only to carbon-based lifeforms whose evolutionary survival relied heavily on sexual reproduction. It did not take her up on the offer, but Red felt a little better.

Grabbing a plate, Red piled up some snack-size yozzies, a couple tiny nintha sandwiches with the crusts cut off, and a handful of cnothu puffs. She settled back into the couch and tucked her legs underneath her, managing to dribble only a little yozzie grease onto her robe. Fritzi handed her a napkin without a word.

"You know," Red said around a mouthful of puffs. "The last person who wanted to make a deal with me over coffee, it didn't work out so well. What a goddamn nightmare," she continued, oblivious to everything except the food she shoveled into her face hole. "Not much for rules, myself, but I tell ya, that whole experience taught me that there's one rule you never, ever break: don't work with family." She burped, then picked up a nice fat yozzie. "Of course, that's pretty easy to do, for me. I don't have any family now except for Granny, and she's hardly the type—"

Red glanced up to see Sam staring at her. The agent's hand hung in midair, shaking, the nintha sandwich it held forgotten. Startled, Red looked at Fritzi. The Andarian's scales had turned a dull grey. She put down her own nearly empty plate and took her wife's hand between her own. "You need to tell her."

Dread wrapped cold tentacles around Red's gut. "Tell me what?" She tried to swallow a chunk of yozzie but it stuck in her throat. Coughing, she sputtered, "Seriously, you need to tell me what in the nine hells is going on, because I swear on Shugga Mia's grave, if it turns out that you're, like, my long-lost cousin, I'm going to assume I'm in a coma somewhere and this whole thing is my dying brain playing episodes of *Port Desire* before it gives up entirely."

Sam sighed. "The reason I need to know how you got free of John Smith is . . . I need to get free of him too." She buried her head in her hands, blue hair falling in a curtain across her bandaged cheek. When she looked up again, her eyes shone with tears, but her jaw was set, defiant. "What I told you before is true: I'm a lot like you. Red, this may come as a shock, but Smith is your father. He's my father, too."

Chapter 18
Plenty More to Break

Red snorted. "*Port Desire* coma fantasy it is, then," she said, scooping up another round of cnothu puffs.

"I'm serious. Smith is your father. I'm your half-sister. I have documents to prove this, if you'd like to see them."

"Ha, no, that's okay," Red said. Damn, these puffs were *good*. She'd have to stock up next time she did a supply run. "I believe you. Smith already told me I'm his daughter."

Sam blinked. "Wh—you knew—"

Red shrugged. "I think he thought it'd convince me to join his life of crime. But I had my own life of crime, you know? Working for him would be a demotion. Plus I'm not into the whole murdering family thing."

"Did he . . . did he tell you about me?"

"Nah, but it makes sense he'd have another kid out there somewhere. I mean, he knocked up my mom, whoever she was, and dumped me on Granny's doorstep as a baby. Never saw him again until a few years ago. He's probably got dozens of bastards out there."

"Actually, no."

Red raised an eyebrow. "And you know this because?"

"I suppose I don't," Sam admitted. "Smith was—is—a master of deception. Still, I grew up knowing about you. Why would he hide others from me, but not hide you?"

Good question. *You have all the characteristics that I value in myself.* Smith's words echoed in Red's memory. At the time, it all sounded like grass-fed, Grade-A grumshit. She didn't want to be anything like Smith. But it was flattering, too, in a way. Resourceful and self-reliant, he'd said. Intelligent and clever. And he'd wanted *her*, chosen *her*. Being chosen for something—even a shitty something—felt good. Even if he didn't give half a dead fazzer about her until she'd proven herself.

Wait. "You knew Smith growing up?" Red asked.

"Of course. He raised me." Sam hesitated. "He wanted me to take over his business. His criminal business. He said he was grooming me. Damn, that word turns my stomach. I was five years old, maybe six, when he said this. I knew right away I'd never be like him. But what could I do at five years old? Even then I knew my life would be forfeit if he found out I wasn't one hundred percent loyal. What kind of a thing is that for a kid to live with? So I kept my mouth shut. I pretended every day to be the good little girl happily following in her beloved daddy's footsteps."

Red felt like several tons of molten slag crashed down on her, crushing her, making it hard to breathe. So much for being chosen. The one good thing she'd managed to scrape out of that whole Smith mess, gone. Whatever she'd thought made her special to him, skills and qualities she'd worked hard to develop in herself? Her independence, her badassery? Clearly it was nothing compared to whatever Smith had seen in Sam as a freaking *baby*.

"Red," Fritzi said tentatively. "I can see that this bothers you."

"Bothered? Me?" Red scraped cnothu crumbs from underneath her fingernails as if it were the most important thing she could be doing in that exact moment. "Why should I be bothered? It's not the first time I've had someone worm their way into my life before announcing they're my long-lost family. I've seen that episode before. Just another wonderful day in the life of Red Darkling." Fritzi said nothing and Red sighed. "But he raised *her*." She tilted her head at Sam without taking her eyes off Fritzi. "Why not *me*? What's wrong with *me*?"

"What, you think I wanted this?" Sam spat. "You think it was easy, to know what he was, and love him all the same?"

"How could you love him?"

"He was my dad," Sam choked. "I was a kid. I had no choice in the matter. Just like you. And when I *was* given a choice, I chose no. Just like you."

"So if you told him to eat grumshit and die, why do you need my help? Obviously he hasn't killed you yet either."

Sam's eyes shifted. "I . . . haven't actually told him."

"I knew it!" Red threw her plate against the bathroom door, where it shattered. Not nearly satisfying enough, but she was just getting started. There was plenty more to break. Messier things. Bloodier things. Like Sam's face. Her hand itched for that D4 screwdriver—she had a theory about popping eyeballs out of sockets that she'd like to try out—but it was buried in that sack across the room. "I freaking knew it. I'm so goddamn stupid. You're working for him! This whole time, trying to get me to talk about Smith. You *are* just like him—a lying sack of grumshit."

Sam's face flushed, her eyes sparking with fury. "You're right about one thing, Red Darkling. You are goddamn stupid."

"Please," Fritzi interrupted, holding out her hands as if to separate a couple of angry dogs. "Just listen to each other."

"Think about it," Sam continued with visible effort to collect herself. "If I'd told Smith the truth, I'd be dead. Even now, with all my military training and S.E.C.S. experience, I'd be dead. Worse, Fritzi would be dead. You said this place is shielded to protect us from random bad guys, but you're wrong. It's to protect us from one very specific bad guy. It's to protect us from *him*."

Red barked a laugh. "There's no way in seven systems that I believe this." She turned on Fritzi. "And you think I should trust her?"

"You can, and you do," Fritzi said simply. "Sam, tell her how you came to be associated with S.E.C.S."

"It was a bargain I made with Smith when I finished school," she said flatly. "I convinced him that I'd be a better asset to him as an informant than as a successor. And what better place for Smith to have an inside informant than an agency whose sole purpose is to hunt down and kill people like him?

"Can't you see?" she continued, leaning forward. "The reason I joined S.E.C.S., the reason I became a . . . an assassin, as you call it, isn't because I want to be like Smith. It's because the only thing I've wanted since I was five years old is to *take him down*. I just have to find out how. Which is why I need you. *We* need you." She squeezed Fritzi's hand.

Red raised an eyebrow. "You're a professional assassin sanctioned by the government, and you need my help?"

"I've tried!" Sam said, throwing up her hands and falling back against the couch. "Management won't sign off on it unless I've got evidence. Smith's too good, and my word's not good enough. I don't dare press any harder on the off chance I'm not the only mole Smith's got in the agency." She shook her head. "No, if I'm going to get rid of him, I need to do it off the books."

Red thought about what Sam was proposing. She had a point—Red's whole life depended on staying off the books, and she was damn good at it. She could count on one hand the number of outstanding warrants with her name on them. And after all, she'd already outwitted Smith once. That proved he could be beaten. He wasn't invincible. Right?

Plus, Sam was her only lead on Bonk. She watched the cat picking its way through the cups, dishes, and bowls, investigating each one like there was a nest of weevils hiding somewhere among the snacks. That warm rush of affection returned. The cat saved her life—more than once—and Red didn't walk away from anyone who had her back. Especially if it turns out to be a killbot, which, given Red's lifetime of luck, was probably pretty likely. But she needed to know for sure if she'd ever be able to sleep around it again. If it meant working with Sam and Fritzi, breaking that one rule, well . . .

She found herself nodding. "Let's do this," she said. "I tell you what I know about Smith, you help me figure out what's going on with Bonk." She extended a hand before she could change her mind. "Deal?"

Sam shook it enthusiastically. "Deal."

"Wonderful," Fritzi said, her scales rippling pink and green. "Now, let's have some coffee while you strategize. It's not very warm anymore, but it'll do." She arranged three cups at the edge of the table and began pouring coffee from the carafe. Bonk watched intently.

Just as she'd finished filling the third cup, Bonk stretched out a paw and carefully, deliberately, pushed each one to the floor, pap pap pap. Coffee splashed over the table, couches, and carpet, causing everyone to leap back with various shouts of surprise and alarm.

"Goddammit, Bonk!" Red shouted, shoving the cat off the table. It ran under the bar and crouched there, hissing. She mumbled a curse under her breath and turned back to help Fritzi and Sam wipe up the steaming mess.

Chapter 19
Score! Two Points

Steaming mess?

"No!" Red grabbed Fritzi's wrist to stop her from blotting the carpet with a napkin. She threw her other arm out to block Sam from bending down to pick up the cups. "Don't touch it—there's something wrong with it."

"What do you mean?" Sam asked. Then her eyes widened. "The steam . . ."

Fritzi looked at her wife, puzzled. "I don't understand."

"It's not hot," Red explained. "You said so yourself."

"So, then, why . . ."

"Look!" Sam pointed to the table. The bowl of mixed nuts was now a bowl of slurry. Pulpy sludge quivered on a plate—that must've been the nintha sandwiches. The cnothu puffs were completely liquified. The dishes, cups, carafe, all fine. Not so fine were the table and carpet, where ragged holes were growing everywhere the coffee had splashed. "It's eating through everything organic. Food, fabric, everything."

Fritzi wrapped her arms around herself and shuddered.

"Whiskey never would've done that to us," Red said. "Just saying."

Sam knelt down to peer at Bonk, who still lurked in the shadows under the bar. Suddenly she stood up, face grim. "We've got to get out of here." She tossed the sack of weapons at Red, who managed to catch it without too much awkward juggling.

"What about my clothes?"

"No time," Sam said. "Come on, Fritzi. We need to go. Now."

Fritzi nodded. "I'll inform Imon."

"Are you kidding?" Red spat, tightening the robe yet again and wishing like hell she had her jacket. "He brought the coffee!"

"She's right," Sam said. "We can't trust him."

"Let's just go already." Red threw open the door.

Sam pushed past her into the hallway. "You'll just get lost. You don't know your way around the C.L.I.T. like we do."

"Fair enough," Red conceded. "Wait, I need to grab Bonk."

But she didn't. Bonk raced out from under the bar like a gazellope on amphetamines, wove nimbly through everyone's legs, and flew out the door. It disappeared around a corner at the end of the hall, running into absolutely nothing along the way. Red exchanged a quick glance with the others. Fritzi shrugged. "It's going the right way."

The three made their way through the maze of nondescript halls and out into the nondescript street. Night had fallen in a big way, darkness blending with the shadows and a dank chill hanging in the air. Red squinted into the gloom, scanning the area for any potential threats, the hair on her neck standing up with either fear or cold. All she saw was the familiar green and gold glow of Bonk's eyes across the street. It growled.

"Look, cat, we made it as fast as we could." Red turned to Sam. "What's the plan? You got another safehouse around here somewhere?"

The agent stared into the distance, chewing her lower lip. "Our best bet is to get the hell off this planet," she said. "Where's your ship?"

"Near the theater," Red answered with a shiver. "What if they're still watching flights?"

"Then you'll get to practice your evasive maneuvers," Sam said, flipping open the strap on her shoulder holster. "I'm going to move fast. Try to keep up."

~ ~ ~

By the time they arrived at the *Wart*, Red's bare feet were numb, her teeth chattered, and, annoyingly, sweat poured down her face from running after Sam. She thought longingly about the coffee she didn't get to drink and the whiskey she was never offered. Right now, she'd be happy with either one, poison or no.

Once Sam completed a quick but thorough inspection of the outside of the ship and gave the all-clear, Red popped the hatch and they climbed in. It felt good to be back on her own turf. She dumped the bag of weapons in a corner. "Make yourselves at home," she said, sweeping a pile of laundry to one side and kicking an empty duoofish can through the portal to the kitchen. Score! Two points. "I'll get us going."

Fritzi perched delicately on the edge of a chair, her feet dangling awkwardly halfway to the floor. Sam followed Red into the cockpit.

Red plopped into the captain's seat and worked her way across the control panel, flipping switches, turning knobs, and pressing buttons. Sam stood behind her. "You'll want to check both low- and high-res bands before we take off," she said.

"What do you think I'm doing?" Red scowled. "Not my first bavit shavah ceremony, you know."

Sam put up her hands. "Hey, just trying to help."

"Sit down," Red grumbled. "You're making me nervous hovering like that."

Sam sank into the copilot's chair. "See anything we need to worry about?"

Red took a moment to scan the displays. She punched in a few numbers, then shook her head. "Nah, just the normal traffic alerts for this sector. We should be good to go." She started up the engines, which thrummed comfortingly. "I'll keep it on manual until we're ready for sublight, just in case."

Sam nodded. "Anything I can do from here?"

"Just figure out where we're headed and keep your mouth shut about my flying."

To Sam's credit, she did keep her mouth shut, though there was a sharp intake of breath and subtle white-knuckled clutching at the armrests when Red got the ship caught in the wake of a sewage freighter. It wasn't her fault, though. Sure, she wasn't technically supposed to be in that lane, but the freighter's top speed maxed out at half of the *Wart*'s, and they were in a hurry. She'd give the pilot a break, though. This time of night, they were probably the newest ones on the roster: young, exhausted, less than a thousand hours of flight time, and stupid enough to believe the Gamboran cops gave a shit about lane restrictions and speed limits.

They broke atmosphere without further incident. Red settled into orbit and turned to Sam. "Okay, you got any other safehouses in this sector, or are we going sublight?"

"I don't . . ." Sam bit her lip and tucked a strand of hair behind her ear. "Anywhere," she said finally. "It doesn't matter. Zaldron."

Gee, how specific. "New Az? Uk Voth? Please don't say Gozgor Toth, the locals already don't like me there. Big misunderstanding, but hell if I can convince their city council that the solar array was messed up before I got there."

"Wherever you want."

"Ooooookay, I pick . . . New Az. The weather's nice this time of year, and I could go for a good chocolate moonrabbit split." Red searched up the coordinates and fed them into the navcomp, which spit out a flight time. "Eighty-five hours. That's, what, three days?"

"Three and a half."

Great. Three and a half days with three people and a possibly murderous cat (not cat) crammed into a ship designed for one. Or two, if the two were friendly enough to share a bunk. Red sighed heavily at the realization that she'd be a complete asshole to keep the bed for herself while her married guests camped out on the floor of the main compartment. At least she was used to that sort of thing. Somehow, she didn't think anyone who stocked Plestene bogmeadow soap in their guest bathroom would have much practical experience sleeping among the weevils and gnars Bonk hadn't gotten around to exterminating yet.

Red activated the sublight drive, stood, and stretched. "I'm grabbing some clothes and a smoke."

Sam shook her head. "We need to finish our discussion about Smith."

"And Bonk."

"Yes, and Bonk, of course."

"Look," Red said. "I know we've got a metric ton of grumshit to shovel through, but we've got eighty-five freaking hours to do it before we need to figure out our next move." She plucked at the collar of the robe. "This is great and all, even if it *is* a bit flappy at times, and I appreciate not being, you know, totally naked running through the streets of Gambora, but I need pants." She cringed when she heard herself say that, but the expected dirty joke didn't appear. One of the benefits of hanging out with people other than Woodman.

Sam nodded. "I could use some sleep," she said, throwing a hand toward the main compartment. "And I'm sure she feels the same."

"Yeah, about that." Red led the way back to where Fritzi sat stroking Bonk's chin. A twinge of jealousy burst through her chest, but she quickly shook it off. Stupid cat can get its dumb chin rubbed by whoever it wants. "There's only the one bunk, so you guys can take that," she said, nodding at the door to the room. "I'll be good out here."

"Oh, no," Fritzi said. "We won't take your bed."

"Nah, it's fine." She waved a hand dismissively. "I'm still too jazzed up to sleep anyway."

"Well, since you insist, thank you."

"Don't thank me yet," Red snorted. "The sheets are probably dirtier than the floor here. Just ignore any crispy bits, it's not what you think. Or maybe it is, I dunno what your life's been like. But hey, on the bright side, at least this mattress doesn't have a giant hole chewed out of the middle like my last one."

The couple exchanged a glance. "That sounds like a story for another time," Fritzi said. She took Sam's hand and together they disappeared into the bedroom.

"What d'ya say, Bonk?" Red said, digging through the laundry heap for clothes clean enough to bend. "What should we do until they wake up?" She shucked the robe and pulled on one of Woodman's old Vulvato concert tees and a pair of engine oil-stained jeans. She looked around for the cat. "Bonk? Where'd you go?"

That's when she heard the distinctive gurgling purr, muffled behind the closed bedroom door.

Fine. Glitchy little bastard. She lit a cigar and collapsed into the captain's chair, bare feet on the control panel, and watched the stars streak by the viewport.

She had a sister.

Chapter 20
Dirk Who?

Red's guests emerged a few hours later. Neither one looked particularly rested. Fritzi's hair flattened on one side of her head, but shot up twice as high on the other. Her scales were pink but dull. She brushed what looked suspiciously like FlinkBar crumbs off the back of her wife's shirt. Red made a mental note to stop eating in bed, at least anything she couldn't cram in her mouth in one piece.

"There's coffee," Red said, gesturing at the kitchen. "It'll destroy your insides, but not because it's poisoned." She shrugged. "It's just cheap."

"I'd prefer tea, if you have any," Fritzi said, patting her hair back into some semblance of shape.

"Probably a good choice." Red searched an overflowing cabinet of half-empty boxes. "Aha!" she announced. "Fauas Finest." She dropped a bag in a chipped Crolinian Psycats mug and ordered up some hot water from the dispenser. While the mug filled, she turned to Sam. "You?" She waggled a second tea bag by its string.

"I'd rather get straight to business," she said, pulling on her jacket and rolling her shoulders. "We've wasted enough time already."

Red groaned. "Jeez, you really know how to bring a party down in flames." She handed the mug of steeping tea to Fritzi, who wrapped her hands around it gratefully. Then Red made herself a double-big coffee with milk, sugar, and a shot of whiskey.

Bonk wandered out of the bedroom. "Well, look who decided to show up," she said, holding her mug close to her body. "You're not knocking this one over." The cat ignored her and headed toward the kitchen. The speed and accuracy of the escape from the safehouse didn't help it avoid the wall. Red sighed, nudging the cat toward the door with her foot. Some killbot.

"So," she began, as they all arranged themselves in various chairs around the table. "While you two were wasting time sleeping or, you know, whatever, I did some thinking."

Sam paused in mid-stretch. "About?" she asked in a carefully neutral tone.

"Everything." Red sipped her coffee, wincing as she burned her tongue. "First, I know you're hot to talk about Smith, but if I'm going to trust you with what I know, I need to be sure you're able to hold up your end of the deal and actually help with Bonk."

Red could hear Sam's teeth grind at this, but the agent gave a sharp nod. "Does that mean you agree that the cat is probably S.E.C.S. tech of some kind?"

"It's the only theory we've got, really." Red shrugged. "We don't even know what Bonk *is*. The vet tech was sure it's not a cat, not on the inside. And the panel with the missing chip says SECS, so it makes sense to start there. If we're wrong, we're wrong. But SECS is where we go to find out."

"No," Sam said, shaking her head vigorously. "Impossible."

"Why?" Red asked. "I thought you and the R&D guys were all buddy-buddy."

Sam ran a hand through her hair. "If I haven't encountered this before, it's because I'm not supposed to. Management would have my head on a spike if I showed up asking questions about something I'm not supposed to know even exists."

Red rolled her eyes. Amateur. "Well, you don't just make an appointment and say 'Hello, I'm here to find out if this cat is really a killbot you built to assassinate politicians and cult leaders.' Don't you know anyone outside of work? Someone who hates their job? Oo," she continued, "even better, someone who could be bribed or blackmailed, maybe gambling debts or a piece of ass on the side?"

"People like that don't last long at S.E.C.S."

It took every ounce of self-restraint Red had left to let that one go. "Fine, but you get the idea. There's always someone."

"No. There's not."

"Sam," Fritzi said, peering casually into her mug. "There may be someone."

"Who?" Red asked.

Sam's scowled. "Fritzi, no."

"But Dirk might be able to help."

"Dirk who?"

"No way," Sam said forcefully. "We can't bring Dirk into this."

"If this is what you suspect it might be, he may already be involved," Fritzi said softly.

"Would you both shut up!" Red roared. The ship fell awkwardly silent. "Thank you! Now, who the hell is Dirk?"

Sam sat back in her chair, arms crossed.

Fritzi glanced at her. "Dirk Largo," she explained, turning to Red. Sam growled, but Fritzi raised a hand and continued. "He and Sam served together in their early days at the Academy. They were close. They spent almost a decade together at S.E.C.S." She sent a pointed look at her wife. "In fact, Sam is the one who got him a job there."

"Perfect!" Red clapped her hands. "He trusts you, you trust him, and best of all, he owes you. Let's talk to Dirk. Where is he?"

"You don't understand." Sam shook her head. "Dirk disappeared. He had some kind of disagreement with Management and quit. Just up and quit. No one's heard from him since." She fell silent a moment, then continued: "People don't just quit S.E.C.S. without consequences. Rumor is, they took him out. But I don't believe it, *can't* believe it. He's too smart for that."

"You think he might be holed up somewhere?" That's what Red would do.

Sam shrugged. "Maybe. But if so, he's deep enough underground that Management can't find him."

Red thought. Where would she go in that situation? Laying low in one place meant you could get comfortable and lazy. One day you skuttle out of your hidey-hole for FlinkBars and coffee to find a phaser melting your face off. Skipping around the galaxy, though, meant too many fueling stops in too many places with too many faces.

Too many faces . . .

"Does Dirk like to drink?"

"Um. Sure, as much as anyone, I guess. Why?"

"I might know someone who could help us find him."

"Wait," Sam objected, holding up a hand. "I never agreed we *should* find him. There's got to be another way."

Red slammed her half-empty mug on the table. "I thought you were helping me with this cat business."

"In return for information from you," Sam reminded her. "We had a deal."

"It's hardly a deal if you refuse to do your part."

"Don't you understand that it's more than just you and me in this thing? It's bad enough that Fritzi is mixed up in this grumshit. And you want to get Dirk involved too? Sure, he's probably the only one who could help us, but he's off-grid for a reason. If he's managed to avoid Management's agents this long, I don't want to be the one to help them finish the job."

"Pardon me," Fritzi interrupted. "Kindly do not use me as an excuse. I am fully capable of making my own decisions about which, ah, grumshit I mix myself up in. In this case, I'm eager to do whatever I can to help both of you find the answers you need."

Sam flushed. "You're right," she muttered. "I'm sorry. But you can't speak for Dirk. He's not being asked about this. And we can't ask him without possibly exposing him."

"Think about it, though," Red said. "If he's already dead, then there's no reason not to look for him. What're they gonna do, kill him twice? And I can't blame you for not helping me if the guy's dead. You'll have satisfied your end of the deal and no harm done to anyone. But," she continued, "you said yourself he's the only one who might tell us something. If we don't try to find him, you can't hold up your end of the deal. No deal, and not even a hundred rabid fazzers with souped-up plasma cannons could get the Smith story out of me." She picked up her mug and drained it in a single gulp. "Your move."

Chapter 21
The Best Lie is Mostly Truth

Sam got to her feet, a dark look on her face, and stormed into the bedroom. If the portal was a regular door, it would have slammed shut in full, overly dramatic *Port Desire* fashion. As it was, it simply slid closed with a whoosh.

Red helped herself to another coffee, double whiskey, to give her sister time alone to realize that it made sense to find this Dirk guy. It would save a lot of time if people just did what Red wanted in the first place, without all this pacing around and ineffective door-slamming.

"So," Red said, returning to her chair and folding her legs under her. "How did you two meet, anyway?"

The Andarian's scales flushed a radiant yellow. "It's a funny story. Are you familiar with the philosopher Exaius?"

Red managed to keep herself from spraying coffee out her mouth, but it was a close thing. "Yeah," she said casually, wiping her chin on her shirt sleeve. "Smith mentioned him a few times."

"Ah," Fritzi nodded. "Well, both Sam and I planned to attend—separately, of course—a lecture on his juvenilia. Fascinating subject. Anyway, the university oversold the event, and Sam and I both held tickets for the same seat." She laughed, a gentle trill that rippled her gills in an admittedly adorable fashion. "You can imagine our faces. We decided we'd both skip the lecture and have drinks instead. The rest, as they say, is history."

Red wasn't sure how funny the story was, exactly, but she chuckled a bit to be polite.

"How about you, Red? Are you married?" Fritzi asked, sipping her tea.

"Ha! No."

"Is there someone special in your life?"

"Uh." Red shifted. "Not—there's this guy. Woodman. I mean, Mark. Mark Woodman. I guess you could say we're kind of dating. It's weird, though. You know?"

"Weird in what way?" Fritzi smiled encouragingly.

"Just weird-weird." Red swirled her mug. "It's like, the sex is great, he's always got my back, and he gets me better than anyone. But he's also annoying as hell, always wanting to take care of me and shit. But I take care of myself, you know? I don't need him or anyone else to keep me safe. I'm not sure I even *want* to be safe, not all the time." She scowled at her coffee. "I'm rambling, sorry."

"Don't apologize. What is it you *do* want?" Fritzi asked, back in Shrink Mode. Maybe it was the Andarian's intense gaze, or narrowly missing being blown up and poisoned in the same day, or the caffeine-boosted whiskey making her head buzz, but Red didn't mind.

"I dunno," she shrugged. "I guess I want to settle down. That's what normal people do, right?" She snorted. "If not him, then who? We've known each other so long, it makes sense."

"You guess?" Fritzi tapped her mug thoughtfully. "If you are not sure what you want, it will be impossible to make a healthy decision about your personal relationships." She caught Red's eyes with her own. "How does Mark feel?"

Red looked away. "You'd have to ask him," she mumbled. *He owes me twenty-five from the ShiqShaq*, Chuck had said. Who goes to a place like that if—but did she even—

Thank the Fourteen gods of Penthos and half the Anaplastic saints, Sam chose that moment to reappear. "I'm willing to try contacting Dirk. Wait!" she said sternly. "Don't say anything yet, just listen."

Red shut her mouth with a dramatic pop and mimed a zipper across her lips.

"I have some conditions." Sam sat on the edge of her chair, elbows on her knees, hands twisting together like a colony of dugger mites on vacation on Ophesus. "First, we do this my way or not at all. If I say stop at any time, we stop. No arguments." Red nodded.

"Second," Sam continued, "if he says he can't help, or won't help, we let it go. No arguments." Red nodded again.

"Finally, Bonk is the only topic we discuss unless Dirk brings it up first. No questions about his S.E.C.S. work, nothing about why he left, nothing about his favorite brand of toothpaste. Nothing. Understood?"

"I can agree to that." Red stuck out her hand, and Sam shook it.

"And, in exchange," the agent added, "you will tell me everything you know about the man who goes by John Smith—including his favorite brand of toothpaste. You will also tell me everything that went down between you two, including that final meeting at the house in Magross and why you're still breathing. Understood?"

This time it was her hand extended across the table. "Deal," Red said, shaking it. "You really have no idea where this Dirk guy could be hiding out?"

"No!" Sam said, frustrated. "I've been racking my brain ever since he disappeared." She started pacing again. Her foot hit an empty Old Wo'hall'a can. It bounced off a crate of Rhuatan Fizzdrops (homona-bark sedatives that were until recently the drug of choice among the galaxy's sleazier aristocrats; now the whole lot was barely worth enough to pay Red's monthly cigar budget) and into the kitchen. Jeez, a perfect trick shot, three points, and she wasn't even trying.

Red leaned back in her chair, hands behind her head. "Golly, if only I knew a cross-dimensional being who personally ran every bar worth a damn in a dozen systems who could tell us if anyone matching Dirk's description wanders in."

"Do you mean Chuck?"

Red's jaw dropped. "You know Chuck?"

Sam rolled her eyes. "Of course I know Chuck. He's one of Smith's closest associates. I've known him forever. I held the candle at his son's gifting ceremony. You think I just happened to show up in that bar the day we met?"

Dammit, Chuck. Red really needed to hang out in fewer bars. Or different bars. "So you know he's good at what he does," she pointed out.

"Sure, but what makes you think he'd help us?"

"A hunch. He and I still do business, even after I shook Smith. He's a good dude. And if this guy Dirk drinks somewhere he thinks he won't get found, he's probably in one of Chuck's places. That's the kind of place Chuck runs." Heh. It would have to be that kind of place, wouldn't it? If people knew their bartender was the eyes and ears of the biggest criminal in the galaxy, he'd sell a hell of a lot fewer nintha mojitos.

"And what if Chuck reports to Smith about what we're up to?"

"Why would he do that? And anyway, so what if he does?"

"He works for Smith. We can't risk Smith finding out where Dirk is."

"He doesn't work for Smith, though, right?" Red asked. "He told me he's an independent contractor. And I get the feeling he's not Smith's biggest fan. Smith likes things all to himself, and Chuck doesn't want to be anyone's pet." She shook her head. "I really don't think he'd rat us out if we asked him to keep it quiet. And we don't even have to tell him who Dirk is. If you've got a picture, that'll be enough. If he asks, we can tell him he stole your dog or something."

"I don't have a dog."

"It's a cover story. It doesn't matter if there's really a dog." Red narrowed her eyes. "Are you sure you went to assassin school? Because this is pretty basic stuff."

"You're right, it is basic stuff. 'The best lie is mostly truth.' They teach it the first week of assassin school."

"Wait, is there really an assassin school?"

"No."

Fritzi interrupted. "I think we're getting away from the main issue. Sam, do you have any other ideas for how to find Dirk?"

Sam frowned, but shook her head.

"Red?" Fritzi asked. "Can you think of another way that doesn't involve Chuck?"

"Nope. This is all I've got."

"Then I think the decision is clear."

"Fine," Sam sighed. "We'll talk to Chuck."

"Huzzah!" Red shouted at the ceiling, hands thrown in the air. "Welcome to the Red Was Right After All Club. It's small, but exclusive. I really need to get merch made up. What size t-shirt do you wear?" Sam shot her a dirty look. Red grinned. "I'll go ping Chuck."

"No," Sam said firmly. "We do this in person. We can't trust vidchat. Anyone could be listening."

Good point. Wouldn't be the first time Red's communications were compromised, wouldn't be the last. "Well," she said, "we're already headed to Zaldron. He's got a place there, in—ah, hell, it's in Gozgor Toth." Of course it was. She blew a strand of hair out of her face. The city council probably forgot all about the solar array thing. Besides, it was years ago; whatever warrants had been issued would be long expired, right? What's the statute of limitations on vandalism of public property in Gozgor Toth, anyway? Damned if she could remember. Well, she still had almost eighty hours to look it up. If she wanted to.

Eighty hours, ugh. A long time to make small talk over coffee. That's one good thing about someone trying to murder you all the time—it broke up the endless talking. There had to be a way to pass time that didn't involve explosions or psychoanalysis. At least real-life ones.

Maybe there was . . .

"Anyone up for a few episodes of *Port Desire*?" she asked, getting to her feet and looking around for the vidscreen remote. "The Grand Duchess Gloogle Vander Sklorp just started her life sentence for stealing her identical twin sister's prize-winning orchids for the insurance money, so we'll finally find out if she—what?"

If looks could kill, Sam would be filing paperwork for a month to explain how Red's smoking husk ended up in twenty-six different pieces, and what exactly happened to her liver, anyway, was it that greasy yellow stain on the hull?

"I think," Sam said, her voice terrifyingly calm, "it's time you told me what you know about Smith."

Red sighed, returning to her chair and lighting a cigar. "You sure? Cuz I'll help with the paperwork."

"Huh?"

"Never mind." She blew a stream of blue smoke at Sam and began. "When I was twelve . . ."

Chapter 22
Now With Added Menace

Anyone who checked the *Wart*'s chronometer could confirm that the remainder of the flight to Zaldron took approximately eighty hours in standardized galactic time units. However, in terms of lived experience, the trip stretched out into months or even years. Red felt herself growing older as the time ticked by. Not because of any glitch in spacetime or temporal rift, but because Red spent most of it explaining, describing, sharing, and otherwise talking about stuff she'd spent the better part of the previous year purposely *not* explaining, describing, sharing, and otherwise talking about.

Each time Red thought she had said absolutely everything there was to say about Smith, Sam would come back with a question. Why did you do that? Why didn't you do this instead? Where were you at that point? Where was Smith? What were his exact words? Do you think he could have meant this? Why not? Can you go back to that other thing you said earlier? Sam didn't take notes or record anything—Red wouldn't have allowed it anyway—and Red had the terrible suspicion that she'd have to go over it all again soon.

Then there was Fritzi. Red had been afraid she'd try poking around in her brain with that psychology nonsense, but she didn't. Oh no. It was far, far worse. She *cleaned*. Crusty old dishes? Scrubbed, dried, stacked in newly-disinfected cabinets. Filthy laundry? Washed in the bathroom sink *by hand*, standing on the Rhuatan Fizzdrops crate. Piles of rotting trash? Bagged and thrown in the ship's incinerator. Red hadn't even known the ship *had* an incinerator. Humiliating. Worst of all, Fritzi cleaned graciously, without a single tut or tsk or wrinkled nose.

It was all new to Red. Woodman never complained about the mess (or cleaned, for that matter), and Granny definitely tsked and tutted. If this extended-visit thing got to be a regular deal, Red would have to set some boundaries. It's not that she liked living in filth. She took full advantage of Granny's fungus-free kitchen and clean sheets every time she visited. But years ago she'd come to an arrangement with her inner (and outer) slob: it could devolve into vermin breeding grounds all it wanted, as long as said vermin didn't interfere with whatever it was she would rather do than scrub a floor. Which was pretty much anything. It helped that Bonk kept the vermin problem at an ignorable background level.

But after so much time living this way, the trash and clutter felt like home. It was part of who she was, as weird and as sad as that might be. Without the mess, the *Wart* felt like an insurance office—nice enough, but not somewhere you could fart comfortably. And dammit, it was her ship, after all. If she wanted it filthy, it should be filthy. It's about respect, really. Boundaries. She'd never leave her crap all over someone else's clean space, at least not on purpose. Okay, maybe on purpose, depending on the person, but two wrongs don't make a right and all that.

Well, if Fritzi liked cleaning so damn much, Red would give her plenty to do. She staged a full-on silent war against the Andarian's oppressive tidiness. She hid half full beer cans under the bed, tossed cigar butts in the bathroom sink, and smeared electroputty on the refrigerator door. The sabotage distracted Red from Sam's endless grilling and gave her a satisfying, if false and petty, sense of control. Fritzi, meanwhile, just kept cleaning without a word about it. Red wished she'd either give up or get angry or do *something*, but no. Probably some psychologist trick.

To round out the party, there was Bonk. Bonk was still Bonk, but now with added menace. Probably just Red's imagination. Sure, it watched her pee. Sure, it sat in the bathroom when she showered so she could see its shadow through the curtain. Sure, it stared at her, unblinking, from under the control panel in the cockpit, on top of the refrigerator, and behind furniture. All cats did that stuff. Right? It wasn't *actually* stalking her through the ship like she was a wounded gnar with no place to run. Still, the only time Red felt she could breathe easy was when Bonk followed Sam and Fritzi into the bedroom and the door swooshed shut.

By the time the navcomp announced their arrival at Zaldron, the tension in the *Wart* was thicker than a Crysallian cloudbank. Red tossed a homona core over her shoulder on her way to the cockpit. She flumped down in the captain's chair, checked the scopes, and punched in the coordinates for Gozgor Toth.

Time to get the hell out of this ship for a while.

~ ~ ~

Red cracked the door to The Painted Pony, Chuck's place in Gozgor Toth, and stepped hesitantly into the gloom. The bright afternoon light did little to illuminate the dark recesses of the bar, so she couldn't make out every face behind every glass or bottle. No one jumped to their feet and pointed at her shouting about solar arrays, so it was probably safe enough. She'd just play it cool, try not to draw attention to herself, and trust everyone drinking in the shadows at that time of day to do the same.

She nodded to Fritzi and Sam, hovering behind her in the street.

The Painted Pony could've been any one of a dozen other Chuck places. Maybe he bought them pre-assembled from some cross-dimensional catalog service. A "hello, I'd like to order a sweaty-smelling dive bar, heavy on the beer stains, and you know what, give me the Everything's Vaguely Sticky Package" sort of thing. Business must be damn good if he can afford the shipping. Red wondered if Fritzi would try to clean up this place, too, or if she reserved that passive-aggressive service for her in-laws. At least there wasn't a TuneBot blasting inane pop music and encouraging everyone to "get funky."

"Hey, man," Red said, sliding up to the bar. Her elbow, of course, found a puddle of what she sincerely hoped was zuran cider and not urine. She considered sniffing it to find out and decided she'd rather not know; it was too late in either case. "You ever consider upgrading to a model people actually *want* to spend time in?"

The bartender half-turned, looking at Red from the corner of one bloodshot eye. "I see enough of you already."

"Aw, c'mon, Chuck," Red said. "I class up the joint, and you know it." To make the point, she belched loudly.

Chuck wrinkled his nose, but then he saw the other two women behind Red. "Sam," he nodded. "Fritzi."

"It's so nice to see you again," Fritzi said warmly, climbing into a stool with the quickness and grace of a person who has spent her life in a world built far too large for her. She held out her hand and Chuck—get this—kissed it.

Sam sat next to her. "How's Ron these days?" she asked.

The oddest thing happened: Chuck smiled. At least Red assumed it was a smile. The corners of his mouth turned up, raising his cheeks and exposing a row of pungent yellow teeth, which on anyone else would be a smile. On Chuck though, it was like a quashtoad wearing a pink sundress. She didn't even know he *had* teeth.

"He's great," Chuck said. "Just started preschool. He loves that stuffed orl you two sent for his birthday, by the way. Named it Flippy." He filled two glasses with icewine and placed them in front of Sam and Fritzi. "On the house."

Red stared at the glasses. "I was just gonna have an Ol' Wo'hall'a, but if you're giving away drinks, I'll have a Finebock. A double Finebock. In fact, just gimme whatever's left in the bottle."

"Like hell you're getting free drinks." Chuck pointed at Sam and Fritzi. "They don't run up a tab they never pay." He turned to Sam. "You that hard up for company these days you gotta hang out with this deadbeat?"

Sam laughed. "You know how it is," she said, taking a sip of her icewine. "You can't choose your family." She nodded at Red. "Have pity on her and give her a drink. I'll pay."

"Hang on," Red protested, throwing up a hand. "Chuck knows about us? The whole sister thing?"

He slammed a visibly dirty shot glass on the bar and slopped some whiskey in it. Not the Finebock, Red noticed, and not even a full shot. "Everybody knows. You're probably the only one who didn't know."

"You could've told me," she muttered under her breath. "I thought we were friends. I didn't even know you have a kid."

"Friends? Ha. And it's two kids, not that you ever bothered to ask." Red pouted. Who asked their bartender about their family? No one, that's who. The best bartender is one who pours big drinks, listens to you bitch about your life, and never mentions your tab. Common knowledge. But even on a good day, Chuck only hit one of those three, so Red supposed it was unfair to expect more now.

"Yeah, sorry about that, I guess." Red threw back her whiskey and gestured expectantly but fruitlessly for another round. "Look, I need your help."

He snorted. "Of course you do," he said. "You always need something. 'Chuck, I need you to buy this stolen booze.' 'Chuck, I need you to tell me top secret stuff.' 'Chuck, I need you to cover my ass again.'"

"What Red meant to say," Fritzi interrupted gently, "is that *we* need your help."

"There's a man we're trying to find," Sam said. She pulled a tattered photo from her jacket pocket and slid it across the bar. Did she carry a pile of photos everywhere she goes? "It's an old picture, I know, and he might look a bit different now — longer hair, maybe, or simple plastic surgery. The kind of thing you'd do if you were avoiding unwanted attention."

Chuck glanced at the photo, but didn't touch it. "Who is it? Anyone I should know?"

"He stole her dog," Red interjected.

Sam shot her a scowl but said nothing.

Chuck's squinty eyes flicked back and forth between the two. Finally, he said, "Okay. But this is for you, Sam. Not *her*." He picked up the photo and studied it from behind the oily hair that hung across his face. Then he faded out a bit while he got his other selves on the cross-dimensional vidscreen for a group chat. A few seconds later, he snapped back into full-fleshed reality.

"Yeah, I know this, ah, dog thief," he said. "Started coming in about ten years ago, at The Lucky Seven Saloon, over in Jutu'un on Ru'ur. Not really a regular, but he'd show up every couple weeks. Then he disappeared for about a year before turning up at the Crossroads Pub in Xyflar Bluff, then again a few years later on

Luforia. On and off like that. Looked pretty much the same as in the picture, though." He handed the photo back to Sam and moved down the bar to serve a round of Pergolian sweet tea shandies to a clutch of women in raunchy bachelorette hats.

Sam stared at the photo, then reached for her icewine with a hand that shook just the tiniest bit.

Fritzi put her hand on Sam's arm and squeezed. "We know he's alive," she said in a low voice. "That's a good thing. It sounds like he's moving around to avoid detection."

"What she said," Red added, standing up and reaching for the whiskey bottle to pour her own refill. "If he's right, the guy's got a pattern, and he's bound to pop up again somewhere. We just need Chuck to tell us when and where."

Sam fiddled with the stem of her wine glass, staring at the puddles of condensation and other moisture on the bar. "When Chuck comes back, let me do the talking," she said. "You're not very good with people."

"That's not what the defensive line of the Crolinian Psycats said."

A smile quirked the corner of Sam's mouth, and Red realized why it was so familiar—it's what Smith would do every time he couldn't help but find Red's stupid jokes amusing. Maybe Sam actually had a sense of humor after all. Maybe this cnothu could be cracked. She was about to follow up with a detailed description of the offside blocker's birthmark (shape, size, and location) when Chuck came back with an armload of empty glasses.

"This guy we're looking for," Sam said as he piled the glasses in the sink. "Would you let us know next time you see him?"

Chuck snatched the shot glass and bottle away from Red, dousing her with suds. "Sure," he said, tossing the glass into the sink with the rest. He put the bottle on the shelf behind him, well out of Red's reach. "He's at The Meaty Noodle in Uk Voth right now, ordering another Fuzzy Fazzer on the rocks."

"You're telling me that this guy—" Sam held up the photo again— "is currently drinking Fuzzy Fazzers at a strip club only a couple hours' flight away?"

"Yup."

"This exact guy?" Sam asked, waving the photo.

"That exact guy."

"Right now?"

"Right now."

"Fuzzy Fazzers?" Red asked.

"On the rocks."

"Gross." Red shuddered.

Sam slammed her hand on the bar. "Why didn't you just tell us this before?" she demanded.

Chuck shrugged. "You didn't ask."

Sam crumpled the photo in her fist, knuckles white. "Can you hold him until we can get there?"

"How do you expect me to do that? It's a titty bar, not a jail."

"Just keep pouring drinks for him. Get him a lap dance or something. On me, of course." She slapped a pile of credits on the bar.

"Oo, can I get a lap dance, too? OW! What was that for?" Red pouted, rubbing her arm. "I never get to do anything fun."

"I bought you drinks," Sam hissed through gritted teeth.

"One drink," Red grumbled.

"You've been most helpful, Chuck," Fritzi said. "Please give my love to Babs and the kids."

"Will do," he said with a nod.

"Oh, and Chuck?" Sam leaned across the bar and took Chuck's sweaty hand in hers. "Don't tell my father. I know it's a lot to ask, but this is none of his business. It's . . . a personal project. Do you understand?"

The bartender pressed his flabby lips together. "I got you, Sam."

Chapter 23
Bright, Dirty, and Sticky

Places like The Meaty Noodle weren't Red's usual go-to as a hangout, but it was definitely a nice change of pace. Instead of dark, dirty, and sticky, it was bright, dirty, and sticky. And loud. Neon lights pulsated and music thumped. Small tables surrounded the circular stage at perfect credit-stuffing distance for most species. A pair of Orgullan women in six-inch platform heels spun on the twin poles, their miles of blue hair flying in wide arcs that almost, but not quite, brushed the faces of the eager spectators. Other women in spangled hot pants wandered through the tables, delivering overpriced, watery drinks and laughing too loudly at the ass-slaps and dirty jokes.

Sam, in full Business Mode, ignored all this while scanning the room. "You see Dirk anywhere?" Red shouted in her ear over the throbbing beat of a Pink Chenille remix. Sam shook her head, then made her way to the bar, where this manifestation of Chuck was busy sticking paper umbrellas into a tray's worth of Fuzzy Fazzers—glasses filled to the top with ice cubes and a splash of slightly boozy fruit juice thrown in, mostly for color.

Chuck didn't say a word, but shot a look at a curtained booth to the left of the stage. He pushed the tray of drinks at them and turned his back. Whatever was about to go down, he didn't want to see it—maybe in case Smith did come sniffing around, he could truthfully say he didn't see what happened. What did Sam say— the best lie is mostly truth? Something like that.

Red picked up the tray. Sam took a deep breath, then nodded and strode toward the booth. Red and Fritzi exchanged a look, then followed.

Sam pulled back the plastic privacy curtain a few inches. Red stood on her tiptoes to see over her shoulder. A Glorreen woman in a spangly g-string writhed on a man's lap, her cartoonishly large and very naked breasts obscuring his face. Her lips curled into a smile and she batted her double-thick fake eyelashes at them. "If this is turning into a party, I'm gonna need more credits," she said without stopping her gyrations.

"You can go." Sam jerked a thumb over her shoulder, nearly poking Red in the eye.

The Glorreen's smile disappeared. "Hey, Chuck said this guy is mine," she snarled. "Get your own."

"Yeah, geyyer own," the man slurred. "Typhanee n I're havin a goo' time."

Sam flashed her badge at Typhanee. "Go tell Chuck to give you the rest of the night off and add it to my tab." She held up a few credits, which the Glorreen snatched and tucked away somewhere Red wished had been left to her imagination.

The dancer pushed past the agent. Her eyes widened at Red's tray of Fuzzy Fazzers. She picked one up, tossed the little umbrella on the floor, winked, and downed it in one gulp. She replaced the glass and took another.

"Here," Fritzi said, handing a business card to towering Typhanee. "I know sex work can be difficult. Call me if you ever need to talk to a professional. No charge. Tell your coworkers too."

Typhanee glanced at the card, then down at Fritzi. "Thanks, honey."

"Take care of yourself," Fritzi said, but the woman had already gone.

"Wherr'she go?" The man tried to stand up, but his legs buckled under him and he collapsed back in the chair.

"You sure that's our guy?" Red whispered to Sam. "He looks like a used ship salesman." She sniffed one of the drinks on the tray, then ventured a sip. "How many of these did you have, dude?" she asked. "There's, like, zero alcohol in here."

Sam squatted next to the man. "Dirk?" she said. "It's really you, isn't it."

Dirk's head swung toward her. His eyes struggled to focus. "Who're you? D'I know you?" His head swung around again. "Wher's Typhanee? Th'guy said—"

"Cut the crap, Dirk." Sam's voice was hard. "I've seen this fake drunk bit too many times."

His eyes cleared scary fast. "You shouldn't be here, Sam." He glanced over his shoulder. "Close that curtain, you morons," he hissed.

"Okay, okay, jeez." Red shoved the drink tray at him and pulled the curtain shut.

"I thought you were dead," Sam said, her voice barely audible over the music.

"That was the idea," Dirk shot back. He fidgeted the tray in his lap and glanced again at the curtains. "How did you find me?"

"Never mind that for now," Sam said. "We need your help. Let's get out of here to someplace we can talk."

Dirk wiped beads of sweat from his balding scalp. "No way," he said. "You should know better." He eyeballed Red and Fritzi. "And you brought a couple of strange broads? Dammit, Sammy, why not just post on the high-res bands? 'Dirk Largo found alive and unsatisfied in Zaldron strip club. His massive boner could not be reached for comment. Better come quick, ladies, he won't last long.'"

"I'm not some strange broad," Red protested. "I'm her sister!"

"I don't care if you're the Queen of—sister?" he choked. "*That's* Mildred Darkling?"

"Red to you, asshole."

"Well, well, I guess hotness runs in the family." He left Red sputtering and leered at Fritzi. "Who's she, another sister? I don't normally go for Andarians, you know. Scales ain't my kink. But I'd make an exception for that one." His eyes caught on Fritzi's expansive cleavage, which Red had pretty much forgotten about. Funny how you could get used to something if you see it enough.

"That's my wife," Sam said coldly. "You can trust both of them." She glanced at Red. "I do."

Dirk narrowed his eyes. "I do not need this. Two of Smith's kids—one a freaking SECS agent and the other who smells like a duuofish milkshake?"

"Hey!"

He threw back a Fuzzy Fazzer. "I'm dead. I'm so dead. Never deader. Order up a headstone, Sammy: 'Here lies Dirk Largo, sex god.' On second thought," he added morosely, fiddling with the umbrella from his drink. "Just cremate me and turn my ashes into body glitter and send me to Typhanee."

"Please, Dirk. Just come with us. We'll keep you safe." Sam pulled Dirk to his feet. The tray of empty glasses crashed to the floor. Red peeked through the curtain, but no one seemed to have heard the noise. Thank the Fourteen for loud music, hot strippers, and industrial-grade stain-resistant curtains.

"Dammit, I'm not coming!" Dirk shouted, wiggling in a fruitless attempt to escape from Sam's iron grip. The sleeve of his white polyester jacket tore a bit at the shoulder. "Aw, man! This is my favorite suit!"

"You're making a scene," Sam snarled. She looked at Red, who shrugged.

"What you need is an ARSE," she suggested.

Sam rolled her eyes. "Fine," she sighed. "But you'll have to do it. My hands are full."

"That's what my last girlfriend said," Dirk grunted, still twisting.

Sam ignored this. "Just be careful with it," she said, turning her body so Red could reach the weapon under her jacket.

Red greedily plucked the weapon from Sam's shoulder holster and examined the dials.

"Don't change the settings," the agent warned. "I've got it calibrated for humans. We don't want to turn his brain to jelly."

"Jelly!?" Dirk renewed his squirming.

"Just hold still," Red said. "It's my first time." She aimed the ARSE at Dirk, stuck her tongue between her teeth, and pulled the trigger. The wiggly bits twitched, there was a silent whoomp of energy, and Dirk slumped, unconscious.

Red whistled. "Oh man, that was soooo cool."

Sam lowered Dirk's limp body to the chair and felt his wrist. "Okay, he's stable. Let's get him to the ship." She caught Red slipping the ARSE into the waistband of her pants and held out her hand.

Red reluctantly handed the weapon back. "Aw shucks, sis, you're no fun."

"You're lucky you got to use it at all," Sam said. She stuck a shoulder under Dirk's armpit and wrapped an arm around his back. "Get the other side, will you?"

Together, they lifted him up and managed to balance him between them. His head lolled to one side. "Shit," Red said. "How are we going to get him out of here without anyone seeing us?"

"Actually, that might not be a problem," Fritzi said, gills rippling thoughtfully. "It looks like he passed out from too much alcohol. I'm sure he's not the first patron of this establishment to do so. I doubt anyone will pay us any attention."

Chapter 24

It's Not Her, It's *That*

Fritzi was right, of course. A new act, this one a human redhead, had taken the stage and was in the 'revealing the psycat tattoo on her torso' portion of her performance. This occupied most of The Meaty Noodle's patrons. The only one who noticed their stumbling struggle to get Dirk's inert body out the door was Chuck, who barely glanced in their direction before returning to refilling the display of scented novelty condoms.

Back on the *Wart*, Red set a more-or-less random course out of the Zaldron system, fast but not suspiciously fast, just in case. Meanwhile, Sam tied Dirk loosely to a chair with the sash of the robe and a belt that Red didn't recognize but had probably belonged to Woodman at some point. "To keep him safe until he wakes up," she'd claimed, but Red detected a nonzero amount of wariness. Made sense—Red spent enough time around angry drunks to know precautions rarely went too far.

"How long before he comes to?" Red asked, plopping on a chair in the main compartment.

"Should be soon," Sam said, feeling Dirk's pulse for the sixth time. "It's intended to temporarily incapacitate, not have long-term effect."

Bonk jumped up on the couch next to Fritzi. The Andarian absently ran a hand over its back. "Have you thought about how to approach this conversation once he does wake?"

"Oh yeah, I have it all planned out," Red said. "'Pardon me, good sir, but do you perchance happen to possess knowledge of or pertaining to this particular cat-like contraption?'"

Fritzi smiled thinly. "If I may venture a professional opinion," she said, "Dirk is likely experiencing some degree of psychological trauma, from both his time in hiding as well as the shock of being 'found.' Keep this in mind when talking to him. If you push too hard or too fast, you may cause further damage and lessen his willingness—and, frankly, ability—to assist you."

"Just let me do the talking," Sam said wearily. "I mean it this time, Red. Don't be cute."

"Who, me?" Red placed one hand on her chest. "That's probably the first time anyone accused me of being cute. I usually get 'not bad' or 'needs implants.'"

"That's exactly what I'm talking about," Sam scolded. "Can't you ever just be—"

No one got to learn her likely entirely unrealistic expectations for Red's behavior because Dirk chose that moment to groan to soupy consciousness. He attempted to raise a hand to rub his face but the robe sash stopped him short. "What the—hey!" He struggled briefly, then relaxed when he saw Sam. "You told me you weren't into this sort of thing, Sammy."

"It was just to make sure you were safe during launch," Sam said, reaching for the knots. She hesitated. "You're not going to make me regret this, are you?"

"Sammy, baby, you are safe with me." He leered at Red and licked his lips. "Can't say the same for your sister, though. She's one fine slice of pie, if you know what I mean. Once you get past the grunge."

"You haven't changed a bit, Dirk." Sam shot a look at Fritzi as she untied the sash and belt. "And you thought he'd be traumatized."

Fritzi shrugged. "Everyone processes things differently."

Dirk rubbed his wrists and turned in his chair. "Ah, yes, the third kitten in my basket. Why don't we—" He froze in mid-entendre, eyes huge.

"What?" Red asked, following his gaze. "You already met Fritzi, back in the club."

He scrambled out of the chair, knocking it over in the process, and backed himself against the wall, as far from the couch as possible. "It's not her, it's *that*." He pointed a trembling finger at Bonk. Fritzi put a protective hand on the cat's cranial hull, but it blinked unconcernedly.

Sam tilted her head. "You've seen that cat before?"

"No, no, you don't know, you can't know . . ." Dirk moaned. His eyes darted around the compartment like a corn-fattened shiq confronted by a hungry clomis.

"Dude, calm down," Red said. She stood slowly and began edging toward the bedroom. There was a pair of holocuffs under the mattress, if she could only get to them before Dirk did something stupid like open the airlock so they all joined the frozen debris that made up Zaldron's outer rings.

"Calm? Calm, she says! I'm plenty calm, baby, believe me," he gibbered. "But I need to get the hell off this ship. Drop me anywhere. Ru'ur, Ophesus—hell, strip me naked and leave me on the doorstep of the SECS building, just get me away from that *thing*."

Sam got between Dirk and Bonk, hands up in a gesture of concession. "Look, Dirk, it's okay, I promise," she said in a soothing voice. "Just sit down. Please." Red assumed that voice was the last thing people heard before taking a SECS-issued blaster to the face. She inched closer to the bedroom door. Dirk's eyes shot to her.

"You too, Red," Sam said. "Sit. Let's just talk."

Reluctantly, Red sat, wishing she hadn't dumped her weapons in the ammo box when they got back from The Meaty Noodle.

Sam took Dirk's hand and guided him back to the chair, which she righted. "You need to trust me, my friend. Like you used to, back at the Academy. Remember when old man Peterson almost caught you on the judo range with that nurse?"

A smile twitched on Dirk's face. "Patti. Man, she was something else. She did this thing with her toes . . ."

"She was hot," Sam agreed. She dragged her chair next to Dirk's. "And remember who you asked to take the heat? Who told Peterson *she* was the one who left that thong hanging from the gun rack?"

"You did, Sammy."

"And who pretended to be the provost's daughter so you could sneak into the Tau Lambda house on initiation night?"

He sighed. "Okay, okay, you saved my ass more times than I can count. You win. I owe you. So what do you need from me?"

"We need to know what you know about that cat."

Dirk let out a shrill laugh. "First of all, that's no cat."

A flurry of glances flew among Sam, Red, and Fritzi. "It's not?" Sam asked.

Red pulled a cigar from her bra and clenched it in her teeth. She patted her pockets, looking for a lighter. Dirk whipped out a gold-plated one shaped like a dick and lit the cigar for her with a wiggle of his thick eyebrows. Red wondered where he got the lighter, and if he could get her one just like it. If she had a chance later, she'd ask. She deserved a little treat.

"Thanks," she said, blowing smoke toward the ceiling and held out the cigar. "You want one?"

"Nah," he said, slipping the lighter back into his shirt pocket. "I don't smoke. This body is a temple, baby. Gotta keep it pure for all the ladies, gents, and anyone else lucky enough to get a taste." He ran his hands over his protruding pot belly and the thicket of chest hair protruding from his open collar.

Red swallowed a little vomit. "Uh huh."

Sam cleared her throat. "Dirk? You were saying it's not a cat?"

"Definitely not a cat." Dirk threw a nervous look its way. "That, my fine-ass friends, is a FUKR."

"He's not that bad," Red said defensively. "No worse than any other cat."

"Ha, no," he said. "A Feline Universal Killing Robot."

Chapter 25
General Screw You-ery

Red dropped the cigar in her lap. "You've got to be shitting me," she said, frantically beating out the ashes that threatened to catch her pants on fire. Flaming pants were best kept to a once-a-week experience.

"Nope." Dirk laughed nervously. "That FUKR is the reason Management's been trying to crawl up my ass the last ten years."

"Maybe you'd better start at the beginning," Sam suggested.

"Okay, see, my mom and dad played a quick game of hide the yozzie in a Shellchucker's bathroom and nine months later--"

"Dirk," Sam said, scowling.

Red elbowed Sam in the ribs. "And you were worried about *me* being cute," she said.

"No sense of humor, Sammy. That's your problem." Dirk fiddled with one of the giant medallions hanging from a gold chain around his neck. "Red, baby, did hot cheeks here tell you what I used to do at SECS?"

"Something in R&D," Red said.

"Something in R&D," he repeated, shaking his head. "Every time Management had one of their brilliant ideas, who did they come to?" He jabbed a thumb into his chest. "Me, Dirk Largo. I was the man who could make all their dark little dreams come true." He started ticking things off on his fingers. "ARSE, BUM, CLIT, KUM, ANUS, all mine."

"Wait," Red interrupted. "You're the one who came up with all those acronyms?"

"You bet your sweet tits, I did," he said proudly. "Management hated it, but what could they do? They needed me."

Red grinned. "Hey, Sam, I think I like this guy."

Sam sighed. "I told you you'd get along with R&D."

Red took a drag on her cigar. "You're sure that Bonk is your FUKR?"

His face turned sour. "It isn't mine," he growled. "Not now. It was until Management and I had . . . creative differences."

"What does that mean?" Sam asked.

Dirk leaned forward in his chair. "See, the whole purpose of the FUKR is to be the perfect assassin. It can infiltrate anywhere, hide in plain sight. Because it looks just like a cat, see? No one would ever suspect. And it worked. Oh, god, did it work. It was perfect, the best thing I've ever done. Except maybe that time I crashed Ephrasia Pfeff's bridal shower and scored with every single member of the wedding party. Everyone goes for the bridesmaids, but it's the groomsmen you really want. Good times, baby. Good freaking times."

"Dirk . . ." Sam prompted.

"I'll tell you the whole story later, doll," he told Red with a wink, "when Ms. Buzzkill isn't around." Red gave him a thumbs-up.

"Anyway," he continued, "That FUKR worked just like they wanted. Killed anything you told it to in sims. But then I found out who their first field test target would be." He paused. "It was not a target I could get behind, so to speak."

"You assassins all have the weirdest moral code," Red said. "'We're okay with killing people, but not that person, he's cool; or that other one, her dog let me pet him once.'"

"Look—" Sam shouted, pointing at Red.

Fritzi hmmed, interrupting what was clearly going to be an epic rant. Red flinched; the Andarian had been so quiet, she'd had forgotten she was even there. Sneaky bastards, those psychologists, always listening and thinking and shit.

Sam threw herself back in her chair, crossed her arms, and stared angrily at the floor.

Fritzi spoke up. "Dirk, please continue. What did you do when you learned the intended target?"

"I sabotaged the FUKR, of course." He glanced at Bonk. "Ever try to get it to do something it doesn't want to do?"

Red thought back. "Yeah, Bonk's not the greatest at following directions. I mean, it's pretty good at taking out gnars and dugger mites and stuff, but it's like it has its own schedule. I assumed that was just a glitch."

Dirk laughed. "Oh, no, baby," he said, wiping his eyes. "That's not a glitch. That's a design feature, courtesy of the fine piece of man meat you see before you. 'We want it to be just like a real cat,' they said. Well, they got it. Hoo boy, did they ever."

The women exchanged confused glances.

"You don't get it?" Dirk asked. "Figures. Okay, I'll use small words. What is the one thing that's fundamental to every cat's programming?" He was met by a trio of blank looks. "Anyone? Hello? Is this thing on?" Dirk tapped an imaginary microphone. "None of you ever had a cat before?" He sighed. "It's independence. Contrariness. General screw you-ery. It's what everything else a cat is derives from. You can't have a truly believable cat without it. And once it's in there, you can't take it out without the whole processing system going into a catastrophic cascade of failures until you're left with a cat-shaped hunk of junk."

"I still don't understand," Sam said. "Why is that sabotage?"

"Sammy, sweetheart," he said. "Imagine an assassin that doesn't follow directions."

"Oh."

"Yeah. Oh." Dirk twirled the biggest, sparkliest medallion around a finger.

"Malicious compliance," Fritzi nodded. "You were given a premise—make a real cat—and simply followed it to its logical conclusion. In doing so, you made the project untenable."

Dirk shrugged and picked at the torn seam in his jacket. "I told them I was just following their own orders, but you can imagine how well that puppy flew. So I split town like a hooker with bus fare. I figured they'd either abandon the idea or destroy it entirely. I never expected them to reassign the project to Tod."

"Who's Tod?"

Dirk spat on the floor. "Todhunter Balzac. A whiny-ass douchebag with the skid marks of the Academy still gracing his tighty-whities. He'd've dry-humped a C'longi to get my job. Tried to do just that, in fact. Of course, there's nothing wrong with dry-humping a C'longi. Done it several times myself. Those tentacles, yowza! Talk about hot. But that particular C'longi was our supervisor. Now, I'll screw anything that moves and most things that don't, but screwing your boss is bad business."

Yeah. Red definitely liked this Dirk guy. "So Tod fixed Bonk? Got around the programming problem?"

"I doubt it," he snorted. "The guy's a tentacle-sucking twerp. He lost IQ points every time he creamed his jeans over a Slook's underwear catalog. Wouldn't be surprised if he'd managed to shoot himself in the face with his own blaster by now."

"No, he's still with S.E.C.S.," Sam said. "At least, I still see him having lunch with the other R&D guys. Gnvrk, Carl, sometimes Umansi."

"Those wankers. I've been cured of sexually transmitted diseases that had a better grasp of advanced robotics than all of them put together." Dirk polished his nails on his jacket. "None of them could manage to extricate the primary drivers from the underlying matrix to bypass the relevant conundrum."

"You mentioned that it wouldn't follow directions," Sam said. "How did it get those directions?"

Dirk leaned forward again, clearly eager to show off. "I designed the FUKR to respond to a unique combination of target and trigger," he explained. "Safer that way, more accurate, less likely to end up with the wrong person turned into a puddle of goo. I do have *some* ethical standards." He shot Red a look. "The target, of course, is whoever you want neutralized in a horrible and extremely permanent fashion. That's based on physical proximity. The thing measures appearance markers, biometrics, pheromone signature, the whole deal, to see through disguises and physical mods and make sure it's the right target."

"And the trigger?"

"That can be anything, really," Dirk said. "A song, a particular sequence of flashing lights, an uncommon word or phrase. It's different for every target. But without the trigger, the FUKR won't move on the target, even if it's in the target's immediate presence."

"That sounds like a complicated piece of coding," Fritzi observed.

"You ain't kidding, kissy lips. But that's why they came to me with the project in the first place."

Sam wouldn't be distracted. "And how was that information transmitted to the device?"

"We'd program everything onto a Directive Infomatics Chip. It's basically a souped-up data chip that delivers the instructions —"

"HA!" Red shouted, slapping her knees and drumming her boots on the floor. "I knew it!"

Sam glowered at her. "You said it was a slow jams playlist."

"Pretty sure that was you, not me."

"As I was saying," Dirk cut in, "you gently but firmly insert the DIC into the proper slot in the FUKR's abdominal cavity. No DIC, no target and no trigger. No target and trigger, no murderous rampage. It just does cat stuff."

"So why did you freak out when you saw it?"

His face went dark. "Management may have given it a DIC that targets me."

"Doesn't really matter right now," Red said.

"What? How do you know?"

"Because Bonk's DIC slot is empty." Red dug the chip she'd gotten from Tom out of her pocket and slapped it on the table. Everyone stared at it.

Dirk's tongue flicked out like a lizard's. "Where did you get that?"

"From the C'longi who sold me the cat last year."

He reached out a finger as if to touch the chip, then pulled back his hand with a shudder. "What did this C'longi look like?"

"Ugly, goopy, big-ass eye, lots of wiggly bits. The usual C'longi jazz. He did like flowery scarves."

Dirk stared at her. "I will give you a night of sweet sensual passion unlike any you've ever experienced if you tell me the C'longi's name *isn't* Tom."

Disappointing people was nothing new to Red but the overwhelming relief at doing so was. "Yeah, that's him. At least, that's what he called himself. It never seemed like a particularly C'longi-y name to me. Why?"

Dirk buried his face in his hands. "Tom was my supervisor at SECS."

"You've got to be shitting me." This whole ball of electroputty just got a lot more complicated.

"Cupcake, if I were shitting you, you'd know it." He peeked through his fingers at the chip lying innocently on the table. "That DIC could have my name on it, or ... You never tried plugging it in, did you?"

"Of course not!" Red exclaimed. "We're not stupid."

Sam cleared her throat. "If I recall correctly, I had to stop you from plugging it in, back at the safehouse. Because *you* thought it was a slow jams playlist."

Red waved a hand. "The important thing is, we didn't."

"Good." Dirk wiped sweat from his scalp.

"Even if your biojunk is on the chip, so what?" Red said. "As you can see, we've got the chip, and it's not in the cat. You're all good."

"But Tom!" Dirk cried. "He's still out there! Any of those fazzer dildoes I worked with could whip up a new DIC. It's not that hard. Even Tod couldn't screw that up. Tom could be on our tail right now, coming for me. Or, you know, someone." He shot a panicked look toward the main portal, as if he expected the C'longi to burst through with a DIC in each tentacle.

"Oh, hey, you're in luck," Red said. "Last time we saw Tom, he was a puddle of burning grey goo. There was this bomb, see, and--"

"You think one dead supervisor matters to Management?" A hysterical wave of laughter burst from Dirk like the contents of an overripe spaceherpes pustule. "DICs and bureaucrats are cheap and plentiful. They'll just send more, and more, and more, until one of them succeeds in making me a sexy smear on the tarmac of life."

Sam shook Dirk by the shoulders. "You've got to calm down."

"How can you say that, Sammy?" he wailed. "You know as well as I do that we—I mean, I don't stand a chance."

"I think you're overestimating S.E.C.S.," Sam said. She squatted next to him and took his hand in both of hers. "They don't do anything without filling out paperwork in triplicate, checking it, drafting a resolution, running it through committee after committee, then tearing it all up and starting over from scratch. Even if they want to send someone else after you, it'll be a year before they get around to authorizing a vote on whether or not to make a plan."

"You don't understand. You just don't." He put his face back in his hands. "Why did you have to find me, Sammy? We were all doing fine, we were all safe, and . . ."

He keeps saying we. Why does he keep saying we?

"Tell me what's going on, Dirk!" Sam begged. "I can't help you if you don't tell me."

That's when all seven hells broke loose at once.

Chapter 26
Rookie Mistake

The lights on the *Wart* cut out, plunging them all into darkness for a few terrifying seconds until the emergency backups could flicker on. Alarms wailed, beeped, flashed, blinked, and otherwise made themselves known. Bonk launched off the couch in a flash of rusted metal. Dirk squealed and cowered, but it ran past him into the bathroom.

Red ran to the cockpit and frantically scanned the displays, trying to sort through the dozen alerts to find out what was causing it all. She cleared them one by one until there was only one left: the plasma damper. They'd just replaced that stupid thing and now it's acting up again? She cursed at the unfairness of it all. Why couldn't it be something new and interesting, like the electrical panel or life support system?

She silenced the final alarm, shut off the plasma damper, and went back to the main compartment. "There's good news and bad news," she reported to the group as she rummaged through piles of dirty clothes to find her toolbag. "Bad news is, there's something screwy with the plasma damper. I had to shut it down so we'll just have to limp along at impulse until it's fixed. Hopefully it's something simple, like the injector pump jiggled loose." She flicked a dried clump of slak sauce off her ancient proton welder and stuffed it into the waistband of her pants. "Pass me that sonic wrench, wouldja, Sam? It's under that stack of skin mags. Don't worry, the two aren't related. At least not recently."

To Sam's credit, she did pass her the wrench, though not without wrinkling her nose and holding the wrench between two fingers like it was diseased. "What's the good news?" she asked, looking around for a place clean enough to wipe her hand.

"I lied," Red said. "No good news."

"Au contraire, mon sexy ami," Dirk said. He unfolded himself from his ball of terror and shot his cuffs. "The good news is, you've got Dirk Largo."

Red raised a skeptical eyebrow. "What do you know about engines?"

"What do I know about engines?" he asked, offended. "Honeypants, I was fixing ship engines in my uncle's garage when I was four years old. I'm what they call a 'mechanical prodigy.'" He winked. "It's one of the many, many talents I'm willing to demonstrate."

"Great." Red tossed him the sonic wrench. "Prove it."

"Anything we can do while you two are busy with the damper?" Sam asked.

Red thought a minute. "You know your way around a navcomp?"

"Sure."

"See what's nearby. We might need to land somewhere to get parts. Look for a big market, a salvage yard maybe." Sam nodded.

"Will Bonk be all right?" Fritzi asked, frowning at the bathroom door.

Red snorted. "Oh, yeah, it's fine," she said, hoisting the strap of the toolbag over one shoulder and coiled power cable over the other. "It hides behind the toilet when its startled. Everything's gotta be soooo dramatic, you know? It'll come out when no one's paying attention anymore."

Dirk followed her to the engine room. "What's up with the towels?" he asked, eyeing the crusty pile.

"Dude, you don't even want to know."

He gestured to the rigged-up plasma damper hanging precariously off the engine block. "This was your work?" he asked with a low whistle.

"Pretty impressive, right?" Red said, dumping the tools on the floor and admiring her handiwork. "Did it myself."

Dirk rubbed a hand over his chin. "Impressive. Sure. The same way a rich C'longi hooker is impressive." He squinted at the mess hanging off the engine casing. "Is that a Twist series? You know they stopped making those back in oh-three because they had a habit of catching fire, right?"

"You think I'm stupid?" Red protested. "Look." She pointed to a set of wires sprouting from a blob of electroputty. "I bypassed the heat sump circuit and used an insulated power coupling on a grounded bracket to pick up the slack. No way this thing's catching fire."

"Okay, that's actually kind of clever."

"I know." Red fished another cigar from her bra and lit it with the pilot light on the temperature control mechanism.

Dirk squatted and poked the blob thoughtfully. "I assume you used alkaline electroputty to seal the connections?"

Uh oh. "Let's pretend I didn't."

Dirk sighed. "Rookie mistake. Without alkaline electroputty, the iridium foam used in that type of insulation begins to decay almost instantly." He took off his jacket and rolled up his shirt sleeves. "Gimme that proton welder. No, just the beam generator. I'm going to try melting off this putty to see how bad the damage is."

Red sat on the floor and crossed her legs. "You and Sam go way back, huh?"

Dirk shot her a sideways look. "Yeah."

"Like me and Woodman," she thought aloud. She tapped her ash into a scrap of aluminum sheeting, then stuck it under the damper to catch the dripping putty. "You must be really close."

"Well, yeah. I love her."

Red fiddled with her cigar. "That must be hard, what with her being married and, you know, into chicks and all."

Dirk snorted. "For someone who talks as much shit as you do, you've got a pretty narrow idea of things." He adjusted the beam on the welder. "First off, just because someone's married to a woman doesn't mean they're only into women. It takes all kinds to make this galaxy spin, you know?"

"Point taken."

"Second, you can love someone without getting everyone's genitals involved. Lots of times genitals do get involved, sure. But it was never like that with me and Sammy. It could've been, but it just wasn't." He shrugged. "We're friends. Good friends. Probably the best friends two people can be in this oozing pus bucket of a galaxy."

"And there was never anything more? For either of you?"

"More? Nope."

"No way. I hear how you talk. And Sam's super hot. I mean, I'm totally into guys and whatever, but even I can tell. There's no way you didn't at least try to hit that at some point."

Dirk flicked off the beam generator and looked Red in the eye. "You never had a friend who knew you inside and out? Saw all your dark nasty parts and didn't care? Who always had your back? Who could always make you smile?" He turned back to melting putty. "Sex is one of the greatest things out there. I know that from plenty of experience. But trust me, having a friend like that is better."

Red blew a smoke ring toward the ceiling and thought about that. "I guess I never knew that could happen."

"Well, it does." Dirk snapped off the beam generator and tossed it to the floor. "Lemme ask you something. You and this Woodman guy. You're friends, yeah?"

"Yeah."

"And lemme guess—you're also something else?"

"I mean, maybe?"

"Are you something else because you want to be, or because you think you're supposed to be?"

Red ground out her cigar butt in the makeshift ashtray. "You sound like Fritzi."

"Angelface, I'm not telling you what to do or how to feel," he said gently. "Just keep in mind that reality is a lot bigger than you might think." He turned back to the plasma damper. "Speaking of bigger, you got a magnifier?"

She pulled one from the toolbag and handed it to him silently. He inspected the exposed coupling through the lens. "Yup, just what I thought," he said. "Take a peek, sugarbutt." He handed her the magnifier. Sure enough, the coupling looked like a quashtoad nest with clusters of scooped out holes pocking the surface.

"We need a new coupling, at the very least," Dirk said. He lay on his back and scooted under the awkwardly jutting damper.

"But I'd feel a hell of a lot better if we redid this entire thing. You done good, don't get me wrong. But there's better ways to do it. I can show you."

Red barely heard him. "Let's say I buy this whole friends thing," she said, picking at a hole in her sock. "Friends don't keep secrets from each other."

"I have no idea what you're talking about. See this?" He pointed at something on the underside of the damper. "This is what *I'm* talking about. You rerouted the coolant vector when you could've just—"

"Don't change the subject," she snapped. "You gotta admit, it's kinda weird that you won't tell your super bestest friend in the whole entire universe what's really going on with this Bonk business."

Dirk slid back out and glared at her. "You're going to lecture me on what friends do?"

"It's bad enough you made her think you were dead all this time," Red pointed out. "Do you think she keeps secrets from you?"

Dirk glanced at the closed engine room door. "You don't understand," he hissed. "She can't know. It's the only way I can protect her."

Red suppressed a scream. "When are you men going to learn?" she snarled. "Women don't always need or want your stupid protection. Quit thinking we do. It's not macho, it's infuriating. We can take care of our own damn selves. And if we can't, we'll let you know."

Dirk scowled. He snatched up the sonic wrench and started banging away at the engine casing. "You don't understand."

"Oh, I think I do," she said, her voice deadly calm. "Woodman, Smith, it's always the same. 'Poor little Red, we just want to keep you safe.' It's grumshit! I've never needed anyone to save me. And when I need help, I ask. Like a freaking adult."

Dirk gave the casing one final whack with the sonic wrench and the damper suddenly came loose and crashed to the floor. He dropped the wrench and slumped. "The original field test was *Sam*," he whispered. "That FUKR was meant for *her*."

Red choked on her own spit.

"So you see why I had to sabotage it," Dirk continued in a rush, his words practically falling over each other in an attempt to be heard. "Otherwise she'd be dead. Horribly dead. Torn to itty bitty bloody pieces dead. So dead that—"

Red held up a hand. "Yeah, I get it," she said. "I don't need the gory details." She processed this a minute. "But why would Management want her gone?" she asked. "She seems like a model employee, in a paid assassin kind of way."

Dirk snorted. "Who said it was Management that ordered the hit?"

"Who else would it be?"

He pulled himself up on one elbow. "I think you know."

Dammit. "Smith," Red spat. "It's always Smith."

"Bingo," Dirk said, shooting her a pair of finger guns. "Sammy told daddy dearest she was his faithful little bad girl spying on the government for him. But he didn't believe that anymore. Never did, probably. Too smart, the bastard. But he used her anyway, made her do . . . things that benefited him and his business. Until she started getting restless. Then she went from manageable asset to risky liability."

"How do you know all this?" Red asked.

His eyes shifted away. "Because I was working for Smith too."

Jeez, was there anyone in the freaking universe who wasn't working for Smith? His payroll expenses must be gargantuan. "So? What did he have you do? Change the oil in his ships? Get him laid?"

Dirk lay back, head on the damper, and stared at the ceiling. "Spy on Sam."

"Oh."

"Yeah, oh. He needed someone and I volunteered. I thought, better me than some stranger, right? I thought I could, I dunno, manage him. Feed him just enough intel to satisfy him, without putting anybody in real danger. Just like Sam tried to do with him."

"Rookie mistake," Red said softly.

Dirk rolled his eyes. "You got that right, babydoll. When he came to me with the FUKR project, I didn't know it was his way of dealing with the Samanthya Anyanama problem. If I had known the whole thing was just a big setup to take her down, I would've made some excuse and refused the project from the beginning."

"You were okay with creating a killing machine as long as it killed someone you didn't know?" Red hissed. "What is wrong with you people?"

"Hey, space babe, I don't know where you live, but here in this dimension? It's never that simple. People die all the time. Some people deserve it. Others don't. I do what I can to tip the scales so the ones who do, do, and the ones who don't, don't."

Red ran a hand through her hair. "You never told Sam any of this?"

"Are you kidding? Of course not. As far as she knows, Smith has no idea she's playing him and I'm just good ol' Dirk from R&D." He laughed bitterly. "I had to protect her. Yeah, I know, I know. But if she knew what Smith wanted from me, she'd only have accelerated her plan to escape his influence."

"To protect you," Red observed.

He nodded. "And anytime you move too fast, you make mistakes. Even Sam. So I took the Smith job and hid it from her to buy her some time."

"Maybe you should've trusted her to make her own decision about that."

"Now who sounds like a shrink?" He chuckled softly and sat up. "Okay, okay, you've convinced me. Sammy needs to know. Deserves to know. But Red," he said earnestly, "swear to me that you'll let me tell her myself. Don't go blabbing any of this."

"I don't blab." Red smiled wickedly. "But don't wait too long to tell her, or I could make an exception."

"Deal."

Red looked at the Twist series plasma damper lying in a mess of melted electroputty. "Is any of that salvageable?"

"Oh yeah," Dirk said, picking up the damper and weighing it in his hands. "You don't even need most of the stuff they put in these things. The manufacturer adds all these bells and whistles to sell more product. 'Get the latest model, it's got sixteen more microbursts per minute and a coffee maker!' What really makes this puppy tick is the inducer. If that's good, you can slap it in any engine and it'll damp your plasma like a Vortex-brand FeatherLite

DildoPlex 9001 with the Auto-Lube package and solar charging option."

"That's ridiculous," Red scoffed. "The 9001 doesn't have a solar option." She waved a hand at the damper. "But we can compare toys later. Let's get to work on this thing."

"Not so fast," Dirk shook a finger at her. "The inducer's intact, but it's still a Twist series that could roast us. We need another coupling and *alkaline* electroputty."

Red stood up and clapped her hands. "Let's see what Sam and Fritzi found on the navcomp," she said. "There's gotta be a market within a day or two on impulse."

Chapter 27
The Hidden Gem of the West

"What d'ya mean, there's no market within a day or two on impulse?" Red stared at the local map displayed on the vidscreen. "That's not possible. There's always a market. It's, like, physics or something."

Sam spun around in the captain's chair. "You're welcome to give it another look."

"Outta my chair," Red growled. Sam shrugged and moved to the copilot's chair. Red plunked down and wiggled a bit to get the padding back to fit her own butt shape.

"Is there no other way to fix the plasma damper?" Fritzi asked. Bonk swirled around her legs, having overcome its fit of drama-rama.

"Ask the engine expert over there," Red said, waving a hand at Dirk.

Dirk shook his head. "It needs a new coupling. No way around it."

"But do you need to buy one?" Fritzi pressed. "Or could you fabricate one?"

"Huh." Dirk swirled his fingers through the chest hair poking out of his unbuttoned shirt collar. "I could, but I'd need some stuff our dear hostess probably doesn't have on board."

"Try me," Red said. "I got a lotta weird shit on this ship. You never know what someone's willing to overpay for, so I grab whatever I can find."

"Let's see," Dirk said, ticking off each item on his fingers. "A standard set of dies, about 500 grams of tribunium-copper alloy, and something I can use to coat the threads of the gaskets. Oh, and the alkaline electroputty." He paused. "I suppose I can make the dies if I have to. You've got enough crates around this trash heap that I can carve up."

"Hey, it's not that bad," Red said. "Fritzi cleaned." The *Wart* wasn't some fancy ship, and yeah, she could be tidier and scrape the mildew off the bathroom floor and do laundry, but now she could at least incinerate her garbage and . . . she forgot where she was going with that train of thought.

Dirk continued. "I can make the alloy too, if I can get my hands on tribunium- and copper-rich ores and a smelting furnace. But I really don't want to do that, because smelting sucks fazzer balls."

"Okay, I got none of that." Red thought a moment. "What seals the gaskets?"

"Anything that spreads smoothly when wet, like—"

"Don't," Sam said with a scowl.

"Anyway," Dirk continued, unfazed, "epoxy, spackle, paint, even creamed zuranfruit would do the trick. There's no chemistry involved. It just needs to be thicker than water and sticky enough to stay in place until the gaskets are screwed together, to make the seal airtight."

"Slak sauce?"

"Maybe, if it's the original flavor. Salsariffic and Tahitacular have chunks."

"Okay, cross that off the shopping list," Red said. "I got a case of the stuff no one wants because it's, ah, slightly out of date."

"How slightly?"

Red squirmed. "Um. Not sure. Maybe a couple, uh, years?"

"Hm," Dirk said to himself. "More viscosity."

"Then all we really need," Fritzi said brightly, "are the putty and the metals."

"Oh sure," Dirk scoffed. "You have any idea how hard it is to find tribunium, let alone tribunium-copper alloy? It doesn't grow on trees, honeytits. And without it, no coupling. That's why it's easier to just buy the damn thing."

"That might not be an option," Sam said grimly. "Unless you're willing to spend the next month on this trash freighter."

"HEY."

"Did this trash freighter come with a scientific scanner package?" Dirk asked Red.

"How would I know?" Red pouted. "I'm no scientist. I just use the basics, like comms and ballistics."

"Lemme see." He reached across Red to access the scanning controls. His musky cologne—she hoped it was cologne—made her eyes water. "Okay, yeah, this is good," he said, swiping through a few menus. "Right here, 'scientific suite.' I'll just check the box to enable it, and blammo!" He slapped Red's thigh and pointed at the display. "Scientific scans. Now I'll tell it what we're looking for . . ." He tapped in a complicated chemical formula that was mostly symbols from a section of the keypad Red had never noticed before. A second later, the display flashed a single result.

"Loniwell Gor? Why does that sound familiar?" Red scrolled down to read the full entry. "Wait a minute!" She snapped her fingers. "The Whore's Knuckles!"

"The what?" the others chorused.

"You never heard of the Whore's Knuckles?" Red glanced from face to face. "Come on, guys," she groaned. "Hidden Gem of the West? Gateway to the Fingerlands?" Nothing but blank looks. She pulled up the link. "It's like an old-fashioned vacation place in the mountains. See?" She pointed to a professional promotional picture put out by the local tourist bureau. "Granny talks about it all the time. She used to go there with her grandparents before it was bought by some corporate conglomerate that made it all cheesy. You know, two-for-one buffet specials and 'I rode the Knuckles and all I got was the clap' t-shirts." She flipped through the images. "Looks like they've added a couple water parks." She flipped some more. "And a casino." Another flip. "And a brothel?"

"What? Lemme see." Dirk stuck his head over Red's shoulder.

Irritated, Sam switched the display to show both the Whore's Knuckles area map and the scanner results. "They also have the tribunium-copper alloy."

Red entered the coordinates into the navcomp. "It's less than a day away at impulse." She looked around at the group. "Whore's Knuckles, here we come!" she whooped.

Chapter 28

A Big Steamy Gawk

Red spent most of the uneventful trip to Loniwell Gor craving cnothu puffs and thinking about what Dirk had said about his friendship with Sam. It had to be grumshit. That sort of thing never, ever happened between men and women. Sex always got in the way, for better or worse. And someone like Dirk? Jeez, the dude hit on everyone and everything. They must've hooked up at least once.

But the more time she spent with them, the harder it was to deny. Red sat in the cockpit, a can of Ol Wo'hall'a undrunk in her hand, listening to them talk and laugh together in the main compartment. They had an entire lost decade to catch up on. Dirk told Sam about his life as a dead man, hopping from one place to the next, always thinking three steps ahead. Sam told Dirk about her brushes with death on the job, and other agents who hadn't been as lucky. This inevitably turned to reminiscing about their Academy days, telling inside jokes Red didn't understand, gossiping about people Red didn't know. Before long, she recognized the hot, sick feeling creeping up from her belly and curling her lip.

Jealousy.

She took an angry slug from the can and grimaced at the warm, flat taste. She tossed it away in disgust, splattering beer she hoped Fritzi wouldn't clean up. What was she jealous of, exactly? She and Woodman had those kinds of conversations all the time. They usually ended up naked and sweaty, but that was okay.

Better than okay. Still, it's not like he's the only one who can do that thing with his tongue. Plenty of guys did that. She knew. She'd taught them. She'd considered patenting the move, but it was like a hundred pages of paperwork, and anyway, it was a community service. If she paid taxes, she'd deduct it.

The beep of the nav interrupted her sulky thoughts. They'd arrived at Loniwell Gor. Red took a deep breath. "We're here," she called over her shoulder. The laughter died down. "Dirk, you wanna do another scan for me?"

"Sure thing, Red baby," he said, entering the cockpit and wiping a tear from his face. "I'll scan anything you want."

"Just see if you can pinpoint where this alloy is," Red snapped, getting up so he could take the captain's chair. "It's a damn big planet."

"Gotcha." He pulled up the scanner and ran another search. "Okay, here's the coordinates." He rattled off a string of numbers that Red fed into the navcomp. "That should get us within a few miles."

Red flipped the controls to manual and started the descent through the upper atmosphere. "You guys were talking an awful lot," she said under her breath. "Did you tell her?"

Dirk stared out the viewport. "No. But I will."

"Soon."

"Yeah, sure, soon."

The navcomp guided them to the piney woods at the foot of the mountain range. Canyons snaked out between the peaks, zigzagging across the landscape. Red landed the *Wart* on a sunny clearing well outside the sprawling strip of budget hotels, souvenir stands, tour offices, overpriced theme restaurants, and cheesy attractions promising the biggest this and the tallest that. Everyone stretched, cracked their various joints, and generally got ready to explore an unfamiliar place. For Red and Sam, that meant attaching weapons to every possible limb. Dirk popped his collar, spritzed some breath freshener, and rearranged the few strands of hair that he kept plastered across his bald head. Fritzi applied a thin layer of sunscreen to her exposed scales and tied a thin scarf over her cloud of hair.

Red popped open the hatch with a flourish. "Welcome to the Hidden Gem of the West!" she announced as they clambered down the ramp through the billowing cloud of reddish grit kicked up by the *Wart's* landing cycle. The immediate area was littered with rocks vomited out by several steep, narrow canyons that opened nearby. Behind that, the Knuckles rose up against the midday sky, shimmering in the heat.

Sam raised a hand to block the sun from her eyes. "What am I looking at, exactly?"

"Those are the Whore's Knuckles!" Red pointed. "See how the mountains kind of look like fingers folded over? The peaks are the knuckles?"

"Huh," Fritzi said, pulling her scarf around her gills to keep out the dust.

"You have to use your imagination," Red insisted. "It helps to see it at sunset. When the sun sinks down behind the mountains, it looks like a big-ass jeweled ring sitting on the back of a hand." She shrugged. "At least, that's what the brochures say."

Dirk crossed his arms. "Very nice. Well, now that we've all had a big steamy gawk, can we get to business finding that alloy?" No one objected, so he continued. "The scanner says there's only one deposit, but it's compact and right on the surface. Should be pretty easy to spot once we're close."

He squatted down, picked up a handful of gravel, and sifted it around in his hand. He plucked out one rock, touched it to his tongue. "This is hargonite," he said. "This is usually found two to three thousand feet below the surface. The only way it would get here is being torn loose from one of these canyon walls by a flash flood. That's probably what happened to our alloy too." He dropped the gravel back to the ground and brushed off his hands. "We'll start in the canyons. Sam and I can take the first one on the left. Red, you and Fritzi start on the right. The material we're looking for is shiny and black. If you find it, bring what you can back here and wait for the others. Got it?"

"And keep your eyes open for wild animals," Red added. "Hikers get their faces torn off by psycats all the time. It's in the news every year during breeding season. The ones here aren't as big as their Crolinian cousins, but that just gives them something to prove." She glanced around. "And psycats are the least of it. Granny always talked about something else out here in the mountains, something that would take people. A monster."

Sam laughed. "You've been watching too much *Port Desire*."

"There are no monsters on *Port Desire*." Red tipped her head. "Unless you count Hunk Bestial, the carny with the lazy eye who —"

"Psycats are one thing, but monsters?" Fritzi asked. "Do you really believe that?" She placed a hand on Red's arm.

Red shook it off. "People disappear out here," she insisted. "Something happens to them. Maybe it's a pack of clomis. Maybe it's a monster. What's the difference?" She loosened the strap on her blaster. "I'm not taking any chances."

"She's got a point," Dirk said. "I'm not ready to be psycat scat. Hey Sammy, lemme borrow that biometric pulse gun you used on me."

She pulled it from its holster and handed it to him. "It's still in the testing stages," she warned.

"Damn, they do move slow over at SECS. I had the schematics for this done before that whole FUKR fiasco." He whistled, turning the weapon over in his hand and stroking the wiggly bits. "I haven't held an ARSE in ages," he said, pointing it experimentally into the distance. "Pew pew pew!"

The sound of a rock tumbling down a slope echoed through the air. "Dirk," Sam said wearily. "Rocks are inanimate. It won't work on them. You're just wasting the charge."

Dirk looked at the ARSE, bewildered. "But I didn't fire it!"

"Then what—You hear that?"

Red froze. She did hear it: a skittering, scrabbling noise, and getting closer.

"It's the monster!" Dirk dropped the ARSE with a clatter and threw his hands over his ears.

Fritzi put her arm around him. "There's no monster," she said soothingly. "It's probably just a gazellope or rock albahar going about its business."

"Business like eating our faces!" he whimpered. He shrunk down and tried to hide behind the short Andarian.

"Shh!" Red hissed. The sound had stopped. Only one boulder, about ten yards away, could hide anything big enough for them to worry about, animal or monster. She looked at Sam and raised her blaster. The agent nodded once and unholstered her own. Together, they crept forward, trying not to disturb any loose rocks with their footsteps, fingers twitching on their triggers. When they got close enough, Red held her breath, glanced at Sam, and peered behind the boulder.

Chapter 29
Westward Ho, I Guess

Up rose a creature unlike anything Red had seen outside of a horror vid. Its flat, segmented body was the color of old rust. Each segment had a pair of short grabby-looking appendages that appeared to serve as arms or legs or both. It reared up like a snake, sitting on its rear segments, the rest towering above them. It clacked a wickedly pointy set of mandibles and waved its antennae as if enjoying the smell of fear gushing from Red's pores.

She fell backward in surprise, dropping her blaster to more effectively scramble away. From the corner of her eye, she saw Sam swing her own blaster to bear on the creature.

"Just shoot it already!" Dirk shrieked from behind Fritzi. "What are you waiting for?"

The ten-foot monstrosity tilted its round head to one side and blinked its several pairs of flat black eyes. "Forgive me," it chittered. "We don't get many visitors out here. I forget how my appearance must startle those who are unfamiliar with my species."

"What are you?" Sam asked, still aiming her weapon at the creature.

It pulled itself straight up to its full height. "I'm not a what, I'm a who," it said sniffily.

"Okay, then who are you?"

"I am The Serendipitous Teh," he intoned, "Most Elevated of the Sequestrian Order of the Hind Leg of Fardus and abbot of the Entropic Monastery of the Temple of the Singular Eye." He clasped several sets of hands in front of his midsection and spread the others in a gesture of welcome.

Sam lowered the blaster but didn't put it away. Red grabbed her own from the dirt and stood, brushing dust off the back of her pants. "Nice to meet you, Teh—"

"Serendipitous Teh, please," he scolded mildly. "I did not scale the Several Celentine Staircases to forego my honorific."

Great, one of these guys. She slid the blaster back into its holster. "Sorry."

"Apology accepted," he nodded. He relaxed into a more S-shaped posture. "You are not the first to make that mistake, and I suspect not even the power of St. Cripps herself could make you the last."

Red ground her teeth. This is why she never bothered with religion. Eh, might as well have some fun with it. She gestured at the group. "Let me introduce my friends. The blue-haired one is Sam ARSE-Hogger."

"Hey!" Sam objected, but Red continued. "This is her wife, The Incongruous Fritzi."

Fritzi dipped into a small curtsey. "Pleased to meet you, Serendipitous Teh."

"And the bald guy here is—"

"I," Dirk said, pushing his way to the front and bowing low enough that his medallions brushed the ground, "am The Tumescent Dirk." He took one of The Serendipitous Teh's hands and pressed it to his moist lips with a lascivious smirk. "You have a lot of hands. The possibilities abound."

The Serendipitous Teh coughed and waved his antennae uncomfortably. He wrestled his hand away from Dirk and wiped it delicately on a handkerchief he drew from an opening in his carapace. "And you are?" he asked Red.

"I'm just Red."

"It is a pleasure to meet you, Just Red."

"No no, I'm nothing."

"Ah, my apologies, Just Red the Nothing." She heard a trio of snorts from behind her. The abbot looked confused for a moment, then continued. "It is truly an honor to be in the company of such illustrious persons. I assume from your honorifics that you are among the Elevated? Members of the Integrated Order of the Feminine Side of Fardus, perhaps?"

What the hell did any of that even mean? "Uh. No, I don't think so," Red said, nodding at the *Wart*. "Our ship is busted. We just need to camp out a few days until we get it running again." Best not mention the tribunium-copper alloy they needed. If it's as rare as Dirk said, they didn't need any competition for it.

"Camp!" The Serendipitous Teh exclaimed. "That I cannot allow. You must stay with us at The Entropic Monastery. Why, just moments before you arrived, my fellow monks and I completed the traditional Fardic Blessing of Welcome on a new visitors' dormitory. It features 500-count Luforian cotton sheets, in-room minibars, complimentary scented soaps and lotions in our signature scent, and a full room service menu. We would be delighted to have you as our inaugural guests."

Red glanced at the others. Sam scowled but no more so than usual. That could be just how her face looks. Fritzi didn't seem concerned, and Dirk mumbled something about testing out the sheets. That was reason enough to decline the offer, but Red had a better one. "We'll just stay in our ship," she said. "We don't have the credits for all that fancy stuff."

"Ah, you misunderstand." The Serendipitous Teh smiled. "There is no charge for any of our hospitality services."

Hold up. "You've got to be shitting me," Red said, narrowing her eyes. "What's the catch?"

"No catch," he explained. "We of the Sequestrian Order of the Hind Leg of Fardus consider it a sacrament to provide the very best in luxury accommodations to satisfy every desire."

Red shook her head. "There's always a catch. Do we have to work for a year in your dilithium mine? Bring back the right kidney of some mythical three-headed goat? Become part of your cult in a dark midnight mass of the damned?"

Fritzi reached out a hand but Red flinched away. "I swear by the Fourteen Gods of Penthos, if you touch my arm one more time, you'll pull back a bloody stump."

The Andarian's scales flushed purple as she withdrew her hand. "What she means," Fritzi told the abbot, "is that we respect your belief system, though it is strange to us. We would be honored to help your Order fulfill its holy calling by accepting your hospitality with no expectation of payment."

The Serendipitous Teh's mandible dripped something pale and viscous. "Is this true, Just Red the Nothing?" he asked. "Is that what you meant? I am not always good at understanding human metaphors."

Red sighed. Nothing in the galaxy was ever free. "Yes, fine. We'll stay. But," she pointed a finger at the abbot, "it's just until we get our ship fixed up. What do you think, Dirk? Two days?"

Dirk nodded. "That should do it. Unless it takes longer than usual to satisfy my every desire. I do have more than the average number of desires." He winked at the abbot.

Red shuddered at the mental image of Dirk and all those legs. Still, if all the monks were as resistant to his, ah, charms as The Serendipitous Teh, it wouldn't be a problem. "Should we take the ship with us now?"

The abbot considered this. "Given the terrain, I suggest making the journey on foot. When we arrive, I can send one of my colleagues to collect your ship. It will be perfectly safe here until then."

"Yeah, no," Red objected. "I'll come back for it myself. No offense." She glanced back at the *Wart*. It seemed so small against the towering pines. No one flew her ship but her. Maybe Woodman if she was busy with something. But that sounded petty, even to her. Luckily, she had another valid excuse ready to go. "It's just my cat has a complicated history with giant insects. I'd hate for anyone to get hurt."

"Of course," he said. "We are grateful for any opportunity to center our worship on you." He closed his eyes and bowed his head. "Now, if you would please follow me, I will show you to the monastery." He dropped down to all legs and skittered away into the widest and most inviting canyon.

"Westward ho, I guess," Red muttered, and entered the canyon with the rest. The Serendipitous Teh was hard to see winding among the rocks, but they had no problem following the clicking and clacking of his feet on the stony ground.

Fritzi fell into step beside Red. "You seem tense," she observed.

"I don't want to be the center of anyone's worship," Red said in a low voice. "That's how you end up with your organs in jars made of your own skin."

"Don't be so dramatic," Fritzi's gills fluttered with agitation. "I assure you, there is nothing to worry about. I've worked with Fardic monks many times over the years. They are among the most highly respected sects in the galaxy. Peaceful."

"Peaceful." Red snorted. "That's what everyone says before they find the stack of skulls in the basement." She lowered her voice further. "Besides, we don't know for sure he's a Fardic monk. I mean, he says he is, but that's what any death cultist would say if they wanted to lure you to their murder bunker for a ritualistic bloodletting. Don't you think it's a tiny bit convenient that they happened to have finished this wonderful dormitory just in time for us to stay there? For free?"

"It's clear you've never studied comparative theology," Fritzi said, shaking her head. "It's not your fault. Most public schools do not include it in their curricula. That's why many Fardic monks fund schools: to provide a foundational understanding of diverse cultures and faith communities in an effort to promote tolerance and peace throughout the galaxy."

Red didn't buy it. "Sam?" She beckoned for her sister to join them. "This whole thing about leaving our ship and following a stranger to their hidden lair doesn't get your secret agent paranoia senses all tingly?"

"Eh," Sam shrugged. "Fritzi knows this stuff. I'm not letting my guard down, but if she says it's safe, I'm inclined to believe her."

"It's just so damned convenient."

The Andarian almost managed to not look smug. "It's all a string of coincidences that will make perfect sense when you understand—"

The Serendipitous Teh poked his head up several yards ahead. "It's not far now," he said, then disappeared around a bend.

"Even if he is what he says he is," Red said, kicking at an anthill. "That doesn't mean there aren't monsters out here, or worse. Woodman and I have this saying: do it right, do it careful, do it smart. It's kept us out of trouble — like, serious trouble — since we were kids, and I don't see why it wouldn't now."

The Andarian shook her head. "Trust me. I'll explain once we're settled in the dormitory."

"I hope they have a pool," Dirk panted, wiping sweat from his eyes. "You know, I could be the first outsider these people have seen in years. Lots of sex-starved nuns looking to score. Good thing I always carry a selection of high-quality, waterproof prophylactics in my wallet."

Sam punched his arm.

"Hey, not all of us have a smokin' hot piece of Grade A prime Andarian ass all to ourselves," Dirk pouted, rubbing his arm. "Of course, if you're willing to share . . ."

"Dude, monasteries have monks, not nuns," Red said.

"Potato potato." Dirk waved a hand. "Nothing wrong with a little variety. You always drink the same beer?"

"Yeah, pretty much."

Sam punched Red this time. "Shut up, you idiots. Look!"

They had reached the end of the canyon.

The Serendipitous Teh's antennae quivered with barely suppressed pride. "Welcome to the Valley of the Temple of the Singular Eye."

Chapter 30
No (Visible) Piles of Skulls

The walls of the canyon fell away sharply on both sides to reveal a small valley nestled in the mountains like a green bowl. A waterfall spilled down one end and formed a river that burbled through lush wildflower gardens and groves of flowering fruit trees.

The Serendipitous Teh led them along a path of glassy black pebbles and over a simple wooden bridge to the temple itself, tucked neatly between a bend in the river and the sheer wall of rock on the far side of the valley. Red wasn't sure what she'd thought a Fardic temple would look like, but whatever it was, a pile of dull grey stone being swallowed by a tree wasn't it. The trunk of an enormous jiljala tree jutted crookedly toward the sky, its roots twisting down around the stone walls in ropes like taffy.

As they drew closer, Red could see elaborate carvings etched into the walls. Thick roots covered most of it, and blankets of blue-green moss obscured the rest, but Red could pick out a figure here and there. She pointed to one.

"See?" she hissed at Fritzi. "A three-headed goat!"

Fritzi squinted at the carving. "That's an Ulatan on horseback."

"Yeah, well, how many kidneys does it have? Huh?"

The Serendipitous Teh curved his head over Red's shoulder to peer at the carving. "I believe that is L3at and Pr8n, allparents of the Ulatan people."

Red elbowed Fritzi. "You said you were Fardic monks, not L3at!an," she said to the abbot.

"We did not build this temple," he explained. "We discovered it, abandoned, soon after I received my honorific from Fardus, many human generations ago. It serves our purposes well."

Red looked skeptically at the decaying temple. "I suppose if you're looking for a fixer-upper, you can't get much better than this."

The abbot clacked his mandibles curiously but was interrupted by a human monk in a plain brown robe emerging from a doorway hidden in a gap among the roots. "Most Elevated, your ass is required in the council chamber. That bastard The Impatient Taht says there's some urgent godddamn matter that needs your attention."

"Thank you," The Serendipitous Teh said. He turned to the group. "You must excuse me. The Vulgar Adn will show you to the visitors' dormitory." He dropped to all legs and skittered into the temple.

The Vulgar Adn smiled. "Welcome to The Entropic Monastery," he said. "This way, assholes." He ducked back through the doorway. First Fritzi, then Sam and Dirk, disappeared after him.

Red crossed her arms and stayed where she was. The last time she'd followed a monk into a derelict temple she'd ended up hanging by her ankles over a pit of ravenous fireworms—and this time she didn't have a can of duuofish in her pocket to distract them. She considered that lesson good and learned. Well, not good enough to always keep a can of duuofish in her pocket, but really, how much stuff could one person carry, anyway? Easier to avoid the pit of fireworms in the first place.

But sometimes, there was greater danger in being left behind and alone. One time, years ago, she'd waited for Granny outside the senior center rather than join her for bingo. Marge Blattz had cornered her for over an hour with suspiciously glowing stories about her grandchildren, complaints about the high price of fresh produce, gossip about whose husbands were in jail, and recaps of particularly titillating *Port Desire* storylines. Okay, that part hadn't been so bad, but still, Red knew which of Granny's friends had bladder control problems and she could never go back to the blissful state of not knowing that. Give her fireworms any day.

With a heavy sigh and a hand on her blaster, she chose potential fireworms and followed her companions into the ominous darkness of the creepy temple buried under a tree.

There were no (visible) piles of skulls, pits of fireworms (in plain sight), or even talkative old women (in the immediate area). Instead, Red found herself in a cozy room filled with overstuffed chairs in various shapes to accommodate the anatomy of most known sentient species. Thick rugs softened the stone floor and a cheerful fire crackling in the fireplace added warmth and light to the space. Next to a surprisingly tasteful rack of colorful tourist brochures, a bookshelf overflowed with everything from worn leatherbound volumes to trashy pulp paperbacks. Red spied Indar Skjov's sultry pout splashed across the cover of his autobiography, *La Vie en Throb*. Against another wall, a table held simple refreshments: pastries, coffee, pitchers of still and sparkling water, and a variety of teas. Dirk already had a mouth full of what Red hoped was whipped cream filling. Red wanted to immediately sink into one of the chairs with a giant mug of coffee and the Skjov book. She'd heard the second chapter alone was worth the sticker price.

Red inhaled. "Is that Plestene bogmeadow?" she asked The Vulgar Adn.

He smiled. "It's the potpourri. Do you like it? It's our signature scent. Some people think it smells like grumshit, but goddamn it, it always reminds me of home."

"You're from Plestos, then?" Red asked, edging toward the coffee.

"Yes, but the monastery is my home now," the monk replied, a sad look flickering across his face. "I haven't been back to Plestos since joining this fucking Order, but some goddamn memories refuse to fade."

"Why do they call you The Vulgar Adn?"

"Isn't it obvious? I lead the Salacious Obscenity Services on St. Cripps Eve."

Fair enough.

"Are these the new guest quarters?" Fritzi asked.

The Vulgar Adn laughed. "Hell no. This is just the lobby. Right through here."

Red hurriedly sloshed some coffee into a mug and took a scalding sip as she followed the monk to the dormitory.

'Dormitory' didn't begin to describe it. More like 'ten-star hotel' or 'resort for the disgustingly rich.' It made the Modern Mandrake look like a quashtoad breeding sump. No mossy stones or invasive tree roots here. Everything glittered when appropriate and shone when not. It somehow managed to be wildly sophisticated and welcoming at the same time. Maybe it was the helpful signage directing guests to various amenities ("They have a pool *and* a hot tub!" Dirk exclaimed), or the way the babbling of the river could be heard through the open windows.

The monk assigned them rooms, suggested they clean the shit off themselves, and directed them to dial zero with any questions about the room service menu or to schedule spa services. Red's paranoia twitched as everyone separated behind closed doors, but it settled down pretty quick at the opportunity to spend quality time alone with a minibar and unlimited hot water.

Red kicked off her boots, throwing clouds of dust and grit into the air, and downed the rest of her coffee. Damn good stuff. A few hundred lightyears from the instant battery acid crystals she'd become accustomed to on the *Wart*. If she saw any lying around unattended, she'd have to snag it. People would pay big credits for this, even on Gambora or Glor.

She flopped on the bed. Something dug into the back of her head; reaching up, she found a chocolate opaxnut truffle. She popped it in her mouth, stretched, and instantly decided to add 500-count Luforian cotton sheets and anakadown pillows to her wish list. Maybe Granny could swing it if they counted as Christmas and birthday for the next few years.

The truffle awakened her stomach. Red leaned off the bed and popped open the minifridge. Oo, premium liquor! These monks didn't mess around. She snagged a bottle of Tolmarine wine, then something else caught her eye: a snack-sized bag of cnothu puffs. She had just been craving those. She hesitated a moment, then grabbed the puffs too. Might as well take advantage of these coincidences while she could. In for a moonrabbit, in for a clomis, they always say.

As she munched the crispy puffs and washed them down with wine, she thought about Bonk stuck back in the *Wart*, all by itself. Was it lonely? Did it miss her? Heh, probably not. More likely curled up in the kitchen sink to recharge, oblivious to the fact that she was gone at all. Or maybe it was finally getting around to hunting down those weevils taking over the storage compartment. She wished she could be there to see it. Dirk was right—Bonk was a FUKR through and through—but Red found her initial fear had turned to fascination. Sure, it was pretty pants-filling to watch it dismember a gnar, but it had never turned its teeth and claws on her, not in any serious way. And if Dirk's sabotage worked the way he said it did, then even if Bonk had a DIC with her name on it, it wouldn't necessarily hurt her.

Red shook the last of the cnothu puff crumbs into her mouth and crumpled the empty bag. She tossed it across the room to the wastebasket—and missed by a mile. She wished Bonk were there so she had someone to complain to about her epic fail. It would like these sheets as much as she did. She imagined it kneading the blanket like Granny's biscuits before laying down next to her, purring its weird-ass purr and blinking its mismatched eyes. Actually, it probably was best that Bonk was on the ship. She'd seen what its kneading could do to bedding. Red didn't want to know what the monks would do if they discovered holes in their expensive worshippy sheets. Probably put her to work wrapping truffles or replacing toilet paper rolls.

Speaking of toilet paper, that coffee must've been stronger than it tasted because it was already doing its job. She stood, picked up the empty cnothu puff bag, and slam dunked it into the wastebasket. "Two points!" she cheered quietly. But it wasn't the same.

Chapter 31
Fardicism for the Unelevated

It quickly became apparent that half a roll of quilted triple-ply, a steamy aggrippinia-scented shower, a dozen tiny bottles of booze, and an enormous room-service pepperoni-and-nintha pizza weren't enough to distract from the loneliness. So, Red left her room to find the others.

Sam answered her knock wearing a plush white bathrobe. "Nice," Red said, gesturing at the robe. "Better than the ones at your safehouse. That's something I'd be happy to wear when fleeing assassins through the streets of Gambora."

"Ha ha," Sam said. "We need to talk about our next few days."

Red groaned. "More talking?"

Sam ignored this. "Fritzi just got up from a nap. Let's meet in the sculpture garden in fifteen minutes."

"This place has a sculpture garden?"

"Didn't you see the sign on our way in? Tell Dirk too."

"Ugh, what if he's in the middle of shagging The Vulgar Adn?"

"Then tell him he's got fifteen minutes to finish up and meet us in the sculpture garden."

Red threw up her hands. "Fine!" she said. "But if I see anything emotionally scarring, you owe me counseling. Or at least a six-pack."

It turned out to be a non-issue, since Dirk didn't answer Red's repeated and increasingly thunderous knocking. She refused to consider any reason other than he wasn't in there and headed to find the sculpture garden.

The helpful signage led her to a glass-roofed indoor space filled with immaculately trimmed shrubberies interspersed with sculptures of all sizes and media. Red never thought much about art beyond the occasional tattoo, so she didn't recognize anything. But after spending most of her life smuggling goods from one system to another, she knew Fancy Important Stuff when she saw it, and this was all Fancy Important Stuff. She wandered around, evaluating the collection, testing herself. That bust carved from a single laprocrystal? A million credits for the laprocrystal alone. The pair of towering concrete monoliths, though, probably got their value from artistic merit rather than raw material. She idly checked the educational placard. Holy shit, who knew Funk Wagnar, who played the head doctor and his evil pirate twin on *Port Desire*, was a sculptor? Red regarded the monoliths again and told herself she saw something evil-twinny about the piece.

A grunt interrupted Red's ruminations on the subtle metaphors of celebrity artists. She spun around, hand not quite hovering over her blaster, then heard it again, from behind an abstract piece that definitely looked like a three-headed goat. This time, the grunt turned into a giggle, then a sigh. A voice said, "Does that tickle?"

She knew that voice. "Dirk," she called, turning away to avoid any accidental glimpses of flesh. "Sam and Fritzi will be here in a few minutes. Sam told me to tell you to finish who—*whatev*er it is you're doing. I'm going to walk over to the far side of the garden and study that fascinating statue of Vladmir IX. I'm going to study it really, really closely. I'm not going to stop studying it until you say it's safe for me to stop. Okay? I'm going now."

She didn't wait for a response, but strode purposefully across the garden. The statue was quite interesting, actually. According to its placard, the artist attempted to reinterpret Vladmir's warrior-poet mystique through the lens of post-Quazlian pseudo-sardonicism, though the controversial addition of an illuminated crown of quashtoad bones seemed to contradict the symbolism of the—

"You can stop pretending to care about art now, cupcake," Dirk said from behind her.

Red refused to take her eyes off the statue. "Are you sure? Because apparently there's some really interesting debate about whether the artist succeeded in capturing her subject's—hang on, let me get this right—'grimly imposing corpus' given her use of 'aesthetically and morally offensive day-glo tones.'"

"I'm fully zipped and The Eager Liek has departed," he said. "We were in the cuddle-and-chat phase anyway. Quite the coincidence that I'd discover a novel and exceedingly gratifying sexual experience with a fun new partner at a monastery, of all places." He winked at Red.

"You told me they'd be sex-starved. Why are you surprised?"

"I'm not surprised," he said. "You still don't know the deal with these Fardic guys?"

"No!" Red snapped, her face hot. "I wish someone would just tell me already."

"Tell you what?" Fritzi and Sam walked hand-in-hand into the garden. The Andarian's scales shimmered pink, and Sam actually had a smile on her face. Red scowled. Everyone was getting laid but her. Did she miss a memo somewhere? They all settled in a set of benches encircling a low fountain.

"I don't get this Fardic stuff." Red complained. "Why is everything working out so well for us? It's not right. The last time that happened to me, it turned out to be Smith." She spat in the shrubbery to get his name out of her mouth.

"Haven't you read any of the informational materials our hosts provided in the lobby?" Fritzi asked. "Never mind, I brought a couple for you." She handed Red some glossy brochures with titles like 'Fardus, St. Cripps, and You' and 'So You Want to Be a Fardic Monk: What You Need to Know Before Signing on the Dotted Line.' Red opened one called 'Fardicism for the Unelevated: A Beginner's Guide.'

> Thank you for your interest in the fascinating and increasingly popular Fardic faith! Your understanding is very important to us. We are thrilled you have chosen to spend a few moments perusing this brochure in search of

enlightenment, entertainment, or a satisfying bowel movement. We hope to share the truth about our religious beliefs, dispel rumors, and promote tolerance and acceptance. So sit back, relax, and enjoy your journey through the essential tenets of Fardicism.

<u>History</u>

Fatnyg Ny Fardus was born six thousand years ago on an unknown planet in the Cwumwyl Nebula. Few records exist from his youth, but we do know his parents were shiqherders who had been rejected by the dominant Mormosoanism religion of the region for their unorthodox beliefs and practices.

Fardus was an intelligent child, full of curiosity and a desire to achieve a higher state of consciousness than a life among the shiq could offer. He left home soon after successfully completing his coming-of-age diorama (see Figure 1 for an artist's rendering). Friendless and penniless, he relied on the hospitality of strangers, often staying on a host's couch for months before moving on (see Figure 2 for a map of his travels).

His wandering path eventually brought him to Glor and the home of Theodolorosa de la Montaigne della Cripps. The two quickly realized their shared disdain for current religious practices and delight in salty language. They disappeared into the jungle to consummate their newfound friendship and did not reappear for eight years. It is unclear whether this was a purposeful retreat from society or the result of poor orienteering. Whatever the case, the two reemerged with stories of staircases and mystical powers granted by the colorful fungus found growing at the top.

Fardus and Cripps felt compelled to share their experiences with the galaxy. They chose the honorifics The Fundamental Fardus and Cripps the Crapulent and spent their remaining years guiding hundreds of others up the staircases to partake of the fungus. Cripps received posthumous sainthood from Fardus and remains the only individual to be so recognized.

On his deathbed, Fardus swore to be reborn in glory at such time as the living galaxy is properly prepared for his return. There is much debate among scholars about when this might be, exactly (see Figure 3 for a handy calendar of most commonly predicted dates, times, and venues).

What Does This Mean?

Today, those of the Fardic faith continue to ascend the Several Celentine Staircases (the exact number of which is unknown and may vary from one individual to the next). Once this occurs, and the fungus is consumed (see Figure 4 for a delicious recipe for Sweet & Savory Fungus Flambé), the individual takes an honorific that befits the spiritual powers they have been granted.

Many sects have arisen since the days of Fardus and St. Cripps—six thousand years is a long time!—but the underlying beliefs remain the same. These are:

- Hospitality, to honor those who opened their homes and refrigerators to Fardus during his travels

- Friendship, to promote peace through tolerance of differences and prepare the galaxy for Fardus' return
- Vulgarity, to celebrate the joy Fardus and St. Cripps found in earthy language

Fardic monasteries and Cripptic abbeys may choose to join one of several sanctioned sects. Each one remains grounded on the foundational Fardic beliefs, but expresses those in ways that are most meaningful to them. Some examples include:

- The Defenestrated Order of the Broken Elbow of Fardus
- The Sequestrian Order of the Hind Leg of Fardus
- The Quincunxian Order of the Left Eyebrow of St. Cripps

As you can see, no matter your gender, species, or socioeconomic status, there's a Fardic sect just right for you! Interested? Contact your local monastery or abbey for more information about the application process. (See Figure 5 for a complete list of locations.)

Fardic FAQ

Q: When is St. Cripps Eve celebrated, and can anyone participate?

A: St. Cripps Eve, the central holiday of Fardicism, is celebrated on the third Friday of the sixth month of every eighth year. The Unelevated are welcome to join their local monks or nuns at their services. However, due to the nature of the worship, it is the official policy of the Contentious Council of the Most Elevated (CCME) to limit attendance to adults only. Proof of age will be required at the door. Minors and Mormosoans will be turned away.

Q: Why did Fardus grant sainthood to Cripps?

A: The reason for Cripps' sainthood is unknown, despite considerable scholarly research on the subject. However, there is no evidence it was due to losing a bet. This is a hurtful rumor perpetrated by the Mormosoans in retaliation for the CCME's recent manifesto condemning their oppression of the Fardus family.

Q: Can women become Fardic monks? Can men become Cripptic nuns?

A: Yes and yes. Several hundred years ago, the CCME passed a resolution eliminating gender as a factor when assigning candidates to either Fardic monasteries or Cripptic abbeys. Still, it is rare to find men and women practicing Fardicism together, outside of the Integrated Order of the Feminine Side of Fardus. Scholars assure us that this lends credence to the opinion that women and men prefer to live in worship among their own kind.

Q: What about people who diverge from the gender binary system, like Ulatans?

A: As previously stated, the CCME has long prohibited consideration of gender when assessing candidates. It is the official policy that all are welcome to participate in the Fardic faith as they so choose.

Q: Why is the religion called Fardicism and not Crippsicism?

A: This is an excellent question, and one which the CCME is scheduled to consider at a future meeting.

Q: When and where does the CCME meet?

A: The CCME meets according to a secret schedule at secret locations that are constantly changing without notice.

Q: Can anyone attend meetings of the CCME?

A: Unfortunately, anyone not expressly invited to attend will be shot on sight. We regret this inconvenience, but it is essential to maintaining the integrity of our bureaucratic processes.

Q: Why are you so evasive about gender issues within the faith?

A: We're not evasive. We included these questions in our brochure, didn't we? You're just looking for an argument and are probably paid by the Mormosoans to make us look bad.

This is an official publication of the Contentious Council of the Most Elevated. Any use of the content herein is prohibited unless with the express written consent of the Contentious Council of the Most Elevated. Have a question for us? Deliver it to your friendly neighborhood CCME representative or submit it in writing to the address below.

Red stuffed the brochure in her pocket. "Okay, the hospitality thing makes sense. But what does any of this have to do with the cnothu puffs in my minifridge?"

"Cnothu puffs?" Fritzi gave her a puzzled look, then shook her head, causing her hair to bounce vigorously. "Just like Fardus and St. Cripps, monks and nuns today take their honorifics to reflect the powers granted them by the fungus," she explained.

Red snapped her fingers. "That's why The Vulgar Adn swears so much, and The Eager Liek was so willing to hump Dirk behind the three-headed goat statue."

Sam's eyes flicked to Dirk. She smashed her lips together, trying not to smile. "You didn't."

He smirked and smoothed his jacket. "Not my fault there just happened to be a horny monk looking for a piece of what The Tumescent Dirk has to offer. Blame the Most Elevated. I'm just along for the ride." He winked. "Pun most definitely intended."

"So," Fritzi continued with strained patience, "since the abbot is called The Serendipitous Teh, that means . . ." She waited a moment for Red to catch up, saw her blank look, then suppressed a sigh. "That means the fungus granted him the spiritual power to make good things happen by chance."

"Oh, so that's what serendipitous means," Red said. "I thought it was some kind of lizard."

"It's an extremely useful gift," Fritzi mused. "And powerful, if its range is wide enough to bring us here. I wouldn't be surprised if that's why he was named the Most Elevated and put in charge of this monastery. Anyway," she continued, "I believe Sam wanted to discuss our next moves?" She crossed her legs and smoothed her skirt over her knees. Hey, that wasn't what she was wearing when they arrived. Must be more serendipitous crap. Red made a mental note to check the closet in her room for something less crusty, if not outright clean. Maybe she'd find some cool vintage Deltonic Implosion merch to add to her collection. There was a limited-edition signed grumskin vest she'd heard rumors about from their second   tour . . .

Sam cleared her throat, dreamy smile gone, back to full Business Mode. "The way I see it, our immediate concern is getting the plasma damper back online. Dirk, that's your job."

"Actually, Sammy," Dirk said, "I have something else I need to do first."

The agent blinked. "What's more important than the damper?"

"The cat."

Red sat up. "What do you want to do to Bonk?"

Dirk shook his head. "It's just an idea rolling around in my gorgeous noggin. It came to me," he waggled his eyebrows lewdly, "during my time with The Eager Liek. I do my best thinking after an outdoor shag, and apparently an indoor sculpture garden counts. Don't ask me, ask my libido. But I don't want to say anything about the idea until I have a chance to unzip its pants and see what it's packing, if you get my drift."

Red's hands tightened into fists. "You better not hurt my cat," she growled.

"Don't get your lacy underthings in a twist." Dirk waved a hand dismissively. "If this works out the way I think it might, that FUKR will be just fine. Trust me."

For someone who trusted no one, Red sure was having to trust a lot of people lately.

"What do you need from us?" Sam asked.

"I need Red to get the ship back here and find that alloy," Dirk said. "I just hope these monks have the tech and high-res access I'm gonna need to make this idea happen."

"I'm sure the abbot's power will provide," Fritzi said.

Dirk nodded. "That's exactly what I'm counting on, hotcakes."

Red looked around to make sure they were alone. "About that," she said in a low voice. "We definitely need to take advantage of it as long as we're here. Do you think if I made a list—"

"That's not how it works," Dirk said. "Haven't you read Exaius?"

"Why does everyone ask me that? It's on my list, okay?" Jeez.

"And you've never heard of the conundrumatic matrix? Causality in the quantum foam? Anyone? Anyone?"

Fritzi interrupted before Red could get her hands on Dirk's throat. "How it works is irrelevant," she scolded. "We will not be exploiting The Serendipitous Teh. This is his holy gift we're talking about. We should only graciously accept the help we really need."

"It's a matter of need, then. Okay, I can work with that." Because Red really needed that vest. It was, like, a deep, spiritual need. Yeah. So deep. Bone deep.

Sam crumpled a brochure and tossed it at Red. "Cut it out," she said. "Fritzi's right. We can't piss these people off, at least until after we have the ship fixed and Dirk's done with whatever he's got to do."

"How come it's okay for Dirk to—you know what? Never mind," Red pouted. That's fine. She wouldn't say anything to The Serendipitous Teh, but inside she thought hard in his direction about how much she needed that jacket. And two—no, three million credits in her account. And to get laid. Hell, it worked for Dirk. Why not her?

Fritzi slid off the bench and picked up the discarded brochure. "It's only late afternoon," she said. "Plenty of time to get started. We can touch base over a late dinner. I'll work out the details with our hosts. Does anyone object to soup and sandwiches?"

"Wait a minute," Red said. "What are you and Sam gonna do?"

"Ah." Fritzi seemed to suddenly realize that smoothing out the wrinkled brochure was extremely important. "We've got a full schedule."

"Doing what, exactly? Sam?" Red asked. Sam flushed and looked away. Red snatched the brochure from Fritzi. She glanced at it. "The Singular Eye Salon and Spa," she read. Several services were circled. "Tell me you're not lounging around while the rest of us are working our asses off."

The Andarian didn't have to respond. Her quivering gills and flushed orange scales told Red all she needed to know.

"So much for only accepting help we really need," Red muttered to Dirk.

Fritzi pulled herself up to her full, if unimpressive, height. "Need?" she snapped. "What do you know about my needs? I shouldn't have to remind you that I was happily sipping tea in Gambora when you showed up at the door with my wife bloodied and bruised. Since then, I've been nearly poisoned by a trusted employee and forced to flee my home in the middle of the night, only to be dragged from one planet to the next, and for what? To figure out what's wrong with your *cat*? I'm tired, Red. Tired of fixing everyone else's problems. Tired of running. Tired of *you*." She snatched back the spa menu. "So if I can get a Glorreen sea salt scale scrub for free, and spend quality time with my wife, I'm going to do it."

Red put up her hands in surrender. "Okay, okay, no need to go full fazzer about it. Jeez." Note to self: don't get between an Andarian and her scale scrub. She shuddered to think what would happen if Fritzi had scheduled the full-body Orgullan scrum-oil massage instead.

A blue flicker rippled across Fritzi's face. She opened her mouth to say something, shut it again, and spun away toward the door back to the monastery. After a few steps, she paused, turned back, and shoved the brochure at Red. "You should try their quusberry foot soak," she said through clenched teeth. "It looks delightful." She left before anyone could respond.

Red stuffed the spa brochure in her pocket next to the Fardic propaganda and exchanged awkward glances with Dirk and Sam. "Guess I should go get the ship, then."

"I'm sure she didn't mean all of that, Red," Sam said, rubbing the back of her neck. "She's been under a lot of stress lately—we all have, of course, but she's not used to this kind of life. It's a lot for her to adjust to."

"Pfft," Red said, shuffling her feet on the cobbled path. "Welcome to the club, Fritzi."

"Well, this has been a delightful little extravaganza of family bitterness and bile," Dirk said briskly, "but I'm going to poke around the closets of this place and see what I can find. You two sex dumplings know what you need to do. So go."

Chapter 32
Migwyrn P'tan

Sam left Red at the helpful signage with a flurry of further apologies. Red waved these off and mentally thanked the Fourteen that she didn't have a wife to order her around.

She found The Eager Liek restocking the refreshment cart in the lobby. He readily agreed to accompany her back to the *Wart* and guide her to the parking garage. If he felt embarrassed about getting caught with Dirk in the sculpture garden, he didn't show it. He chatted the entire hike back through the canyon, pointing out unusual rock formations, local wildlife, and sites of historical or ecological interest.

"Tell me about the monsters," Red said when he paused for breath.

The Eager Liek frowned. "It's very sad. The psycats who used to inhabit these canyons were pushed deeper into the wilderness by the encroaching tourist developments."

"No, not psycats," Red clarified. "There's supposed to be a monster that eats people. Or maybe just their faces? At least that's what my Granny said. She used to come to the Whore's Knuckles with her parents."

"That's ridiculous," the monk chuckled. "There's no monster."

"But people do disappear in the Whore's Knuckles," Red said. "What happens to them?"

The monk's voice got serious. "The native peoples of this land don't like that name for these mountains. It's offensive. They prefer the name Migwyrn P'tan."

"What does that mean in plain old GalactiStani?"

"It's difficult to translate." He thought a minute. "Roughly, it means 'hand bones of a morally unconventional woman.'"

"Uh huh. Totally different. Hey," she narrowed her eyes. "You didn't answer my other question."

He bent down to inspect a flowering shrub. "Which other question was that?"

"About what happens to people who disappear. I'd've thought you'd be, you know, eager to clear this up for me."

The monk sighed. "Most people who stumble across The Entropic Monastery never leave."

"Never leave, huh?" Red edged away from The Eager Liek and dropped a hand to her blaster, casual-like.

If the monk noticed, he didn't say anything. "You have experienced only the briefest taste of what our hospitality can be," he explained. "People intend to pass only a few days with us, but many decide to become our Friends in Fardicism. You've already met one—The Vulgar Adn. I'll introduce you to the others later, if you like."

"You're saying there's no monster."

He shook his head. "Not that we are aware of. We don't discourage the rumors, though. We're a very popular Order and cannot possibly accommodate everyone who applies for membership. It's embarrassing, though Fardus knows we do our best with the resources given to us."

"Heh," Red chuckled. "They say you eat people's faces off."

"Oh, we totally do," The Eager Liek grinned, "but only if they get mud on the sheets—No! Don't shoot!" He threw his hands up across his face. "I'm kidding!"

"Funny." Red holstered her blaster slowly. "There's my ship."

She slapped a hand on the ID panel and the hatch opened. Even before the ramp had fully descended, though, she was knocked on her ass by a metal blur colliding with her lower legs. She cursed heavily and steadily with a well-bitten tongue as Bonk swirled around her, gargling and butting her with its head.

The Eager Liek's jaw dropped. "Have you been studying with The Vulgar Adn?"

"Nope, I'm a natural." Red stood, picking gravel bits out of her palms. "Meet Bonk. Don't worry," she added, spitting a mouthful of blood on the dirt. "This is just how it says hello." She grabbed the cat by the gap in the hull behind its head and hauled it up the ramp to keep it from escaping into the foothills. "Welcome aboard the *Wart*," she said over her shoulder. "It's not much, but then again, neither am I."

"I like it," The Eager Liek said, glancing around the interior. Red sealed Bonk in the bedroom. It yowled in protest and thumped rhythmically against what sounded like the wall a foot or so to the left of the door. The monk blinked. "I like cats, too, generally speaking. This one seems to have an exceptionally fresh battery pack." The thumping increased in speed and force, rattling the dishes all the way in the kitchen sink. "Are you sure you don't want to power it down?"

Red plopped into the captain's chair and picked up an open beer from the floor. "Nah," she said, shaking the can. Empty. She tried another—bingo. "It'll settle down in a minute. Let's get to the garage." She poured the few remaining drops of stale beer dregs into her mouth and swished it around a bit before swallowing. She squinted through the viewport at the brilliant red sun setting behind the Whore's—Migwyrn P'tan. It could look like a gem, she supposed, if you kind of crossed your eyes and had never seen a gem before. She waved a hand at the landscape. "The valley's just over that ridge, right? Second knuckle from the left?"

"It's a little more complicated than that," The Eager Liek said, brushing cigar ash off the co-pilot's chair with a corner of his robe before sitting down. "The canyon takes a more direct path than we're able to navigate from the air. And once we arrive, the parking structure can be hard to see if you don't know what you're looking for. It's set into the mountains behind the monastery, designed to blend in with the rock."

"Sneaky." Red powered up the *Wart* and glanced at the readings coming from the engine to make sure the thing wasn't leaking too many neutrinos, what with the plasma damper disconnected and all.

The Eager Liek's eyes widened. "We're not trying to be sneaky," he explained hastily. "It's just that we like The Valley of the Temple of the Singular Eye to maintain its natural beauty. There's nothing beautiful about a parking garage."

"You need to travel more. I've seen parking garages that would make angels cry."

"Really?"

"No." Red engaged the surface thrusters and the ship lifted off the ground. When they got high enough, she found the canyon that led to the monastery. The monk was right; it was too narrow to accommodate the ship, so she had to follow it from above. Problem was, all the damn mountains kept getting in the way. She had to keep going around this peak and that outcropping. A few times she lost the canyon entirely and needed the monk to correct her course.

The sun had completely sunk behind the mountains by the time they reached the valley. The monastery—the whole valley, really—nearly disappeared in the deep shadow, only a few cones of soft light from the dormitory windows to tell Red she was in the right place. She parked the ship in the nearly invisible garage. The Eager Liek was right; there was no way she could've found the entrance on her own.

Much like the main entryway to the monastery, the garage walls featured intricate carvings from ceiling to floor. Red squinted through the viewport. "Is this more Ulatan stuff?" she asked.

"Oh no," he said brightly, "our Friend The Artistic Moar, whose soul has departed this plane of existence to dwell atop the Staircases, carved these when we built the parking garage. They're scenes from the life of Fardus. My favorite part, the first meeting between Fardus and St. Cripps, is depicted over there, right next to the fuel pump. Come on, I'll show you. It'll only take a minute."

Red rolled her eyes as she shut off the engines and locked down the control panel. Another art history lesson, bleh. Still, she wasn't exactly looking forward to scouring the valley for ore to smelt into a coupling. And who knows? Maybe she'd learn something she could throw in people's faces next time they brought up freaking Exaius. Oh yeah, well, did you know that

Fardus and St. Cripps once went back to Mormosa and ended up inventing sublight travel? No? Huh, I thought everyone knew that.

She continued this fantasy until The Eager Liek stopped short at the base of the wall. He pointed to a scene with two figures pouring wine down each others' throats. The sculptor obviously knew what drunk people looked like. "My kind of people," she said.

The monk jumped on this with both tongues, spinning an endless monologue of biographical details, traditional Fardic recipes, and dirty jokes St. Cripps tattooed on her skin. When he shifted to an examination of religious doctrine, Red zoned out, eyes unfocused, shuffling along beside him. That's why she didn't see the crate until she'd tripped over it, sending it skidding across the floor.

The Eager Liek rushed to help her to her feet. Red brushed off her hands and shook her head. "Sorry, man, I kind of spaced out there for a minute. I hope I didn't break any of these —" She tilted her head to read the printing on the side.

```
Plasma Damper Couplings
Omni-Adjustable
100% Tribunium-Copper Alloy
Guaranteed to Fit!
Includes Electroputty
```

"What the — does that say what I think it says?"

"That depends on what you think it says," the monk replied with a nod he probably thought made him look wise and philosophical.

Red tore open the crate and pulled out a coupling. The metal glimmered dully in her hand. She dug around in the packaging and found a tube of electroputty. Sure enough: it said ALKALINE in big red letters.

Okay, this was getting just plain weird.

She turned to The Eager Liek. "Can we buy one of these?" she asked.

The monk shrugged. "You'd have to ask The Serendipitous Teh, but I don't see why not. The CCME sends the same supplies to each monastery once a month, but we don't necessarily have an immediate use for everything they send."

Red sent a quick thank-you up to Fardus, St. Cripps, and whatever other galactic forces conspired to save her from smelting ore. She stuffed the coupling and putty tube into her pocket. "Let's go find the abbot, then."

Chapter 33
That Thing has TITs and ASS?

At the entrance to the tunnel leading back to the monastery, they bumped into The Vulgar Adn. His eyes darted between Red and The Eager Liek like a couple of weevils in a trap. "Dammit, I'm so glad I found you bastards. Our system picked up something you need to fucking see, Just Red the Nothing." The monk darted back down the tunnel. Red exchanged a concerned look with The Eager Liek.

"Go," he said. "I'll talk to the abbot about the coupling."

"Thanks, man," she said, then jogged after The Vulgar Adn. She hated jogging. It always reminded her that she should quit smoking and drinking and eat healthier, and that wasted a whole thirty seconds of her valuable time feeling guilty before reality reasserted itself.

He led her through the tunnel back to the monastery, then through a series of hallways to a door labeled Observation Room. Inside, a bespectacled monk sat at a giant screen surrounded by dozens of smaller displays showing various readouts and vids. Red recognized the vids as surveillance footage from around the monastery and the surrounding valley: the pool, lobby, canyon entrance, sculpture garden, shuffleboard court, kitchen, and more flashed in sequence. Elaborate security for a bunch of monks.

The Vulgar Adn excused himself and hurried away, mumbling something about another cluster, as the monk at the displays glanced over his shoulder. "I'm The Observant Yuo. Don't touch anything," he said, slapping Red's hand away from the control panel. "You'll mess up my system. Normally this area is prohibited for the Unelevated, but I found something extremely unusual and I'm hoping you can explain it."

The Observant Yuo used a touchpad to drag an image from one of the smaller displays to the large main screen. "This is our long-range scope." He zoomed in and pointed to a section of space. "See?"

Red squinted. "Dude, I don't see anything."

"Of course you don't," the monk said, pushing his glasses higher on his nose. He enlarged the image again. "That's because it's completely devoid of stars, nebulae, planets, asteroids, bhoot spores, and anything else that's floating around out there. Nowhere in space is that empty of stuff."

"You're saying you know there's something there because there's nothing there."

"Exactly."

"So how did you notice—never mind." Red rubbed her temples. "Okay, there's nothing there. What does that mean?"

"It means someone's got themselves a cloaking device." He tapped a series of keys. "I traced the outline of the anomaly and knew immediately I'd seen that shape before. I ran it through the database to compare it to known craft, just to be sure. And I was right—there was just one match." The display split into two images—the empty space on one side, a ship on the other—that The Observant Yuo then merged together so they overlapped. "That, my friend, is a Class XIV stealth transport. See those two round structures protruding from the hull? Those are the Troop Interstellar Transports. And this?" He circled what looked like a gun turret. "That's an Anti-Shielding System. This thing is built for moving a lot of people and blasting straight through anything it finds. And it's headed this way."

"That thing has TITs and ASS?" Red's heart dropped. "That's a SECS ship."

The Observant Yuo nodded appreciatively. "You know your tech."

She sighed. "No, just the pervert who designed this stuff."

"You know Dirk Largo?" the monk gasped, spinning in his chair to look at Red directly for the first time. "*The* Dirk Largo? What's he like? As cool as everyone says?"

"Find out for yourself. He's probably in the hot tub with The Eager Liek right now."

"Are you serious?" Red didn't think eyes weren't meant to pop out that much—not without severe damage to the optic nerve, anyway. "I thought he was dead! Can you introduce me? Wait, no, that's silly, he's probably far too busy. Can you get me his autograph at least? Have him write 'to my good friend The Observant Yuo.' No, that's stupid. Maybe, 'to The Observant Yuo, from the most bodacious babe magnet in seven systems.'"

"Dude," Red said. "I'm sure he'll sign whatever you want. Just focus a minute. Why did you call me down here to show me this class whatever ship?" Because it can't be that a ship full of government assassins is coming for them. It's probably just a coincidence. There's got to be plenty of reasons they'd be headed for the Migwyrn P'tan. Maybe there's a team-building retreat at one of the resorts. Or they're hoping to recruit the monster for their company jatball game. Hell, they could be filming a music video for all she knew.

The Observant Yuo flushed and turned back to the main screen. "Because of this," he said. A few quick taps at the controls and the ship images were replaced by a message. Red grabbed the back of the monk's chair to keep from sinking to the floor. Four simple words loomed down at her, each letter a foot tall on the screen, casting harsh green light over her face.

HAVE THE CAT READY

Chapter 34

SECS is Coming

"What does that mean, 'have the cat ready?'" The Impatient Taht asked. His blue Orgullan hair swung as he rocked back and forth. Red wondered if he had to empty any of his bladders.

A handful of monks, including the abbot, had joined Red, Sam, and Fritzi for what Sam called 'an opportunity to formulate a plan' but Red thought of as 'a potential group freak-out and panic attack.' They gathered in the sculpture garden—the only indoor space at the monastery that was large enough to hold them all besides the pool area, which Red rejected because of the possibility of seeing Dirk in a mankini. It turned out not to matter, though. Dirk, who hadn't been in the hot tub at all but in his room, hunched over a tangled mess of patched-together tech, refused to take a break. Something about being two (hopefully metaphorical) extra-sensitive shiqskin rubbers away from a breakthrough. A breakthrough to what, no one knew.

Red gave a brief rundown of the Bonk situation for everyone not already in the loop. She caught several of the monks looking at the cat with undisguised disbelief. Red didn't blame them. The way it curled up on the bench next to Fritzi, its legs telescoped up into its hull so tightly its feet disappeared, its eyes lazily blinking—everything pointed toward a simple cat, low-battery and harmless, though pretty damn pleased with itself being the center of attention. No, if she hadn't seen it at work with her own eyes, she'd never believe it was a vicious assassin with a sabotaged behavior circuit that was one thin DIC away from turning all of them into a pile of sloppy joes without the buns. The only hint of its violent nature was the tip of the tail flicking jerkily back and forth which, Red had to admit, was hardly uncommon for regular cats.

". . . and they're heading straight for us," she finished, her voice cracking. She wasn't used to making speeches. She fumbled a room service Hamstel Lite beer from her pocket and gulped it down. She chased it with a minibar Finebock whiskey to give the group time to process the infodump.

The Vulgar Adn broke the silence. "This is some fine goddamn grumshit you've piped up our asses," he said. He crossed his arms and scowled under his eyebrows at her.

"Dude, we didn't do it on purpose," Red protested. She patted her pockets only to realize she'd already gone through her entire stash of booze. If she'd known there'd be pushback, she'd have emptied Sam's minibar too. "In fact, we wanted to stay on our ship. Blame him." She waved a hand at The Serendipitous Teh. "He practically begged us to come here."

Fritzi raised her hands to quell the surge of angry murmuring among the monks. "There is no reason to place blame," she said. "Our enemies are coming regardless. Our time would be better spent working on a solution to the problem."

"How do we know they're actually enemies?" The Eager Liek asked with a hopeful look. "Maybe they're headed to town for a relaxing vacation."

"I thought of that," Red said. "But no. The message confirms it. They want Bonk."

"I say we give them the goddamned cat so they'll leave us alone."

She turned on The Vulgar Adn. "No. That's not on the table."

"Destroy the fucker, then."

Red's hands clenched into fists. "No. Way."

"Then you four assholes leave and take the cat with you."

Red got up in his face, close enough to smell the coffee on his breath. "Did you miss the part about how they killed the C'longi who sold it to me? I've still got his guts under my fingernails. It may never come out. Let's not forget the vet tech who started asking questions. He and most of his staff were gas-leaked into oblivion. Oh, and were you dozing off when I said we were almost poisoned in a shielded government safehouse by a trusted employee? Or maybe—and this is my personal favorite—you're stupid enough to believe these people will take the cat, say thank you very much, and fly off into the sunset so you can get back to folding towels and cleaning the pool." She paused, eyeball to eyeball with the monk, only breaking away when he dropped his gaze to the floor.

Red turned to the rest of the group gathered in the garden. "SECS is coming. They won't hold back because you're monks. They won't wait for you to explain that you were just offering us your hospitality. They won't show mercy because you're minding your own business out here in the Whore's Knuckles."

"Migwyrn P'tan," The Eager Liek muttered under his breath.

"Whatever," Red spat.

"She's right," Sam interjected. "You've seen the cat. Hell, you *know* about the cat. That's more reason than they need to justify violence to themselves. Even if we destroy it, you're a loose end, a threat. They'll burn this place to the ground, with you in it, and never look back, whether we're still here or not."

The garden fell silent as everyone took this in. Red studied the faces gathered around her. Sam was Sam: calm, but ready for action, eyes flashing behind her perpetually glossy sweep of hair. The Serendipitous Teh radiated grim determination from every appendage, each antenna. The Vulgar Adn scowled but looked resigned. The other monks shifted uncomfortably, stealing glances at each other. Fritzi's lips pressed together in a thin line and her scales flickered between yellow and green.

Bonk cleaned its exhaust port. Because of course.

The Impatient Taht broke the tense silence. "How long do we have?" he asked, his leg jiggling. "Do we know? Observant Yuo, how long will it take to calculate their arrival time?"

"I already did that." He wiped his glasses on his robe. "We have forty-six hours and eleven minutes until they land at Migwyrn P'tan. And before you ask, yes, I did adjust for orbital alignments and local time zones."

"Forty-six hours?" The Impatient Taht's other leg joined the first in its jigglefest. "Gah, I just want to get this over with."

"No, you don't," Sam said flatly. "The ship that's coming? It holds at least twenty personnel per Troop Interstellar Transport pod. That's forty agents, plus whatever Management they have giving the orders from the command deck. Far more than they'll need to neutralize the likes of us. They'll all be highly trained and carry the best weapons your galactic taxes can buy. And by best, I mean worst for us. We can't underestimate their potential firepower." She paced the cobbles. "Of course, the agents might not be a problem if the ship's Anti-Shielding System is fully operational. That's designed to take out the generators for any type of energy-based shield just like that." She snapped her fingers. "No generator, no shields."

"We rely on physical barriers, then," The Eager Liek said. "We could build a wall. Or a dome?"

"Don't be ridiculous," said The Impatient Taht. "There's no time."

"Besides," Sam sighed. "That's what government-issue bunker-busters are for."

"Oh. They have those too?"

"Yes."

"Of course." The Eager Liek slumped on the bench. "Sorry."

"Don't apologize," Fritzi soothed. "Your input is valuable. It's important to talk through all the options. We won't know what will work unless we know what won't."

Red thought his input was as valuable as a weevil's toenail, but instead of picking that fight, she said, "Let me get this straight. If we stay, we die. If we go, we die. If we peacefully agree to their terms, we die. If we fight—actually, they won't give us a chance to fight. One bunker-buster from orbit, we die. Did I miss anything?"

The Observant Yuo shook his head. "They're not going to blow us up from space," he said. "Think about it. They could do that without the two TITs' worth of troops even if we had a shield."

"Which we don't," The Impatient Taht interjected.

"That's not the point," The Observant Yuo insisted. "The cat would be destroyed along with the rest of us. They want it undamaged. It's the only explanation."

"You're right," Sam said thoughtfully. "Which is better for us, because at least we have a glimmer of a chance in direct combat. Worse for galactic security, though, because that means they think they can undo Dirk's sabotage and have their weapon back under control. We can't let that happen."

Another uncomfortable silence. This time, it was Fritzi who broke it. "Can we all agree that our primary goal is to keep Bonk out of S.E.C.S. hands?" she asked, looking around at the group.

The abbot clacked his mandibles in agreement and The Eager Liek stuck two thumbs up. One by one, the other monks nodded reluctantly, even, thank the Fourteen, The Vulgar Adn. Fritzi nodded at Sam, who looked at Red, who also nodded at Sam, who squared her shoulders and briskly nodded back. Business Mode engaged, captain! Full speed ahead, take no prisoners. How the hell did she do that? Was it like a switch in her brain that flipped when a certain number of nods happened? Red imagined a tiny gnar counting on its paws and working a bank of multicolored switches inside Sam's skull, peeking out through her eye sockets. She wished she had a Business Mode setting. Totally not fair, Sam got all the good genetics, like great hair and Business Mode, and Red was left with split ends and —

" —ideas. Red?" Sam asked expectantly.

Oops. Probably best to pay attention right now. Imminent invasion, life and death, all that. Red shrugged and picked a cnothu kernel out of her teeth with a corner of 'Fardicism and You.' "Uh, you go first."

"All right," Sam began. "Our position isn't terrible, but it isn't ideal either. This valley is hidden but it's not impossible to find. Especially for these people. So, hiding isn't our best option. Another strategy might be to fortify what we can and shelter in place. Now—don't take this the wrong way—" she shot an apologetic look at the abbot, "but this monastery isn't exactly built to withstand an attack of any sort."

The Serendipitous Teh dismissed her apology with a clack of his mandibles. Sam resumed her pacing. "The final option is to evacuate everyone to a more defendable position elsewhere, either on this planet or another."

At this, the abbot rose to his full height, antennae quivering. "We, the Sequestrian Order of the Hind Leg of Fardus, do not run," he said. "We stand firm in our faith that The Fundamental Fardus and St. Cripps the Crapulent will protect and guide us through this challenge." He turned to his fellow monks. "We may die, but if we do, we die in worship."

Red was torn. On one hand, she knew just enough galactic history to recognize religious zealotry as a sure-fire way to get blasted into oblivion. On the other, it couldn't hurt to have more friendly hands on blasters and, being completely honest and not a small bit selfish, more targets to draw enemy fire away from her. On another hand, she liked these guys and didn't want them to get hurt. Still another hand argued that they were gonna need the abbot's holy gift if they were going to live to see next week.

This is why she didn't like working with others. Too complicated. Too many hands with too many arguments, too many skins to worry about saving. Better to die alone in a blaze of glory. Which might not actually be a bad idea? Not the dying part, of course, but—

"We could bring the fight to them," she suggested. "They'd never expect that. A single small ship, like the *Wart*, with a good pilot who knows how to fly casual, like me, could easily get close enough to do some real damage. I bet Dirk could rig up some sweet weapons systems for us, juice up the shields, maybe even throw together a cloaking device. Not that I'd need it, but it would be pretty cool to have."

"This isn't the movies," Sam frowned. "And you're no Indar Skjov. Confronting that ship head-on without the entire galactic army would be suicide. First they'd hit you with their A.S.S., then shoot you from the sky. They might not even waste a bunker-buster on you. For a crappy little ship like the *Wart*, all they'd need is an off-the-rack plasma cannon and you'd be toast."

"All right, I get the point," Red pouted. "No need to be rude about it." Then she snapped her fingers. "I know," she exclaimed. "The monster!"

Fritzi threw up her hands. "Red, for the last time, there is no —"

"No, I get that, but it doesn't matter, just listen," she said. "We can use the legend to scare these government doofuses away. I guarantee they've heard the same stories I have. We could, like, put up a bunch of signs saying, 'beware of face-eating monster,' or, 'do not enter: monster on the loose.' Not that exactly, I'm not a writer, but I'm sure one of you can come up with something good.

Splash some red paint around like blood. Get someone to hide nearby and make snarling noises. I bet these canyons echo like crazy. Or, wait, no, do you think we could trap a psycat to dress up?" She ran a hand through her hair. "Nah, that's ridiculous. You said they moved away, right? Loss of habitat or whatever. Okay, so, what we do is, we make a big monster cutout to throw a shadow. Be sure to give it lots of big claws and — what?"

She hadn't had this many people staring at her since that time when she was eight, lost a stupid bet to Woodman over whose feet were bigger, and had to run naked through the Magross marketplace shouting, 'I am a big stinky fazzer brain.'

"Don't worry." The Eager Liek smirked. "We're just talking through options. Your input is valuable."

"Shut up. Just shut up." Her face burned. "You too," she said to Sam, who bit her lip to smother a laugh before visibly shifting back into Business Mode.

"The only feasible course of action I can see," Sam said, "is to shelter here and force them to fight our way. To do that, we're going to rely on our greatest advantage: the monks."

"Pretty goddamned slim advantage," The Vulgar Adn grumbled.

"You live here," Sam continued, unfazed. "You know this monastery, its grounds, and the surrounding area inside and out. That's knowledge S.E.C.S. doesn't have. We can use that to control the situation. Maybe funnel their approach so we can pick them off one by one, minimizing their advantage of numbers. Doors we can block off, fortified interior rooms where we can centralize our defense. Any thoughts? Serendipitous Teh? Observant Yuo?"

The abbot clacked his mandibles thoughtfully. "The storeroom off the kitchen has reinforced soundproof walls, a locking door, and enough rations to sustain us all for some time, if necessary."

"Why would you make your pantry into a bunker?" Red asked.

The abbot shrugged. "It seemed like a good idea when it was built, so we went ahead with it. Serendipitous, wouldn't you say?"

"I don't want to hide in a closet and wait for them to find us!" The Impatient Taht burst. "There's got to be something we can do."

"We don't have to do anything," a confident voice rang out. All heads spun to see Dirk Largo, eyes bleary, comb-over flapping in the air. He held something small and flat over his head between two fingers. "There's a new DIC in town."

Chapter 35

That's a Pretty Big Ask

Sam pushed through the crowd of monks and threw her arms around her friend. "I've been so worried," she said, squeezing.

Dirk squirmed, but not too much. "Hey, hey, hey, not so tight, Sammy. I may want children someday."

Sam snorted. "Poor kid who gets you for a father."

"Poor kid?" Dirk said. "You mean lucky woman honored with the opportunity to carry my succulent seed."

"Ew," Red gagged. "Can we talk about that DIC in your hand?" She cringed inside as soon as the words left her mouth. She couldn't believe the things she had to say these days. Hard to take anything seriously when you have to talk about DICs and TITs and ARSEs all the time.

Juicy though it was, Dirk didn't take the bait. "This may be my finest achievement, engineering-wise," he said, puffing up his chest and swaggering around the garden. The monks stared at the chip in awe, like it was a lump of Fardus's holy earwax. "I didn't know if I could pull it off. Normally I'd need a full lab with anti-quark chambers to enable interface between the berylite cathodes and—well, never mind all the technobabble. Point is," he said dramatically, "I've reprogrammed it."

Red narrowed her eyes. "Who's the target?" she asked warily.

"Don't be so squeamish, honeylips," he said. "Remember what I told you about tipping the scales?" He waved the chip so close to her nose that her eyes crossed. Irritated, she slapped his hand away.

"We've got the FUKR," he continued, "and thanks to me, we've got a chip. Why not use em?"

"You said you'd sabotaged the cat to make it uncontrollable," Fritzi pointed out.

"Ye of little faith," he scoffed. "I sabotaged it; I can unsabotage it."

"Can you?" Sam asked.

"Who do you think I am, Todhunter flipping Balzac?" He stabbed a thumb at his chest. "Hell no! I'm The Tumescent Dirk Largo, and don't you forget it." The Observant Yuo sighed. Dirk winked at him and continued. "It'll take five minutes. Every tech saboteur worth their dilithium leaves a key for the back door under the mat, to mangle a metaphor."

"I don't know, Dirk," Sam frowned. "This seems like a bad idea. If you unsabotage it, and S.E.C.S. does get their hands on it, they've got a fully-functional F.U.K.R."

"We've already deduced they want the cat intact because they think they can reprogram it," The Observant Yuo said. "Doing it ourselves gives us the benefit of a powerful weapon without adding to the overall risk."

"Besides," Dirk said, "I'm sure it'll work out. Right, Your Most Elevatedness?" He waggled his eyebrows at the abbot.

The Serendipitous Teh waved his antennae and sniffed. "I couldn't say. Any attempt to predict a particular outcome resulting from my Fardic gift would negate the unanticipated nature that constitutes the true heart of holy serendipity."

"Way ahead of you," Dirk assured him. "I studied Exaius' Third Paradox of Prophecy at the Academy." He put a hand over his heart. "I solemnly swear on my lucky pair of underwear not to unravel the underlying conundrumatic matrix or disturb the diluvian currents in the quantum foam by making explicit requests."

Red's head spun at this philosophical vomit, reminded of why her copy of Exaius had collected several inches of dust under the bed. *Port Desire* was better. They didn't use words like 'conundrumatic matrix,' for starters. No, *Port Desire* stuck to the stuff that mattered in the real world: paternity tests, twins separated at birth, and faked deaths. Even that one storyline where Hunk Bestial cloned his dead wife using DNA found in spit she used to seal the envelope of her suicide note.

'Cloned from spit' buzzed in Red's head. "Back up a second," she said to Dirk. "I still don't get how you could even have a target for the DIC that will get us out of this mess. Don't you need, like, biometrics and shit? We have no idea who's going to step off that ship."

"Got that under control. Trust me."

"That's a pretty big ask, man," she said.

Sam raised a hand. "It's good enough for me."

"And me," Fritzi added, raising her own.

The Serendipitous Teh glanced around at his monks, then raised all the non-load-bearing appendages on one side. "On behalf of my fellow Elevated of the Entropic Monastery of the Sequestrian Order of the Hind Leg of Fardus, I put our defense in your hands, Tumescent Dirk. We are at your service."

Red lit a cigar. "Well, since it's my cat and you're all asking so nicely, I guess you can count me in, too." She blew a plume of smoke toward the ceiling. "Dirk, what do you need from me?"

"Just the cat." His eyes shot to it and his fingers fiddled nervously with his medallions. "But turn it off before you bring it to my room, okay? I like my internal organs to stay internal."

"I've been watching the clock," said The Observant Yuo. "We've spent forty-nine minutes talking, which means that ship will be here in only forty-five hours and twenty-two minutes—wait, twenty-one minutes."

"Then let's get to work!" The Impatient Taht exclaimed, clapping his hands together. The monks began talking amongst themselves in urgent voices.

"Agreed," The Serendipitous Teh said. "Let us all go our separate ways to prepare for our guests' arrival in whatever way we see fit." He dipped his head to Sam and Red, then led his chattering monks away.

Red hung back as the garden emptied. She plopped on the bench next to Bonk. It hopped on her lap and circled around, bruising her thighs with its absurdly heavy feet and waving its exhaust port in her face. "Lay down already," she complained, but not with any feeling behind it. As far as exhaust ports go, it wasn't too bad. At least it was freshly cleaned.

"I'll get this thing powered down and bring it to your room in a minute," she told Dirk. "I just need to . . . I dunno."

"No problem, babe." He flipped the DIC in the air like a coin, then tucked it into an inside pocket of his jacket.

"You're absolutely, positively sure you know what you're doing?" she asked, rubbing her fingers behind Bonk's auditory collection dishes.

"Absolutely, positively sure," he replied. "I'd even go so far as to say I'm totally, utterly sure."

When he got no reply, he left the garden with Fritzi and Sam.

Red and Bonk were alone. "It'll be okay," she told it, or maybe told herself. Not sure. Could be either one. She pressed the power button and savored the sound of its circuits clicking off one by one. She heaved it into her arms with a grunt and staggered off under the weight of her own guilt.

Chapter 36
A Goddamn Crisis of Faith

Red left the inert Bonk in Dirk's hands only after yet another ill-concealed threat of violence if anything bad happened to it and still more reassurances that he knew what he was doing.

Unsure what to do with herself for the next forty-five hours and change, she wandered back to her room in the dormitory. A fresh truffle decorated the pillow. She ate it mechanically, barely tasting it. The minifridge had been restocked but nothing looked good, and anyway, she needed to stay sharp, or at least not get any less sharp. She checked the closet; no Deltonic Implosion limited-edition grumskin vest, but there was a pair of rad black boots and a stack of clean, neatly-folded, and gnar-hole-free t-shirts and pants in the dresser drawers. She tried everything on, selected the most comfortable set, then sat on the edge of the bed and stared at the wall, slowly turning her D-4 screwdriver in her hands.

She hated having to wait for a battle she couldn't avoid. It didn't happen often, because she could almost always find a way to avoid it. When she couldn't, her standard Plan B was to go full fazzer, her biggest, baddest blasters blazing and a snarl curling her lip. Not pretty, not subtle, but it worked—most of the time. She was still alive, anyway, and that's the main thing when it comes to battles.

Today, though, there was far too much empty lead time (she'd have to ask The Observant Yuo for the current numbers). It left her to sit and stew in her own thoughts, and this stew was especially gristly. She wished Woodman were there to help pass the time. Stupid, but there it is. And, really, why not? He's fantastic in a fight, never let her down. If he were there, right now, she wouldn't be moping in her room and fondling her screwdriver. They'd be gearing up, comparing arsenals, arguing about who's buying the post-fight beer. He'd make a snarky comment about her flying; she'd tell him where he could stick that opinion. He'd call her *Mild*red with that special tone he reserved for just such occasions, knowing how much she hated it.

Instead, he was probably in some hospital room watching his dad die and his mom pretend he wasn't. A horrible realization washed over her, chilling her to the bone. What if he was already dead and Red didn't know? When was the last time she'd talked to Woodman—before she and Sam met Tom at the Gambora marketplace? That couldn't be right. So much had happened since then. She had a sister! She'd almost been killed at least twice! Her cat was an assassin! What kind of shitty person didn't share that with her best friend or her . . . whatever?

Red knew what kind. Her kind.

She threw the screwdriver across the room. It hit the wall point-first and stuck there. She stared at the handle quivering from the impact and felt suddenly claustrophobic. Had to get out. Had to move. Had to hear something besides her own thoughts. She left the screwdriver in the wall and slammed the door behind her.

Red went to the lobby, hoping to grab the Skjov book and a cup of that amazing coffee to clear her mind of, well, everything. She pulled up short when she heard hushed voices—The Vulgar Adn and The Impatient Taht. She crept to the doorway and peered through. The two monks were busy tidying the room and talking. They didn't see her, so she slid behind a decorative plant to listen.

"I understand what the abbot is saying." The Impatient Taht fluffed a pillow. "But I'm not sure I'm ready to die for these people. They're not even our Friends."

The other monk straightened a few brochures in the rack. "They will be soon enough. You know what the abbot's cooking up." What the hell does that mean? Instinct twitched Red's hand toward the blaster on her hip, but she squelched the urge and stayed put to listen.

"I thought you'd agree with me, after your comments in the sculpture garden earlier."

The Vulgar Adn folded a shiqwool blanket and draped it across the back of an overstuffed chair. "I prayed about it, dipshit. Fardus spoke to me, reassured me that we are on the right path."

The Impatient Taht's eyes narrowed into a shifty look. "I've never heard from Fardus. Maybe what you're really hearing is the nonsense our dear abbot has been whispering in your ear."

"What the hell, Friend?" The Vulgar Adn said, wheeling around. "Are you having a goddamn crisis of faith?"

The monk immediately deflated. "No, I—" He bent over to prod the fire with a poker. "Maybe you're right. It's not easy for me, you know. Never has been." The fire brightened, casting more light on his face. Even through the leaves of the plant, Red could see the dark circles under his eyes. "My Fardic gift seems more like a curse. I struggle with that. The abbot says that struggle is simply part of the gift, and I should meditate on what the fungus intended when it granted me this impatience. But . . ."

"That 'but' is your best quality, you bastard," said The Vulgar Adn. "It's what makes you so damn valuable around here. Imagine if we didn't have you around to kick our asses into making decisions? We'd still be talking about whether the dormitory bathrooms should be painted butter yellow or quashtoad eggshell pink." He shook a bowl of potpourri to refresh it. The flowery scent of Plestene bogmeadow tickled Red's nose and she had to concentrate not to sneeze.

"I suppose. What about you?" The Impatient Taht turned to his companion. "Don't you ever doubt the path you've chosen?"

The Vulgar Adn joined him at the fireplace. Together, they gazed into the dancing flames. "Of course I do. I abandoned my family at the Knuckles Family Funstravaganza Mini-Golf and Ice Cream Parlor when I joined you assholes. Don't get me wrong, I have a great life here. You guys are better than family, and I thank Fardus every goddamn day that he called me here. It's just that choosing one thing always means turning your back on something else." He paused. "I have a niece and a nephew I've never met. Hell, my parents fucking died and I never got to say goodbye."

Red flinched. "It just never seemed like the right time to go back. There was always something, some goddamned excuse. Oh, there's an android uprising, it's too risky. Oh, I'm too busy right now, I'll go after St. Cripps Eve. I just never fucking made the time." He sniffled angrily and ran a sleeve across his eyes.

"Do you wish you had?" The Impatient Taht asked gently, putting his arm around his fellow monk.

Crackling logs filled the silence and Red slipped out the door.

Chapter 37
Have Faith. Trust Fardus.

Next, Red's wandering took her to parts of the monastery she hadn't yet seen. The exposed stone, chilly drafts, and musty smell were a stark contrast to the warm, welcoming areas she'd seen so far. These were clearly rooms meant for the monks themselves to use, though she encountered nothing so inhospitable as a locked door or 'keep out' sign.

She took a few random turns and peeked through several doors before discovering a large, bustling kitchen. The Serendipitous Teh appeared to be supervising the preparation of an extravagant meal. He leaned over a steaming pot to taste the thick soup bubbling within. A strand of viscous saliva dripped from his mandible, and Red was relieved to see it hiss harmlessly in the flames rather than in the pot.

"A touch more nintha, I think," the abbot directed a monk wearing an apron and wielding a large spoon. The monk nodded and turned to chop more of the vegetable.

"Never enough nintha," Red observed.

The Serendipitous Teh startled, then waved his antennae in a friendly manner. "Ah! Just Red the Nothing!" He dodged a monk carrying a tray of sliced darna as he crossed the room to greet her.

Red winced at the honorific, but decided it wasn't worth the energy to explain. She looked around the kitchen. "Do you guys eat this well all the time?"

The abbot chittered. "By St. Cripps, no. Our normal fare is simple: bread, fruit, perhaps some cold meat on festival days."

"So what's all this, then?"

The Serendipitous Teh straightened up. "This is a special meal prepared only when we host our dearest guests. In our faith, it is known as the Feast of Perpetual Friendship. Few Unelevated receive such an honor. You and your companions are the first in over a decade." He leaned down to whisper in Red's ear. "I'm afraid our techniques are a bit rusty. The biscuits may be too dry, the gravy not dry enough."

"I'm sure it's fine," she assured him. Her stomach growled in agreement.

"You are too kind," the abbot said. "We are still in the early stages of preparation, but fear not! It will be ready in plenty of time to enjoy with you, our dearest guests."

Red wrinkled her nose. "Why do you keep calling us that? 'Dearest guests,' I mean."

The abbot tilted his head. "I don't understand."

"We don't deserve all this." She gestured to the monk piping dozens of sugary pink rosettes onto an enormous cake. "We don't even deserve to stay in your dormitory—which is gorgeous, by the way. And thanks for the clothes, they fit great." She picked at a hangnail. "It's just that, you know, The Vulgar Adn is kind of right. We dropped a steaming pile of crap at your front door. You're all probably going to die, and it's all because of me and my dumb cat."

The Serendipitous Teh clacked his mandible in concern. "You are the finest guests it has ever been my honor to host," he said. "Every one of your group epitomizes the teachings of our faith. Strong bonds of friendship, joyful delight in vulgarity, an appreciation for physical ease and comfort: these are sacraments here. If we are to die in this battle—and, you must understand, I do not believe it will come to that—then we could not do so in better company than yours. Tomorrow, you become more than our guests. Tomorrow, when we share this feast together, we shall become Friends."

"But how? You just met us."

"Have faith. Trust Fardus." He wrapped his upper appendages around Red in a surprisingly soft embrace that lasted forever. When he pulled away, he bent over to look her in the eyes. "It is truly serendipitous that you found us, Just Red the

Nothing." He held her gaze a moment, then turned his attention to a monk peeling quusberries.

Red watched the monks, chatting with one another as they chopped and mixed and baked, and walked out of the kitchen.

Despite the rad boots, Red's feet ached from roaming the hard stone floors of the monastery. She followed the faint smell of chlorine to the swimming pool to dip them in some cool water.

She wasn't the only one with that idea. Fritzi sat on the tiled edge of the pool, scaled toes barely reaching far enough to dabble.

Red spun on her heel to see if the abbot's serendipity would produce a second Fritzi-free pool, then spun back out of stubbornness. She chose a section of pool calculated to be close enough to the Andarian to not be rude, but far enough to make it clear she didn't feel like talking. She pulled off her boots and socks and sank her feet into the cool water with a sigh she couldn't keep to herself.

As she soaked, she refused to look at Fritzi. It was enough to feel her sitting there, her shrink eyes trying to bore holes through her skull and into her brain. Wait, Andarians couldn't read minds. Or could they? Just in case, Red filled her head with random thoughts: grocery lists, *Port Desire* characters, the starting lineup of the Crolinian Psycats' Proboscal Cup-winning team . . . Finally, the awkwardness got too much.

"I'm sorry about—" "Red, I wanted to—" They both stumbled over each other's words.

Red chuckled. "You go first."

Fritzi smiled gently. "I must apologize for my outburst earlier. It was unfair."

"Nah, you're right," Red said. "I screwed up your deal. I screw up everyone's deal." She kicked at the water. "Sorry about that."

"I—" Fritzi hesitated. They sat quietly a few moments, then: "How are you holding up?"

"I'm fine."

The Andarian sighed. "I don't have to be The Observant Yuo to see there's something bothering you."

Red opened her mouth for a snarky remark, then closed it again. She thought a minute. "Don't you think it's weird that Dirk won't say what he's up to?"

"I'm sure he has his reasons."

"Yeah, but that's what I want to know—his reasons."

Fritzi flexed her toes. "Red, it's understandable that you have difficulty with trust. Your entire life, you've been lied to, used, and manipulated by the very people you're supposed to be able to trust."

Red concentrated on picking tiny bits of grit from the treads of her boot.

"Betrayal hurts us at the deepest level of our being," Fritzi continued. "You're a strong person, Red, but being strong doesn't mean you don't get hurt. In fact, strong people are often the ones who get hurt the most. Others see your strength and think it's like armor, deflecting any blaster fire that comes your way. What they don't know is, that blaster fire is bruising you underneath the armor."

"You make my life sound terrible."

"You've had some terrible things to deal with," the Andarian said.

"You're not supposed to agree with me."

"The good news is, it's not all terrible. Some of it is wonderful—or, it could be. You have a lot of people who care deeply about you."

"Who, Granny?" Red snorted. "Great. One old woman who has to care about me because we're related."

"That's not true, and you know it." Fritzi gave her a pointed look. "Sam cares for you. So do I. Dirk too."

Red loosened a small stone, tossed it over her shoulder, and started on the other boot. "You guys hardly know me."

"And yet, here we are, putting ourselves in personal danger to help you. Why do you suppose that is?"

Red shrugged. "Sam's fulfilling her part of our deal. You and Dirk got caught up in the mess."

"As I recall, the deal was information on Smith in exchange for information on Bonk. Don't you think you've both fulfilled your respective obligations a long time ago?"

"I appreciate what you're trying to do, Fritzi. I really do. But now isn't exactly the time to get my head shrunk. You know, the whole impending invasion thing?"

"There is never a right time for anything. There is only this moment and what we do with it."

Another tiny stone flew over Red's shoulder to plink on the tiles. "Let me guess — Exaius again?"

"You can continue to deflect and hide behind sarcasm, but it won't work forever. Someday, you'll let someone into your heart. The question is, will you survive long enough to see that day?"

Coming from anyone else, Red would consider that a threat. Coming from Fritzi, it was somehow worse.

Red pulled her feet from the pool. "I'm going to go before I get pruney," she said stiffly, and struggled to pull on her socks over her wet skin.

Fritzi watched her in silence for a moment, then said, "Please, think about what we've talked about."

"Oh, yeah, sure. Of course. I'll definitely do that." She gave up on the socks, grabbed the boots, and strode away, her bare feet slapping the tiles.

Chapter 38
Dirk Is a Genius, He'll Save Us All

Red paused in front of the helpful signage to let her feet dry enough to force them back into the socks. As she tied the laces on the boots, she scanned the list to see if there was anyplace she'd missed. Pool, check. Sculpture garden, check. Lobby, dormitory, parking garage, check check check. The only places she hadn't already seen were The Erudite Library and The Singular Eye Salon and Spa. Might as well complete the tour before SECS and their bunker-busters turned it all to a smoking hole in the ground.

She pulled a Hamstel Lite bottlecap from her pocket. Right-side up, the library. Upside down, spa. She flipped it toward the ceiling. Light from the windows glinted off the metal as it spun to the floor. It landed with a clink. Red snatched it up, stuffed it back in her pocket, and turned down the hallway toward the library.

She'd expected to see a monk or two poring over crumbling parchments, but no—the only one in the library was Dirk. His head bent over an ancient tome at least six inches thick. The light of the reading lamp on the desk shone on his bare scalp.

Dirk heard her footsteps and looked up. "Hey, sugarlumps," he said, taking off his reading glasses.

Red sank into a chair across the table from him. "What're you doing here? I thought you'd be busy with Bonk."

"Pfft." He waved a hand. "I told you, five minutes was all I'd need. Consider the cat uncatted."

"I assume you still won't tell me what you put on that chip?"

He crossed his arms and grinned.

Worth a shot. She pulled Dirk's book closer and flipped over the cover. "'Fardicism on a Budget: A Step-by-Step Guide to Ascending the Several Celentine Staircases on Just Ten Credits a Day,'" she read. "What're you doing with this?" She blinked. "Wait a minute, are you going to become a *monk*?"

Dirk pulled the book back from her. "No. Yes. Maybe. I don't know yet," he said defensively. "I'm considering my options."

Red's jaw dropped. "Why? Was The Eager Liek really that good at . . . whatever it was he did?"

He frowned. "Not everything is about sex, you pervert."

Um. Okay, that was unexpected. "Then why? You don't seem the religious type."

Dirk thought a minute, running his hand over the yellowed pages. "You're a lot like me, I think. Always looking for the next good time, never looking back, responsible to no one but yourself. But did you ever get the feeling you're missing out on something important?" His eyes burned into her, but when Red only shrugged, he continued. "My time as a dead man gave me a new perspective. Always on the run, always looking over my shoulder, cut off from everyone I knew. I missed people. Don't get me wrong, I had all the tail I could handle, but it wasn't enough. It was never enough. I wanted my friends. I wanted Sammy. Do you get it?"

"I don't even know, dude."

"Neither do I." He patted the book. "This may be how I can find out."

"Speaking of friends, did you talk to Sam yet?"

"Uh."

Red threw up her hands in frustration. "You're running out of time. SECS will be here soon and if your super-secret plan doesn't work and we all end up flatter than a quashtoad. . ."

"I know, okay?" Dirk crunched up his eyes and rubbed his temples. "I know. You don't have to tell me. I screw this up, we're all dead. But don't worry, Dirk is a genius, he'll save us all." A bitter chuckle bubbled up from his throat.

"You said it's all under control." She paused. "It *is* all under control, right?"

"Don't you get it?" he moaned. "I'm no different than anyone else. Sure, I know some mechanical tricks—and they're good ones—but do I really want to stake my life on it? The lives of my friends? Who the hell am I that everyone is counting on me?"

Shit. Their only hope of survival was in the hands of a glorified grease monkey with imposter syndrome. "You don't have to do this alone, you know. Maybe if you told me what the hell your plan is, I could help."

Dirk snorted. "You can't help."

"How can you know that?" she demanded. "Sure, I haven't read Exaius or invented any sophisticated biometric detection algorithms or whatever, but I'm not a bad mechanic. You said so yourself." When he didn't respond, she continued. "Can you at least tell me *why* you can't tell me the plan?"

"Because it's a crazy dangerous risk and you wouldn't understand why it's worth taking."

"I'm not liking the 'crazy dangerous' part."

"I don't like it either, okay?" he shouted, slamming his hand on the table hard enough to make the heavy book jump. "I didn't ask for any of this. I was happy getting my lap dances and drinking my Fuzzy Fazzers when you showed up and dragged me into a stand-off with goddamned SECS, of all people." He swiped at his eyes. "I know SECS. Hell, I *was* SECS. This isn't a game."

"Whoa, calm down, man." Red reached awkwardly across the table and patted Dirk's hand. "Don't cry. It'll be fine."

He slapped her hand away. "Go away. Just go away."

Red started to leave, then hesitated a moment, hand on the door. "For what it's worth," she said over her shoulder, "I trust you."

"Yeah, right."

"I mean it." And she did.

Chapter 39
Stupid Snoodslime

Red's head ached. Doubt, faith, trust, more doubt. Did Vladmir IV think about this stuff before his son's army kicked his ass at Ehlar? She should've paid attention in history class. Or read that book Smith gave her. The library might have a copy, but Dirk needed space more than she needed tips on coping with pre-battle jitters. Luckily (or serendipitously?) her last stop, the Singular Eye Salon and Spa, might have something to take the edge off.

Of course, that's where she found Sam, sprawled in a chair, face slathered in thick white goop. A monk knelt at her feet, massaging oil into them with slow, firm motions. He greeted Red with a nod.

Sam cracked an eye. "This snoodslime mask is amazing," she said. "My face feels like it's on fire, only from ice, but in a really good way."

"I can't believe I'm actually saying this," Red said, "but can we talk?"

Sam exchanged a glance with the monk, who wiped his hands on a towel and excused himself from the room.

Red trailed her fingers along the assortment of little jars and bottles on the table next to Sam. She picked one up, sniffed it, and put it down. She rubbed some lotion on the back of her hand, enjoying the swirls it made before sinking into her skin. Then she examined the label on a glass pot of gunk. "Is this what you've got all over you?"

Sam stood and took the goop from Red. "That's it," she said. "You want to try it?"

Red shrugged.

"Sit down and close your eyes." Sam pushed her gently into the chair. She took a cloth from a bowl of warm, fragrant water and pressed it to Red's face. "Just relax," she said. "I'm going to take off my own mask."

Relaxing was never really Red's thing, especially without chemical assistance. She did manage to unclench her jaw, which she hadn't realized was clenched to begin with.

After a minute or two, Sam pulled away the cloth. "Keep your eyes closed," she warned, dipping her fingers into the pot of snoodslime. "I'm not an expert aesthetician like The Gentle Tehy, and I don't know what would happen if I got some of this slime in there."

Red scrunched them tight. Putting slime on your face was weird. Having someone else put slime on your face while you couldn't even watch? Even weirder. Still, it smelled pleasantly of mint and honey, and Sam's fingers were light and soft.

"I don't know what I'm supposed to do," she mumbled.

"Just sit still," Sam said, smoothing slime over Red's cheeks.

Red shifted in the chair. "No, I mean, with you. I've never had a sister before."

Sam's fingers paused, but quickly resumed their work. "I'm almost done." She spread a final bit of slime across Red's forehead. Then she heard some splashing—probably Sam rinsing the slime from her hands.

"What do you mean, what you're supposed to do?" Her voice was close. Red guessed she was sitting in the next chair.

"I dunno," she said. "I don't know how to do all the sister stuff. Like, shouldn't we be doing each other's hair and whispering secrets about cute boys?" Red found it surprisingly easy to talk when she didn't have to look at who she was talking to. Or maybe it was the snoodslime starting to tingle-burn. Or the FlinkBar jingle that was stuck in her head. *You'll love the nutty taste*

. . .

Sam chuckled. "Where did you get that from?"

"You know. Around." She didn't say *Port Desire*, which, despite being the truth, she knew was silly.

"Well, if that's what we're supposed to do, then we're screwed. I'm married to a woman, so whispering about cute boys is probably not going to happen."

Red snorted. "And you really don't want me anywhere near your hair."

"Why? Yours isn't so bad," Sam said, running her fingers through Red's mousy brown tangles.

"You should've seen it when I cut it for Smith's big fancy concert." Red smiled at the insides of her eyelids. "It was so lopsided."

"I remember."

Red's eyes flew open. "You were there? Seriously?"

"Eyes shut!" Sam scolded. When Red complied with a grumble, Sam continued. "Of course I was there. I'm not surprised you didn't see me, though. You were practically drooling over Indar."

"Oh, like you wouldn't be." Red thought a second. "Wait, no, I suppose you wouldn't, would you?"

Sam chuckled again, but when she spoke, her voice had shifted back to a serious tone. "That concert wasn't only about you," she said. "It was about me, too. Smith wanted me to see you. He wanted me to see who he'd chosen to replace me."

"Shit. That sucks. I'm sorry."

"Not your fault at all." Sam's voice got wistful. "You had this glorious dress and the most god-awful boots I've ever seen on a living person."

"The dress was a gift from Smith, but he didn't give me shoes. I had to improvise with what I already had."

Sam burst out laughing. "Oh, that's so perfect. I bet he loved seeing those boots." She paused. "You were beautiful."

Red squirmed. "It was a great dress. But you didn't see my hair after the gnar chewed off a big chunk while I was sleeping in the Scarpio's storage room."

"That sounds like quite a story. I'd love to hear it sometime."

"If we get through this invasion thing, sure."

"One time when Dirk and I were at the Academy, he got it in his head that I needed to dye my hair pink. The Fourteen only know why, or why I let him talk me into it. He mixed up a bunch of stuff in the lab. A special recipe, he called it." She chuckled.

"My hair fell out. All of it. I was completely bald. Took a month for my scalp to heal enough for it to start growing back."

"I'd've killed him. Got any pictures of bald you?"

"Ha, no, I pretty much turned into a hermit. It's exactly as embarrassing as you'd imagine. Ask Dirk, though. He might have one someplace."

Red twitched her nose. Who knew snoodslime was so itchy when it dried? Better not be an allergic reaction. She folded her hands across her stomach to keep from scratching. "Okay, I need to ask you about something that's been bugging me. It's stupid, but I gotta know." She took a deep breath. "This thing with you and Dirk. I don't get it, like, at all."

"We're friends. What's to not get?"

"It's just that you've known each other forever, but you've never taken it that next step. You know, a relationship. Commitment. Love or something. Is it just because he's a dude?" Red couldn't help but scratch. A clump of half-dried slime buried itself under her fingernail. Terrific. She opened her eyes and sat up. "Gimme a towel, will ya? This stuff itches."

Sam handed her a fresh cloth from the basin. "I do love him, but not in a romantic way. And it's not just because he's a dude."

Red scrubbed slime from her face. "What about Fritzi, then?"

"What about her?"

"When did your friendship turn into something more?"

Sam took the towel from Red and dropped it in a hamper. "There's a million kinds of love out there, Red. Family, friends, lovers, even pets, like Bonk. They're all different, but they're all powerful, and they're all real. Yes, I love Dirk. And yes, I love Fritzi. I don't love one more than the other. It's not a competition. I don't have to choose. They're just different kinds of love."

Red picked a slime flake from her pants. "I always thought you like someone, then one day it hits you that hey, you love that someone. Then if they feel the same, you get married and have kids. That's what people do."

Sam nodded. "Some people, sure. But that's not what happens for everyone."

"How did you know it was different with Fritzi? That it wasn't friendship but something else?"

"I just knew." A flush crept up Sam's face. "I felt it."

"That's not an answer, dude."

"I know, but it's hard to explain." She frowned. "Like . . . all I wanted was to be with her. To make her happy. To be worthy of her. It all sounds like a crappy soap opera, but it's true."

"And that's different from how you feel about Dirk?"

"Oh, yeah."

"How?"

Sam smirked. "This is about that Woodman guy, isn't it?"

"No. Well. Maybe."

"I can't tell you what to do—"

"That's what Fritzi said."

"Smart woman," Sam nodded. "Anyway, to me? If you're not sure if you love him That Way, that seems like a pretty good sign that you don't. But that isn't necessarily a bad thing. Friendship is fantastic too." She waved a hand. "And don't worry about what you should and shouldn't do. What makes sense for you? Do that."

"What if I don't know what that is?"

"I think you do. You just need to give yourself permission to recognize it."

Red lobbed a handful of bogmeadow-scented swabs at Sam. "You've been married to a shrink too long."

"You have no idea." Sam tossed a few swabs back at Red. "Hey, remember how earlier you said you didn't know what sisters do? Now, I can't say for sure—I've never had a sister either, you know—but it might be this. This is what sisters do. Talk. Laugh. Cry. Snoodslime facials. We even talked about boys."

"Hey, I didn't cry," Red protested. "I had slime in my eye."

"Next time."

"If there is a next time."

"Fair enough." Sam spread her arms wide. "I think this is where we hug?"

Red grinned. "Next time."

"If there is a next time."

"Fair enough."

The spa door cracked open and The Observant Yuo poked his head in. "The abbot asked me to tell everyone the Feast of Perpetual Friendship will begin in an hour in the dining hall."

Red stretched. "How long until the SECS guys get here?"

"If they maintain their current speed and course, they will arrive in our sector somewhere between forty-three hours and fifty-nine minutes and forty-four hours and eleven minutes from now." He pushed his glasses up on his face. "I'm sorry I can't be more accurate."

Sam and Red exchanged a glance. "Thank you, Observant Yuo," Sam said, a hint of a smile quirking up the corner of her mouth. "That is accurate enough for our purposes."

He nodded. "Do you require anything before the feast?" he asked.

Sam shook her head, but Red said, "Actually, yeah. Is there anyplace I can do a vidchat? If not, that's cool. I can always hike out to my ship, but—"

"Oh no," The Observant Yuo protested. "The parking garage is far too great a distance to travel, especially when our time is so limited. Fortunately, each guest room in the dormitory is equipped with a high-resolution vidscreen for your entertainment and communication convenience. Simply dial nine to access a secure outside line from the privacy of your room. If you have any further questions about these features, please dial zero to speak to our guest services coordinator. He will be, ah, eager to assist you." He nodded and ducked back out the door.

"Who are you planning to ping?" Sam asked gently.

Red shuffled her feet. "Granny. This could be the last chance I have to . . . . But she doesn't need to know about the whole imminent death thing. She'd only worry about me, and what could she do? Knit me a scarf?"

"I agree. Best to spare her the worry," Sam nodded. "Anyone else?"

Red shot her a look. "Maybe."

Sam's mouth twitched again. "Keep in mind that we might actually get out of this alive," she said. "So make sure whatever you say is something you'll be okay with tomorrow."

Red surprised herself by throwing her arms around Sam in a fierce hug. "Sorry I got you into this mess."

"Oh, Red." She returned the embrace with equal force. "You don't have to apologize. There's no one I'd rather fight off the legions of bureaucratic violence with than my sister."

Red pulled away and sniffled. "Stupid snoodslime."

Chapter 40

You Can Never Go Back

Red settled onto the plush armchair in her room and switched on the vidscreen. Hopefully Granny wasn't at bingo. Was it Thursday back on Magross? Sunday? Four in the afternoon or two in the morning? Interstellar time zone conversion always made Red's head spin. She'd just have to ping her and hope for the best.

Granny responded almost immediately. "Mildred!" she cried, drying her hands on a dishtowel. "It's so nice to hear from you, dear. I just finished cleaning up after dinner. Are you in the area? I have leftover meatloaf with mashed parplips."

Red's stomach rumbled and her heart ached. Would she ever have Granny's meatloaf again? "Thanks for the offer, but I'm not anywhere near Magross."

The old woman sat in her rocking chair and folded the towel in her lap. "That's all right," she said, picking up her knitting. "I'll reheat it for lunch tomorrow." Her fingers, bent with age but agile, clicked the needles cheerfully. "What is new with you, dear?"

She wanted to say: I've got a sister, a SECS agent, who kills people for a living. She's married to an Andarian shrink named Fritzi, and her best friend, Dirk, is a complete pervert who knows his way around tech. Oh, and Bonk is an assassin bot, but don't worry, he hasn't killed anyone I know lately.

What she actually said was: "Nothing new, really. Same old stuff, you know."

Granny tutted. "No exciting adventures?"

Yes! I'm hiding out in a remote valley with a bunch of monks because those SECS guys Sam works for are on their way to take Bonk by force if they have to. We've got no real defense and we'll probably all die cowering in a hole. No one will find our bodies. You won't even know I'm dead, isn't that exciting? "Not really. Pretty boring over here. What about you? Been winning at bingo?"

Granny chuckled. "Oh my, no. Marge is on a streak lately. I think she's cheating. Her son-in-law has been pulling the numbers, you know. Very suspicious. The man who usually runs the game is out for several weeks because his gout is flaring up. It's not fun being old, Mildred."

"Aw, Granny, you're not old."

"Of course I'm old!" she chided. "Being old has its problems, but it also has its advantages. I've met so many wonderful people in my life, lived so many wonderful experiences. I wouldn't trade it for anything, not even a chance to be twenty-two again."

Red swallowed. "Granny, this may be a weird question, but who's your best friend? Marge?"

"'Best friend' is a strange concept to me." Granny tied off her yarn and plucked a new ball from the basket by her feet. "I think our friends all have their particular places in our lives. It's not a matter of having one above all others. Sometimes you need a Marge Blattz, but sometimes you need a Louise Ferguson. Does that make sense?"

"I suppose so," Red said. "I've been thinking about friendship a lot lately and . . ." Granny knitted and waited patiently for her to collect her thoughts. "I just, it's like, I'm not sure I have any friends."

Granny laughed. "Why Mildred, that simply isn't true. What about Mark?"

"That's what I mean," Red said, leaning toward the vidscreen. "We're not just friends."

"Not just friends?" Granny smiled. "Whatever do you mean?"

Red squirmed. "You know what I mean," she said. "We, you know . . . Don't make me say it, you're my grandma! I just don't know if we're friends or something else or both or neither or —"

"Sweetheart." Granny put down her knitting. "Relationships don't always need to fall into a particular category. You can just . . . be." She picked up the needles again. "I never told you this, but I almost didn't marry your grandfather. Today lots of couples never marry, but back then, that was a big deal. 'Living in sin,' my parents called it. But we felt, he and I, that making our relationship officially a marriage would be narrowing it to something it wasn't."

"What made you change your mind?" Red asked.

Granny shrugged. "We got tired of people complaining. It seemed easier to go along with what everyone expected of us than continue fighting."

"Do you regret it?"

"Regret is a strong word," Granny said thoughtfully, rocking. "It's more that I feel cheated of something bigger and better. I loved your grandfather, and he loved me. But it was a love bigger than a piece of paper on file in Magross City Hall."

Red thought about this. "If you could go back, would you do it differently?"

"Maybe. Maybe not. Luckily, I don't have to make that decision, because you can never go back."

You can never go back. "I love you, Granny."

A warm smile lit up the old woman's face, somehow both creating more wrinkles and making her look decades younger at the same time. "And I love you too, Mildred. When do you think you'll be visiting again?"

Red shifted her eyes away and rubbed the back of her neck. "I, uh, don't really know. I have some stuff I gotta do. But soon, okay?"

Granny nodded. "Give me a few hours' notice and I'll make that spoo aloo again. Or roast a darna, if you'd rather."

Red stomach rumbled more forcefully. She checked the time. Only half an hour until the feast! "I'll definitely let you know. But I have to make another call, okay? I'm sorry, I wish I could talk longer."

Her grandmother dismissed this with a wave of one gnarled hand. "I need to concentrate on this sock anyway," she said, holding up the project hanging from her needles. "The heel is always the trickiest part. Do you like the colors? I'll save them for you."

"Thanks, Granny. That'd be great. I'll talk to you—" if I survive tomorrow— "soon, okay? I love you."

"You said that already, dear."

"I know," Red mumbled. "But it's still true."

"Good. I love you, Mildred. You take care, now."

"Bye, Granny." Red clicked off the chat, leaned back in her chair, and stared at the ceiling to keep the tears from running down her cheeks.

~ ~ ~

After a quick potty break and face-splashing, Red returned to the vidscreen and pinged Woodman before she could talk herself out of it. She sat in the chair, staring at the blank screen, chewing on a fingernail and hoping he wouldn't ping back.

But he did. He always did.

"Hey, darlin!" he drawled, smiling. "How's my favorite space babe doing?"

"I'm not a space babe," she grumbled, but she smiled, too. "I'm doing all right. How's your dad?"

Woodman's face fell. "His surgery's tomorrow. It was originally scheduled for Friday, but his blood pressure was creeping up and they wanted to get in there before it got worse."

Dammit. "Do they still think it could be the rikk?"

He snorted bitterly. "They won't say," he spat. "You know doctors. 'We don't want to speculate,' blah blah blah."

"That sucks," Red said. "How's your mom holding up?"

"Okay, I guess." He ran a hand through his shaggy hair. "She keeps planning stuff for after the surgery. Like, a week's vacation on Glor or remodeling the living room. It's driving me crazy. I keep telling her, don't plan for that stuff because it may never happen."

She shrugged. "But maybe it will happen."

"He might die, Red," Woodman growled.

"Dude, I know!" she snapped. "You think I don't know that we all could be just hours from a horrible fiery death in a hole somewhere?"

He frowned. "Uh, Red?"

She got up and paced the room. "I'm just saying, you don't know if he will die or he won't die, and if he doesn't, you have to make sure whatever you do now is something you'll be okay with later. And once you've done it, you can't go back. You can never go back."

"You're not making any sense. Are you drunk?"

"I'm not always drunk!" She threw her hands up. "Just listen. None of us know what's going to happen tomorrow, or if we'll even have a tomorrow. We might not even have the next five minutes. So what we say and do right now, *right now*, is everything. But you have to get it right, because what if we don't get tomorrow, or—oh god, even worse—what if we *do* get tomorrow? You have to live with whatever decision you make for the rest of your life, whether it's five minutes or fifty years."

"Are we still talking about my mom planning a trip to Glor?"

"Yes. No. I don't know. I can't say what I mean." Red sank into the chair, exhausted from the stress, from the confusion, from the emotional crap, from everything. Everything.

Woodman squinted through his side of the vidscreen. "Are you okay? No," he said, his forehead crinkled with worry. "You're not okay. What's going on?"

Shit. "Nothing," she said quickly, clearing her throat. "I'm fine. Just, you know, uh, tired. I've had a long couple of days."

He looked skeptical. "You sure about that?"

"Yeah yeah," she replied, waving a hand. "Lots going on over here, that's all."

"Here?" Woodman leaned to one side, as if to see behind her. "Where are you, anyway? That's not the *Wart*. Are you in a hotel?"

"Uh." Think think think. "Yeah, a hotel. Really cool place. Thought I'd take a break from, uh, you know. Stuff."

"You're acting super weird, babe. What's wrong?"

Red forced a laugh. "Nothing's wrong, you doofus. Just taking a little break."

"Okay."

"You don't believe me."

"It's not that I don't believe you. It's just—gah, never mind." He ran a hand over his stubbled cheeks. "How's Bonk? Have you figured out what's going on? What did the vet tech say? Did you ever meet up again with that Sam person from SECS?"

Wow, it *had* been a while since she'd talked to Woodman. "I'll tell you all about that later." If there was a later. "But I have been doing some thinking about stuff lately."

"Stuff." He nodded solemnly, but a glint in his eye betrayed his teasing.

She fiddled with the hem of her jacket. "We're friends, right?"

"Pfft." He rolled his eyes. "Babe, we've been friends since, what, first grade? Kindergarten? I can't even remember that long ago. I've always got your back."

"Sure, but . . ." she paused. "Are we friends or . . . something else?"

"That's what's gotten you so worked up? Wait, is this about the ShiqShaq thing?" He snorted. "Because it was just me and a few guys from the bar going out for Jason's birthday."

"No, it's not that." She sighed. "I mean, it is, but it's not. I feel like, I dunno, like I should be mad about you going to the ShiqShaq, and pinging that Orgullan chick with the fancy shower every time you're out in that sector, but I don't. I don't know why I'm not mad. Should I be mad? Would you be mad if it were me?"

He blinked. "I'm so confused. Are you asking if I'm your boyfriend?"

"Yes. No. Yes?"

He shook his head. "Look, Red, I care about you a whole lot. You know that. And damn, we're pretty hot in the sack, right?" She snorted, but he wasn't wrong. This would all be a lot easier if he was. "What more do you want?"

"I don't want *more*, I just want to know what it *is*," she said, exasperated.

"Well, I told you what *I* think. What do *you* think?"

"I don't know," she said miserably. "I think I love you, and I think you love me. But there's so many kinds of love, you know?"

He scratched his chin. "D'you mean like two dudes, or—"

"No, you idiot!" she shouted. Jeez, was he always this stupid? "I'm talking about friends! Do we have friend love, or boyfriend/girlfriend love?"

"Oh."

There was a knock on the door, and The Eager Liek poked his head in. "I'm sorry to interrupt," he said, glancing at the vidscreen. "The feast is about to start."

Ugh, the freaking friendship feast. "I'll be right there," she said. The monk nodded and closed the door.

"Who was that?" Woodman asked. "What feast?"

"Look, man, I can't explain everything now, I don't have time. I shouldn't have even pinged you. Tell your dad I hope his surgery goes okay." She moved to disconnect the chat.

"Wait, Red," he interrupted. "Hang on, don't go yet." He sighed. "Dammit, I wish we weren't doing this over vidchat. I don't know what's going on, but whatever it is, you need to understand that I . . . I do . . . I love you. I'm not sure what exactly that means, but I do. Maybe it's friend love, like you said. I'd need time to think and figure it all out. You kinda dumped this on me here." He paused. "I just know that you make my life better and I don't know what I'd do without you."

Red touched his face on the vidscreen. "Same, man," she said. "Same."

He touched the screen too. "You should go," he said. "Never miss a feast. Promise you'll ping me back later? Maybe tomorrow?"

Tomorrow.

"Yeah, totally. I'll ping you tomorrow. Promise." She swallowed the lump of that lie, suddenly a lot less hungry than she had been.

"Okay." He grinned. "I'm gonna hold you to that promise, *Mild*red."

"Ugh. I hate when you call me that."

"I know. Why do you think I do it?"

"Fine." She smirked. "Then I'm gonna start calling you Father Skulkington."

"That's *Reverend* Skulkington," he said.

"Whatever." She touched the screen again. "I gotta go. Goodbye, Mark."

"Later, space babe," he said, then disconnected.

Red pressed a button and the vidscreen sank back into its pocket behind the desk. Well, that went as well as a glob of snoodslime in the eye. Why did this shit have to happen now? She couldn't afford to be distracted when SECS arrived. She could just hear herself: 'Could you please hold your fire until I can figure out all my relationships from scratch? Kay, thanks.' Sure, that would fly. She had to focus. She scrubbed angrily at her face in a desperate attempt to clear her head. It didn't work.

Well, if she couldn't have an empty head, at least she could have a full stomach. Red hoped the feast would be well underway so she could sneak in unnoticed, and there would still be a piece of that cake with her name on it.

Chapter 41

Let's Do It Tonight

Alas, the feast had waited for her. "Sorry," she said, squeezing past a bench full of people to the only remaining empty seat, between The Observant Yuo and The Vulgar Adn. Sam shot her a questioning look, but Red just shrugged and turned her attention to The Serendipitous Teh, who clacked his mandibles at the head of the table.

"Now that we are all present," he said, looking over the crowded room, "I can begin the liturgy."

Liturgy? Damn. Red eyeballed the covered platters of food and jugs of beer and wine. Her stomach voiced its impatience again, but she tore her attention away from the spread as the abbot began.

"My dearest Friends," he said, "we gather today under the singular eye of Fardus, awash in the buoyant laughter of St. Cripps. As we partake of this glorious feast, The Feast of Perpetual Friendship, may we remember the bond that united Fardus and St. Cripps, in life and also in death. May we strengthen our existing ties and extend our hands to new Friends with equal gusto. The bread we break together represents the most holy act of hospitality; the wine we pour together represents the carnal joys with which this life has blessed us." He spread his appendages. "And now, my friends, let us follow St. Cripps' most sacred commandment: let's do it tonight, because we might not get tomorrow. In the sacred name of Fardus we pray, amen."

The monks chorused their amens, and even Red managed to mumble one. It was the least she could do, considering.

Red had never eaten so much so quickly: roast meats, crisp salads, fragrant gravies and sauces, steaming casseroles, and rich pastries, each dish more delicious than the last. And the booze! Red started with wine at the abbot's suggestion, then quickly switched to the monastery's nameless but strong home-brewed beer, which was excellent. It made the food slide down her gullet ever so nicely.

When she finally slowed down, uncomfortably stuffed but pleasantly buzzed, Red's eyes drifted over the crowd gathered around the table. The meal had long since been devoured, but everyone continued to pick morsels of darna off the bones and swipe their fingers through the frosting left behind on the serving platter. Every hand held a glass of something: wine, beer, water, or some fizzy concoction called soquem doce that The Vulgar Adn insisted was his people's national drink back on Plestos (Red suspected it was just fermented bogmeadow potpourri, but she said nothing).

But neither food nor drink stopped anyone from chatting and laughing together. Dirk was telling the abbot a story that apparently required a series of rude hand gestures. Sam and Fritzi pressed together comfortably on the bench, half-smiles on their faces. The Impatient Taht had challenged The Vulgar Adn to a game of jester's snap using empty coggle shells and bits of napkin as game pieces. The tone of The Vulgar Adn's expletives suggested he was losing badly. The Gentle Tehy and The Eager Liek, along with other monks whose names Red couldn't remember through her beer haze, sang a boisterous but off-key hymn with a catchy refrain that she feared would be stuck in her head for days—assuming they had days. At least it would be a change from the FlinkBar jingle. *Before you blast off into space . . .*

Red raised her stein to take another swig of beer in desperate hope of drowning that jingle for good. But then, she heard a single "ahem" from the seat next to her. It was The Observant Yuo. He wrung his hands and attempted to get the room's attention.

"Excuse me," he said, but his voice was lost in the noise. He cleared his throat and tried again. "Please, this is important—" A fresh chorus from the singers drowned him out.

"OI!" Red shouted. Silence descended instantly and all eyes turned to her. She nodded at The Observant Yuo. "Our friend has something to say." The monk gave her a grateful smile before standing to address the crowd.

"They're here," he said simply.

"Who?" The Impatient Taht demanded, throwing down his coggle shells and scattering napkin scraps across the improvised game board. "Who's here?"

"SECS. They're here."

The Impatient Taht rolled his eyes. "How do you know? You haven't left that seat in hours."

The Observant Yuo pointed to his glass of wine on the table before him. "Those ripples on the surface? Those are from a slight disruption to the normal air pressure in the area—the kind of disruption caused by a powerful ship's engine."

The Vulgar Adn leaned across the table and squinted at the glass. "That could be any goddamned thing, you bastard. Maybe there's a thunderstorm over the foothills."

"I could be wrong," The Observant Yuo admitted. He pushed his glasses up. "But this particular pattern is too regular to have a natural source. The frequency aligns with the type of engines that are typically used in government-issue Class XIV stealth transports. Given what we know, the possibility of this disruption being caused by anything other than the SECS ship is diminishingly small."

The abbot's antennae quivered. "It's too early, isn't it? I thought we had more time."

The Observant Yuo squirmed miserably. "It *is* too early," he said, mostly to himself. "They weren't due to arrive for another forty hours and twenty-seven minutes or so. There must've been a factor I failed to consider in my calculations."

Dirk bounced in his seat. "D'you think they could've coated the hull with high-shabolitic panels? That would give them the extra slip to account for the difference, or—"

"Or," Red interjected, "we could just go look out the window and see if it's them."

The Serendipitous Teh raised himself to his full height. "An excellent idea. However, I believe there is a safer option.

Observant Yuo, Sam ARSE-Hogger, and Just Red the Nothing, please join me."

Hushed whispers from the others followed the abbot's group out of the dining hall. He led them to the Observation Room, then gestured for The Observant Yuo to take his seat at the control panel. A few taps brought the security camera feeds up on the main screen. Sure enough—there was the ship they were waiting for, its bulk squatting across the river from the monastery's main entrance, TITs sparkling, the words *The S.E.C.S. Rector* etched near the main hatch. Dirk whistled between his teeth.

The Observant Yuo dropped to his knees before the abbot and pressed his forehead to the floor. "Most Elevated," he said, "I cannot express my shame at failing the Order so utterly. My calculations—I must have forgotten to carry the three, it's the only explanation. My foolish error has placed us all in far greater danger than we anticipated. I beg you to intercede with Fardus on my behalf."

The abbot clicked his mandibles. "You have nothing to be ashamed of, Friend," he said. "Fardus does not require perfection. He grants us holy gifts so that we might use them to the best of our ability. And after all, yours is observation, not calculation." He placed several upper appendages on the monk's arms and gently lifted him back to his feet. Tears streamed from The Observant Yuo's eyes.

"We don't have time for this," Red said through gritted teeth. "We need to tell the others and get everyone into position."

"Agreed," Sam said. She tore her eyes from the ship looming on the screen and turned to the abbot. "Red, Dirk, and I will get the cat. Can you get the rest of the group to that pantry you mentioned earlier?"

The abbot gave a tight nod. "Fear not. We will act as demanded by our faith." Red didn't like the sound of that. 'Yes, we'll go straight there and hunker down' would've been more reassuring. Or even 'of course, how stupid do you think we are?'

"Wait!" The Observant Yuo said. "I've been working on something that we can use to keep an eye on what's going on outside." He opened a drawer and withdrew two handheld devices, each with a small screen and series of colored knobs. He handed one to the abbot. "I call it the Feed-Accessing Remote

Televid Surveillance, or FARTS for short," he said. He handed the second device to Dirk without making eye contact. "It's strictly video, and not nearly as good as some of your products, but I thought—"

Dirk examined the FARTS in his hand and grinned. "No, I like how you think," he said, twisting one of the knobs. "And these control the—ah, of course!" The screen lit up and began cycling through the security feeds, mirroring the large screen above. "I assume this is encrypted?"

The Observant Yuo flushed a deep red. "I used roetogenic algorithms. Not impenetrable, but it should slow down anyone trying to get in."

"Excellent work, Friend," said the abbot. "But Fardus has equipped you to use it better than I." He handed the device back to the monk.

"Hello?" Red interrupted. She waved her hand at the screen, where a hatch had opened in the belly of the ship. "Suck each others' dicks later. Right now we need to *move*."

"Indeed." The Serendipitous Teh wrapped several appendages around The Observant Yuo. "Have faith," he said. "Fardus will protect you. St. Cripps will give you strength."

Red wished she shared his optimism.

~ ~ ~

Bonk lay on its side on the worktable Dirk had improvised by laying the in-room ironing board across the backs of two chairs. Dirk pressed the cat's power button to initiate the warm-up cycle, then started stuffing various tools and gadgets into a canvas tote bag with the monastery logo embossed on the side. Another serendipitous find, Red assumed. Sam paced outside the door, eyes glued to the FARTS.

The run to the dormitory had burned Red's beer buzz right out of her, along with most of her breath. She sank onto the bed to pant quietly to herself. She really needed to quit smoking. But right now, she mostly needed a smoke. Time to put that serendipity to work. She closed her eyes and pictured a thin, black Crolinian cigar—her favorite. Then she opened the drawer of the bedside table. Apart from a grumskin-bound copy of *The Marvelous Life and Times of Fardus (V.1)*, it was empty.

Damn.

Wait, it didn't work if you asked, right? She lay back on the bed, folded her arms behind her head, and hummed the FlinkBar jingle. Then, casually, she reached back into the drawer and picked up the book as if she actually wanted to read it. Underneath was a single Crolinian cigar.

Dirk was right: maybe there was something to all this Fardic stuff after all. She snatched up her find before Fardus could pull a fast one and disappear it up the Staircases or whatever. She unwrapped the cigar, stuck it in her mouth, and started patting her pockets for a match.

Something hit her in the forehead and fell into her lap—Dirk's golden dick lighter. "Ow," she grumbled, rubbing the spot. "But thanks."

"Keep it," Dirk said, winding a length of wire into a coil and adding it to the tote bag. "You're already getting more use out of it than I ever did."

"Thanks, man," Red said. She turned it over in her hands a few times before lighting the cigar in a flash of butane. She only managed one deep drag before Bonk extended its legs to full length, tail in the air, and opened its oral port wide enough to showcase each and every razor-sharp tooth. Its green eyes blinked.

"Its eyes!" Red sputtered. "What did you do? They match!"

"That was the key to uncatting the cat," Dirk said smugly. "Old programmers' proverb: 'The best back doors are those in the front.'"

Red rubbed Bonk's skull casing behind its aural receptors, causing its eyes to dim in appreciation. It'll take some getting used to. Maybe Dirk could put them back the way they were after . . . whatever was about to happen.

Sam popped her head in the door. "We've got a problem."

"Another one?" Red groaned theatrically.

Sam tossed her the FARTS. Red glanced at the screen and her stomach dropped into her boots. "Holy hell."

"What?" Dirk snatched it from Red's hand. His jaw fell open. "What the hell is that Fardic fool *doing*?"

Chapter 42
Abbot-Rolling Duty

Dirk spun a knob and zoomed in on the vid. The image became grainy, but it was impossible to mistake what was happening: The Serendipitous Teh walked down the black pebbled path, approaching the bridge leading to the menacing ship. His appendages extended outwards, as if to offer an embrace. So far, though a ramp had been extended from the open hatch, it seemed no one had ventured out of the ship. There was probably still time to avert disaster.

Probably.

But it meant more running.

Shit.

At least Red had managed to suck in a couple lungsful of nicotine before these most recent fazzers hit the viewport. It helped give her legs the extra boost they needed to haul her ass back through the monastery.

Through the atrium and into the lobby she ran, not bothering to see if the others had followed her. She skidded to a halt at the stone doorway they'd walked through such a short time ago. A stabbing pain shot through her side as her body objected to its unexpected call to action. Clutching the cramp, she poked her head around the corner to take in the situation outside.

Not even The Vulgar Adn would have words to adequately describe her reaction to what she saw. The Serendipitous Teh was no longer alone. At least two dozen fully-armored soldiers flanked him on the near side of the bridge, weapons in hand but not yet raised. The abbot himself seemed perfectly calm, his appendages still extended in a gesture of welcome. Red's heart slowed its pounding enough for her to hear that he was talking to someone at the foot of the bridge that she couldn't see.

"On behalf of the Sequestrian Order of the Hind Leg of Fardus, I welcome you all to The Entropic Monastery," he said. "I am The Serendipitous Teh, the Most Elevated of this chapter. Hospitality is our holy calling. We invite you to partake of our services during your stay, and, in so doing, allow us to worship as our faith commands." He paused, clicking his mandibles softly. The troops remained motionless. "We offer a delightful snoodslime facial in our spa," he suggested. "Or, if you prefer, take a relaxing stroll through the sculpture garden. Our kitchen staff can provide a variety of snacks and refreshments for your enjoy —"

"Enough," the unseen person said. "You know why we are here. Where is the cat?" He sounded bored.

The Serendipitous Teh's antennae quivered, but his voice remained steady. "Yes, we did receive your message. It pains me deeply to be unable to accommodate your request immediately, but I must respect the privacy of our other guests. I'm sure you understand. I am confident a solution can be reached that is agreeable to all parties. Perhaps we can discuss the issue over tea?"

"No discussion necessary. Commander? Find the cat. Let nothing stand in your way."

"I know that voice," Dirk muttered, causing Red to jump.

"Don't sneak up on me!" she hissed. "Who is it?"

A sharp crackling cut him off before he could answer. Red spun back to see the abbot collapse to the ground and roll his long body into a tight coil, head wedged firmly in the center.

"NO!" She ran headlong toward the abbot — toward her Friend — without a thought to spare for the inherent danger of running toward a small battalion of trained fighters armed to the gills and under orders to flatten her if necessary. She simply ran. Some remote part of her mind heard Sam yelling at Dirk and saw blaster fire erupting in the air around her, but she didn't care. She slid the last few feet to the abbot's side on her knees.

He wasn't moving, and no wonder. The blast had blown open the chitinous plating on one of his segments like a can of duuofish, exposing globs of viscous brown goo never meant to see the light of day. The abbot's coiled posture slowed it down from a gush to an ooze. The Feast of Perpetual Friendship gurgled halfway up Red's throat, but she didn't have time to be sick. The abbot's antennae twitched feebly; he was still alive, if barely. He had to get back inside. Hell, *she* had to get back inside. No way were they dying out here.

Red shoved her arms under one side of his outermost coil and hauled backward, trying to drag him toward the relative safety of the monastery. Who knew ten feet of sentient arthropod could be so heavy? She pulled for an eternity, legs straining, boots slipping against the damp grass. A blaster round hit near her foot, sending up a shower of burning turf. Red yelped, then glanced over her shoulder—she'd barely moved. She'd never make it.

Suddenly, somehow, Dirk appeared at her side. He grabbed the abbot next to Red and caught her eye. He mouthed 'one, two, three' and they heaved in unison. The massive coil rose onto its edge and wavered there, like an enormous wheel. Dirk raced around the other side to keep the abbot from tipping over, then together they rolled him across the lawn and through the stone archway without gaining any new or bloody holes.

Once inside, Red and Dirk braced The Serendipitous Teh against the wall and took a few seconds to catch their breath. As Red arched her back to loosen the muscles, she saw who was responsible for her lack of blaster damage: Sam, silhouetted against the light streaming in through the door, double-fisting twin scatterfire handrifles. She was screaming through her curtain of blue hair, spit and sweat flying from her like rain. She swept the monastery lawn with wide swaths of destructive flame. She looked like a warrior goddess descended from hell to visit bloody vengeance and fiery death upon her enemies. She was utterly, utterly beautiful.

It's not fair. Not fair at all.

"Get him back to the others." Sam didn't interrupt her rhythm.

"But what about you?" Dirk shouted over the crackling rounds.

"If I stop now, they'll swarm the place." She tossed a drained handrifle aside and pulled out a standard blaster to replace it. The maneuver took only a few seconds and she never once took her eyes off her targets. "I'll be right behind you."

Dirk shook his head violently. "Sammy, I'm not leaving you here to—"

"*Go.*"

Red grabbed Dirk's hand and dragged him away from the doorway. "Sam'll be fine," she said. "It's the abbot who needs us now."

With a strangled growl, he pulled The Serendipitous Teh's coiled body upright from the wall. Together, he and Red made their way through the lobby. The abbot's size, even curled up, made it difficult to navigate among the overstuffed chairs, doily-covered tables, and rack of brochures. They made it through the opposite door and were halfway down the hallway to the kitchen when an explosion shook the building. The sound of crashing rock was followed swiftly by a billowing cloud of dust and grit pouring through the door from the lobby.

"Sammy!" Dirk wailed, leaving Red staggering to balance the entire weight of the abbot against her shoulder. He started back to the lobby, coughing and waving his arms to dispel the dust.

Red cursed, managed to get The Serendipitous Teh's coil standing upright, and hoped he'd stay that way long enough to get Dirk back. She lunged out and grabbed Dirk by the arm. He turned and snarled at her, kicking at her to free himself.

"Dirk," Red said, his polyester sleeve slipping from her clenched hand as he continued to pull away. "Whatever happened back there, there's nothing you can do about it. We have to trust Sam. Dirk, please," she begged. "Please, I can't move him myself."

He yanked his arm out of Red's grasp but didn't continue into the settling debris cloud. Instead, he let out an anguished, wordless wail that echoed through the stone halls of the monastery. Welp, that was it for Dirk Largo. He'd given up. Broken. Bye-bye. Red steeled herself to do what she could to get the abbot to the kitchen storeroom by herself—then Dirk shook himself briskly.

"What're you looking at, tittybritches?" he smirked. "Let's go already."

Thank the Fourteen. Fritzi would split her wig over whatever industrial-grade repression was going on in Dirk's psyche right now, but at least he was functional enough to get back to abbot-rolling duty.

Chapter 43

Uh, About That . . .

The rest of the way to the kitchen was uneventful—well, as uneventful as can be expected when you're wheeling the injured body of a Friend to safety while being pursued by armed soldiers through a crumbling monastery's back hallways. At least nothing else blew up, and whatever happened back in the lobby kept those same soldiers from following them.

For now.

True to the abbot's word, the pantry door was tightly sealed—with palmprint locks. A problem, since neither Dirk nor Red had their hands scanned for access. Dirk balanced the abbot with one hand and tapped lightly with his knuckles on the door with the other. There was no response. He knocked louder. "It's us!" he called. "Let us in!"

"Shh!" Red looked nervously over her shoulder. "You want the entire SECS army to know where we are?"

"If it's soundproofed like he said," Dirk replied, jerking his head at the abbot, "they probably can't hear us anyway." He wiped grimy sweat from his head and leaned back against the door. "Guess we'll just have to wait and hope—"

The door suddenly swung inwards. Dirk fell on his ass with an oof. The Vulgar Adn helped him to his feet.

"Did you hear us knock?" Dirk asked as he brushed himself off.

"No, we saw you on the FARTS," the monk explained, waving a hand at The Observant Yuo. "We saw the whole shitshow: the abbot, the firefight, the explosion, the hallway . . ." He turned to the abbot. "Is he fucking *dead*?"

Red elbowed Dirk to help her roll the abbot into the pantry. "I don't think so," she panted. "Not yet, anyway." She took one last glance back through the kitchen, saw nothing but dirty dishes and crumb-covered countertops, and kicked the door shut behind them. "But he's pretty badly hurt. I mean, he did take a blaster to the middle at close range. Not many people can survive that."

The Gentle Tehy stepped forward from the cluster of monks huddled among the shelves of food. "Lay him down, please," he said. "Carefully. Try not to jostle him." A handful of monks helped Red and Dirk lower the abbot to the floor.

"Don't you work in the spa?" Red asked, confused. "What are you going to do, give him a manicure?"

The monk frowned. "I am a trained medical professional," he said. "My skills are applicable in many settings, including nontraditional health modalities such as spa treatments."

The Impatient Taht gave Red a stiff shove. "Get out of the way and let my Friend work."

Red put her hands up in surrender and backed away.

The Gentle Tehy approached The Serendipitous Teh cautiously, brows knit in concern. His hands fluttered over the abbot's body, feeling his antennae, tapping the protective shell that had snapped shut over his eyes, and finally touching the goo that had squeezed between the coils from the damaged segment. He raised his fingers to his lips and, to Red's disgust, licked them. And she thought putting slime on someone's face was a weird job. Better that than being whatever kind of doctor had to taste his patient's guts.

"He is still alive," the monk announced. Relieved murmuring broke out among the crowd. The Gentle Tehy raised a hand for silence, then continued. "His autonomic conglobation has done its job—the wound is no longer draining synovial fluid and the damage is contained. At this point, any attempt to uncurl him to access the injured segment for direct treatment would interfere with his body's natural attempts at healing and repair."

"What does all that mean?" demanded The Impatient Taht.

"There is nothing more to be done," the monk replied. "He is in Fardus's care now."

"Fuck." The Vulgar Adn ran a hand over his face.

"What do we do now?" The Eager Liek asked, wringing his hands.

"We can't just stay here," said a voice from the back. "We've got to get out."

"Did you see what they did to the abbot?" another replied. "I'm not leaving this room."

The monks started arguing amongst themselves in fierce whispers. Dirk sat beside The Serendipitous Teh, one hand lightly resting on his coils. Red's skin prickled with rising panic. This situation was in grave danger of escalating to full red-alert, rhombus-shaped chaos, and fast. If Sam were here, she'd know what to do.

Sam.

Red looked around frantically for Fritzi, and found her sitting in a corner against a barrel of pickled quusberries, hands limp in her lap. Her scales throbbed a dull yellow as she looked up at Red with puffy red eyes. "Sam's not with you," she whispered. "I had hoped . . ."

"Did you see what happened?" Red asked, sinking to the floor next to her and crossing her legs.

The Andarian sniffled. "She'd run out of ammunition. The soldiers knew it. They were advancing. She set some kind of explosive, I assume to collapse the doorway so they couldn't get in. She started to run, but the entire lobby fell in. The camera cut out, and we couldn't see. I thought maybe she'd made it through somehow, but then we saw the feed from the hallway, it was just you three, and . . ." Her voice broke.

Shit.

"Look, Fritzi," Red said, patting her awkwardly on the back. "I'm sure Sam's fine. You know better than anyone how tough she is. No way she'd let a stupid pile of rocks stop her."

"She's not invincible, Red."

"I know," Red said. "But this wouldn't be the first explosion I've seen her walk away from, remember? And I've only known her a little while. I bet Dirk knows tons more stories just like that. She's not Smith's daughter for nothing, you know." Red snorted. "We kick ass. It's in our genes."

Fritzi forced a smile. "You're probably right, of course."

"Of course I'm right," Red said briskly. "One day everyone will learn this and it'll save a hell of a lot of time. Now, I need your help with something."

Fritzi raised an eyebrow. "Red Darkling, asking for help? From me?"

"Yup. This is right up your alley." Red gestured to the monks, whose arguing had reached a fevered pitch. No punches had been thrown, but it was close. She could smell the testosterone fug pouring from their glands.

"Ah, of course," she said. "Panic is anathema to survival. De-escalation is necessary." She stood, sighing. "Can you get their attention? Like you did for The Observant Yuo at the feast. I'm afraid my presence isn't as, ah, commanding as yours."

Red grinned. "Yes, ma'am." She cracked her knuckles, cupped her hands around her mouth, and shouted. "OI!"

The monks fell silent.

Fritzi smiled. "Could you please boost me up on the barrel?" she asked Red. "I need everyone to see me clearly." Red obliged, happy to pass off the metaphorical baton of leadership to someone else.

"My dearest Friends," Fritzi began. "I know you are afraid. I am too. We all are. Our enemies are at our very doorstep. They have already incapacitated or . . . separated us from two members of our party. These are extremely serious matters. But hope is not lost. There is good news. *We are still here*." She paused, letting this roll around in everyone's heads.

"And who are we?" she continued. "We are powerful. We are strong. We are The Observant Yuo's attention to detail. We are The Impatient Taht's drive to act, The Gentle Tehy's medical expertise, The Eager Liek's enthusiasm. We are Dirk's mechanical problem-solving and Red's . . . My point is, we have all these things because we have each other. We have our Friends. And that is not to be underestimated."

"Great," The Impatient Taht grumbled.

"But most important of all," Fritzi added. "We have Bonk."

Red's heart dropped. "Dirk," she said slowly. "When you and Sam left the dormitory, what happened to Bonk?"

All heads turned to Dirk, still on the floor next to the abbot. He jerked to attention and looked around anxiously. "The cat?" he stammered, fiddling with his medallions. "So, funny thing, actually . . ."

Chapter 44

I Hope It Doesn't Stain

"Where is it, Dirk?" Red advanced across the room. Monks recoiled on either side, clearing a path for her and her barely contained rage. "Where is my cat?"

Dirk's eyes darted around the room like a cornered fazzer. "I mean, it's probably still in my room. Where would it go?" he babbled. "We can check the FARTS, make sure it's there before we—"

"You left Bonk behind!?" Red shrieked. "How could you—Why—"

"Hey, you left it behind too, you know." Dirk retorted. "You took off after the abbot, leaving Sam and I to make a split-second decision about what the hell to do. I'm so very, very sorry we chose to keep you from getting blasted into orbit rather than babysit your stupid cat."

Red threw herself at the prone man but only managed to land one good punch before several of the monks pulled her away. She struggled against their grip, her appetite for violence only whetted by the blood pouring from Dirk's nose.

"You brode by doze, bidtz," he said as The Gentle Tehy knelt at his side to examine the injury.

"Good," she spat, shaking off the monks and retightening her fists. "What should I break next?"

"Stop it, Red," Fritzi snapped, hopping down from the barrel. Then her voice softened. "Look at him."

Red blinked. In that moment, she saw Dirk not as the bumbling pervert who ditched her cat and threw away their one shot at surviving this disaster, but as a man who cared enough about her to risk everything. Her Friend. Dammit. Her anger deflated and she stepped back. She let her hands relax. Her knuckles ached; she'd bruised them.

"I hope it doesn't stain," she muttered, gesturing to the blood streaming down his suit.

Dirk started to laugh, then cringed in pain. "Dat's duh beaudy of polyesder, babe," he said. "Easy do clead."

The Gentle Tehy tutted and pinched a folded napkin over Dirk's nose. "It's not broken," he said. "But no more talking until the bleeding stops."

"Are you all done now?" The Impatient Taht interrupted. "Can we get back to the part where the cat we're all depending on to save us from certain death is, you know, not here?"

"Gimme the FARTS," Red said, grabbing the device from The Vulgar Adn. She cranked a couple of the knobs back and forth, then slapped the side and shook it upside down. "How do you make this thing scroll through the other feeds? I wanna see if I can find Bonk."

The Observant Yuo snatched it away from her. "You're going to break it," he said, then adjusted it to the proper setting. "See, there's the pool, and that's the — wait, what's — is that?"

They all pressed around the monk, each trying to see the small screen. "Is that the lobby?" Red asked. She elbowed The Eager Liek out of the way so she could get a better view of the crazy bursts of static cutting through the image.

The Observant Yuo pushed up his glasses and nodded. "The camera was damaged by the explosion, but it must still be sending a signal. It's not great, but every few seconds you can see . . . there!" He jabbed a finger at the screen. "Did you see that?"

"Yes!" The Eager Liek shrieked in Red's ear. "Just for a second, but it looked like — there it is again!"

This time The Observant Yuo pressed a button on the FARTS to freeze the image. Red snatched it and held it close to her face, squinting. She could make out the mountain of crumbled stone and jagged roots from the jiljala tree above, obviously, but there was something else, too: a two-legged something with a familiar sweep of hair obscuring the face.

"Fritzi!" she whooped, shoving the screen at the Andarian. "It's SAM!" Red punched the air. "I told you we Smiths kick ass. Let's go get her."

"No," Fritzi said softly. She traced the image with a finger. "It's too risky. Sam will know to come here if she can without endangering us." She handed the device back to The Observant Yuo. "Can you pull up the other feeds? We need to know what S.E.C.S. is doing, and hopefully find out where the cat is."

"Of course." He twisted some knobs and the display cycled through the feeds. He stopped on the view of the monastery's front lawn. The *Rector* still crouched across the river with its ramp extended. A handful of soldiers lay on the grass near the bridge, obviously dead. Good job, Sam. A few others sat nearby, receiving care for their injuries from a pair of soldiers wearing medic armbands. Another pair of soldiers pulled down chunks of rubble that blocked the collapsed archway, while a third paced the lawn, gun in hand, scanning the area for something to shoot at.

"How many did you say those TITs could hold?" Red asked The Observant Yuo.

"Each one has a maximum capacity of twenty."

"Twenty per TIT, and there's two TITs," Red said under her breath. "That's forty altogether."

"Hang on," The Vulgar Adn interrupted. He scrunched his face in concentration. "Yes, that math checks out on my end."

Red ignored him. "There's probably ten soldiers out there we don't have to worry about anymore, because they're either dead or too injured to continue."

The Observant Yuo nodded his agreement.

"The medics and front door patrol make another three," Red continued, counting on her fingers. "That's thirteen. Plus the ones clearing the doorway, that's fifteen. I didn't see anyone but Sam in the lobby, did you?" He shook his head. "Let's assume the worst, and none of these fine members of our armed forces got their heads flattened by a boulder." She paused. "So where's everyone else?"

A nervous murmur rippled through the crowd of monks as The Observant Yuo set the FARTS to cycle the feeds again. He stopped on one. "There's six circling around the south side of the monastery," he reported. "They're probably looking for another way in."

"Will they find one?" Fritzi asked.

"No!" The Eager Liek bounced with excitement. "The only doors into the monastery are the front door, which Sam blocked off, and the emergency exit at the far end of the dormitory, which we barricaded before the feast."

"You forgot the tunnel to the parking garage," The Impatient Taht pointed out.

The Eager Liek dismissed this with a wave of his hand. "They'll never find the parking garage," he said. "It's far too well hidden. And the other end of the tunnel is right here in the heart of the monastery. We can access it, but they can't."

"Is there a security feed that monitors the exterior of the parking garage?" Fritzi asked. The Observant Yuo nodded and pulled up a vid of the blank rock wall at the back of the valley. Even having flown the *Wart* into the hidden entrance herself, Red couldn't find it. Luckily, there was no evidence anyone else could find it either — no soldiers in sight.

"They might not need to find a door," The Observant Yuo said, switching back to the feed to the south. The original six soldiers had been joined by another four guiding a large machine along the uneven turf using an antigrav dolly. "They'll just make their own."

Red twisted her head. "What is that thing?"

"There doesn't appear to be any mountings for a rotational assembly, which means it's a Directional Ionizing Laser Delving Operation." He pushed up his glasses. "It's a fancy drill."

Oh great. "Where are they taking it?"

"Hard to tell."

"Keep an eye on that group," Fritzi warned.

No shit, Exaius. Red hmphed. "There's still, what, fifteen soldiers unaccounted for? Is there anywhere in the monastery or on the grounds that isn't covered by security cameras?"

The Observant Yuo shook his head. "We were very thorough."

"And none of the other feeds show any soldiers," Red pressed.

"No."

"Then the only place they can be is still on the ship."

Dirk, nose swollen and red but no longer bleeding, approached the group with the second FARTS in his hand. "Hey, Red," he said through is swollen nose. "D'you rebember earlier when I said I regognized thad voice?" He handed her the device. "It's Todhunter Balzarg."

"Todhunter who?" The Impatient Taht demanded.

"Balzac," Red answered, eyes locked on Dirk's.

"Who the sweet living fuck is Todhunter Balzac?" asked The Vulgar Adn.

"I used to worg wid himb," Dirk replied as Red examined the tiny figure on the screen. It was one of the injured on the lawn by the bridge. As she watched, he gestured to the monastery and barked something at the medic wrapping a bandage around his head. The medic said something angrily back, then moved on to a man writhing on the ground with an arm bent the wrong way.

"That's not Todhunter Balzac," Red said.

"Of course id is," Dirk snapped. "I'd dow thad smug face andywhere."

"I'm telling you, that's the guy who poisoned our coffee. Fritzi? You look." She handed her the FARTS.

Fritzi studied the image for only a second before the color drained from her face. "That's Imon," she whispered. "He was our personal assistant."

"So which one is it?" The Impatient Taht growled. "Balzac or Imon?"

"Both," Red said simply.

Fritzi shook her head. "I hired him six months ago. He came highly recommended. I never thought . . ."

Red cleared her throat and took back the FARTS. "It looks like he's the one in charge."

"Thad's whad I'mb afraid ob," Dirk replied grimly.

"Why?" Fritzi asked. "Surely it's better to have an enemy you know than face an unknown."

"Becaudse," Dirk said, "this beans by plan didn'd worg."

Chapter 45
Poor, Stubid Dirg Largo

Seven . . . eight . . . nine . . . ten. Red opened her eyes, but her nails still dug into her palms with the strain of not throttling Dirk. "Your plan didn't work," she said, her voice tight. "Maybe it's time you shared this plan with the rest of us, yeah?"

Dirk sank to the floor. "Id doesn'd madder dow," he groaned.

Fritzi sat beside him and took his hand. "Why does Imon—I mean, Todhunter's presence mean your plan didn't work? Did you expect someone else?"

He mumbled something.

"Uh, we're not orls," Red said. "You're gonna have to speak up."

Dirk sighed. "Id was supposed do be Smidth."

Red laughed. "No, seriously, come on."

"I amb serious," he snapped. "I - I called Smidth." He slumped, staring at his hands. "I told himb where we are, where the cad is. He was supposed to come ged id. Thad's who I programmed into the DIG. Bong is primed and loaded for John Smidth and ondly John Smidth."

"Ah," Fritzi said. "And instead, he sent Todhunter."

Dirk nodded. "Smidth is probably sibbing icewine on a beadch somewhere a hundred lide years away, laughing hids ass off ober how he trigged poor, stubid Dirg Largo."

Red stabbed a finger at The Gentle Tehy. "Isn't there some ice you can put on that damn nose so he can talk like a regular person?"

The monk mumbled something about the best cure for a swollen nose was not punching it in the first place, but went to rummage around in a subzero storage cabinet.

"Let's go back a click," Red said. "You know, to the part where you called the *one person* we didn't want to see and told him *exactly* where to find the *one thing* he's looking for."

"Dis ids why I didn'd wandt to dell you by plad." The Gentle Tehy returned with a bag of frozen peas wrapped in a cloth napkin. Dirk pressed it to his face and winced. "I dew you wouldn'd udderstad."

"What in seventeen systems made you think he'd come himself?"

"He dew you and Sam were bodth here, doo." Dirk refused to meet Red's eyes. "I figured he couldn'd resist the chance to pull the trigger himself. Or ad least see the loogs on your faces when he had someone else do the wetworg for him."

"And when Smith got here?" Red asked. "Wouldn't Bonk need to know his pheromones and bone structure and shit?"

"I eggstrapolated the genedic information I needed fromb samples of his close biological reladives," Dirk explained. "Being half-sisters, you and Samb have enough of his DNA bedween you to make a reasonably reliable reblica of Smith."

Red couldn't help but be a little impressed. "That's actually pretty clever, Dirk."

"You did that here at the monastery?" The Observant Yuo gasped. "Is that why you needed to borrow my centrifuge?" Dirk nodded, and the monk sighed, fanning himself.

"What I don't understand," Fritzi said, "is why you thought to call Smith in the first place."

Red stood stiffly and crossed her arms. "Go on," she said. "Tell her."

Dirk sighed and adjusted his pea bag. "Because I've been working for Smith for years. No, nod like that!" he protested when Fritzi's scales flashed a deep crimson. "He wanted someone to keep tabs on Samb at SEGS. He didn'd trust her, was looking for any excuse to take her out for good." He shook his head. "No way was I letting anyone hurt Sammy, especially not that arrogant douchebag. I toog the job so I could cover for her."

"And Sam never knew about this," Fritzi said. "She never knew that Smith doubted her, or that you were ostensibly his spy."

"I'm lost," The Eager Liek said. He exchanged a puzzled look with the other monks, who murmured their agreement.

"It's simple," Red said, turning to the group. "Sam was spying on SECS for Smith, but not really. Dirk was spying on Sam not really spying on SECS for Smith, but also not really. Smith probably knows that Sam is not really spying and may or may not know that Dirk is also not really spying, but Sam definitely doesn't know about Dirk's spying, really or not really, though she may know that Smith knows she's not really spying. Got it?"

Everyone frowned except The Observant Yuo, who nodded vigorously.

"Any sign of Sam?" Fritzi asked Dirk.

"Lemme check," he replied, twiddling his FARTS. The feeds flipped by every few seconds: piles of dirty dishes abandoned in the dining hall, the glasslike surface of the pool, Sam waving her hands frantically at the kitchen camera, the destroyed lobby—

"She's here!" Red shouted. "Open the door!" The Eager Liek scrambled to let a filthy and battered but remarkably whole Sam stagger into the pantry. She still looked amazing, dammit. Freaking Orgullan genetics.

Fritzi pushed her way through the crowd and flung her arms around her wife, who returned the embrace after a few startled seconds.

"By turn," Dirk said, tossing aside the peas and gathering Sam into a giant bearhug. Gross. Red peeked out the door to make sure no SECS soldiers were lurking among the ovens, then shut it again. She breathed a small sigh of relief when the lock engaged.

Sam managed to extricate herself from the lovefest and stuck out a hand to Red. Red looked at it, then pushed it away and gave Sam her own quick hug. "Okay, okay, okay," she grumbled as she pulled away. "We're all happy you're not dead and all, but can we save this for later?"

Sam grinned, her teeth unbelievably bright against her smoke-stained and dust-caked face. "I'm happy you're not dead too."

"What happened out there?" The Impatient Taht demanded. "What did you do to the lobby? How did you escape? Did you see the cat? What—"

Fritzi held up a hand. "Give her a moment to catch her breath," she said gently. Someone passed up a flask of water, which Sam chugged in a single go.

"Are you injured?" The Gentle Tehy asked.

Sam burped. "Nah," she said. "A few scrapes and bruises. My leg took a hit." She indicated a singed hole in the thigh of her pants, then waved away The Gentle Tehy and his seeking fingers. "It missed the joints and major blood vessels, and isn't deep, but it'll be a wicked cool scar one day."

The Impatient Taht coughed. "*Now* can we ask questions?"

Sam shrugged and shook the last drops from the water flask into her hands to try to clean off a layer of grime. "My main blasters were almost out of juice," she explained, leaning against the quusberry barrel to take the weight off her injured leg. "When I slowed down my rate of fire to conserve ammo, they realized it was just one person defending the door. Not too bright, these guys, considering. So they rushed it. I had a random arc grenade left over from a previous mission, so I tucked it into the archway, pulled the pin, and ran. Did I get any of em?"

Red nodded and held up both hands, fingers out. "More or less."

"Good." Sam chuckled. "Didn't quite make it out before the roof came down. But I did manage to duck into that giant fireplace, which protected me from all but the smallest stones. Once everything settled down, I had to dig my way out and find another way here to the rendezvous point. This place is quite the maze. You should definitely remodel." She gestured to the rapt audience. "Your turn. Is anyone hurt?"

"Just one," Red said. "The abbot, well, he's been better." She shot a look at the coiled body in the corner. "The Gentle Tehy says he's still alive and his automotive congregation—"

"Autonomic conglobation," the monk sniffed.

"Potato, potato." Red rolled her eyes. "Point is, he's healing himself and there's nothing we can do but wait and see."

Sam nodded. "What about you?" she asked Dirk, pointing to his nose. "Hope my stunt in the lobby didn't lob a rock at you."

"Nah," he said with a grin. "Got hit with something even denser than that." Red shifted uncomfortably, but Sam must've engaged Business Mode because she didn't pursue it. "And Bonk? Any idea where it is?" She looked around at the group. "You've got to be kidding me. We don't know where it is?" No one quite met her eyes, and more than one monk shuffled his feet. "Well," she said briskly. "Let's find it and get Dirk's plan back on track."

"About that," Red said darkly. "Dirk has something to tell you."

Color drained from Dirk's face, even his swollen nose. But before he could stammer another excuse, a deep rumbling shook the pantry. Boxes and cans and paper-wrapped packages jittered off the shelves and rained to the floor. Everyone struggled to brace themselves against walls or simply fell down in a heap.

"W-w-what the hell-l-l is this sh-sh-shit?" The Vulgar Adn cried. "Another exp-p-plosion?"

Red thought Dirk shook his head, though it was hard to tell with the entire room shaking. "This is t-t-too prol-l-longed to b-b-be an exp-p-plosion."

"It-t-t's the d-d-drill," The Observant Yuo said, pressing his hands to the wall. "They're c-c-coming through."

Chapter 16
Anywhere But Here

These guys were definitely starting to get on Red's nerves. First they had some super-stealth tech on their ship to sneak up on them, plus the bunker-busters that would make Sam's arc grenade look like an off-brand mail-order Christmas cracker. Now they had some big-ass drill that goes through walls? It just wasn't fair.

"They're h-h-here." The Observant Yuo jumped back from the wall. "They're r-r-right on the o-o-other s-s-side."

Everyone scrambled toward the door to the kitchen—then the lights cut out, along with the rumbling. The silent darkness was almost tangible, pressing down on Red until she could barely breathe. She strained for any sign of their enemies—a smothered cough or light seeping through a crack—but there was nothing. The oppressive tension swelled like Dirk's nose. She groped for the door handle.

Then a sharp crack echoed through the pantry and a light flared. A pale visage loomed to life in the sickly yellow glow. One of the monks screamed and Red's hand flew to her blaster. But it was just Sam, shaking an emergency ion flare to get the streams mixed together completely.

"Everyone stay calm," she ordered as the light expanded to illuminate most of the room. "I don't know what happened, but they seem to have stopped drilling. We need to use this time to evacuate. You two," she pointed at The Gentle Tehy and The Eager Liek, "get the abbot. Impatient Taht, you're with me up front. Bring one of those F.A.R.T.S. The rest of you, stay close and we'll all get out of this alive." She turned to Red. "You take the other F.A.R.T.S. at the tail. Make sure everyone's accounted for and . . ."

"Got it." Sam didn't need to say the rest. Red knew her main job was to watch their asses for any SECS bastards who tried to take them from behind. "Where are we headed?"

"Anywhere but here." With that, she opened the door cautiously, waved to the group, and disappeared into the silent monastery beyond.

The lights had gone out here, too, and as they crept through the kitchen and into the warren of rooms and hallways, it became clear that power was out everywhere. Great. Thank the Fourteen for Sam's flare.

They made quite the parade in the little pool of flare light: Sam, limping but still a grim-faced warrior goddess; the monks jumping at shadows and yelping every few seconds; The Serendipitous Teh rolling and bumping along; Red walking backward with blaster in hand, eyes glued to the darkness closing in behind them, trying not to trip on her own feet.

To keep herself from firing randomly at anything that twitched her senses, Red tried to figure out how many SECS guys were left who could be back there for her to deal with. But mental arithmetic wasn't her strongest subject at the best of times, let alone when she was fleeing a small army through a darkened monastery. There had been ten with the drill, but would they all have come through? Too many, regardless. This wasn't *Port Desire*, where the bad guys got picked off one by one with impossible shots by a single dude who barely knew which end of the blaster to hold and which end to point. This was real life. In real life, she'd be lucky to take out two or three of these dickbags before their buddies inverted her carefully-maintained hole-to-body ratio with some exotic weapon she'd never get the thrill of firing herself.

This led to an extended fantasy of collecting one of every weapon in the galaxy (she'd need a place to store them all, no way the *Wart* could ever be big enough, even if she turned the kitchen into an arsenal and added another bedroom). Her plans to wheedle Sam out of that nifty ARSE cut short when she bumped into one of the monks whose name she couldn't remember — The

Forgettable Hlep? Something like that. Anyway, the group had come to a halt in a hallway with bare stone walls and a damp funk that called for a few bowls of potpourri. Red recognized it as the one that turned into the parking garage access tunnel.

Sam made her way back through the crowd to Red. "Anything?" she asked, stretching her flare out into the darkness to illuminate as much as possible.

Red shook her head. Her neck cracked, its sound echoing alarmingly through the narrow hall. She flinched.

"What about on the F.A.R.T.S.?"

She'd forgotten about that. Pulling it from her pocket, she checked the feeds. "Holy shit."

It was the drilling squad. Or it had been, anyway. Mostly there were pulpy piles of limbs surrounded by shredded uniforms and a mangled lump of metal that was once the drill. Something suspiciously like intestines festooned the shrubberies.

"What is it?" The Vulgar Adn interrupted. He poked his head at the screen and gagged. "What could've done so much damage?"

"Bonk," Red said. "It was Bonk."

The monk paled. "No goddamn way one dinky-ass cat did all that," he said. "Look at the fucking drill, for Cripps' sake."

"Bonk's not a real cat, though," Red pointed out. "Trust me: I've seen what it leaves behind. This is its work." She studied the image. "I don't see it anywhere. Must not've stuck around for dessert. Well, now we can be pretty sure that if SECS did have it, they don't anymore."

"They probably never made it through to the pantry," Sam said. "That takes a little pressure off, but not much. Their buddies will find them sooner or later." She gestured toward the front of the group. "The Impatient Taht says this leads to the parking garage. It's really our only option. My thought is, we get everyone into the *Wart* and lock it down. Worst case scenario, we fly like hell and hope we can lose them in the Knuckles."

"What about Bonk?"

"It seems to be taking care of itself so far," Sam said dryly. "Maybe it'll finish the job so we don't have to."

"Or maybe Todhunter Balzac is better than Dirk thinks and will manage to turn it against us."

"That's certainly a possibility," Sam admitted. "But I'm not sure what choice we have."

"Excuse me, Sam the ARSE-Hogger?" The Eager Liek appeared at their side, wringing his hands. In the dim light, Red saw the abbot's coil leaned up against the wall. "The Impatient Taht told me to tell you that the soldiers at the front of the monastery have gone back into their ship and the ship is firing up its engines and that we need to, uh, get our asses moving or . . . oh no, I forgot the rest."

One corner of Sam's mouth twitched in that Smith way. "That's okay. I think we got the gist. How's the abbot?"

"The Gentle Tehy says his conglobation is loosening up a bit. Which is a good sign, I guess?" He shrugged. "He's kind of floppy now. Makes it harder to roll him."

"Hang in there." She squeezed his shoulder. "Please tell the others we'll be moving into the tunnel shortly." He nodded and worked his way back through his fellow monks, sharing the message.

"What d'you think SECS is up to?" Red asked Sam once The Eager Liek was out of earshot. "Giving up and running away?"

Sam snorted. "Yeah, that's probably it." She dropped her voice and edged Red further away from the group. "Seriously, though, if they're on the move, that means they've got new intel or a better plan or both. Either way, we're probably screwed. But that's just between us. We can't afford to have everyone panic." Red agreed nine thousand percent. Sam raised her voice back to conversational level. "The Observant Yuo says we'll likely lose reception in the tunnel," she said. "Keep your eyes on your F.A.R.T.S. as long as the signal lasts. It'll be dark, but if you see anything, give me a shout." She turned to go, but Red grabbed her arm.

"Did Dirk talk to you about his plan?" she asked.

"No time," Sam said. "But we'll have time to revise our strategy when we're safely on the *Wart*."

"But—"

Sam sighed. "Let's just get these guys through the tunnel first," she said in a tired voice, and left to do just that.

Sure, why not? Who needs to know the only plan for their survival is an utter failure, anyway? Not like the plan ever had even a quashtoad's egg of a chance of working in the first place. If Dirk was lucky, they'd all be blown to bits before he had to tell Sam what he'd done. Then they could fight about it in hell for eternity while Red got drunk with Vladmir IX and waited for Woodman to show up.

I just know that you make my life better and I don't know what I'd do without you. The way things were going, he might have to find out.

Red stuffed that train of thought deep down in her subconscious with the rest of her emotional crap. If she did end up in hell, she'd deal with it then. Why should Dirk get all the luck? She kicked at the wall before turning her attention to the vids cycling across the FARTS.

Almost as soon as she crossed the threshold of the tunnel, the signal degraded to jumping, buzzing static. Red stuffed the device in her jacket pocket. She didn't see the feed from the monastery's front lawn flash once before the screen went black, so she didn't see that the *Rector* was gone.

Chapter 47
TITs and All

The tunnel was lower and narrower than Red remembered from her previous trip, or at least it seemed that way. Maybe it was the crowd of whispering monks, or the dripping darkness, or the impending doom that could be approaching from any side. The abbot's coil scraped the ceiling at times, and light from Sam's flare had trouble making it past his bulk. Red spent most of the time fighting the urge to run screaming back toward the imaginary safety of her guest room and burying herself in those Luforian sheets. She kept on trucking, though, shuffling her feet through shallow puddles and groping the walls on both sides, wincing each time a cold drip of groundwater ran down her neck.

And now she had to pee. Great. Thanks, monastic homebrew.

Eventually the tunnel began sloping upwards and widening, and the quality of the light changed from the eerie yellow of a dying ion flare to the comforting warmth of natural sunlight. Red's eyes adjusted, and she could make out the silhouettes of the robed monks against the rocky walls. Somewhere along the way, The Eager Liek and The Gentle Tehy had turned over abbot-rolling duty to Dirk and The Vulgar Adn. The abbot himself was indeed floppy, his tight coil relaxing into an irregular oblong, though his injured segment was still pressed up against the others and his antennae flopped in limp circles.

They approached the end of the tunnel slowly. At the front of the group, Sam hesitated, favoring her injured leg more than before. Fresh blood spread across the fabric of her pants. The stumbling trek must've reopened the wound. Red hoped they wouldn't have to make a run for it. She didn't fancy the idea of carrying Sam. She could barely carry Bonk.

The FARTS flickered back to life in Red's jacket pocket, but she was too busy trying to ignore the pressure in her bladder to notice.

"Dude, what's the hold-up?" she asked, pushing her way to the front. "Some of us gotta take a leak. Dibs on the bathroom, by the way."

Sam threw a hand back at her to shut her up. "Something's not right," she said in a hushed voice.

Red craned her neck, but all she could see was the carved cavern walls and her ship, her beautiful *Wart*, with its beautiful toilet, waiting for her across an empty expanse of pavement. "Why? I don't see anything."

Sam shook her head. "I don't see anything either. It's more of a feeling. I dunno. Maybe The Observant Yuo—"

Red shifted in urinary discomfort. She couldn't wait for the monk to point out a chip in the paint that wasn't there before or a shadow that didn't match the angle of the others just right. None of it meant anything anyway. No one was out there; the place was empty. Sam said so herself. Something tickled the back of Red's mind, but she shook it away. There was no time. They had to get everyone on the ship before SECS *did* show up and before Red wet her pants. Definitely more because SECS might show up, though.

"I'm going for it," she announced to no one in particular. She half-ran, half-crouched toward the *Wart*. She heard Sam hiss a warning but she ignored it. She'd follow, and so would everyone else, when they saw Red enter the ship without a scratch. By then, Red would be blissfully doing her part to return the monks' tasty homebrew to its place in the water cycle.

She made it to the ship and slapped the palmprint lock to open the hatch. While the ramp descended (she needed to lubricate those servos, it was taking far too long), she crossed her legs and looked back across the garage. The Observant Yuo and Sam waved their arms frantically just inside the tunnel entrance. Sam caught her eye and gestured urgently at something across the cavern. Red frowned and followed Sam's pointing finger. She didn't see what the big deal was. There was nothing there, just the empty —

The *S.E.C.S. Rector* dropped its cloaking device and shimmered into existence, TITs and all. Its hatch was already open, its ramp fully extended. A double line of soldiers marched out, fewer than before but still way, way too many. They took position on the pavement, and Red could hear the low hum of their weapons brimming with a charge as full as her bladder.

Then a single figure dressed in an exquisitely tailored suit and brilliantly shined grumskin shoes descended the ramp. Suddenly peeing was the last thing on Red's mind.

Chapter 48

I Want the F.U.K.R.

"Ah, Red Darkling. It is delightful to see you again." Smith moved among the soldiers with his hands casually in his pockets, like he was strolling through the sculpture garden, deciding which pieces to buy for his Glorreen beach villa. "Though I must confess, I had hoped our reunion would be on less . . . antagonistic terms."

Red spat on the pavement. "Did you forget our arrangement, *Dad*? I get one little scratch from you or your goons and that info drops on every low- and high-res band there is. Every two-credit gangster in the galaxy will be fighting to have your head on his barbecue before sundown." Her eyes flitted around the cavern, looking for anything that might help her get the hell out of this. Everywhere except the tunnel entrance, that is. No reason for Smith to know the location of a dozen potential hostages. "I should put it on blast just for showing your face." Just play it cool, keep him talking, give Sam a chance to get everyone back through the tunnel. Where could they go, though? She'd long lost track of how many of these bozos were running around and where they all were. Eh, Sam would figure something out. Red just had to buy her some time.

Smith's cool blue eyes flickered with amusement. "I see you are still playing this game." He tutted. "I overestimated you."

"It's no game, Smith. I'll do it. You know I will." Red reached into her pockets. The soldiers tensed, raising the scopes of their blasters to their eyes, but Smith held up a hand and they stood down. Slightly. Red pulled out a FlinkBar she'd lifted from the pantry. She waggled it at Smith. "You want any?"

"Thank you, no."

"Good," she said, peeling off the wrapper and taking a gooey bite. "I just have the one and I don't like sharing. Especially not with murdering bastards like you."

The amusement disappeared. "I see."

Red licked chocolate from her fingers. "Seriously, you're missing out. They're terrific. You know what the ads say: You'll love the nutty taste of FlinkBars." She hummed the last few bars of the jingle through another bite. "So," she said, picking a glob of nougat from her teeth, "I'll give you thirty seconds. I don't see your taillights by then, I'm initiating the broadcast."

"If you were going to do that, you would already have done so." He took another step. "Let us forego the inane banter. You know why I am here."

Red took her time chewing the last of the FlinkBar. She swallowed dramatically, neatly folded the empty wrapper, and tucked it back in her pocket. No reason to litter. "I do?"

"Yes." His gaze somehow managed to sharpen even further. Red consciously stopped herself from wincing. "You are not stupid, Red. Acting as though you are is a waste of my valuable time and yours."

"Or," Red said, tapping a finger against her temple. "Or, maybe—just maybe!—you could quit with the lame insults and just freaking tell me what you want."

Smith stared at her so long that one of his soldiers yawned. But Red'd be damned if she'd be the one to break. She examined her fingernails and wondered how much farther her friends had to go before they'd be back in the monastery.

Eventually he laughed, twice as dry as sandpaper and half as contagious. "The F.U.K.R., Red. I want the F.U.K.R."

"Aw, come on," Red whined. "I'm not enough of a FUKR for you?"

"Your attempts at humor exhaust me. I want the cat."

"What cat?" Red raised her eyebrows and looked around the cavern. "I don't see any cat." She waggled a finger at Smith. "You haven't been drinking that blood rum again, have you? Nine out of ten doctors say it'll rot your brain, and the tenth guy is probably on your payroll."

"Indeed." Smith's lips curled in a thin smile as he took another step. "Allow me to be blunt. We know it is here. A reliable source informed us of its presence at this precise location. We have seen the . . . fruits of its labor." Red thought this was a very nice way to put it. Far nicer than 'liquified corpses it left behind to congeal into a thick jelly.'

"I will make it simple," Smith continued. "The F.U.K.R. is here. It belongs to me. I want it. You will give it to me. We will leave. There is no further discussion necessary. I trust you have yet to read Exaius?" He cocked his head. "Pity. There is a relevant quote from his ninth treatise on the primacy of order over chaos, but I fear its richness would be lost on you without proper context."

Red rolled her eyes. She'd forgotten how much this guy loved to hear himself talk. "Look, if it'll save me from another Exaius quote, we can talk about Bonk. Hell, I'd eat a gallon of quashtoad shit, without a spoon, licking the bowl clean, if it meant I never had to hear the name Exaius again. But man, I gotta be honest, I'm about to pop my cork, if you know what I mean." His face remained a blank slate of disdain. "Make water. Break the seal. Unleash the tides. Paint the porcelain. Urinate. Pee. Like an incontinent racehorse." She made a shooing gesture with her hands. "So why don't you send your cute little army men back to their cute little TITs. Then you and I can go inside the *Wart* here, I can dump my load, and we'll both be more comfortable."

"As charming as that sounds," Smith said, "I am satisfied with our current company." He paused. "Of course, things are rather one-sided. Perhaps we should level the field by inviting your companions to join us as well." He gestured to the tunnel entrance.

"I have no idea what —"

Smith ignored her. "Come out," he called. "You have my word that no harm will come to you if you do. If you do not, however   ..."

Red couldn't help but look at the tunnel. Her heart sank. Sam hadn't retreated. None of them had. They all streamed out: Sam, her face murderous, fists clenched; Dirk, scuttling behind; Fritzi, scales a pale red, speaking in a low, comforting voice to the monks cowering in their robes. Even the abbot appeared, fully uncoiled and obviously weak but crawling along under his own power, his mandibles clacking in proud defiance.

If it were just her and Sam, Red would give them even odds against Smith and his remaining ammo dumpsters. But there were the others to consider. None would be useful in a fight. Most would be a distraction or, worse, a liability. People not used to being shot at tend to react in unpredictable ways when blasters started firing. Not their fault, of course, but there it is. Even with Sam's calm expertise and skill, they'd be constantly splitting their attention between offensive maneuvers and protecting their Friends. Unless she could somehow remove everyone but Sam from the equation, the best thing would be keeping the conversation gunfire-free.

Red purposely didn't think about how The Serendipitous Teh's gift might come in super-duper handy right now.

She caught her sister's eye. Sam glanced back at the group and muttered something to Dirk and Fritzi. They gathered the group protectively around The Serendipitous Teh. Sam positioned herself directly between the huddled monks and Smith. Her posture, loose but ready, told Red that she'd come to the same conclusions. She noticed, too, that Sam wasn't favoring her injured leg. Red smiled to herself. Smart move. Never show your enemy a weakness, especially an enemy like Smith.

Red regretted every crack she'd made about Sam being an assassin. When (if) this was all over, she'd be sure to apologize.

First things first.

Smith.

"My dearest Samanthya," he said. Red searched his face for a glimmer of affection, pride, sadness, anger—anything that they could use as a lever—but his tone and demeanor were unreadable.

"Hello, father," she replied coolly. "I didn't expect to see you here."

"The feeling is not mutual, I can assure you," he said. His eyes flicked to Red. "I confess, I often wondered what would happen when you inevitably succumbed to temptation and made contact with your sister. May I be so bold as to ask your opinion of her?"

Sam's jaw tightened but calm quickly replaced the concern. "I can see why you'd consider her for your successor, if that's what you mean," she said. "Especially since your first choice turned you down."

"Hey!" Red protested. "I can hear you, you know."

They both ignored her. That's fine. If Sam could keep him busy, maybe she could sneak inside the *Wart*, pee, and find some random item that would miraculously save their asses. She edged toward her ship's ramp.

"You are my greatest disappointment, Samanthya. My greatest failure," Smith was saying. "You were everything a man could want in a daughter: intelligent, strong, self-possessed. What did I do wrong?"

Sam barked a bitter laugh. "Don't you ever get tired of having this exact same conversation? You know why I work for S.E.C.S."

"I do indeed. In fact, I suspect I know more about your professional ambitions than you realize."

Red slid a few inches more and got one foot on the ramp.

Sam crossed her arms. "You're obviously dying for me to ask. I'm feeling generous, Smith, so I'll indulge your need for power. What do you think you know about me?"

Instead of answering her, Smith turned to the nearest soldier. "Go collect the man in the hideous suit." The man nodded tightly and moved toward the group. Dirk whimpered.

Sam, on the other hand, pulled out her ARSE and leveled it at the soldier's head. "What do you want with Dirk?"

"How do you know he's talking about me?" Dirk asked, peering from behind The Vulgar Adn's sleeve.

Without taking her eyes from the advancing soldier, she said, "Come on, man. That suit's awful. That's why you wear it."

"I like it," Dirk pouted.

"Call him off, Smith," Sam warned. "Dirk's not going anywhere with you."

Red was halfway up the ramp now. Just a few minutes more . . .

"Your faithfulness to your friends does you great credit, Samanthya," Smith said. "But do your friends return your loyalty in equal measure?"

"You're trying to distract me. It won't work." The soldier circled to one side. Sam had to shift her stance to track him with the weapon, forcing her to turn away from Smith. Red didn't like this development, but as long as everyone was still just talking, it would be fine. Just a few feet from the hatch now.

"Let us ask Mr. Largo what he knows about betrayal," Smith said.

Sam thrust her chin out defiantly. "Dirk would never betray me."

At that point, Dirk stepped forward. "It's all right, Sammy," he said, putting a hand on her ARSE. She allowed him to push it down. "I'll go. It'll be okay."

Sam blinked. "Wh-what?"

"I can explain," Dirk choked out around the tears brimming in his eyes. He put up his empty hands and walked toward the soldier. The man grabbed him roughly and held him in front of his body like a human shield, blaster now pointed at his temple.

"There is no need for violence, lieutenant," Smith chided. "I am certain Mr. Largo will cooperate, much like he has always done. He is, after all, a close friend of the family." The soldier released Dirk grudgingly, then nudged him back toward Smith with the muzzle of his blaster.

"What's going on? Dirk?" Sam's voice cracked. Business Mode was failing. Not good. Red would have to make a break for it soon. If Sam lost her shit, things would get bad. Like, really bad.

Red risked a glance inside the *Wart,* sending up a silent prayer to Fardus or whoever happened to be listening that she'd find something, anything that could help.

She did: two glowing green eyes. They blinked, and she smiled.

Chapter 49
The Firefight Symphony Orchestra

Back on the pavement, Smith was just getting warmed up. "Oh, this is a delicious turn of events," he said, eyes sparkling. "I could not have asked for a more satisfying conclusion to our visit. Naturally, I had my doubts when I received the message from Mr. Largo informing me of the cat's whereabouts. It was simply too perfect a trap, the bait irresistible. Given Mr. Largo's history of cowardice—"

"I'm no coward," Dirk muttered.

Smith gave him a withering look, then continued. "I found it reasonable to assume he was not acting alone. I even considered that it might not have been his idea at all. No, he was most likely acting at the behest of the one person he has ever trusted: his childhood friend, Samanthya Anyanama. Perhaps, I thought, Mr. Largo loved you more than he feared me. A dangerous mistake." He smiled like a hungry clomis when it sees an injured shiq. "But now, to learn that you were utterly ignorant of his deception? It is positively delightful. Even if I fail to secure the cat—and I will secure the cat—this trip will not have been wasted."

Okay, Dirk's plan was back in play. Smith was here. Bonk was here. All Red needed to do was to use the trigger Dirk programmed on the DIC to initiate Bonk's murder mode. But what was it? She tried to think of some phrase that only Smith would use, but like a bad case of spaceherpes, the stupid FlinkBar song kept popping up. Dammit, with her luck, it was some Exaius shit. Of all the decisions Red regretted in her life, she didn't want this to be one of them.

Meanwhile, Sam stared at Smith. "You're a liar. You've always been a liar."

"I assure you, I speak the truth." Smith rubbed his hands together. "Mr. Largo's regular reports on your actions at S.E.C.S. have been instrumental in my attempts to discern your true motives." He paused. "Did you believe I trusted you? That being my daughter would earn you a special place in my esteem?" He frowned. "You are as much a fool as your sister."

Maybe it wasn't Exaius. Maybe it was Vladmir IX. Or V. Or some other old dead dude. Smith liked those.

"Dirk, tell me this isn't true." Sam's voice wavered. "Please."

"I meant to tell you," he whispered. "I really did—"

"No!" she screamed, spit flying from her lips. She raised her ARSE again, but this time, she pointed it at Dirk.

"Sammy, please," he gibbered. "Please, trust me—"

Smith held up a hand. "Kindly leave Mr. Largo unharmed. We need him to reset the cat before we leave and its original target is again out of reach."

"Out of reach?" Sam whispered. "Target?"

Smith's cold eyes glinted. "Yes, my dearest Samanthya. I had the cat created with you in mind. I have long known your duplicity. Did you think you could possibly hide it from me? Did you think our common blood would save you from my wrath?"

"Dirk made Bonk," Sam stammered. "He'd never—he couldn't have known—"

"Oh, he knew," Smith said, smiling. "He was a willing participant in the process. Then his cowardice asserted itself and he disappeared. I assumed he took the F.U.K.R. with him for protection."

"I didn't!" Dirk cried, trying to break away from the soldier's grip.

Smith turned. "Your failure to take even the most rudimentary precautions with your deadliest creation became clear once my surveillance devices detected the cat aboard Red's previous ship. Tom was a better associate than you ever were, Mr. Largo. He understood my goals. He knew the value of patience. He spent nearly ten years in one decrepit market after another, but he persisted until an opportunity arose—an opportunity in the form of Red Darkling."

"Hold on one goddamn minute," Red interrupted, her mind distracted from the fruitless search for Bonk's trigger. "Tom? Tom with the muumuus?"

Smith smiled thinly. "Indeed."

She raked her hands through her hair. "Tom planted Bonk with me because he knew Sam would show up at some point?" She paused. "But he took the DIC out. I had to go through a ton of crap to get it from him. Why? What's the point of me having a cat without a DIC?"

"I intended to ask him that very question," Smith said tightly. "It is possible he understood you well enough to use your stubbornness for his own ends. Or perhaps his financial greed overtook his judgment. In any case, his death made it impossible for me to seek definitive answers. I underestimated the unpredictability of the unregulated F.U.K.R."

"It was you," Sam said softly. "You planted that bomb."

Smith said nothing.

"And the coffee," she continued. The ARSE shook in her hand. "You had Imon poison our coffee."

"Who?" His eyebrows knit briefly in confusion. "Oh, now I remember. That is the name Todhunter used to seek employment at your alleged safehouse." He tutted. "You are far too trusting, Samanthya, and naïve. There is nowhere in the galaxy I cannot penetrate to protect my interests."

Red snapped her fingers. "The gas leak," she said. "Dr. Oe knew Bonk wasn't a cat, so you had to kill him."

Again, Smith said nothing. The dude couldn't be more obvious if he had a TuneBot behind him blaring Vulvato's "I Hate That Bitch (She's Always Right)." Wait, could that be the trigger? A long shot, but still a shot. How did the opening lines go?

"You tried to kill me," Sam said, her voice rising, "in my home." She swung the ARSE back to Smith, though it was shaking so much she'd never make the shot. "You tried to kill my wife. My *wife!*" she screamed.

This was it—Sam officially discovered Emotional Freakout Mode. No more time for figuring out the trigger on her own—Red had to go straight to the source. "Hey, Dirk!" Red shouted. All eyes turned to her, and she gulped.

Smith frowned. "Your manners have degraded significantly since our last encounter. Most cultures consider it the height of rudeness to interrupt a conversation."

"A conversation?" Red snorted. "Everyone's either monologuing or screaming." Smith opened his mouth to speak, probably to make an insulting observation, so Red rushed ahead. "Dirk, remember that plan you had? What a joke. That never would've worked."

Dirk flinched. "Hey, now, Red baby, that stings."

"Yeah, well, too bad," Red continued, desperately thinking how to ask what she needed to ask without tipping Smith off. "I wish I had my finger on a *trigger* right now." Come on, Dirk, pick up the hint. "I'd show you just how dumb your *plan* was."

Smith narrowed his eyes. He knew something was up. But Dirk did too. "Oh. Uh. You're right," he said, glancing nervously around the garage. "It never would have worked. Boy, I sure am stupid, wow. Ha ha. Just call me Mr. Stupid. Uh. Okay, so, I'm going to go with Smith and these guys now." He jerked a thumb over his shoulder toward the *Rector*. "But man, you know, I sure am hungry. I don't suppose you've got another one of those FlinkBars, do you? You know, before I *head off into space*."

You've got to be kidding.

"Before you head off into space, stuff a FlinkBar in your face!" Red sang at the top of her lungs. "You'll love the nutty taste of FlinkBars!" She ducked to avoid the ball of claws and teeth that would come flying out of the hatch to shred Smith into hundreds of itty-bitty pieces.

A ball of claws and teeth that never came.

Red turned to Bonk. "Come on!" she hissed. "Before you head off into space, stuff a FlinkBar in your face! You'll love the nutty taste!" But the cat didn't respond. "What's wrong with you? Before you head off into space, stuff a FlinkBar in your face! You'll love the nutty taste of FlinkBars! *Do something!*"

Despair flooded her when Bonk merely blinked.

"Enough of this nonsense," Smith said with a dismissive wave. "Lieutenant, take Mr. Largo into the *Rector*. Give him every courtesy. He has redeemed his earlier mistakes by delivering my daughters to me for disposal."

"DIRK!" Sam's primal scream reverberated through the cavern.

Then things happened real damn quick.

One of the soldiers, probably a noob on his first assignment out of the Academy, fired off a shot in Sam's direction. The blast blew past her head and struck the far side of the cavern wall, releasing a cascade of shattered rocks. The monks ducked in a single amorphous blob of pure reflex.

Sam had reflexes, too, only hers threw her into an evasive roll across the pavement. She came up on one knee already firing. The ARSE did its wiggle-whoomp thing and the impatient soldier slumped over. His fellows, including the one in charge of Dirk, were relieved to finally have an excuse to shoot at something, so they shot at Sam. Or, more accurately, shot at where Sam had been just seconds before. Their reflexes couldn't match hers. She dove behind a stack of crates and leaned back against them to regroup. She set aside the ARSE, reached into her coat, and whipped out a wicked-looking snub-barrel thing. She didn't even flinch when splinters exploded around her from the barrage of blasterfire eating its way through the crates.

Warrior Goddess Mode: far more interesting than Business Mode, and a vast improvement over Emotional Freakout Mode.

Dirk, free from the lieutenant's grasp, bolted back across the field of fire toward the monks. By some miracle he managed to avoid being hit by so much as a stiff breeze. He and Fritzi argued, him gesturing wildly at the tunnel entrance, her at the *Wart*. Red couldn't hear their words over the Firefight Symphony Orchestra playing at full volume around them, but Fritzi must've won, because the two got the monks to their feet and moving across the garage toward the ship. Red drew her own blaster and laid down some cover fire. Probably unnecessary; all the soldiers' attention was on Sam.

When the last of the group was safely aboard the *Wart*, Red turned to the open hatch to duck inside herself. Something tugged at her shoulder as she did so. She spun through the hatch and pressed her back against the wall. Only then did the pain catch up with her. She braced herself, then took a quick glance at the slice in her cool new jacket, with a matching slice in the meat of her shoulder. The blast cauterized the wound, at least, but it burned like she'd dipped it in magma. The burnt flesh kind of smelled like it, too.

Queasy, she looked around the crowded main compartment, then grabbed Dirk. His eyes lit up when he saw her, but his expression turned to shock when he saw her injury. She shook him with her good arm. "I'm fine," she insisted. "Have you seen Bonk? It was right here a minute ago."

Dirk shook his head, still staring at her shoulder. "Maybe it's hiding from all the new people?"

"Maybe. Hey," she said, "the FlinkBar jingle? Really?"

"Ugh, I couldn't help it!" He squeezed his eyes shut and wrinkled his nose. "It's been stuck in my head for days."

She lowered her voice. "Why didn't it work?"

"I don't know. I'm sorry. I really thought I had it."

"Well, nothing for it now," she said, glancing over her injured shoulder out the hatch. "I'm going back out there. Close this behind me and jam it shut. Break the mechanism, I don't care."

"How will you get back in?"

Red didn't think that would be something anyone would need to worry about. "Jam it. Then power up the shields. Use your Dirk Largo powers to boost em up, if you can. That should keep you all safe so Sam and I can concentrate on Smith and his army. If something happens to us, like worst-case scenario shit, you can get everyone out of here."

Dirk gave her a quick hug, careful to avoid the injured arm. "Take care of Sammy for me, will ya?"

"I doubt she needs me to, but okay. Have Fritzi keep everyone from panicking in here. Maybe get the abbot to lead a prayer or something, if he's up to it. Oh," she said, poking him in the chest with a finger. "Don't let anyone go into that box under my bed. You'll know the one. That's my private stash of limited-edition skin mags. Some of them are signed, and not in ink."

He chuckled humorlessly, then sighed. "Thanks, Red," he said. "I got this mess. You go get that one."

She looked longingly at the bathroom, but a sudden shrill scream cut through the blasterfire. Gotta go.

Chapter 50
In or Out!

She found Bonk.

The cat was working its way through the soldiers, one by one. Five already lay dead on the pavement, internal organs rearranged in ways incompatible with continued existence, let alone battle. The rest had split into two camps: one grimly committed to fulfilling their primary objective, firing round after round at the mechanical fury making yozzie filling of their cohorts; the other fleeing in horror as they realized the primary objective was super pointy and definitely going to kill them, and kill them messy.

Bonk didn't care. It moved so fast that most shots missed it entirely. The shots that did land seemed to ratchet up its speed and power. If robots could get mad, Bonk would be. But they can't, which made the cat's intensity that much more frightening. And to think that this all came from the sex-soaked mind of Dirk freaking Largo, lounge lizard extraordinaire. Note to self: don't get on his bad side.

Still, Red was less worried about the soldiers than their leader. Between Bonk and Sam, who was doing her share of picking off enemies from the shelter of the crates, there'd soon be more dead than alive anyway. But where was Smith? She crouched behind the *Wart*'s landing gear and scanned the cavern. No sign of that smug bastard. He must've scurried back into the *Rector* when the fighting started. Figures. And he called Dirk a coward?

Red crept toward the *Rector*, keeping her injured arm as still as possible, sticking to the edge of the cavern. No need to get too close to the mayhem. She knew Bonk wouldn't hurt her — right? — but the more bodies piled up, the more the remaining fighters panicked, and Red knew from experience that panicked dudes with guns did the most dumbass shit imaginable. If she was gonna die, she wanted it to be at the hands of an expert, not some rando with a pantload of adrenaline.

Do it right, do it careful, do it smart.

It only took Red a minute or two to reach the enemy ship, but by the time she did, Destruction Concerto #9 for Blaster and Not-Cat had petered out completely. Her ears rang in the silence. She caught Sam's eye across the bloodied pavement, pointed to her wounded shoulder, and waggled her hand. Then she shot Sam a questioning thumbs up. Her sister responded by pointing at her leg, repeating the waggling gesture, then returning the thumbs up. Red did her best Smith impression, serious face and hands in pockets, then gave an exaggerated shrug and gestured at the *Rector*. Sam gave another thumbs up.

Okay, he was in there. What was he doing? Were more troops arming up right now? Did he have some secret weapon? Something better than Bonk?

One way to find out. Red rolled her neck, cracked her knuckles, and stepped onto the ramp.

A metallic streak flew past her, nearly knocking her down. "Goddammit, Bonk," she hissed. The cat stopped at the entrance to the ship and looked down at her, tail waving lazily, as if blood wasn't dripping from its teeth. "I guess you're coming too?" she said, climbing the ramp and running her fingers under its chin. "Fat lot of good it'll do me, but I guess I can't really stop you."

She drew her blaster again, wincing at the pain that shot through her arm. She checked the charge, flicked off the safety, and slid into the *Rector* to find her father.

Red hadn't spent a lot of time on government ships, and none outside the holding cells, but as it turned out, that was all the experience she needed. Utilitarian, spartan, nondescript in a non-CLITed way, everything the same monotone grey and all right angles. There were few doors; instead, the hallway widened periodically, making niches for control panels, rows of benches, or, in one notable case, a series of cages made from plasma-reinforced steel mesh. This was a ship designed for transporting people like cargo, voluntary and involuntary, and not an extended vacation cruiser or permanent residence.

All the open space made Red feel more exposed with each echoing step. Her nerves jangled. Her back itched. Her bladder weighed in her gut like a stone. Her shoulder, thank the Fourteen, had gone numb for now. She missed Woodman or Sam—anyone halfway decent with a blaster, really, who could cover her ass. She constantly looked back, poked her head around corners, and jumped at her own footsteps, expecting a blast to the face that never came.

She moved methodically through the ship but found no one— not Smith, not the injured soldiers, not even a cleaning bot. Bonk kept pace, occasionally poking its nose into a random corner or staring intently at the ceiling. In other words, being absolutely no help whatsoever. Red wished she had something of Smith's she could rub on its Senso-Trak device so it could guide her to him. Oh well, next time. If there was a next time.

Swallowing that thought like a glob of week-old spoo aloo, she approached one of the few actual doors in the place. It was closed, because of course it was. Maybe it was a bathroom! She raised her blaster and pressed her empty hand against the panel to activate the door mechanism.

The door slid open with barely a sound to reveal the cockpit. Banks of monitors, switches, keypads, gauges, and other spaceship junk sprawled across three walls. A table in the center of the room held a few piles of papers and a partially unrolled map. The fourth wall was dedicated to a massive viewport that, from the angle, must be in the center of the ship. The two TITs on either side narrowed the view, but thankfully the *Wart* was dead center. The ramp had been retracted, the hatch sealed. Red could even make out the slight haze of the shields emanating from its hull. Good job, Dirk.

Apart from a few chairs anchored to the floor around the table, the room was empty. No Smith and no soldiers, but also no toilet. Damn. Red took a step in, grateful for the chance to have a closed door behind her, at least for a few minutes. Whatever Smith was doing, wherever he was, he could wait for her to catch her breath and maybe suss out some useful intel from the displays. She turned to close the door and found Bonk sitting in the opening.

"Come on, Bonk," Red whispered. She glanced nervously into the hallway beyond. Still empty. "I want to close the door."

The cat didn't budge. Red grabbed it behind the head with her free hand to pull it out of the way of the door sensor, but it dug its claws into the floor. She'd have to put down her blaster and use two hands to haul it in, which seemed like a really, really bad idea. Bonk looked over its shoulder, then began idly cleaning a chunk of soldier meat from between its back claws.

"What the hell is wrong with you?" Red snapped. "In or out! I don't care which, just pick one." Bonk moved on to cleaning its other foot.

"You're supposed to be on my side here," she grumbled. She reluctantly set her blaster on the floor—careful to still be within reach—and took a deep breath, bracing herself for a struggle with the cat.

Huh. Did the air smell like that before? It was sweet, almost flowery. . .

She turned back to the cockpit, half expecting to see one of the monks putting out bowls of potpourri and brewing a pot of tea. Of course, that was ridiculous. She was still alone. Nothing had changed that she could tell. No movement anywhere, not even on the monitors, except for the loose papers rustling gently in a draft of air.

A draft of air that hadn't been there before.

Red forced all the air out of her lungs in a rush and threw herself back into the hallway. She scrambled to her feet to close the door, but Bonk still blocked the sensor. What was it even doing? The gas spread invisibly into the hallway. Her eyes burned and watered in a desperate attempt to save themselves. She blinked to clear her vision, and that's when she saw her blaster, still inside the poison-filled cockpit. She lunged, grabbed it, and spun back out to the hallway, still holding her breath. Bonk yawned and joined her. Red slapped the door panel and it slid shut.

She sprinted away from the cockpit and ducked into the first alcove she came to. It was one with a bunch of benches. She sank to the floor in a heap, only then risking a breath to relieve her aching lungs. No flowery smell, just sterile, government-issue air, Optimum Molecular Mix for Humans and Humanoids.

Bonk walked to her side, bumped her in the leg with its head, and settled down beside her. Red dropped a hand on a relatively cleanish spot of its chassis. The cat emitted an electrical squeal and looked up at her. "Yeah, yeah, okay," she said, catching her breath. "You were right. I'm sorry. And thank you for, you know, saving my life. Again. That's, what, the third time? Fourth? I'm losing count." She stroked the cat's back. "I don't want to tell you how to do your job, of course, but if you really wanted me to be safe? You'd take care of Smith like you're supposed to."

The cat blinked and squealed again.

"I get it," Red continued. "I don't like people telling me what to do either. But this is really important, Bonk. Smith's dangerous. He's the most dangerous thing you've ever met, even if you don't know it. And it's not just me I'm worried about. He's dangerous to you, too. I'm afraid of what Smith might do to you if he ever gets ahold of you." Her voice caught. "Don't you get it? He might destroy you. Gone, erased, turned to scrap. Or he might get Todhunter to make you into the weapon they want you to be. They could make you hurt me, or Sam. Hell, he could turn you against Fritzi. You wouldn't like that, would you? You like Fritzi. If you could just do this one little thing, we could all be free of him. We'd be safe."

The cat shifted to press harder against her leg and started its bizarre purring.

"I can't believe I'm talking to a damn cat." Red chuckled, then something bloomed at the back of her mind, big but unformed. "But you're not a cat, are you?" she said thoughtfully. "Not really. And I don't mean the assassin bot thing. You're . . . you're my friend." Her mind spun. "That's it, isn't it? That's the key!" Bonk was her friend. She replayed her near-death experiences in her head: the hitchhiker last year, the exploding navbox, the poisoned coffee, the team drilling their way into the pantry, the gas in the cockpit. The trigger failed, but it took out the soldiers in the garage . . .

It suddenly made sense. She turned the idea over and over, trying to find a weak spot, excitement growing when she didn't find one. Where was The Observant Yuo when she needed him? Or Dirk, he'd know what she was trying to get at. He'd know some theorem or principle that would explain it. But they were tucked away in the *Wart,* so close but so far. Maybe there was a comms area she could use to contact them. If she could avoid Smith long enough . . .

"All right, Bonk," she whispered. "Let's find a way to talk to Dirk, then see if we can find Smith."

"No need," an all-too-familiar voice said. "Smith, it seems, has found you."

Chapter 51
Like Slime Off a Snood

Red sank back against the bench. No time to get Dirk's opinion. She'd have to trust her own logic on this and hope she wasn't totally screwed over by her utter lack of algorithming.

She casually picked a piece of bone out of Bonk's aural collection dish. "Oh good," she said. "Saves me a lot of wandering around this boring-ass ship." She flicked the shard at Smith. It plinked to the floor at his feet.

He glanced at it, his nostrils flared. "That device is far more impressive in person than in simulation," he said. "My money has been well spent. I must share my thoughts with Mr. Largo when I return it to his care for . . . repurposing." He stepped on the piece of bone with a sickening crunch.

"Take it." She patted her pockets. "Hey, you got a smoke?"

Smith twitched an eyebrow. "You offer it to me freely?"

"No, I'm asking you for one. I'm out."

He frowned. "I mean the F.U.K.R."

"I know, dumbass. I'm playing with you." She waved a dismissive hand. "Sure, go ahead. You can have it. Just step up and take it."

Smith's blue eyes narrowed to slits. "Why fight me this far, only to allow me to take it?" he asked. "Why not simply give me the cat when I asked for it? Why condemn all those soldiers to death? Why put yourself and your friends at risk?"

Red sighed. "No smokes, huh? Bummer." She stretched out her legs and folded her arms behind her head. A stab of pain shot through her shoulder, but she ignored it. Bonk shifted against her side, annoyed at the change in position. "You want to know why I'm letting you take Bonk? Because I'm calling your bluff, Smith."

"Bluff?" Smith hesitated. His eyes flicked between Red and Bonk. Suspicion poured off him in thick waves, like slime off a snood.

"Yeah, bluff. I'm guessing you saw what happened to your team and had to run back here to change your tighty-whiteys. Not so brave, are you, without a squadron of soldiers between you and the enemy. So go on, take it. I dare you. What are you waiting for?" She grinned. "You're not afraid of it, are you?"

"Afraid?" he sneered. "Me? Of my own creation? Hardly."

"It's not *your* creation, though, is it?" Red pointed out. "*You* don't actually do much of anything. Ever. You make everyone else do the actual work. No, this FUKR is Dirk's baby, and even he pisses his pants around it." Speaking of pissing one's pants . . . "Look, take it or don't. Just do something, because either I'm getting up to find a bathroom, or I'm going to make a huge mess all over this floor. And I'm not cleaning it up. I'll send you my laundry bill."

"Your continence, or lack thereof, is of no concern to me. My only interest here is the cat." But he still didn't make a move toward Bonk.

"Oh, hang on. Maybe it's *me* you're afraid of?" Red snorted. "Hilarious." She drew her blaster from its holster. Smith's right hand twitched. Ah, good, he's packing something. She made a show of putting on the safety, then removing the charge pack. She slid both pieces across the floor. "There. I'm unarmed now."

Smith rubbed his jaw. "You will forgive me if I do not trust you."

Red recoiled dramatically. "Why, Daddy!" she cried, placing a hand on her chest. "I'm hurt!" She rolled her eyes and opened her jacket to show the empty pockets. Then she lifted one pant leg, then the other, to reveal bare skin above her boots. "You surprised us, and I didn't have a chance to get my full arsenal. All I had is the blaster." She gestured to the disassembled weapon. "I'm not letting you pat me down, though, because I'm not into that incest shit. This'll have to be good enough."

He started pacing like a psycat, eyes never leaving Red. He was tempted, but unsure. Perfect.

"You *are* afraid," she said. "Actually, legitimately afraid. You're sweating." She threw her head back and laughed. "Oh, I'm sorry, man, it's just so funny," she said, wiping away tears. "You, afraid of me. Mr. Big Shot Gangster, the great John Smith, afraid of a girl and her cat. God, I wish Sam was here to see this."

His mouth tightened. She was on the right track.

"We both were so scared of you. We thought you were this terrifying monster. Really, though, we should've known you'd wimp out." She folded her hands behind her head again. "Wouldn't be the first time, would it? Back in that kitchen — the one where my parents were murdered by your goons, remember? — you had the drop on me good. But I walked right on out of there, didn't I? Even with your entourage of wankers waiting to put a bullet in my head, you were too scared. Scared of me, scared of a little piece of paper, scared of your own shadow."

"You silly fool," he scoffed. "You underestimate me at your own peril."

"What are you gonna do, kill me?" she taunted. "All by yourself, like a big boy?" She paused. "Wait, do you still — no, you can't possibly — I knew you were a coward, but I didn't realize how rock stupid you are. You actually fell for my idiotic 'I've got this paper, oo, better watch out' nonsense?"

If looks could kill, she could stop there. But, since they didn't, she continued. She'd better be right about Bonk. "Oh, Daddy, I almost feel bad now. It must be so hard to be outsmarted by your own kid. And I'm not exactly the bright one in the family, am I? That's Sam. That's why you raised her yourself, isn't it? But she had to come to me, little old Red Darkling, general screwup, because I'm the one who tricked you."

Smith's hand twitched again. "Explain."

"What's the magic word?"

This time it was his eye that twitched. Bonk shifted slightly against Red's leg, aural dishes flattened against its head. It stopped purring.

"Jeez, and you were lecturing me about being polite? Okay, I'll say it slow, so you'll be sure to understand." She looked him straight in the cold, blue eyes. "I lied. There is no file. Never was.

It was all a bluff. And you fell for it. What's worse: feeling stupid because you thought you'd screwed up, or finding out you were stupid enough to believe someone as stupid as me?"

"This cannot be true." He shook his head, still pacing. "If it were, why would you confess it to me? Surely you know I could easily kill you now, with no repercussions."

Red laughed again. Almost there. "I'm not afraid of you, Smith. Why would I be? You don't have the balls to kill me. You never did. You never will. You hide in your beach houses and corporate offices and send minions out to kill innocent people minding their own business. You're nothing but a quashtoad-brained coward, and you know it."

"I am no coward." His lips curled in a snarl, more psycatlike than ever. Bonk shifted again, tail twitching, and emitted a stuttering ekekekek noise.

"Prove it, then!" Red cried. She flung her arms out defiantly. "Here I am. It's just you and me. Do it! *Kill me, Smith!*"

With a guttural roar, Smith finally lost control. His hand flew to his side and pulled an elegant-looking weapon. Red didn't flinch. This was it. Time to find out which one of them was really the quashtoad-brained one.

She didn't have time to finish the thought. Bonk launched across the room in a single leap. Smith's shooting arm flew wide as the cat collided with his body. A single shot echoed through the government-regulation hallways, alcoves, and TITs. His head hit the floor with a crack. Surprisingly, Bonk didn't immediately tear off his face. Instead, it crouched on his chest, eyes shining steadily.

Red stood up and hobbled across to the prone Smith, kicking his weapon away. "Well?" she asked Bonk. "What are you going to do?"

The cat growled deep in its belly. Its metal lip plates pulled back to expose razor-sharp teeth still clotted with blood. Claws extended from its feet, embedding themselves in Smith's body a fraction of an inch at a time. He thrashed, trying to throw the cat clear, but Bonk dug in harder and gave Smith's face a quick series of hits, pap-pap-pap, plucking one of his cold blue eyes from its socket and sending it into the wall with a wet splat. Smith screamed, a hysterical wordless wail, as Bonk slowly began kneading his flesh like biscuit dough.

Red watched until it was over. Bonk extricated itself from the carcass and rubbed against her affectionately, purring again. She grimaced at the gore it was smearing on her pants, then realized she no longer needed a toilet. Urine ran down her leg and spread into a pool that mingled with Smith's cooling blood. There was a metaphor there somewhere, but Red was too tired, wet, and aching to care.

Chapter 52
Such a Good Kitty

Red picked her way across the pavement back toward the *Wart*. She managed to slip in puddles of guts only twice, which was more than she'd hoped, but really, what was another layer of blood at this point? She needed a long shower in her guestroom bath, followed by a longer soak in the tub. Hopefully the monks had restocked the little shampoos and soaps. And the minibar.

She found Sam sitting on the ground beneath the *Wart's* sealed hatch. The Warrior Goddess energy had fled, leaving behind a limp, drained husk of a woman. Her injured leg stuck out stiffly, but it seemed to have stopped bleeding. She looked up, startled.

"What happened?" she gasped. "Where's Smith? Did you find Bonk? Is any of that yours?" She gestured to the blood-soaked clothes. Her nose wrinkled. "And what's that smell?"

Red sank to the floor, wincing as her wounded arm bumped against the ship's shield. "Found Bonk. Found Smith. Almost died. Smith died. Peed myself." She grinned. "Wish you could've seen it. It was rad." She paused. "Not the peeing part. Everything else, though."

"I would've joined you, but I needed to make sure there was no one left to follow you in." Sam blinked. "Wait, did you say Smith's *dead*?"

"Yeah," Red said. "Oh. Sorry. I know he was your dad and all."

Sam stared at her hands in her lap. "It's odd," she said. "I knew this could happen. I knew it should happen. I *wanted* it to happen. Still, now that it's over, I can't help but wonder if—"

"Don't go there." Red dug a glob of liver? spleen? out from under her thumbnail. She nodded to the *Rector*. Nothing about it had changed, but it seemed dead too. The menace was gone. "If you want to see him . . . closure, or something?"

Sam shook her head. "No, I'm good."

"Probably best," Red said. Bonk strutted up and sat between them, proudly dangling Smith's eyeball from its mouth by the optic nerve, like a slimy gnar. Red snatched it away and stuffed it into a pocket. "Gee, thanks for the present, Bonk," she grimaced. "Next time, get me a beer instead, yeah?"

"It did that to Smith?" Sam choked. She turned green as a Glorreen's backside but, thankfully, didn't puke. Puke was the one thing Red didn't have caked into her clothes, and she'd like to keep it that way. A girl's got to have *some* standards.

"Oh yeah," Red said. "That and more." The cat coiled itself up into a tight ball, nose to exhaust port, and entered power-saving mode. "Such a good kitty."

"It looked like the trigger didn't work, though?"

Red shrugged. "It didn't."

"Then how—"

"As far as I can figure, Bonk was never actually un-catted," Red said. "I honestly don't think it can be at this point. It doesn't matter whether it has a DIC or not. It's going to do what it wants. And I think what it wants is to protect me."

Sam glanced down at the inert lump of cat-shaped metal. "Then why didn't it go after Smith right away?"

Red frowned. "I need to talk to Dirk about it, but my guess is, it only bothers when I'm directly threatened. Think about it: the explosion on Gambora, the poisoned coffee. Just now, on the ship, it wouldn't let the cockpit door close until I'd escaped the poison gas with my blaster in hand."

"What about the soldiers?"

"It didn't go full fazzer on those dweebs until they came for us in the pantry, and again when I actually got shot by one of them."

Sam shifted her weight. "Okay, so what did Smith do to you?"

"He tried to kill me," Red said. "I had to talk him into it, actually. It was fun, in a twisted sort of way."

"I thought you'd fixed things so that wouldn't happen."

"I told him the truth," Red said. "That I'd made up the whole thing, that there was no info to expose, and he was perfectly safe to kill me with no negative consequences." She paused. "Well, that last part was kind of a lie. I mean, having your eyeball swatted out and your organs turned to spoo aloo isn't exactly a positive outcome. Still, you know what I mean."

Sam whistled. "That's quite a risk," she said. "You're lucky it worked out."

"Did someone say lucky?" They both turned to see the abbot in the now-open hatchway, shaky but upright, antennae all aquiver, Dirk and Fritzi at his side. Red jumped up and helped Sam to her feet as the ramp descended. She thrust her good arm around Sam's waist and together they limped into the belly of the ship.

"I thought I told you to jam this hatch shut." Red punched Dirk's arm, pointedly ignoring Fritzi and Sam blowing off their pent-up energy with an urgent make-out session.

He grinned. "I needed a D-4 screwdriver but it's the one thing you don't seem to have on this rustbucket."

"Oh," Red said. "It's stuck in the wall of my room in the guest dormitory."

"Serendipitous," Dirk said, winking at the abbot. "You needed a way back in after all. Turns out, you're not the incompetent loser we all thought."

"Speak for yourself," The Vulgar Adn grumbled, smiling.

"Gee, thanks." She looked around at the monks crowded into the too-small main compartment of her ship, and grinned. "I know you're all dying to know what happened in there," she said, "but first things first. Dirk, grab the bottle of Finebock from the kitchen. I'm gonna change into something less grody, and when I get back, I'm having a round of shots with my Friends."

~ ~ ~

One round of shots led to two, then three. These Fardic guys knew how to party. Red's emergency whiskey didn't go as far as she had hoped, but somehow a second bottle turned up in the freezer just when the last shot was poured. When she found a third taped to the wall behind the toilet (once you break the seal, it's all over) she raised it to the abbot with an appreciative nod.

Around the fourth bottle, which she'd thought was an empty rattling around under the control panel in the cockpit, Red started to lose track of how much booze she'd actually had. She also lost track of strictly linear time. Everything blurred together in a boisterous collage of happy tableaux:

Dirk autographing The Observant Yuo's bare chest while the monk swore to never wash it off.

The Serendipitous Teh wearing a zuranfruit peel as a hat and singing the FlinkBar theme song.

The Vulgar Adn vidchatting with his sister and her kids.

Sam and Fritzi ducking into the bedroom and closing the door.

The Eager Liek teaching The Impatient Taht and The Gentle Tehy to play jester's snap with bottlecaps, all three laughing hysterically when their discard stacks clattered to the floor.

Red herself leaned against one wall, Bonk purring in her lap, a cigar burning down to ash in her hand, watching everyone else and feeling perfectly at home.

The death and destruction littering the pavement outside the ship, forgotten for now, could wait.

Epilogue

Morning sunshine peeked over the Migwyrn P'tan, banishing the nighttime chill from the valley. The river babbled contentedly to itself. A few late-season skelterbugs flashed across the water's surface, looking for breakfast. An orl's cry echoed on the breeze gently releasing the leaves from the jiljala tree above.

Red sipped her coffee from her perch atop a boulder on the monastery lawn. Such a beautiful place, no matter what you called it. Something about the mountains made her feel cozy and safe, despite the violence and death she'd seen here just a few months before. She envied Dirk for staying. Red had her secret doubts about his desire to become a monk, but she respected her Friend's decision. The talk with Sam had been tough, and even though they'd worked everything out, the guilt weighed on him. He needed time to sort through it all. And if that meant attempting to ascend a bunch of staircases and maybe eating some trippy fungus, then Red supported that one hundred percent.

She'd considered staying too, but only for a hot second. She couldn't deny the pull of the galaxy waiting for her beyond the valley. Her hands itched to guide the *Wart* through another asteroid field or even rush-hour traffic in Magross. Her feet longed to walk new streets in a familiar city. Her butt missed the comforting embrace of the captain's chair. Day trips to the Whore's Knuckles tourist traps were fun for a while, but they didn't satisfy her anymore. Even the overnight hikes through the canyons and foothills, looking for psycats (or monsters) had lost their thrill.

It was time to go.

"What d'ya think, darlin'? Tomorrow?"

Red smiled and turned to Woodman, seated next to her on the boulder. He'd arrived a few weeks ago with Granny. His dad, thank the Fourteen, had pulled through his surgery like a champ. It wasn't the rikk after all, just a nasty case of Bhoot fever. He'd undergone a full course of antifungals and returned home to complete his recovery under the watchful eye of his wife. Mrs. Woodman insisted her son accept Red's invitation to the monastery, claiming he needed to do something fun for a change and he'd only be in the way at home.

Granny was an easier sell. She had another granddaughter to meet, after all. Poor Sam, catching up on decades of being fussed over and doted on. Neither she nor Fritzi would need a scarf or hat until Fardus returned to the galaxy. Besides, Granny hadn't had a vacation in years. She thoroughly enjoyed reliving her childhood visits to the Knuckles. She'd filled her camera with pictures recreating her memories: posing in front of the peeling "Westward Ho!" sign, eating knuckle sandwiches (boneless barbecue grumribs on a seeded bun), watching the sun set from a bench in Gemview Park.

"Yeah, tomorrow," Red answered, taking another sip of coffee. "I'll leave after breakfast. I think the abbot said something about a new menu they're trying out."

The monks were, of course, delighted to have their dormitory overflowing with guests who needed three meals a day, laundered sheets and towels, restocked minibars, and refreshed potpourri. They were even making progress on fixing up the lobby, which turned out to have sustained only superficial damage, thanks to The Serendipitous Teh's holy gift. Red and Woodman offered to help, of course, but The Vulgar Adn kept shooing them away with increasingly colorful obscenities that made poor Granny clutch her knitting needles in dismay.

"Where will you go?" He stroked his full beard. Woodman hadn't stepped foot in the spa since he arrived or, it seemed, bothered to shave at all. He'd preferred spending his time convincing Fritzi to give *Port Desire* a chance (they'd finished the second season already) and sharing his family's favorite recipes with the kitchen staff. Red thanked the Fourteen that he hadn't stopped showering too. At least the beard looked good.

She shrugged. "Not sure. I mean, I'll drop Granny off at her place, but then—who knows? I'll see where the navcomp takes me." She finished the last, cold mouthful of coffee. "What about you?"

"I'm going home," he said, squinting into the distance. "Mom was right, I needed a break, but she needs me even if she doesn't admit it." It'd been awkward to see him at first; Red didn't know exactly how to act, with the pre-invasion vidchat hanging heavy in the air between them. They'd hugged, he'd leaned in for a kiss, she'd turned away, he'd made a joke about muscle memory, she'd taken his hand. But it was good. Seeing Dirk and Sam together, and spending time with the monks, had explained things better than Red ever could have herself. It just took some getting used to.

Red stood and stretched. High-quality caffeine buzzed lightly in her system. Her stuff was already stashed back aboard the *Wart*, along a dozen bags of Whore's Knuckles souvenirs, chocolate opaxnut truffles, a case of monastic homebrew, tiny Plestene bogmeadow soaps embossed with the monastery logo, and an entire set of Luforian sheets and blankets she'd convinced herself the monks wouldn't mind her borrowing for a while. Yep, she could leave any time. She just needed to trek to the parking garage, fire up the *Wart*'s sublight engines, and go.

Just like that.

"You sure you don't want just one more naked pushy-pushy for the road?" Woodman winked. "For old times' sake?"

"Dude, no!" She smacked his arm. "Friends don't do that."

"Says you," he pouted. "Fritzi says it happens all the time and is perfectly healthy as long as something something mutual consent, something something boundaries." Then he swallowed her in the kind of fundamentally non-sexual hug she hadn't known she'd needed from him. "I love you, Red," he said into her hair. "You know that, right?"

She buried her face in his shoulder. "I love you too. Thanks for understanding."

He pushed her away with a laugh. "For the record, I'm totally down with the occasional hookup. You know, if you ever miss being sexed up by an expert in the field."

"I think I'll be fine," she said dryly. "But if I'm ever that desperate, I'll definitely keep in mind that I have Indar Skjov's private number."

"Hey!" Woodman protested. "What's he got that I don't?"

"Money, for one," she replied, grabbing her empty cup and heading back toward the monastery. "Gobs and gobs of money. A career, for another. Oh, and he's super charming, and he can actually pull off a beard without looking like a homeless fazzer, and —"

"Sorry I asked."

Inside the partially restored lobby, she deposited her cup on the refreshment table and turned to Woodman. "Hey, I'll meet you in the dining hall, yeah?" she said, tilting her head in the direction of the dormitory. "I've got to grab something from my room."

"Sure thing, babe." He gave a little wave. "I'll try not to eat all the pancakes before you get there."

"I don't even want pancakes today, dumbass," she shot back. "Just save me a homona tartlet, would you? One with lots of frosting." She spun on her heel and headed toward the dormitory.

Back in her room, Bonk stretched out on the sunny window ledge, charging up its solar cells. "What do you say, buddy?" she asked, rubbing its chin. "You coming with me? You don't have to, you know. It's your choice."

The cat blinked and hopped off the ledge. At Red's request, Dirk had returned its eyes to their original mismatched colors. It fit better.

"All right, then. Let's go." Red emptied the minibar into her final bag and threw it over her shoulder, wincing out of habit more than actual pain. The Gentle Tehy knew what he was doing with those herbs, and the wound had healed nicely. Sam's had, too, though Sam had a way cooler scar. Bitch.

She took one last look at the room. "I'll miss this place," she said. "But we'll come back to visit sometime, yeah?"

Bonk walked toward the door . . . and missed, instead bonking into the wall. Red pushed it through with her foot. "Cut it out," she grumbled, heading down the hall. "You're not fooling me with that bonking grumshit anymore."

It followed her, burbling.

"I know I said we'd go tomorrow, but I can't stand goodbyes." She hefted the bag higher on her shoulder, causing the bottles to rattle softly. "And don't worry about Granny. Woodman'll take her home. He's going that way anyway."

She ducked down the empty hallway that led to the tunnel. Bonk had no problem keeping up. Red suspected the FUKR never really needed to bonk at all.

The tunnel seemed a lot shorter with the power restored and the darkness banished with cheerful pink bulbs. Red emerged into the garage and took a moment to appreciate her ship, polished and repaired, including the brand-new plasma damper coupling—a gift from the monastery. A tug in her chest made her look back, but she took a deep breath and crossed the thoroughly scrubbed and newly painted pavement.

Aboard, she dumped her bag on the cockpit floor and sank into the captain's chair with a sigh. That felt good. She ran her hands over the familiar control panel. Everything exactly where it should be. Bonk's gift, flash-preserved and set in gold, hung from the communications relay lever. It spun lazily and glittered in the sun. Red poked it and smiled to herself. He liked to keep an eye on her? Well, now he could. Forever. Loser.

"What d'you say, Bonk?" she asked. "Where should we go? Glor? Crysallia? Andar?"

Bonk jumped into the copilot's seat and blinked out the viewport.

"The Meaty Noodle? At this time of day?" She chuckled. "Well, if you say so. I could go for a Fuzzy Fazzer. Straight up, though. None of that rocks shit." She powered up the engines and checked the scopes, more out of habit than actual need. "And play a song, wouldja? Something I can fly to." The repurposed DIC deep inside the cat's hull clicked through several tracks before settling on the Poly Torrents' cover of the *Port Desire* theme, "Sail Away to Love." Heavy guitar licks and throbbing bass pulsed, causing the new microfilament speakers extending from the cat's aural dishes to vibrate. Say what you want about Dirk Largo: he knew his way around a FUKR.

Red closed her hands around the controls, feeling the rhythm of the music merge with the hum of the sublight drive warming up. She lifted the ship into the air and guided it out of the garage.

She hovered a moment, enjoying the view of the valley, before burying the throttle and blasting off into the rising sun.

Acknowledgements

This is a book that almost didn't happen. I started drafting immediately after *Red Darkling* was released back in 2018, eager to tell what happened next. I got to Tom's sticky end and froze, beginning an 18-month creative drought. It sucked, but eventually it sucked less.

Thanks to everyone who read *Red Darkling* and demanded more Bonk, without whom this book wouldn't exist. I hope it was worth the wait.

Double thanks to everyone who left reviews and shared links and otherwise spread the word about my silly little stories.

A few specific call-outs:

Charlie Jane Anders, whose inspiring book *Never Say You Can't Survive* gave me permission to embrace the gonzo direction this story took with no regerts.

Nicole Kornher-Stace, tireless champion of the odd story, whose fierce passion for platonic friendships in fiction made me rethink everything I thought I knew about how this book would go. Sorry, Woodman.

Drew Williams, whose enthusiasm for the Whore's Knuckles made them what they are today.

David X. Hunter, fellow author and best writing partner in seven systems. Without David to bounce ideas off of, Dirk Largo, Fritzi Giggler, and Todhunter Balzac would have boring-ass names like Chuck or Mark or . . . wait.

Troy Bond and everyone else who read drafts in whole or part, showed me where I screwed up, and from whom I shamelessly lifted better ideas than I ever had myself.

Jason Kemp, cover artist extraordinaire, for making my books look *good*.

My daughter Phoebe, whose slay-all-day attitude is contagious.

My son McRib, formerly Spiderbro, nee Drew, whose brilliance at back-filling filthy acronyms is both a surprise and a treasure.

My beloved husband Michael, who dealt with The World while I locked myself in the bedroom with my computer and headphones for days at a time, and who in no way inspired any of the male characters in this book.

My cats, Noodle, Pickles, Billiard, and Zee, who are each in their own way the living embodiment of general screw you-ery.

Finally, my faithful cairn terrier Chewie, whose blindness in his advanced years inspired Bonk's original quirk of bumping into walls. See you at the rainbow bridge, little man. You were the best dog.

About the Author

L. A. Guettler is a freelance technical writer from Illinois. *Bonkpocalypse* is her second novel, a sequel to 2018's *Red Darkling*. Her short fiction and poetry have appeared in several anthologies. When she's not tits deep in writing, she can often be found lying on the couch buried in cats, reading and napping by turns. You can often find her procrastinating on Twitter at @la_guettler or on Facebook at @authorLeaAnneGuettler.